Anchoress
of Shere

Anchoress of Shere

Paul L. Moorcraft

Poisoned Pen Press

Poisoned
Pen
Press

Copyright © 2000 by Paul Moorcraft

First Edition 2002

10 9 8 7 6 5 4 3 2 1

Library of Congress Catalog Card Number: 2001098484

ISBN: 1-59058-011-7 Hardcover
ISBN: 1-59058-028-1 Trade Paperback

Poisoned Pen Press
6962 E. First Ave. Ste. 103
Scottsdale, AZ 85251
www.poisonedpenpress.com
info@poisonedpenpress.com

Printed in the United States of America

To Rhiân: I gâr cu

"Men never do evil so completely and cheerfully as when they do it from religious conviction."

Blaise Pascal, *Pensées*

Author's note for US edition

Many years ago I fell in love with a small English village called Shere. To me, it epitomised peace when I spent over twenty years travelling in war zones. It was a promised haven which helped me to survive many vicissitudes. Shere has rural charm, an intriguing architectural heritage and a resplendent setting in the Tillingbourne valley, deep in a heavily wooded part of the County of Surrey. The village is also an enigmatic place, still brooding in its dark history of witches, smugglers and powerful lords of the manor. Even today, not all its secrets have been unlocked, particularly the story of Christine Carpenter, an eighteen-year-old woman who was walled up alive in the village church in 1329. She was called an "anchoress," which means someone who chooses to live in extreme religious seclusion. But did she actually choose to be entombed? I spent over three years trying to discover the answer, but gradually Christine's story led to the exploration of a much greater modern mystery.

Originally the story was intended for a more local audience, but the book sold throughout the United Kingdom, and is now being produced for stage and broadcast. I have written a revised version, partly based on new information, for this special US edition. I make just one plea, as someone who still lives in Shere, and close by the site of Christine's cell. They say writers often kill what they love most. By choosing to write about and develop the true story of Christine, I have encouraged many more people to make a pilgrimage to a place in which so many of the ancient buildings I describe still stand proud and defiant of the passage of time. If you visit Shere, please treat it with care. And don't block my seventeenth-century doorway with your car!

Dr Paul L Moorcraft
Shere, Surrey
England
1 January 2002

Prologue

It seemed at first mere eccentricity, as with all such things in England. Soon it became a murderous obsession that would span more than six hundred years, and inflict on its victims a terrible fate.

The key to understanding the tragedy was an innocent visit to the village of Shere in the summer of 1967. The season was warm and gentle. The rains had caressed the Surrey woodlands, where the ash, oak and cherry flaunted their freedom in the fertile hollows.

Marda Stewart stopped and impulsively plucked a stalk of honeysuckle, savouring its fragrance before tucking it behind her ear, perhaps because wearing flowers in your hair was considered fashionable. After an eight-mile hike she realised she was thirsty—until then she had been much too engrossed in her thoughts to consider food or drink. The energetic young woman marched along the last leg of the footpath etched in the sandstone escarpment, heading towards a seventeenth-century free house. She stood a little self-consciously in the bar, quickly drank a glass of white wine, and left the pub. Marda had not noticed, sitting in a corner seat, a powerfully built man, in his late forties, who had scrutinised her every movement.

Heading back through the woods, Marda walked briskly; when she had hiked there regularly with her brother, their intense conversations necessitated taking a slower pace. Nowadays Mark was too busy affecting the role of fashionable subaltern in Her Majesty's armed forces. He had left the Royal Military Academy, Sandhurst, and his sister, far behind.

So she was alone on her walk, and to her the woods were a retreat. True, in the deeper parts of the Hurtwood she would sometimes sense, or imagine she felt, a frisson of fear, but that afternoon the combination of sun, exertion and now wine made her light-headed. Humming the tune of "Turn, Turn, Turn," she tried not to dwell on the last volcanic argument with Mark, or to decipher its origins. There was no real substance to their recent antagonism; it had sprung from a clash of moods, perhaps from some subtle shift in their temperaments, but its intangibility made it no less disturbing. Marda resolved to put the acrimony aside, willing herself to luxuriate in the last heat of the day. From the long sloping hill that spilled into the water-meadows of the Tillingbourne river, she surveyed the village which she tried to visit at least once a month in the summer.

Shere was green and wet, brooding in antique loveliness. From its heart, the spire of St. James's church peeped above the tree cover, forbidding and yet enticing at the same time. The church had been built of wood when the Normans undertook the laborious survey of their new lands; a hundred years after the Conquest, stone had replaced humble timber.

Marda was instinctively drawn to this ancient shrine which hung back from the bustle of the village square and the worldliness of the small shops. Assuming an air of conscious modesty, she walked through the lych-gate and then paused to admire the intricate play of shadows and sunlight which stroked the stonework.

Marda pressed her ear against the large oak door to confirm that she was not interrupting a service. Hearing no sound from the inside, she lifted the stiff latch, pushed the door open a few inches, and slipped inside.

For a moment she trembled as the dankness assailed her nostrils and the cool air swept across her bare arms and legs. A handful of curious tourists were whispering their way along the aisle, but they ignored her. To the left of the entrance, framed in the door of the vestry, an elderly man nodded a restrained greeting. She assumed he was the verger. She was inclined to apologise to the man for her casual attire, but it was a hot summer, and if her clothing was not correct, at least her demeanour and intentions were.

The elderly man did not miss her hesitation. He intuitively knew that, despite her T-shirt and shorts, the girl had deliberately chosen a place of worship. Despite himself, he observed the unmuscled athleticism of her body, particularly the strength of her lightly tanned legs, but her obvious sensuality also reminded him of his age, and of his position. With an audible sigh of regret, he returned to stacking the prayer books.

Marda felt the man's admiring gaze on her back as she walked carefully into the chancel, adorned by the twin apertures of a cell that once belonged to a fourteenth-century anchoress. She peered into the quatrefoil and the squint, even though she knew that the interior of the cell had been blocked for decades, maybe even centuries, but this timelessness helped her regain a better perspective on her own inner turmoil.

She sat in the second pew, bowing her head slightly. Marda was not religious in the conventional sense. She would sometimes announce, "I am an atheist, thank God"; but the ensuing tinge of doubt suggested an altogether different kind of spiritual sensitivity.

Marda considered herself modern, a child of the sexual emancipation of the sixties. Like her peers she had adopted the Pill as a symbol of the new libertarianism, but she had not dissipated this freedom in bouts of casual sex: she had *chosen* her two lovers with care, while ensuring a respectable distance of time between the relationships. Her mind spiralled back to the most recent lover in France. The emotions had been too intense, because she had loved him with her mind as much as her body. Perhaps that was too much to give to one man. With all the brittle wisdom of her twenty-three years, Marda appreciated that she was attractive to men, but she rarely allowed her friendliness to descend into blatant flirtation.

And now her thoughts were focused again on her brother, a man who was, in this case, impervious to such devices. His anger had troubled her on the walk, and had brought her to the church in Shere. It was *her* anger too: she both loved and hated Mark. In their childhood, just eighteen months apart in age, they had never inflicted the customary sibling rivalry on each other. They had bonded in defiance of their parents' polite distance. But recently, from nowhere, their amity had been ripped apart. Mark had apparently been transformed by military life. Yet Marda was prepared to concede that she, too, had changed. She wondered whether her recent relationship in France had affected her more than she had realised—perhaps some of her frustrations with the Frenchman had been transferred to her brother.

She hoped that the tranquillity of the church would soothe her anger and hurt, that she would recall something of the near-telepathic rapport that she and her brother had once enjoyed. With an inner eye she perceived that this church could become part of the resolution. Fleeting visions impinged on her consciousness. In one tableau she pictured Mark attending her wedding, dressed in all his regimental finery. Maybe they would sing a hymn in French. She imagined Mark struggling his way through the words.

A bud of a smile came over her face. In that moment she experienced an epiphany, although a full understanding of the revelation would take many years. Then and there Marda made a small vow to herself, and she said it aloud, albeit softly: "Some day—no, *soon*—I will live in Shere." Vocalising the intention transformed the wish into a commitment. The next month she moved into Shere, adopting a tiny flat with high Gothic windows and a leafy view of the Tillingbourne.

No one could know that this decision would savagely transform both her own life and that of the entire village.

I

The Enclosure

The year of our Lord 1329

The bishop's gilded crosier shot into the air like the fist of
God. It came down with a thump on cold stone, alongside his
mud-splattered boots. John Stratford, Bishop of Winchester,
shuffled as he completed the final blessing of the girl's
enclosure.

"*Nomine patre, filii et spiritus sancti,*" he intoned.

The bells of St. James's church accompanied the dying
echoes of the hallowed words as nature itself seemed to applaud
the occasion. The beaten earth of the nave offered up a sudden
surge of dampness and the early morning sunlight paid court
to the eastern window, proudly haloing the rich, if crude,
stained-glass impression of the patron saint. Even St. James
himself nodded his assent, as three villagers later confirmed
on oath.

The final stone was placed and mortared into the northern
wall of the chancel. All the months of instruction and years of
devotion had at last converged in this final proof of God's
grace. Christine had spent most of her eighteen years in the
open air, working in the fields, but now she would see the

world through two small holes. For the rest of her natural life the girl would live behind the stones. And it could be a long life, because she had been told that anchoresses in other shires of England had survived for thirty years or more.

To dwell in the small medieval church was now her destiny. Gone was her previous life, a busy world of light and shade compared with her new inner life in her enclosure, utterly dark, except for two slim shafts of light. The squint and quatrefoil were cut on each side of an extended protrusion in the wall, like the bow of a ship. The squint permitted a sacred view of the altar while the carved clover of the quatrefoil enabled her to participate in the communion. These tiny stone windows would be the focus of her existence, the means of her immersion in total contemplation. She knew that a curtain, decorated with a raised golden cross, had been lifted temporarily to let her share this holy ceremony. Through the quatrefoil, to her right, she saw Father Peter, the priest of the parish of Shere. Pressing her face against the exterior wall, she sensed that she had caught his eye, and he smiled a little through his formal mask of piety, as kindness and weakness danced together in his small brown eyes. Her eyes had been closed in prayer, so had his, but just for a second, in the brief visual exchange, they had celebrated a little of the earthly friendship, that of student and teacher, which had fortified their spiritual endeavours.

As the bishop completed the mass, Christine recited the words she had been taught, the words of St. Gregory: "In order to attain the Citadel of Contemplation you must begin by exercising yourself in the field of labour." She realised clearly that she had not yet cast off all the physical world for, when the chantry priest had reached the top note of the Magnificat, she thought—very fleetingly—of her favourite secular song, "Summer is a-coming in," which she had sung so often to her sister Margaret. She suffered a pang of doubt— but she had a lifetime to exile such baubles of her past. She would be enraptured by heavenly choirs, and her old songs would be like the croaking in the marshes of toads and frogs.

Through the quatrefoil she watched the bishop lead a cowled procession from the altar along the nave of the church, incense cloying the atmosphere. Despite her sense of spiritual elation, she was angry with herself that she should feel frustrated by a column which partially obscured the last view of her family. Behind Father Peter, the girl could just see her mother, tired and fearful. Her father, William the Carpenter, stood absolutely still, betraying no emotion.

The external curtain was dropped and her cell became completely black.

She knelt to begin her initial twenty-eight hours of fasting and constant devotions. Except for a few sips of water, she prayed dutifully throughout all the canonical hours, from Terce to the following Sext. Christine had prepared herself, fully she believed, but she still felt the stiffness in her legs when she stood up after her hours of kneeling at prayer. She was also suddenly aware of the cold. Faintness began to creep over her, and she sat back on her rough stone bench.

She remained sitting to regain her strength, which she tested by rising after a few minutes. The cell was just large enough to allow her to stand fully upright to explore her new domain. As she traced the walls with her hands, she cut her right forearm on the rough masonry, although the hurt was something she would train herself to ignore. She put her left hand over the gash and felt blood with her fingertips, raising them to her mouth to taste the blood now dedicated to her Saviour.

"Bear in your heart the words of Christ, sprinkled with His blood," she quoted from the prayer.

And, without thinking, she ran her bloodied hand over her head. Once she had worn her blond hair down to her waist, but now it was cropped close to the scalp as part of her preliminary penance. She had been proud of her hair, though that pride had been banished.

Despite her vocation, Christine was still the practical daughter of a practical father, the best craftsman for many miles around, so she wanted to establish the precise details of her stone universe. Four feet from the bench, on the opposite outer wall, stood a heavy wooden trapdoor, opened only from the outside but inset with a small sliding iron grille, which she had licence to open and close. During her preparation she had been instructed how the parish priest, in silence, would bring her each week a large pitcher of water and bless it in front of her. She could drink sparingly and keep a little to wash herself. Every day, after Matins, her family would be allowed to donate food, sufficient for that day, and occasionally furnish her with a fresh robe. They would also take out and empty her night-soil bucket.

Some weeks before, the bishop had loaned her a treasured copy of the Gospels. She could barely read the first line in the dim light, but the book had twelve gaudy illuminations of the saints, pictures to nourish her soul. When the curtain was lifted and she held the book to the shafts of daylight coming through her grille, she could see the words and pictures plainly. Except for her robe, her sandals, her bedding and her rosary, she had no other worldly goods in the cell, but that pleased her: she needed few earthly artefacts, for before her lay the immeasurable bounty of serving Jesus Christ. God loved prayers, she reminded herself, and these prayers would ascend to heaven, be stored in a treasury and later returned to her as part of her immortal glory. Her Heavenly Father would not only make her solitude bearable. Birth and death were solitary, so were thought and growth, and spiritual reward. Her single purpose now was to experience a foretaste of eternal sweetness, the mystical union with God, the crown of life on earth.

It was the eleventh of August in the year of our Lord 1329. On the seventeenth of September, the fifteenth Sunday after Pentecost, she would receive an extra woollen blanket for the winter cold. Christine was assured that God would protect His anchoress.

⋘⋙

The telephone rang. The hands paused at the keyboard and reached for the phone. A wrong number. Cursing this intrusion of modern life, Father Michael Duval mumbled to himself about the casual caller who disturbed Coleridge when he was writing the story of Kubla Khan. The poet, he recalled, never returned to his unfinished masterpiece.

"I will finish mine," he muttered defiantly. Stroking the sides of his old typewriter like a prize cat, Duval looked up at the plain wooden crucifix above his sparse, immaculately tidy desk. Focusing on the nine-inch Christ, he spoke to it as he did a hundred times a day: "I can do it; I can prove that God can still act through mankind."

His first task was to complete his *interpretative* history of Christine Carpenter, the Anchoress of Shere. God had told Father Duval that He would guide him. Duval's quest was the pursuit of truth, not a mere collation of historical facts. His story would reveal the inner workings of God and, although he rejected the very idea of female priests, he knew God could speak to and through women, just as God whispered to him. All creation was a book which God had written and Duval's own work would follow His literary precedent.

The priest returned to his work, his love. From deep within the almost suppressed memory of his childhood, he recalled, despite himself, the anguished look on his sister's face when their father ordered her, after a trivial misdemeanour, to "remove yourself to the broom cupboard until you are ready to rejoin civilised society." Duval imagined his sister trembling in the darkness. Involuntarily shaking his head to remove the unwelcome flash of memory, Duval pulled the page out of the typewriter, rolled it into a ball, and threw it very precisely into a wicker basket beside his desk.

He ran both his strong hands through his abundant greying hair, and then placed them on the desk, flat and palm down, as if in Muslim prayer. He stared at the inch of bone and flesh missing from his right index finger. That had been a wound in the service of his mission, but he had also been a little too careless, too confident in himself.

Trying to expunge doubts about his own faith, despite bouts of absolute certainty, the priest's mind swirled with conflicting thoughts. He went back to wrestling with the central issue of the biography of Christine Carpenter: to understand precisely why she opted for permanent entombment in the wall of the church. Was it a depth of asceticism—fanaticism—peculiar to the late Middle Ages? No. Duval calculated that it had to be a peculiarly personal decision. Such utter devotion to Christ could not be dismissed as a helpless sacrifice to the spirit of the age.

He addressed his crucifix again: "Christine had to choose freely, because that is why God granted us free will. But why," he asked himself, "did she choose as she did?"

The priest as writer needed to invent a tormentor, an agency which would provide the motive for Christine's entombment. He felt impelled to create the embodiment of evil, because he had become convinced that Christine's purity required an antithesis. If she came to love Christ in heaven, who better to hate than her earthly lord—to cast him as the central villain of the tale?

Duval had scrupulously investigated the nature of evil. History had taught him that great leaders could dispense with God, but never a satanic scapegoat; the mass movements of recent history—communism, fascism, and for that matter capitalism—could flourish without a belief in God, but not without a belief in a devil. And even for those who presumed to eschew all "isms," nuclear destruction beckoned as a convenient symbol for all that was truly wicked. Evil was innate, the natural condition of man; what fascinated the priest was the really extraordinary facet of the human condition, the origin of goodness.

Duval fingered his typewriter slowly, lovingly, as if it were a venerated church organ. Then he started to type furiously.

December 1326

Sir Richard FitzGeoffrey, despite his relatively humble estates, was an aggressive warrior, and renowned in his county as a crusader in the last doomed efforts to regain a foothold in the Holy Land. His demesne included all of Shere, Gomshall and Peaslake in the shire of Surrey. Sir Richard proudly traced his forebears directly to the Conqueror, and believed his French to be pure Norman, although his curses were base Anglo-Saxon. He saw himself as a warrior of Christ, just as long as the actual battles advanced his favour with his earthly king and increased his landed possessions. His two foreign forays had been careful: very bloody, but comparatively short for the long distances he had travelled. He had served his king in France and in the Levant, but slyly returned as soon as he could in order to secure his holdings at home. Jerusalem he regarded as a tool, not a vision.

Sir Richard's men followed him in fear and awe. At home in his favourite tavern, Sir Richard's squire, Phillip of Gomshall, would often hold court, regaling pilgrims and local villagers with tales of his master's ingenious treatment of captured Saracens.

"It were near Antioch," the squire would always start. He would scratch his mop of red hair, wait for perfect silence, and then continue: "We had been ridin' since the break of day. Ten of us there were, two knights, two squires and six men but lightly armed. We sojourned briefly at a well. Bare slaked our thirst when we were surprised by the enemy—at least a score there were.

13

"Sir Richard and his son Edward flew at the intruders. Sir Richard, still mounted, killed two with his long-sword. Edward—on foot—sundered one unbeliever's head with his axe. Most of the enemy then took flight, run they did like frightened hares, but we seized four, with the grace of Almighty God. Sir Richard said we should feast there and honour our Saviour with a toast.

"Then my master ordered us to render naked the Mussulmen, to shame them before their false god. We bound them fast to trees and whipped them, for an hour, and so, in submission, they did our biddin'. We told them to dig—the earth was sandy—a hole six feet deep and near four feet wide. They did it speedily, too, with their hands and metalled scabbards, despite the heat and bloodied backs, though they knew it to be their grave. When it was done, Sir Richard bade the Saracens descend into the hole. Pricked by our swords, in fear, they did so.

"Sir Richard then told us: 'Bury these men, but leave their heads above. We are Christian knights so we shall leave these men to pray to the true God. Place their heads a foot apart, facing east, west, south and north, so they can see that our one true God is everywhere.'

"And so it was. Their heads were like the round hide-balls we throw on feast-days, but resting there in the sand."

The squire would pause for a deep draught of his ale, and savour the wide-eyed look of expectancy in his audience. He would time his drinking actions to tally with his words: "We drank a little of the wine we had, and Sir Richard bade us share some water with the living heads afore us. The first head, desperate was he for the drops we gave, but the second Saracen—even though his eyes were wide with fear—took the drops and then spat at his provider—that were Thomas, my cousin from Netley. You all know him."

The audience would murmur a rapid assent, eager for him to proceed with his tale. The squire would hesitate just a second or so longer than he ought, to tease his captivated listeners. "Ah, yes," he continued, as though he had lost his way for a moment, "Sir Richard saw this impudence, but said naught. He fell to joking with his son about domestic matters. When the sun was dyin' in the sky, Sir Richard instructed us to light a fire, and we collected some of the wood that lay scattered around. One of our soldiers made to start a fire in the lee of some rocks, but my master said he wanted the Saracens to feel the fires of Hell.

"'Light the fire between their heads,' he commanded.

"I could see that the soldier was not willin', though he did what he had been bidden. The man—Gilbert from London town—lit a small fire that did but heat the Mussulmen a little.

"Sir Richard strode over to the fire and shouted, 'By the Holy Cross I wear, we will teach these Saracens the price of scornin' our Holy Father the Pope.' Those were truly his words."

At this Sir Richard's squire would drink deep of his ale until his leather jug was empty. He would upturn the empty vessel and stay silent until a member of the rapt audience bought him more. Adopting a patrician smile as they rushed to satisfy his thirst, and with a softer—almost conspiratorial— voice, he would return to his tale: "Thereupon, my lord threw stout faggots on to the stuttering fire. As the flames rose, the Mussulmen's hair caught fire and they screamed to Allah. Their eyes bulged and popped out like corks from a jug of shaken ale. I must confess I could not bear the sight nor smell of burnin' human flesh. Just like the smell of roasted pig after Lent, exceptin' that the stench of burning beard and hair was stronger than the pork...but Sir Richard was not discountenanced at all.

"He used the black gargoyles with gaping mouths that before were heads as hearth-stones for the roasting of our meat. I felt I could not eat, but we had ridden long and hard, and hunger was on us, despite our battle and the smell of flesh. We feasted on the fireplace of the Saracens."

The squire was always content with the utter silence that would fall on the tavern, no matter that it was the twentieth telling of his tale.

⋖⋗⋙⋘⋗

Michael Duval was also content with the power of his sadistic invention, or "selective reinterpretation" as he would term it. He would now work this episode into his story of Christine.

The historical evidence for Christine's story was meagre: essentially three letters, written in Church Latin between 1329 and 1332. Duval had researched related histories of the lives of anchorites and anchoresses as well as local records. But nothing had told him why the most well-formed girl in the valley—the priest was fusing spiritual and earthly splendour—had chosen a life of total enclosure in a cell in the wall of St. James's church in the hamlet of Shere. Nevertheless, her story had seized his imagination and fired his intellectual curiosity, finally consuming him as though it were a literary transubstantiation: he could feel Christine's flesh and blood coming alive through him. If evil was caused by the flesh, he asked himself, how could the Devil be explained, the fallen angel who had no flesh? Better to explain evil as integral to man's nature, but goodness, yes, that could be generated by flesh, especially flesh as perfect as mortality would allow. A young girl's flesh. The life of Christine was not so much a history as his own creation, a rebirth of his faith, perhaps even the Eucharist of his soul; he had become a consecrated writer. When he picked up his pen to make notes before he typed, he imagined the blood flowing down through his hands into the pen and on to the pure white paper.

August 1327

Edward II had taken up the Cross fourteen years before, and for a century to come the kings of England were to be absorbed in squabbles abroad, for God in the Holy Land and for Mammon in France. When Christine was born in Shere in the year of our Lord 1311, her village had been racked by famine. Harvests failed and murrain infected the oxen and sheep. Plague, taxes and revolt were to lay waste an England often deserted by her lords, her kings and perhaps even by God.

Very near St. James's, her parish church, Christine dwelled in Ashe Cottage, a house with three large crucks—curved tree trunks—forming a series of arches, with a ridge pole to hold the steep thatched roof. The walls were wattle and daub, strengthened with a solid wooden frame. William the Carpenter had built a screen to divide the cottage into a small open room and a bower, or bedroom. In the main room stood an open fire for cooking and heat, with a space in the roof to let out the smoke. In addition, the cottage boasted four windows with skilfully fashioned wooden shutters. William had also built a small lean-to for his two cows and his goat because, very unusually, he did not hold with animals sharing the house, as was the custom among the English peasantry. His well-crafted cottage was home to his wife, Helene, and his three children: Christine, Margaret, younger by two years, and the last-born, a son also called William.

William the elder, although bonded to the FitzGeoffrey family, also worked as a journeyman carpenter, employing an apprentice of nineteen, a runaway serf who had been caught and branded on the forehead, but who had reformed his character under the stern, albeit fair, tutelage of the craftsman. Recently, William's status in the village had been secured by his election as the headman of his tithing group. Except at harvest time, he paid his obligation in kind or coin. His garden provided some staple vegetables, but his defence against starvation was his mastery of wood. Despite the years of anguish and hunger in the village William had survived, even prospered, and so his salt box was always full. Through the dexterity of his hands he provided whey, cheese, buttermilk, peas and beans, daily bread of mixed barley and oats, and—on high days—wheaten bread, washed down with spicy nut-brown ale. He could even treat his family to salted beef or smoked bacon, too, on many a Sunday.

William sat contemplating his lot in this August of 1327. This year the harvest had been fruitful and he had completed his boon work for his lord and paid his tithes. The reeve had collected all, even the wood-silver for coppicing the lord's timber for his carpentry and for his fire. There was, however, one small debt to be paid: the merchet due to Sir Richard. His Christine was to be betrothed to Simon, the tailor's son. The priest had agreed and all that remained was for William to ask his lord for permission. It was the old tradition, although William knew that in the towns such niceties were being forgotten. It was a relatively small fee, normally six pence, an equivalent in groats or marks, or a gift in kind. So William had fashioned a chair fit for the lord, who, by the reeve's inter-cession, had made it known that such a gift was acceptable.

That particular balmy evening, William sat outside his cottage on a bench, dressed in his best breeches, his serge tunic tucked into a belted waist. And next to him stood the magnificent carved chair, which he stroked almost absent-mindedly. His reverie was partly induced by the jug of ale which had been brought to him by Helene, who smiled indulgently at her husband as he, in turn, looked with love on the face that displayed loyalty in every weathered crease. Sipping at the ale, he pincered a hair-louse between his thumb and the broken nail on his forefinger. He looked up as he flicked the parasite away, and locked his gaze on the in-field, the last to be harvested. The barley and oats had been scythed, the strips of wheat had been sickled, and the binders had gathered the corn into sheaves to stack them into shocks to dry. A few of the old people and younger villagers were gleaning the fields to save the last handfuls of the harvest, while the paupers were foraging in the hedges and end strips. Soon the cattle would be set free amidst the stubble.

The sun nestled in the wooded hills that cloaked the pass to Guldenford as the warm ale settled comfortably in William's stomach. The carpenter was his own man, devout, yet possessed of a fine sense of justice, usually tempered by humour. He was unlettered, it was true, but he had memorised many of the chapters from the Gospel by sheer diligence and attendance at the church of St. James three times each Sunday.

As the trees in the Hurtwood began to turn pink in the scented sunset, he saw Christine walking from the in-field where she had been helping to glean the corn. William noticed that Simon, her betrothed, kept his distance from her, but the young man's eyes followed Christine as the small group of villagers filed out of the main field.

William thought that her blond hair outdid the glory of even the richest cornfield. She was tall for a village girl and her limbs so perfectly proportioned that even a father could decently note her fair looks. He loved his first-born and had planned her marriage into a respectable tailoring family with considerable care, and not without a little consultation with his wife and Christine, although, ultimately, he was a man who heeded his own counsel.

As she entered their gate, William beamed a toothless grin at her and said, "See, Christine, I have finished your chair. All be agreed with the reeve. This gift be better than a handful of groats—not that I couldn't be payin' in coin, what with the good harvest an' all."

Christine kneeled by the chair and touched it as though it were a sacred relic. "I thank you, father," she said, "for all the work. This chair be fittin'—aye, more than fittin'—for a lord."

She suddenly laughed, and added, "And the seat so smooth, no splinters to rip his lordly arse."

William tried to look stern, but he could not control the wide grin that consumed his face. Nor could he resist his daughter's impish sense of humour, although her independent attitude troubled him occasionally. She was too much like himself, he knew.

19

"An arse he might be, but we must bow to him and to the strong arm that keeps the peace here, and the robbers out of our woods."

William leaned over to kiss her forehead. "Red you are in the sun and after labourin'. Take a sip of this, a little ale will not go amiss."

Handing Christine his jug, he spoke through the side of his mouth, in a stage whisper, pretending not to offend his wife: "Now that the chair be done, why even I say you can with Simon tarry."

Christine blushed deeply, even though it was the custom for betrothed couples to tryst before their marriage. She had been teased by some of the village girls because she had insisted she would remain a virgin until her marriage day.

Hilda, the miller's daughter, the girl with the distracting wart on her nose, had shouted at her, "Mistress high and mighty, you are. What makes you better than us girls, then?"

Christine had thought about the remark and wondered whether there really was something wrong with her, or perhaps just something different. They wanted marriage and nothing else while, for her, a husband would be just part of her existence, because she was curious about life beyond the village, beyond England, perhaps beyond this world. These thoughts were half-formed, glimmerings which sprang from her lively intelligence.

But her father would not understand this. "Time enough for tarryin', father," she said firmly. "Rest I need after gleanin', not more rushin' hither and thither."

"Enough, daughter, for I am eager to see my liege. The reeve has appointed tonight for my gift to be laid at the master's door. Then next Sunday, God willin', your name will be fixed on the church door to declare the banns."

An hour later William, dressed in his Sunday clothes and carrying the chair, was standing with the reeve outside the gatehouse of Vachery Manor. The reeve, armed with his customary stave, bustled with self-importance. The Manor had once been a small castle, and the moat remained, although the Norman fortifications had been partly demilitarised and transformed into a grand house. It was built for luxury, admittedly, but still could be a stronghold if necessary—all for the glory of Sir Richard. The drawbridge was down. Facing the gatehouse was the entrance to the main hall, where most of the household slept, ate and amused themselves. The hall was open to the roof timbers, and it had a hearth in the centre of the floor and a louvre in the roof through which the smoke was supposed to escape, but the smoke and ash from the fires of many winters had besmirched the fine display of shields. The largest was painted red with diagonal stripes and topped with the sign of a crescent moon.

The reeve pointed to the shield and whispered, "Saracen—captured by our lord."

William was overawed; he had not been inside the hall since he was a young man.

The two men carefully picked their way through a floor thick with rushes, mixed with basil, sweet fennel, lavender, mint, pennyroyal and violets. And, inevitably, mustard seeds had been sprinkled to ward off the evil spirits. The dead flowers and herbs, however, could not compete with the stench of the grease, bones, spittle and the excrement of dogs and cats that mingled with the rushes.

At the lower end of the hall was an entrance from the courtyard. A large screen, carved with scenes of noble exploits in the Holy Land, shielded the hall from some of the draughts. On the other side of the screened-off gangway were doors into the pantry and the former kitchen, now a small armoury. Over the passage formed by the screen stood a gallery where musical instruments were marshalled, waiting patiently for their masters. As he walked past the gallery, William asked the reeve to tell him what the instruments were.

The reeve wasn't sure, but his pride and position would never allow such an admission: "That be an Irish harp, that a dulcimer and that be a shawm."

They stepped through the hall, skirting the dais and high table, past a fine carved oak chest which served as a travelling box, and on to the door of the lord's antechamber. Here they waited an hour or so upon their lord's pleasure until, eventually, the chamberlain summoned both reeve and William to Sir Richard's presence. Even the antechamber seemed a magnificent hall to William, so rich was it in wall hangings and beautifully embroidered cushions, all from France, or so the reeve said, again in a whisper.

The lord sat alone in a large curved stool without a back, but heavy with carvings in the legs. A good piece of work, William thought. The very last light of dusk filtered through a glass window, set in a transportable frame, above his head, and it was the first glass window, outside a church, that William had ever seen. Noticing the remains of an opulent private meal on the main table and on the two long benches that flanked it, William sniffed approvingly at the smell of roast meat that hung about the chamber.

Sir Richard did not speak; he seemed distracted by the magpie that had flown in through a rear window to peck at the scraps of food lying on the pewter platters. William and the reeve stood silently, uncertain of their master's wishes.

"William, the Carpenter," Sir Richard finally intoned.

William bent his head, as was customary.

"William, the Carpenter, my reeve has instructed me that all your boon work and levies are fulfilled. I thank you for the dutiful service to my house. You have asked for this time with me. What is your request?"

William coughed nervously. Sir Richard's lisp, he thought, seemed more pronounced in the confines of the antechamber. He had heard him speak before, but only at gatherings for all the villagers in the fields.

The carpenter cleared his throat, looked up and recited his prepared speech: "Sir Richard, I thank you for your time. My words will be but brief. I have made with my own hands this chair, a gift for your lordship which Reeve Thomas has said is acceptable as merchet for my Christine's marriage. I trust that this is so."

Sir Richard, a big man, dressed in a russet woollen tunic that reached to the heel of his riding boots, stroked his greying beard. As he stood up, he straightened the jewelled dagger on his belt. William approached his lord and, with a slight bow, handed him the chair.

Sir Richard took the chair and, with exaggerated care, examined the exquisite craftsmanship. He set it down on the floor and sat gently on the gift, as William and the reeve smiled at their lord's gesture of appreciation.

"I thank you, William. Gladly will I accept." The knight paused. "This child of yours, how old is she?"

"Sire, she be fully grown to wed these two years or more. She was born to us sixteen harvests since."

"A pleasing girl, she has a healthy ripeness in her face," said Sir Richard. "I have seen her at work in the fields," he added, a touch too dismissively.

He returned to his own chair, sat down and raised one hand, as if to dismiss his audience. The reeve tugged at William's sleeve as a sign to go, but then Sir Richard spoke with unexpected force: "I have a tallage more for you: I wish to speak alone with your Christine before the marriage date."

William looked at the reeve, who seemed as surprised as he was. "Sire," he protested. "I have obliged in all my taxes. And I have laboured mightily with fashionin' this chair. Is this not suffice? An extra tallage, if I dare say, is not meet. It is not our custom."

Sir Richard laughed. "Well spoken, William. I demand no coin from you. In fact I had in mind to give your fair Christine some small token for her nuptials and good

Christian advice. Tell our Father Peter to accompany her to this hall, when the reeve so dictates to you the time. Farewell."

Sir Richard's eyes narrowed as he watched his servants bow and leave the hall.

⋘∞⋙

Duval smiled as he punched triumphantly at the final full stop, for he knew what was to come. The priest believed that you had to experience evil fully before you could condemn it wholeheartedly. He relished his role as omnipotent historian who could manipulate not only the protagonists' past but also their future.

II

The Abomination

August 1327

On the walk back to the village, William questioned the reeve
until he was reassured that Sir Richard's man was no more
informed than himself.

"Take it as a mark of favour," suggested the reeve. "And
the priest will accompany her. Think on the extra wedding
gift...Besides, his command is law in these parts."

William nodded, but was unconvinced. He kept his doubts
to himself; nor would he trouble Christine with his concerns.

Seven days after her father's encounter with Sir Richard,
Christine accompanied her priest at the appointed hour. She
had bathed in the Tillingbourne stream that ran past Ashe
Cottage and had applied an herbal potion to her hair. Barefoot
all summer, she had put on the sandals that William had
crafted for her the previous winter. Her long hair reached to
the waist of the dark blue kersey dress that he had bought for
her during his first and only visit to the fair on St. Catherine's
Hill, near the castle in Guldenford.

"You have dressed to wed," Peter the priest joked with her as they made their way to the manor house, but he seemed uneasy with his jest.

Christine blushed and replied, "Father, this is my first summons to the lordly house. Should I dress as though to herd pigs or milk our cows?" She had a sense of her own worth, tinged with youthful vanity.

Just as her father before her, so too was Christine made to wait an hour outside Sir Richard's antechamber. When they entered, Sir Richard was alone. This time the windows were all shuttered, and guttering candles lent a comforting warmth to the darkened room. The table was set with wine from Aquitaine, although red stains shamed the exquisite white cloth which covered it. The lord, with his face almost hidden by a green hood, sat on one of the side-benches, engrossed in cleaning his long-sword with a leather strip. For a minute the priest and Christine stood in the middle of the hushed chamber.

The priest coughed. "My lord, I have accompanied William the Carpenter's daughter at your request."

Sir Richard shook back his head and the hood slipped on to his shoulders. Christine, noticing something odd about his eyes, trembled slightly, but told herself she had nothing to fear.

"Thank you, Father," said Sir Richard softly. Rising to his full six feet three inches, he pulled out a small velvet bag. "I have here ten groats. Five for you to carry to William the Carpenter as a gift for the wedding feast and five for extra prayers tonight in my chapel for God's guidance in directing my stewardship of this demesne." Sir Richard handed his man the coins, an addendum to the groats he had bestowed privately upon the priest.

"How long should my devotions in your chapel be?" the priest asked, with as much suspicion in his voice as his position would allow.

"Pray, sire, until I bid you stop," Sir Richard replied impatiently. "Do you presume to measure God's guidance? Pray for Christine's soul, but remember where your earthly duty is bound."

The black-robed cleric, his head bowed and hands in prayer, walked slowly out of the antechamber and closed the heavy door.

Christine had not followed this conversation closely because she had been too overwhelmed by the majesty of the great hall, and was now intrigued by the patterns on the tiles adorning the walls of the chamber. When she realised that she was alone with Sir Richard she felt as though she were but a child, so she fixed her gaze on a wax candle impaled upon a vertical spike with a tripod base.

Flattered by the invitation, she had expected a brief homily on her devotions to earthly and heavenly lords. Instead Sir Richard said, "Will you taste the fruits of Aquitaine?"

Christine's eyes searched for fruit on the table, before Sir Richard offered her a goblet. She had never drunk wine but, surprised, she took it as her lord beckoned her to sit beside him on the bench. She sipped the wine and pursed her lips at the strong taste. Despite the sourness, she found it enticing.

She had not yet spoken, but Sir Richard intruded on her silence. "So you are to marry the tailor's lad? Do you find him handsome?"

Christine did not know how to answer, but stumbled out a reply: "Simon, the son of Andrew the Tailor, is a good man, sire. From a Godly family."

Sir Richard smiled broadly, displaying his stained and broken teeth. "Have you tasted him, Christine, as you now taste this wine?"

"I...I know not...what your lordship means," stuttered the girl.

"Have you coupled with him, girl?" the lord said angrily. "Are you bovine, like the cows? I had thought that God had created a head to match the bounteousness of your limbs. You are the fairest creature I have seen among those who live on my land." He paused, then added more softly, "I have watched you working in the fields."

Christine, clutching her goblet tightly, looked down at the flagstones beneath her feet. She became conscious that her breathing was somehow difficult, shallower, more desperate, as though suffocated by the darkness of the room and Sir Richard's presence.

He shifted down the bench to her side and whispered in her ear, "Are you untouched by man, Christine?"

She could smell the wine on his breath. Looking straight ahead and mustering as much dignity as she could, she said, "Sir Richard, if I am bid to answer to such questions, I will tell you that I am a Christian woman. The sacrament of marriage is as sacred as my prayers to the Holy Mother. Plainly, sir, I am pure in body, although I confess my venial sins readily to Father Peter. I will come to my husband as a maiden."

"Good. That is how the Church dictates, despite the abasement of your rustic life. I am glad you shall go to the altar in goodly conscience, as our Lord demands." Christine let out her breath in relief, but then Sir Richard contorted his face into a half-smile, half-sneer. "And your earthly lord demands his pleasure too..."

Before she could react, Sir Richard had taken her roughly by the shoulders and kissed her hard upon the lips. Her arms pinioned by his great bulk, Christine's pewter goblet fell and clattered across the floor. She let out a strangled cry, staring in terror towards the door in the hope that the priest would hear her distress. Somehow she managed to loosen his grip and stood up as if to run. Sir Richard caught her hem and seized the sword upon the table. He crouched and, holding the weapon low and vertical, raised its tip to an inch beneath her chin.

"Christine," he said calmly to the shaking girl, "I will have my pleasure of you this night. I will not take your maidenhood, but I will take you in Byzantine way. No one will hear you if you scream. There is no man nearby except that sodden priest who receives my stipend besides. You will do what you are bidden and then depart...I would rather there be no force, but if you resist I will have a soldier's way and not that of a courtly knight."

The summer ruddiness in Christine's face had disappeared. She felt as though all the blood in her body had sunk into her feet and all the air had been squeezed out of her lungs. She gasped and cried out to the heavens: "Hail, Holy Queen, Mother of Mercy, our life, our sweetness..."

"You have no rosary, child," said Sir Richard with mocking kindness. "No Hail Marys will help you. You can make your penance after." His tone hardened. "Take off your robe or I will cut if off." He let the weapon just touch her chin. "Take off your clothes now," he shouted, his lips slightly flecked with foam and his eyes hungry with malice and lust. "Now. Now!"

She did his bidding and gently raised her robe over her head, then clutched it in front of her body.

"I will see it first. Let me see your maiden's shame." Again he raised his sword to her neck.

"Let it fall," he shouted, as if to a band of soldiers.

She stood there, naked except for her new sandals, petrified, eyes squeezed shut, trying to cover herself with her hands.

"By the Holy Cross," she heard him scream. "I will kill you now if you do not obey me. Take your filthy peasant's hands away." There was not a bat-squeak of pity in his words.

Tears poured down her cheeks as silently she prayed to St. Katherine the Martyr. Her eyes still shut, as if by not seeing she could not be seen, Christine lowered her hands.

"Aye, a goodly sight, that it is. Fine curves, strong legs and you have cleaned yourself," said Sir Richard, as if he were appraising a fine horse. He took the wine jar off the table and sent his goblet away with a sweep of his arm. "Lay yourself upon the table. You can hide your shame. Lay on your belly along the table. Do it! Now!"

Her legs would hardly obey her, but she kneeled upon the bench and then forced herself to flatten her body across the table. Trembling in every muscle and teeth chattering, she felt utterly exposed, her body as white as the cloth on which she lay. She sensed her tormentor moving behind her and felt something tight around her right ankle and then her left as her legs were forced apart and tied fast with cord to the trestles beneath the table.

"Nay!" she screamed. She squirmed to unloosen the ankle bonds, but Sir Richard was too quick. He seized her wrists and forced them down and apart as he tied them to the thick trestle supports.

For a minute the lord surveyed his trussed prize, reliving his own sexual past. His wife, cold, always absent, thank God, a marriage forced upon him, a coupling of vast estates, not ardour. And before that, the beatings, the endless humilia-tions at the abbey. Isolated in Northumberland, far from family, sent to learn how to read and write about the saints; the bribes of the abbot, a leg of chicken perhaps, some stale bread more often, the whippings if he cried after he was tied and sodomised...Anger rose like bile, and he wanted to kill every living thing in creation, so that no one would know of his ignominy.

He raised his sword and gazed at her helpless, heaving, fleshy rump. Much better to thrust his steel into that instead of the bones in her back, more satisfying...

Sir Richard was brought back from the brink by a prayer he recognised from his schooldays, as Christine wept and prayed to all the saints she knew.

"Hold fast your tongue, and cease that prattle. Cease that noise, I say, or I will cut out your tongue, girl. Do not doubt my words."

Christine did not. She managed to stifle her prayers.

Sir Richard's mood swung back from frenzy to mock sympathy: "Few women of your position have tasted their lords.

Consider this an extra wedding gift." As he spoke, he stroked the contours of her back with the flat of his sword. "Hush, woman, a stallion-ride to hell is better than a feast of swords."

Sir Richard loosened his leather belt and pulled up his robe as he positioned himself at the end of the table. He swallowed a deep draught of wine from the jar and swilled it around his mouth, then projected a mouthful of red spittle into his cupped hands. He rubbed them together enthusiastically, before rolling up his sleeves. Grunting at his own inspiration, the knight scooped a lump of goose-fat from a small wooden tub on the side-bench and anointed her rear, pausing to admire his handi-work. Satisfied with this preparation, Sir Richard pulled the girl towards the end of the table; the bonds stretched her arms and she screamed, but the movement allowed him to bend her almost at a right angle.

Then, legs astride, as if preparing for combat, he thrust himself hard into her. For a second, the breath was squeezed from her body. Then a red-hot searing pain ripped through her insides. The sound that emerged from her mouth was not so much a human scream, but more like the last mortal cry of a hunted deer. A long, eerie animal noise filled the large room. "Sweet Jesus, let me die," she shouted.

"This is the devil's ride, Christine," he gasped. "The coupling the learned Greeks did applaud. I will leave the other to your husband. Be thankful that I leave a virgin for him."

He pushed himself deep inside her, the more savage his penetration the better the revenge on those who had abused him in his youth. Every murder and every rape were steps to the complete oblivion of his shame. In his few reflective moments, he rationalised these actions as his physical confes-sion, an atonement, a purging of his memory. His erect phallus was a sword of redemptive justice. Thus inspired, he grasped her hips to keep himself engaged while her screams and pain stoked his lust. "Aye...aye...this be a ride indeed...scream on then, girl...I...break my horses when they whinny thus."

In his final thrusts, Sir Richard grasped the back of her neck with both his hands; Christine, shouting, crying, choking for breath, prayed for death to end her agony. She felt she was being crucified on her master's table. As he reached his grunting climax, he collapsed on top of her with his full weight and sunk his teeth into the nape of her neck. The extra pain devoured her ebbing strength and she lost consciousness for a few blessed seconds.

As suddenly as he had attacked her, Sir Richard extricated himself from his victim. Half-heartedly, he wiped some of the blood from his stomach, and swiftly adjusted his clothing. His lust spent, he quickly undid the bonds.

Almost tenderly, he said, "Put on your dress."

But she could not move nor speak; her wounded body pulsated with pain and her breath rattled from her parched mouth. With her arms stretched out, as if in rigor mortis, she appeared to be nailed to the wood. Roughly, he pulled her from the table and laid her along the side-bench.

"Compose yourself, girl. Here are five groats. If you speak of this again, you and yours will be ejected from this demesne. Be sure of that. You are a virgin still. Be thankful that I have taken my pleasure thus. Here, take this cloth and sop up those tears. I will summon the priest and he will compose you before you go."

Christine still did not move. Sir Richard picked up her discarded gown and propped her up on the bench. Pulling up her arms, he dragged her clothing over her. Christine slumped trembling back on the bench and, lying on her side, hunched her ravaged body into a foetal ball. In her trauma she prayed silently to God for strength. The sin of Sodom, she knew, was like murder and oppression of the poor, sins which cried to heaven for justice. Her love of God and family had been despoiled by hurt, and anger, and fear. And vengeance. All these emotions ran around her brain like screeching demons.

Sir Richard walked to the antechamber door and called to the priest: "Father, this maid has been bad afflicted by the dropsy. She began to foam and shake and I tied her to the table for the moment in case she did me or self a hurt. I have tended her with wine. Take her with you and pray for her...Call my doctor to her home and leech her well. Charge me all the potions. For her wedding day she must be strong. I will call for a horse and wagon to help her on her way. Be sure my kindness in this event is announced to all who wish to know, and that you were present for all the stages of this fit."

Father Peter thought, but could not say, "To Christine it must have been the Stations of the Holy Cross."

When the priest entered the room and saw the prone figure of Christine, an immense anger welled up inside him. The murder of his patron was his first thought, followed immediately by his concern for Christine. He started to rush to her, but Sir Richard raised the flat of his hand to stop him. The priest ignored him, but the crusader's powerful sword arm propelled the priest to the floor.

Sir Richard strode dramatically to Christine as she lay frozen on the bench. He kneeled in full concern and knightly grace. "Christine, be strong. If I hear that you have not recovered well, I may have to summon you again. I will hear from the doctor how you progress. Farewell."

Father Peter, named after the Rock of Christ, helped Christine stagger to the door while cursing Sir Richard under his breath. The girl appeared to be in a trance, her consciousness swamped by agony.

The priest was outraged by his lord's cruelty to Christine and disdain of the Church. Speak to others of the crime he could not, but Christine would be his charge. Prey sometimes he was to temptation, yet the pure remnant of his vocation would tend to her. All this he swore to God and to himself.

Christine took to her bed and remained there in fevered silence. Apart from murmured requests for a little food or drink she did not speak to family, doctor or priest. Soon the fever worsened with the leeching. The wedding was postponed, for the presence of Christine's betrothed aggravated her illness.

William the Carpenter tried to seek out the priest, but Father Peter skilfully avoided being alone with him. Eventually, he had no choice: William had waited outside the church door for hours.

Eschewing his normal deference, William struck at the heart of the matter: "What has FitzGeoffrey done to my daughter?"

Throughout the difficult interrogation, the priest lied and lied to protect his stipend and his shame. He counselled William not to question their lord, warning of his famous temper.

"Damn his temper, Father. A judge to hang him is the course if I find that he has harmed my girl."

"Hush, man. Fear his sword then if you despise his anger. His sword is the law, remember." The priest reached out to touch the man's arm, but William recoiled.

"Pray for Christine instead. Intercession with a mightier Lord is better counsel, Will," said Peter with utter sincerity.

William grew even angrier at the failure of the priest to look him in the eyes. "If Christine dies, I will kill that knight with my own hands..."

The priest finally accepted the challenge of the carpenter's frenzied gaze. "Your hands may be the strongest in this valley, but they are useless without a sword in them. Sir Richard has killed many men by the sword, and he has armed followers. You have nothing. Hold your temper, Will, and pray."

The carpenter managed to contain his anger as, with one final contemptuous look, he turned and walked away.

Father Peter prayed in earnest, both at Mass and at Christine's bedside, as she slipped in and out of consciousness.

William called a healer from Netley, who at first said that she had had a fit and that it would soon pass. When it did not, the local man summoned from Guldenford a wizened sage who administered a potion concocted from rare mushrooms; he also covered her upper body with an ointment made from juniper berries. For three days many such remedies were applied, but without effect, and finally he resorted to his rarest medicines: borage for ailing lungs, and mastic for heart palpitations.

When Christine did not respond to even these powerful potions, the Guldenford sage, with some insight, announced, "Christine is suffering from what the old monks call accidie, a sickness of the soul, where nothing has meaning, and all days seem the same, in an endless string of pain...until death. Sadly, this is the worst case I have seen, and I fear I can do no more; a priest is best."

He returned home, and left Christine to endure her inevitable fate. Soon, her pale face grew white and mottled like speckled marble. Her breathing became erratic and heavy gasps rattled in her throat. All her courage and joyful independence, every fibre of her being, had evaporated, and so had her will to live. Even the instinct of inhaling and exhaling had almost been lost. Finally, after a month of suffering, Father Peter was brought in to perform the Extreme Unction, the final sacrament.

❧⚬❧

Duval rewarded himself with a large brandy for creating a scene of which he could be proud. He was sufficiently self-aware to realise that many critics might describe his style as stilted, his characters as two-dimensional and his subject matter perverted, but he knew they would be wrong; he did not want the fripperies of style to mask his essential search for truth. Evil had to be exposed, and his writing was his absolution, the way for his soul—perhaps—to pass through purgatory. Heaven, he sometimes suspected, was not waiting expectantly for him.

III

The Vision

Father Michael Duval had thought long and hard about the yin and yang of good and evil, of heaven and hell. Just as capitalism needed the concrete enemy of the Soviet Union and could not survive long without its polar opposite, so too this corrupt world could not explain its own troubles without the existence of another. For two thousand years, the "other" had been heaven or hell. Duval had no truck with contemporary popular variants such as interplanetary aliens. Science fiction was just that—fiction. Duval preferred to read the Catholic fiction of enlightened cynics such as Evelyn Waugh. In *Put Out More Flags*, the priest had underlined the following: "It is a curious thing that every creed promises a paradise which will be absolutely uninhabitable for anyone of civilised taste."

From an early age Duval had been fascinated by the mechanics of religion—the liturgy, hymns and sacred accoutrements—without personally embracing the supposed final moral purpose: a heavenly calling. No matter how much he tried, his spirituality was rooted on earth and in the past, not in some heavenly future. That is why he hated the Vatican's tampering with the traditional Latin Mass.

Perhaps Duval's vision of the future had been corrupted by his own past. He was a scion of an old landed family. At sixteen he had converted from sullen High Anglicanism to ardent Catholicism, shifting his head and his heart from Canterbury to Rome. In doing so, he left behind a family already riven by his sister's miserable death in an asylum. Long before she died, he had prayed to his Anglican God to alleviate her suffering, but his unanswered prayers drove him to what he considered was a fervent, more serious religion, with a far more resplendent heritage, far greater mystical reach and, most importantly, a proven connection to the Almighty.

A little surprisingly, he had chosen to live in Shere, which had a long Anglican tradition. In the past the well-to-do local families had favoured the dissolution of the monasteries and had shared in King Henry's spoils. Later, many had sided with the Parliamentarians in the civil war. The area secured influence because Shere had once possessed an important water-mill, one of eight along a waterway which had supported five industries—corn milling, gunpowder manufacture, iron furnaces, weaving and tanning, an impressive array for what was just a large stream rather than a river, and only eleven miles long. The Tillingbourne also gained a reputation for its famous watercress, but generally the poor, sandy soil preserved the poverty of the small farmers. The eighteenth and nineteenth centuries had been kinder to the neighbouring industrialists, and to the large and wealthy landowners who landscaped much of a valley which the English traveller William Cobbett called "one of the choicest retreats of man." Shere marked the halfway point of the Tillingbourne, which rose from springs on the southern flank of Leith Hill, the highest point in southern England, and flowed past the beautiful villages of Gomshall and Albury to its confluence with the River Wey near Guildford.

By the mid-nineteenth century, much of the manufacturing base had been eroded, and the rural population, often untouched by the commercial wealth of the river, had stubbornly maintained their almost feudal traditions. As the mills closed, many in upland wooded areas might have agreed with Cobbett's claim that the valley had produced "two of the most damnable inventions that ever sprang from minds of man...the making of gunpowder and banknotes."

When the railways arrived, Shere flowered as a retreat for bohemian Londoners, especially artists, and by the beginning of the twentieth century the woodlands of the once remote Surrey hills had been discovered by a rich London merchant class. They came in search of seclusion, but felt close enough to the diversions of the city; and so the grey roofs of grand new houses began to disturb, here and there, the flow of forest green. When Duval arrived in 1962, the largely unspoiled medieval character of the village was attracting motorists and day-trippers and even the occasional foreign tourist. The outside tables of the White Horse Inn, in the centre of Shere, were always full in the summers when the first "yeah, yeah, yeahs" of the Beatles could be heard, sometimes too obtrusively, from the portable radios of young people sitting by the river.

Duval lived in an old secluded rectory near Tyler's Cross, about half a mile outside the village centre. Catholic priests nearly always lived in a church house, close or directly adjacent to their parish churches. If it were a large and important church, especially in an urban area, the clerical accommodation would involve a group of priests tended by a full-time housekeeper. Unusually, the bishop had granted Duval special permission to live in Shere, on the basis that Duval had inherited the house from his aunt and no Church money had been involved in any purchase; perhaps even at this stage, the priest's eccentricity warranted special indulgence or perhaps an isolation which would permit the ambitious bishop some room for manoeuvre when it came to denying responsibility, a chance to distance himself from his awkward subordinate.

Duval appreciated this freedom, because he found it very difficult to live cheek by jowl with others, especially other priests. And he was fond of his home in the former Anglican rectory; a Catholic inhabitant was a redemptive act in itself. The house, which Duval had renamed Hillside, had been built in the 1840s and enlarged in 1859 to include a spacious wine cellar and a large attic. Externally, the house was a hotchpotch of styles: part of it was robust Victorian red-brick although the stables, incorporated into the main structure, suffered from a mock Tudor timber-frame exterior, while the out-of-place Doric porch affixed to the main door was thankfully hidden in ivy. Hollyhocks and nettles as tall as a man filled the garden.

Neglecting the outside, Duval had busied himself with extensive rebuilding of the interior, particularly the unusual cellar which he had spent over a year modifying with his own hands. It was entered from a heavy wooden trapdoor in the kitchen. Twelve steps led down to a narrow corridor. On each side of the corridor, forty-three inches apart, stood three doors with small grilles. At the far end of the passage Duval had secured to the stone wall a six-foot-high crucifix, lit by two lamps at its base.

To his few acquaintances, Duval's life was very staid, his interests appearing to revolve around his part-time work at a run-down Catholic church in Guildford, a good six or seven miles from Shere, and his writing in his spare moments. He was recognised as an Oxbridge scholar, but was considered somewhat lax in his pastoral duties, partly because he refused to live in the parish he served. That, at least, was the gossip in his dwindling congregation. They knew he was not a favourite of the bishop. Some thought the problem stemmed from an arcane theological dispute, although nobody in his congregation had been able to pinpoint anything too unorthodox in Duval's often passionate and occasionally obscure sermons. None of his flock had ever got close to their priest, but some of the younger female members of the congregation had suggested that they found his sporadic house visits uncomfortable, a touch too familiar; nevertheless, no formal complaint had been taken to the bishop. Still, Duval's superiors suspected that he was an odd fish, so allowing him to live out of the parish had some advantages.

Duval had no actual pastoral duties in Shere itself. Apart from the normal pleasantries in the village shops, few villagers knew much about him. At just over six feet, Duval stood erect and athletic, and his mildly pock-marked face made him appear, to some females, as attractively world-weary and interesting. An actress *manqué* in the village had commented on his deep, cultured voice.

"He sounds like Richard Burton," she had insisted.

"Speaks like heaven," replied her companion in a mock Welsh accent.

When Duval had first appeared in the village, one or two of the bridge-playing, charity-organising élite had thought to invite him to their soirées, and some of the bored local housewives had turned their heads at the early-middle-aged, good-looking man with the distinguished grey at his temples. He seemed rather mysterious, but when it was rumoured he was a Catholic priest, perhaps even a defrocked one, the matchmakers forgot him. That was the way Duval wanted it, because he did not deliberately court attention. He had Surrey family connections, twice removed, but they were all prominent Anglicans, and those who shared his Norman surname were strangers. He had no friends, only acquaintances.

Duval always made a point of changing out of his clerical clothing before he returned from Guildford to Shere; he preferred to adopt the uniform of a country squire—buff corduroy trousers, highly polished brown brogues and a tweed jacket. For a while, when he first arrived, old Mrs. Malthus who lived in Pilgrim's Way had worked for him as a part-time housekeeper, but when she died Duval had not looked for a replacement.

He was on nodding terms with the landlord of the White Horse. Once or twice a week, the priest would enjoy a solitary pint of beer in the back bar. The landlord would sometimes ask about Bobby, Duval's border collie, who would curl up under the table in the corner of the low-ceilinged snug. Occasionally Duval would visit the other village pub, the Prince of Wales, but he shied away from the good-hearted friendliness of the drinkers there.

Duval walked Bobby for at least an hour every evening. Starting from Hillside, which stood at the end of a narrow dirt track, he would usually follow the bridle-path to Church Hill. From there he would take the footpath, crossing the Tillingbourne on the tiny bridge, and then traverse Upper Street, making his way towards the steep North Downs.

Other times he would wander around Shere interpreting the history of the village's timber-framed houses. To the practised eye, Shere exhibited scores of architectural treasures: the seventeenth century had been preserved well enough, but Duval enjoyed the occasional Regency flourishes and the pomposity of late Victoriana. The historian in him always smiled at the replica timber-framed shop in Middle Street, designed by the young Edwin Lutyens to fit in with the adjacent houses, hundreds of years older. The quaint fire station, the fragile wooden footbridge across Upper Street, the gentle meanderings of the stream along Lower Street and the ducks near the stone bridge by the

Square; for Duval, Shere was an England which the so-called "swinging sixties" were threatening to engulf.

In his walks, Duval always included a visit to St. James's, an anchor in a disturbing world. The church stood a mere hundred yards from the White Horse via the lych-gate, another piece of Lutyens, but it had to come before alcohol in his perambulations; that was his observance of a daily piety—duty before pleasure. Although St. James's church dated from the twelfth century, the Domesday record demonstrated the existence of a previous Saxon church in what was then known as Essira. It was "held" by Queen Edith, wife of Edward the Confessor, so the dutiful Norman accountants had recorded in 1087. The basic structure of the present building was completed about 1190, in the initial Early English style. Duval had researched the church in detail, believing St. James's to be the finest example of this rare Transitional church architecture. The fundamentals of the exterior had changed little, although the internal arrangements had been altered during the Reformation. Duval, of course, disdained these refurbishments as defamatory. Like all medieval churches, St. James's had not contained seats, only a stone bench set into the walls for the old and lame. The great Lady Chapel, with its twelfth-century arch, deep mouldings and clustered shafts of Purbeck marble, had been filled with common pews. The centre of worship in the Reformation had been shifted from the altar to the pulpit—from God to man—but, with the Catholic revival of the 1830s, the focus moved back to the altar.

Duval also disliked the West Gallery, erected by public subscriptions in the 1740s for the poor of the parish. What did they know of architecture? It had completely skewed the proportions of the church. In 1848 the rood window had been renewed, but it was a poor reproduction of an Early English original. The Victorians, however, did deserve credit for restoring the brasses. And they had introduced a barrel organ, which Duval thought was an amusing touch. New bells had been added as well as a robed choir, very High Church and very revolutionary for the late Victorian period.

The church had survived the Second World War untouched although flying bombs fell near Shere. The real enemy had not been the *Luftwaffe* but the deathwatch beetle: many of the oak beams and rafters had needed to be replaced. After the war the spire had been reshingled with Canadian red cedar and, to renew much of the stonework, Ewhurst sandstone had been taken from local quarries in the surrounding Hurtwood. Duval approved of the recent refurbishment of the oak altar and the flamboyant design of the three frontals, and was pleased that, for the first time since the Reformation, the church boasted a carved figure of its patron saint.

Duval knew on exactly which day in 1871 the clock had been installed in the steeple, and that it had an eight-day, dead-beat escapement, gun-metal gear wheels and a copper dial measuring four feet six inches. It now read precisely 7:10 p.m. The date, which of course the clock did not display, was 17th August 1967.

The clock was still going well, but Duval knew he could not say the same of his writing. Standing attentively a foot from the north wall of the chancel, he peered into the quatrefoil of Christine Carpenter's cell. He never prayed formally for inspiration, but every visit to this place renewed his dedication to his study and encouraged him to continue with the revisionist history of his anchoress. The black holes in the wall were a window into the past. Her past. It was almost as if it were not his invention, his imagination, his creativity, but her will and her energy that spurred him on. But now he was suffering from writer's block: his soul had not sensed Christine's presence for a long time. Was her purgatory over, he wondered. Had she ascended to bless-edness in the heavens? This spiritual block had happened before, Duval reminded himself. His muse had slipped from her prison in the wall. Just for a while.

Duval's sigh in the hushed church was audible. I would rather not do again what I had to do before, he thought. But this contact with living females was the only way he could reinvigorate his writing and his research. And after every experience the voice of Christine had returned. It was a worthy sacrifice to his anchoress. It had worked before, but, he asked himself, what if Christine's soul had left the wall for ever?

He touched the cold stone, seeking to sense her presence. He ran his fingers around the mouth of the quatrefoil, sensually, like a man caressing a woman's body. Duval had tried to understand himself, to probe his true motivation. He knew that he was in the grip of an obsession, almost Dantesque in the absolute purity of its near-impossibility—like the search for the Holy Grail. Dante's beloved Beatrice had been alive at the same time as Christine, but a modern equivalent of Beatrice, a tangible Christine, would add flesh to his literary chimera. And the quest was noble in itself.

Despite its original apostasy against Rome, this church in Shere was Duval's conduit to the true spiritual world, a conduit in some mysterious way to both his inner and outer vision. And the stern but persuasive voices inside his head explained that he could serve God directly, just as his anchoress had. It was Christine who held the key, and it did not merely provide access to his muse. No, his writing, he knew, was just a part of his mission. His fundamental calling was to prove that even in the decadent 1960s a woman could be brought to God, just as Christine had been. She could be helped, but in the end she would have to make a free choice.

Duval prayed for the strength of Christine's presence. He did not need a Church that had blockaded the highways to heaven with obfuscation, dogma and hypocrisy. "I have suffered, I have sinned," he said to himself, "yet it is I who will bring female sinners to God." Not just those who display their new hats on Sundays in a Catholic church, but those who will offer everything up to Him—completely.

"I am merely a tool of God. O Lord, your willing man-servant," he said aloud.

Duval walked out of the church, untied his dog's leash from a tree and marched up the hill at a rapid pace. When he reached Hillside, he did not make his customary cup of herbal tea, nor take his habitual bath. He perched on the seat in front of his great desk, eager to see if it were possible to write without Christine's presence whispering in his ear.

September 1327

A curtain had been erected in the bay of the bedroom to afford Christine privacy. She had not spoken for days, but stirred a little when the priest entered with the oils. Christine's brother peeped briefly around the curtain before the priest shooed him away.

Father Peter raised the cross above Christine's head. With due solemnity, he said, "My dear daughter in God, it seems that you are fast leaving this life and ascending Godwards. Sister, are you glad that you shall die in the Christian faith? Do you in all good faith repent of your sins? If you cannot speak to confess, nod if you can, and I will grant you absolu-tion. Then I will say the *Viaticum*."

Without opening her eyes, Christine managed to move her head slightly. "I have brought to you the likeness of our Maker and Saviour. Look upon it, if you can, and draw comfort from the Holy Cross."

Christine managed to open her eyes and unclench the jaws that had been clamped shut. Her whole body was coursing with pain, and death beckoned as a magnificent release. She was impatient for her life's last hours, even these last minutes, to be over.

Yet, as she peered into the gloom, a light—dim at first—seemed to emanate from the cross, which glowed ever more strongly, and the light, so strong now, flowed in waves from its holy form into her body. Warmth engulfed her feet and her lower body, easing and then dissolving her pain. Gradually, the relief spread to her chest, her neck and finally her head. Above all, the rays pierced her heart, purifying it of all her past ways, making her new. She felt light, as though she could float from her bed and dance with angels.

And then she saw a vision.

A small but breathing Christ appeared on the cross, and then it seemed to grow to full size. The wounds were real, and the blood a vivid scarlet. The pain on His face suddenly disappeared and, looking up, He drew her eyes to the ceiling, which had opened up to present the bluest sky on earth. It seemed an opening to eternity, endless years of bliss, of oneness with the Almighty. She was transfixed by the radiance. An intense ball of light swooped down and beckoned her to fly away into a tunnel of the sweetest and most soothing whiteness...but then a figure dressed in purple, a woman with the most peaceful smile she had ever seen, appeared in the tunnel. The figure, floating on a cloud of blue flashing light, summoned her, and yet, at the same time, raised her hand as if to say, "Go back."

Then, announced by the sound of a trumpet, the holy woman spoke: "Return, and all will be well. Follow me in everything, for all your life." The words were repeated, slowly and very deliberately.

And in this vision Christine saw herself turning back, eager to obey the woman, who was, she knew, the Mother of Christ, and yet she was reluctant to leave the incandescent presence.

Then she seemed to be flying over the earth, seeing below many prosperous villages and towns, with golden turrets and marble spires, and also a large white castle, which she knew was made of parchment. All creation was like a ball in her hand, for understanding had replaced the pain and she could see with different eyes. All her sins had been turned into blessings by God's love, a love sanctified by the vision of Mary, the Holy Mother. Love and understanding had been given to her.

All this she saw so clearly, but then darkness fell upon her, and the vision was replaced by the cruel earthliness of her room. Her vision appeared to have lasted but a second of time, long ago. The memory of the light and the peace, she feared, would fade as well.

Christine felt she was strong enough to raise herself a little. The priest quickened his prayers. As he raised the still-glowing crucifix, higher and higher, Christine was drawn up, too, as though sucked by some irresistible force.

The priest knelt and put his hand behind her head to support it and enable her to drink a little ale. She coughed as the pungent liquid stung her throat.

"Gently, my child," he whispered, cradling her head as her eyes closed and she slept. Father Peter sat by her bed, waiting and praying.

An hour or so later she awoke, and managed to eat a little wheaten bread, her first food for many days. Her eyes were large as she stared at Father Peter and they looked at each other in fear and hope. The priest had shared her pain and her shame, the proof of his weakness. Guilt showed on his face, yet her face was bright for the first time since Sir Richard's abomination.

Minutes passed before she spoke, although serenity still suffused her face. Then, forcefully, she said, "I have suffered, as you can attest, but I believe I have done worse to my family and my once-betrothed. I was so confused...I hated my earthly body...I wanted death, even prayed for it...that is my greatest sin...But now our God has spoken to me..."

The priest smiled and said, "Our Saviour almost granted your wish, but He must have wanted you to live on this earth to do His will. My child, I brought with me the unction of the final sacrament...our prayers, though, and your pain...and His will...have brought God's blessing. So I must hope..."

Christine interrupted him, her voice urgent and hoarse with suffering: "I must now confess what I saw. God's power has come here, to Ashe Cottage. When you raised the Cross, I saw blood, real blood, seep down from beneath the thorns..." She coughed and sipped a few more drops of ale, then retched.

Alarmed, Father Peter tried to calm her: "Sleep, Christine, sleep. And strengthen yourself some more..."

"Nay, Father, speak I must." Christine was sitting up now, the words tumbling out. "Truly, I saw blood flow from the crown of thorns. It was hot and fresh and in full flow, just as in His Passion when the crown of thorns was by evil men pressed on His blessed head. The blood flooded down like the drops of water that fall off the eaves of a house after a great rain. He who was both God and man and suffered for our sins. I saw all this."

The priest was overwhelmed with joy at her recovery. It was only natural she would turn to our Lord in such a mortal crisis, he thought. "Christine," he said softly, brushing back the damp hair on her forehead. "You saw God perchance, and He works miracles still. Or perchance it was your sickness. But, thank God, whatsoever it be, you are stronger. Much stronger. Now sleep a little more and then eat. I will tell all to William and then I will pray at Mass for the deliverance of your body and your soul."

After three more days in bed, Christine was able to rise and break bread with her family at table. She still shivered a little, even though she wore her father's cloak and sat near the open fire to ease the autumn chill.

They talked of minor family matters: Helene's new chickens, the way Margaret had plaited her hair into looped

49

braids, how young William caught a hare. Christine loved her family and all its squabbling intimacy, but she felt herself removed. She knew in her heart that she had been reborn in Christ, but she nodded and smiled inside at all the little family mishaps and adventures that she had missed during her fever.

After a few days spent regaining some of her strength, her father turned to a subject she dreaded. William spoke of marriage: "Sweet Christine, will you now see your intended to speak of nuptials?"

Christine did not speak until William repeated his question. "Father, I tell you plainly. I cannot marry. I have told you of my showing, the showing of the Cross. My life is marked for God so I cannot marry a man. I am now betrothed to Him." She joined her hands in prayer and looked up to the heavens.

William sensed his daughter's own Calvary, even though it was far beyond his imagination and understanding. He had gently and privately asked her to explain her vision, to tell him what had prompted her fit, but Christine would talk only of the power and glory shining from the cross and the words of the Blessed Mary. Christine would shed no light on what had befallen her in the manor house.

⟨≶∞⧽⟩

A week after her recovery, as if from death, Christine ambled along the path that led from her cottage to St. James's church for her first confession with Father Peter. Stepping lightly through the leaves that carpeted the graveyard, she stopped to gaze at the church. She had worked and played beside it since she could walk, but she had never really looked at it as she looked at it now. She had lived, and almost died, in its shadow; now she knew she had to be reborn to her church.

Father Peter was waiting at the great west door, smiling despite the guilt that gnawed at him now whenever he saw Christine. "Are you ready for your confession, child? If so, I would confess to you, outside this church. Come, let us walk to the Queen's glebe meadow, and ponder on God's will."

Christine felt the security that comes with knowing one's path. "Father, I comprehend your hurtin'. There is no need. Instruct me rather in the makin' and meanin' of this church, for I know you are learned in its long story."

As they walked slowly through the heavy autumn leaves in misty sunshine, they talked of St. James's history since the Norman days. The priest interspersed his simple lecture with apologies: that he understood how cruel Sir Richard had been; that no authority would accept her word against their lord's; that he had not witnessed anything except her distress, but could imagine a little of what she must have endured; and that he felt ashamed. It was left unsaid, but understood, that he was too cowardly to give up his living, sacrifice his stipend, for the truth.

"The rector, Mathew de Redemayne, cares naught but for the money from this parish." Father Peter's words were agitated. "The Abbot of Netley, what cares he? The Dean of Guldenford cares only for power, not for souls. I am half-wicked, perhaps all wicked, but were I to protest on your behalf, I would be removed. Then I would grieve for myself, but also for you, Christine, your people...my people. For all my faults I do try to follow the righteous path when I am permitted."

Christine cut short his pleas: "What is, is. I am new. Without my sufferin' I would not have seen the Cross in my vision. I had thought to kill myself when I escaped from Sir Richard. God punished me for the contemplation of this mortal sin with fever and, on edge of death, he has shriven me to be reborn, but I will talk of more in my confession. Let it please you to tell me more of our St. James's."

They strolled back to the church, the priest explaining how Sir Richard had granted monies for the recent restoration. He detailed how the church had frugally used old Roman tiles, but nonetheless had sorely needed further renewal. Sir Richard had paid for the latest Chiddingfold glass in the south aisle, and contributed to the repair of the grisaille ornamentation in the east window. Around the spire a wooden scaffold lashed with ropes still remained, after twelve years or more of intermittent building.

"That is now the finest spire in England, for the size of it," Father Peter said, proud of his church and also calm in the knowledge that, at least, very little of the building funds had gone into his own pocket.

"Should be the fairest in the land, the time that has passed with the buildin' of it," Christine said with a smile, the first outward smile since that awful night. She felt at peace and knew her mind—the vision of the Cross had strengthened her will as well as her faith.

At the south porch, Father Peter explained the finer points of the late Norman decoration, bolstered with marble shafts from Petworth. After pushing open the heavy oak door, studded with brass, they passed the treasury coffer donated by Sir Richard, after Pope Innocent III had ordered each church in Christendom to place a chest for coin and gifts to support the Crusades. Near the confessional bench and screen stood the font. Christine stared at the marble with its stern central stem, angle shafts and foliated capitals. She knew no child of hers would be blessed there, and yet felt no regret.

Sitting upon a very low bench on one side of a simple carved wooden screen, her long glistening hair dangled nearly to the floor; half-nervously, with both hands, she flicked up the hair on the crown of her head, pushing aside the fringe over her forehead. Composing herself before declaring her sins to her priest, Christine fluently confessed to vanity and pride. And she expressed contrition at having hurt her innocent and loving husband-to-be. Above all, she confessed to rage and to a desire for revenge against the cruel and hypocritical Sir Richard.

"For all the wrongs he has done to you, I cannot say how Sir Richard has confessed to me," the priest said with heavy resignation in his voice. "But he will atone or face the hounds of Hell and the fires of eternity. And spending his money on adorning our church is no atonement to me; no, it is almost blasphemy...but the church needs his help, for all that I say."

"Father, I know that God will judge his evil, but I know also that Sir Richard's foul impurity has taught me to be pure...for all time. I have told you something of my showing of the Cross, our Lord and our Holy Mother, such rich blessings for one as lowly as me; there is so much more...but I cannot, dare not, use my blundering tongue to speak of what belongs solely to God. But I can say, as God is my witness, that I wish to be closer to Him, perhaps—if He thinks me befittin'—in holy orders, but I do not wish to be sent away from here. In this church I am safe from Sir Richard, and others like him—if there be such other monsters in our shire. I want to be with God alone, not with other penitents seeking His guidance." With a last spurt of emotion, she ended her utterly heartfelt speech with a plea: "Although I am unlettered, Father, I beg you to teach me."

Father Peter was moved almost to tears. "Truly, I will aid you in all I can," he said, his voice thick with remorse. "It is but a portion of the penance I owe to you and to God. To be God's daughter in full vows is a purchase of paradise."

And so it was. Her father eventually came to understand the girl's desire to become a nun; it was a high calling, especially for someone from a simple family, but only Father Peter could comprehend her gradual insistence on becoming an anchoress, a solitary, rather than a member of an established holy order. William did, however, persuade Father Peter to counsel Simon, her once-betrothed, and Christine, both together. The priest, although he felt it to be a thankless task, summoned them to his humble cottage.

Simon arrived very early and, since there was only one chair in the room, he sat on his haunches, fidgeting, and blinking in the thick smoke of the wood fire. The priest tried to comfort him, but the conversation faltered in the face of Simon's truculent silence. An hour later, Christine walked very slowly into the priest's home. At once the lover jumped up and pleaded with all his heart: "A nun, perhaps, I can believe, but a recluse entombed, all that beauty, that energy, encased in cold grey stone!" Normally Simon was a man of few and simple words, but passion empowered his speech. "Delay your plans for a year or so...please think of me—us, then, the little ones we oft talked about."

Christine's face grew red and tears welled up in her eyes, but she took command of her emotions from the past. Her voice was firm: "Simon, I do still love you...but I must beseech you to find another woman. Many others there be far more suited for the unborn children I see in your eyes. I beg you to avoid my sight; please spare me the hurt. You shall be for ever my only earthly love." Her voice started to break. "I ask Father Peter to request you to go in God's peace. Please, please...I cannot bear the pain..." And she banished him from her presence, though never from her thoughts.

In contrast, Christine's mother and her sister Margaret soon perceived the power of her vision. Although Margaret affected to be the most worldly of the family, she loved her sister and accepted with her whole heart that Christine had a different calling. Finally, so did her father, but her decision cut deep into his belief of what his family should be. He cared not what the village said of the strange honour bestowed upon the home, and he despaired of the lonely years his first-born would endure.

Christine spent more and more time with her priest, who himself struggled to read, comprehend, learn and then explain the *Ancrene Riwle*, the guidance for a solitary life of contemplation. Initially, he described her future life as climbing four rungs of a ladder. The first involved lessons on the Holy Scriptures and the writings of the holy fathers, beginning with the lives of the saints. Then she would be taught to meditate on these lessons. Prayer would be enhanced by this lengthy meditation. And the final rung was contemplation, a state to which the priest had never himself aspired. He felt acutely that he lacked what St. Gregory called the "art of arts"—that of guiding souls. He knew he could barely guide himself; Christine would eventually need to be instructed by a much higher authority than his own.

They discussed the means by which one enters a state of true contemplation, the highest form of union with God that the soul on earth can attain, the wondrous and mysterious act that involved the total occupation of the mind and the will with the thought of God. Christine had to substitute the love of self with the love of God, only then was union between God and her soul possible in this mortal life. Father Peter explained all this as he tried earnestly to grapple with the most powerful but enigmatic tenet of Catholic theology.

An anchoress, he insisted, must return Godwards truly to fulfil the purpose of her creation. She might achieve mystical ecstasy only by contemplating the three levels of the knowledge of God, via His creation of nature, by reading His scriptures, and by understanding God as Himself, in His manhood and Godhead.

The priest warned Christine that the path would be very hard and that Christ was a jealous master. And there would be many difficulties and temptations beyond her studies and the conflicts of her inner life. A woman searching for the truth on her own was anathema to the Church hierarchy, because men ruled the Church, men decided on the paths to salvation. Individual pursuit of God undermined the very foundations of Christendom, the centralised control of Rome. Female saints there were, he said, but usually they had been canonised long after their martyrdom. Respected nuns, usually of noble birth, there were also, but Christine refused to consider a communal route to God.

In the beginning the priest tried to overcome the girl's self-abasement about her lack of schooling, but soon her quick mind outpaced her tutor's. A little defensively, he parried her more penetrating questions by asserting the authority of more learned men over her intuitive insights.

Christine asked, "Is it not possible to learn from the Holy Ghost, and to confirm, in dedication, prayer and good works, a knowledge which the layman might know and yet the priest does not—what the fishermen of Galilee did know and the doctor of theology in Oxford today might not? Is it not possible that lovers of eternity can be taught by the doctor within? I have been taught that St. Francis mistrusted learning as a source of pride; is that not so, Father?"

"Is that not your own pride speaking, Christine?" he replied rather hastily.

Christine pressed her tutor on the central Christian principle of free will. She understood that man could choose between good and evil. God allowed evil, so that mankind could be tested, the priest explained. But was there really free will, if so much was predetermined, so many prophecies to fulfil, she asked. "What if Joshua had chosen to ignore the trumpets at the walls of Jericho?" she asked again. "Or if Abraham and Isaac had raised holy arguments against human sacrifice? Could the Holy Mother have refused to go to Bethlehem?"

Father Peter struggled to refute her logic. Sometimes, though, he laughed at her innocent humour. Once he explained that man was a little lower than the angels. Immediately she said, "Then the angels should reform themselves, and quickly too."

At other times he realised that Christine was deliberately teasing him. When they were discussing abstinence, she asked, "Why did God believe the only humans worthy of salvation in the Flood were a family of winemakers?"

Yet the priest was shaken, nonetheless, by her rapid advances in both vocabulary and perception. They confirmed the power of her vision, perhaps, but he knew that if such changes were discussed in the parish she could be accused of witchcraft, and so might he. Occasionally she claimed to hear voices, and once or twice he reprimanded her, gently to be sure, for referring to herself in the third person. Sometimes he was not sure whether her fervour bordered on madness, but her calmness of spirit sometimes calmed his, too. Frequently he fretted about her, realising that much of what she said to him was arguably heretical. He thus encouraged her enclosure in a place where he could protect her from herself and, more importantly, from her Church.

"Remember how often do shrews find themselves on the ungodly end of the ducking stools," he warned. "Remember how Mistress Le Walshe from Gomshall was taken by the bailiff and her tongue cut from her mouth for speaking out against the Church. She was fortunate. Think on them who have burned in the pit for saying that the Holy Scriptures should be put into our vulgar speech, not Latin."

Christine always listened attentively to the priest's strictures, but knew without doubt that she was embarked on a righteous path.

For nearly two years Christine prepared for her seclusion, assisted by the advice and prayers of Father Peter. As before, she continued to help in the fields and around her father's house, but she laughed no more with other maidens, nor did she dance with the young men on feast days. Every day she attended church to learn scripture, at first by rote. Slowly she learned her letters in English, and even more slowly began to read a little Latin. Father Peter was not himself a scholar and had to work diligently to school himself for his lessons with Christine.

Her education was augmented by occasional retreats at a Dominican friary at Guldenford. It had been founded by Eleanor of Provence, widow of Henry III, in memory of her young grandson, who had died in the royal castle by the bridge across the golden sands which gave the town its name. Because there were no self-governing nunneries in any of the Hundreds of Surrey, Queen Eleanor had requested that the friary offer guidance to pious women, and so a small convent was established nearby. Father Peter was acquainted with the

Abbess Euphemia and introduced Christine to her. It did not take long for the abbess to recognise the piety and intelligence of the humble village girl and Christine was offered a place in the convent, where the sisters soon came to accept that her vocation was that of a solitary.

Christine learned dutifully the offices and devotions of the Church and Father Peter explained in detail the long and careful sequence of prayers. He rehearsed her nearly every day in the timetable of the devotions she would have to perform when she entered her cell: "When you rise at dawn, make the sign of the Cross, saying the *Paternoster*, then begin at once the *Veni Creator Spiritus*, kneeling at your bench and bowing forward. Stay thus throughout this hymn and for the versicle 'Send Forth Thy Spirit.' Next, repeat the *Paternoster* and a *Credo* while you are dressing..."

And so her daily programme of devotions was planned, interspersed by observation of the Mass and occasionally the sacrament of communion.

Father Peter explained to Christine how lenient and at the same time how strict an anchoress's observations could be. Certain high-born women had built elaborate shelters, almost tiny houses, adjoining their churches. They might have one or two maid-servants and could entertain visitors. Some even kept pet cats, he said. Others gossiped with their friends through a grille which faced the street.

Christine, however, resolutely chose one of the most austere rules that Christendom had concocted: no meat or fat unless gravely ill; no visitation through her grille except on strictly spiritual matters, although she was permitted to speak to family members on mundane issues of daily sustenance; but no other contact except for food, water, change of vestment or participation in communion. The priest would shave her head four times a year. But she foreswore the hedgehog skins, spiked belts and thorn adornments to wear next to her flesh or sleep on, as some zealots chose. She refused to scourge herself with nettles or whips to drive away temptation. God, she knew, was love, not pain. She had known pain enough; it was His love she sought.

Christine chose to clothe herself in a simple cap with a white veil instead of a wimple, and a plain dress of coarse flax. Her family would provide her food and clothes, and some church alms would be granted to sustain her. A small cell was built on St. James's dank north wall where the sun never shone, and William helped with such woodwork as was necessary. The squint and quatrefoil were placed in the wall, with a few stones left aside for the enclosure ceremony.

It would be some decades before Guldenford would be designated as a suffragan or subsidiary bishopric, and therefore the dean did not have sufficient authority to approve the enclosure. So the Bishop of Winchester's final approval was sought, and granted: "On the fourteenth day of the Kalends of August in the year of our Lord 1329, and in the seventh year of our consecration...I have sought fit to grant licence to the said Christine that she may be enclosed in the church at Shere in the manner of an Anchoress, so that, aside from public and worldly sights, she may be enabled to serve God more freely in every way, and, having resisted all opportunity for wantonness, may keep her heart undefiled by this world."

He attached his bishop's seal. And the next day, the day after her eighteenth birthday, Christine was sealed within the northern wall for life.

❧⊶⊷❧

The words did not flow with ease, and Duval struggled with the muse for weeks. His writing was sometimes becoming a task to hate, not a pleasurable outlet for his passions, as in the past.

Duval's congregation in Guildford was becoming more disenchanted, complaining that he was cold and distracted even when he finally stirred himself to visit a sick or troubled member of his flock, and his penances imposed during confession raised more than a few hackles. They had become onerous, almost bizarre. The bishop summoned him twice to counsel him: "a self-improvement programme" was the bishop's precise phrase. Bishop Templeton had recently been an enthusiastic participant in a church administration course in New York, and so he talked sociology, not theology; management, not morality. The prelate was a passionate advocate of modernising to preserve the best of the old traditions. Duval suspected that the bishop's real love was not God but sport; that he worshipped at the altar of the Marylebone Cricket Club. And Duval despised him for it, even though he could accept Lord Mancroft's famous argument that the English, not being a spiritual people, had invented the game to give themselves at least some conception of eternity.

The bishop was a short, portly man, and Duval interpreted his superior's dedication to the manly world of sport, albeit as a passive spectator, as a symptom of the small-man complex; "a Wisden Napoleon" Duval was pleased to observe in his diary. The priest found Templeton's obsessions trifling and endured the counselling sessions with poor grace. Templeton, he thought, might have made a good, self-indulgent Anglican bishop, but he rated him poorly as a Catholic. His superior talked about theological possibilities, not faith; religion had become mere philosophy. The bishop would thus never comprehend his subordinate's sense of spiritual mission, even if Duval deigned to try to explain it.

Nothing mattered to Duval except Christine, and she was slipping away from him. Yet there was little he could do. Duval felt utterly compelled to recreate her history, and that compulsion spurred on his faltering steps towards his literary antiphon.

1330

Christine's first winter in her anchoress's cell was the coldest Surrey had ever known. The oldest cottager in Shere, Ranulf the Miller, stiff with rheumatism at sixty-eight, swore to that. Yet despite the severity of the season, Sir Richard was not generous in granting permission for the villagers to gather kindling in the Hurtwood. Some of the sheep which had been brought from the North Downs perished from the cold, even when they were allowed to graze in the water-meadows of the valley. In January and February snow fell a foot deep on the hills and the Tillingbourne froze over. Even Christine accepted an extra coverlet and hide boots from her father, once Father Peter had given his leave.

William could see his daughter succumbing to the cold, and shared his concerns with the priest.

"The Holy Spirit can warm the heart, but not always the feet," Father Peter told William. "She is attendant to all her devotions, but her health is not as strong as her will."

"Cannot God's mercy be extended to my child?" pleaded William. "The mercy of just one visit to our hearth, where fire and meat can heal her soonest? Margaret, my daughter at home, cannot bear to see her sister freezing in the wall."

"Leave she cannot, William," said Father Peter earnestly. "To permit her to leave her cell—unless to see a doctor when she is nearest death or for me to give a final sacrament—is beyond me, and the bishops. Were she to leave, only our Holy Father the Pope could grant her rights of return. You know that she cannot break her solemn vows. Would you have her excommunicated and her soul consumed in the fires of Hell? But she should take meat." Father Peter's face betrayed his concern for his charge. "She fasts without my leave and I have told her this."

William replied sadly, "My wife or I do attend her every day after Matins. She takes her drege, the best mix of barley

61

and oats that her mother can make. Some cheese, too, and pease porridge. And buttermilk she enjoys. Her salted beef she refuses. Fruit she asked for in the summer...such unhealthy food...and now she begs us bring roasted nuts. Speak to her, Father, on this matter. She will parley but little with me except to know a word or two of her brother and sister. I speak of matters spiritual, as is right, but sometimes her voice is weak..." William broke off, his anxiety about his daughter and yet his desire to do right by the Church all too evident.

The priest patted William's hand. "I pray for her each day, Will, but she is in God's heart. I must confess to you that she is much near to Him. I could not reach that grace that she possesses."

"But, Father, must she die of cold to prove her grace?"

"If she dies, Will, no purgatory waits for her. See the Doom painting, the Final Judgement, painted there above our church door? Ascend she will to God's right hand. She will be free of our earthly cares."

"Aye, Father," said William, "and free of one mighty care— Mistress de Kempis of Peaslake."

Father Peter smiled. Anna de Kempis, a wealthy widow, was renowned in the villages of the Hurtwood, and beyond, because she claimed to have the "gift of tears," the ability to feel and share Christ's final agonies on the Cross. At any time this gift might be bestowed, and she would howl and scream and writhe on the floor. Her frequent holy fits did not endear Mistress de Kempis to others. She had recently jour- neyed to a holy shrine in France and, it was said, nearly all her fellow pilgrims tarried in Dover for a week awaiting another ship to avoid the screamer. And when she was not travelling, she sought out holy men and women in her locality.

"Anna de Kempis is touched by God even when she roars. It is not for us to judge His ways," Father Peter said mildly.

"Forgive my blasphemy, Father." William humbly lowered his head. "But I judge her touched by the moon. She wails and splutters to my Christine, and quotes scripture by the hour at her grille. The Devil can tempt us in holy guise, for the fallen angel knows his Bible well. This brings harm to Christine's mind and her devotions, I fear. How can she contemplate when the howlin' of Mistress de Kempis fills church and village? This is purgatory at our door!"

"Hush, Will." Father Peter's hand now returned to his distraught parishioner. "Do you want to be dragged to the bishop's court or be burnt, when livin', in the pit for heretics? Go speak to Christine, while I attend to Mass. It is too cold to speak for long in this yard."

William stomped his feet to regain some warmth and trudged through the snow to the north wall of the church. Stopping at the bulge in the wall which was the cell, he tapped on the small trapdoor.

"'Tis I, William. Please slide the grille."

Christine pushed the grille open and looked through the black cloth with a white cross in the centre which protected her from the prying eyes of those who sought her counsel.

"Pull the curtain aside, Christine," William said, a little more sharply than he had intended. "I need to see your face. Plainly. A father can ask this of his own blood."

The curtain was opened and William stared for a moment, looking for signs that her health might be fading. Gently he spoke: "Pale you are, my girl. Take this, some meat, seasoned by your mother. Father Peter has told me you are in need of this."

"Thank 'ee, my father. Under your instruction will I eat of it, though the smell is overripe for me. How goes it in our house?"

"Your brother is strong as the miller's ox, naught touched by cold," William said proudly. "Your sister is intended for domestic service in the manor next spring when she reaches her sixteenth year..."

Christine felt the very worst profanities rise in her throat, but she swallowed hard. "Father, no." Christine put her face—

her eyes wide in terror—as close to her father's as she could. She wanted to tear down the grille and shake him. "Margaret must never labour in Sir Richard's house!"

William was bewildered by her fury. "Why, my child? It is the only means of climbing from her station. She is to work at day and come to us at nights. Not inside service—that I do not like. Else she must go out of our village to another demesne. Better she is in my sight."

"Father, please heed me close." Christine was near panic. "Sir Richard is wicked...I have prayed for him to repent in all my prayers...but do not tempt him with my sister."

William regarded her quizzically. "Christine, will you or will you not tell me more of that night, at the very least to safeguard your sister?"

Christine could not stop shaking, but she forced herself to speak calmly. "Father, that is my life before I was enclosed. I will not speak, even to dearest thee, on this count. God knows all, but do not willingly let a lamb go to the wolf. Keep Margaret away from Vachery Manor!"

"I will think on your words, Christine," sighed William. "I promise. And I will speak again to you, but Margaret is willin' strong to learn from better folk. Be not agitated. I am concerned for you, not Margaret. Are you warm enough? Shall I beg to Father Peter for a third coverlet for your bed?"

Some of Christine's equanimity returned. "No, father, I am content. If I am too pleasured in my cell, I cannot share Christ's sufferin'. The comfort of worldly goods shall drive away my contemplation and lax will I become in my devotions." She paused and rubbed eyes unaccustomed to direct light.

"I still pray for Christ to show Himself to me," she confided. "As in the showing when I was sufferin' at home. I hold my eyes on the crucifix above the altar and He does not weep, as once I did behold. Perchance my vision was but once, for ever. I confess to you that I await a sign from Him to say that my anchorhold is blessed. That I have taken His path, not one of vanity, chosen by my own pride."

William was much moved. "I cry for you, my child, but I do not doubt now that God has touched you. Pure you are and deservin' of His love. And of life," he added. "So partake well of the meat. Do not destroy the earthly temple of your eternal soul."

The carpenter stopped speaking and looked at his gnarled hands. "But forgive my clumsy words; I am but an unlearned craftsman. Of wood I can advise, but God's mysteries are not for me to divine. I love you, child, and wish only for your best, in this life and that which is to come."

Christine looked fondly at the simple carpenter she loved almost as much as her vocation. "It is a Wednesday, is it not?" Her eyes sparkled. "So, father, I shall with my rosary say the five glorious mysteries for you, to guide you in what I have asked."

"Pray for me, then, Christine," said William rising stiffly. "I need your prayers, as all God's children do. Be well. I shall visit you on the morrow...with more meat." She watched him walk away, head bowed, and realised how much he had aged.

Christine survived that first winter in spite of the intense cold, and became stronger in mind and body as the days grew longer towards the spring. Once she had lived the seasons as the iron laws of nature dictated every mood and method of her village. She had been enclosed at the height of the harvest, just after the Feast of St. Peter ad Vincula, or Lammas Day as the villagers called it, when loaves made from the new wheat had been brought for blessing at the church. She had heard them feasting at Michaelmas, on the twenty-ninth of September, when—given luck and good weather—the harvest was finally all collected. Scot-ale, the brew sanctioned by the Church, had been imbibed liberally, while the noble guests drank wine or convent ale, not the "third-ale" which was given almost free to the rustics.

Michael's feast ended, and yet began, the farming year. At All Saints, on the first of November, the cattle were brought to shelter. But, before this, the evil spirits abroad on All Hallow's Eve had to be banished. Villagers whispered of the Green Man, a human sacrifice, perhaps some poor vagrant, dressed and painted after death, then, deep in the woods, burnt to propitiate the ancestral gods. What mattered the life of one outsider compared with a good harvest upon which all the locals depended? Many in the valley indulged in minor pagan rites and fashioned ancient symbols, away from Father Peter's disapproving gaze. Indeed, Christine's brother had brought her a corn-dolly to keep away the spirits of the dead because he fretted that she was alone next to the graveyard. She cared naught for pagan trinkets, but took the gift for her brother's sake.

Then came the autumn ploughing and the sowing of the winter grain. The high point was the celebration of the Nativity: Christine had rejoiced in the Christmas Mass and the twelve days of festivities, and she felt a part of her village as they crowded into the church. Throughout that week she knew that the villeins would collect their best fowls to present to the manor house. Candlemas followed inexorably, and then Plough Monday, when the spring ploughing began. In the cold of her cell, it had seemed an eternity from Christmas to Easter, but finally the candles were lit and the *Exultet* was sung to celebrate the night when Christ broke the chains of death and rose triumphant from the grave. The praises soared to the rafters: "*O felix culpa,*" "O happy fault, O necessary sin of Adam, which gained for us so great a redeemer." During Easter week, the reeve collected eggs from the villagers as obligations to the lord. Hocktide came on the first Monday or Tuesday in the second week after Easter, when some parishes celebrated the destruction of the Danes by Ethelred, but the nobility frowned on such Saxon legacies. Fallow ploughing, weeding the corn, coppicing and sheep-rearing filled the time to mid-summer, the feast of the Nativity of John the Baptist, the beginning of hay-time...and the cycle was repeated.

Christine could see and feel the seasons change, and added the snippets of news from her siblings to her instinctive sense of the rhythms of rural life. Poets and bards did not sing of autumnal splendour, for the winter often spelled death for man and animal alike. Rarely was there enough fodder to keep all the livestock through the winter and most beasts were slaughtered at Martinmas. Meat, she knew, was always in short supply, so peasants risked the shame of the stocks and far worse to poach a rabbit or the lord's game. The villagers and the surviving beasts became gaunt until the grass began to grow again. Fasting at Lent was often a necessity, not simply a religious observance. Most families had exhausted their smoked bacon and salted beef, dried peas and beans, and the remains of the previous year's wheat and rye and the few winter greens. The lack of milk, butter and cheese, especially during the depths of winter, lowered resistance to the constant epidemics. Christine's kin ate little fruit because they thought it was dangerous to their health, and vegetables were deployed mainly as seasonings for soup and meat. Scurvy afflicted nearly every villager by the end of winter.

So the spring meant life. After a winter of cold deprivation, passed in their dark, draughty, smoky shelters, the light, warmth and vitality of spring prompted great joy for the survivors of winter. Fresh food was received with thanks to the heavens and the songs to the merry month of May were truly heartfelt.

On the first day of May Christine listened to the festivities around the churchyard. She could hear the men shouting over their games—outside the church wall, because Father Peter would not allow wrestling nor dice nor ale within his precinct, but the sounds of bull-baiting and cock-fighting reached Christine from the glebe meadow. She knew that her young brother would watch the shove-halfpenny with fascination, and the new game, new at least to Shere, that was back-gammon.

Christine was sure her father would compete at bowls and win, as he did every year, the first ale drawn from the May barrel. And this year William was also elected the "king of the village"; it was his job to act as judge of the sports and morris-dancing competitions. His second daughter, Margaret, would join the village girls in searching in the woods for flowers and shrubs to decorate their houses for the May Day celebra-tions. The young men would go gathering with them, a courtship ritual since pagan times, and Margaret, almost as comely as her sister, would be covered in garlands bestowed by the bachelors of the valley. The young men would also look forward to their "roping," when women were caught like horses with a rope, and forced to give a forfeit—perhaps a kiss or a love token—to be freed. Sometimes the girls, often led by Margaret, would be allowed—for one day in the year—to rope a youth of their choice, and also demand small gifts before he was released.

There were mummers, too. One of the troupe had kindly lifted Christine's interior curtain, and she did not demur. So the anchoress watched through the quatrefoil as the actors dressed in their gaudy costumes in the nave. She saw one put on the red mask of a dragon, while another donned the rough replica of a bull's head with enormous horns. The mummers would act out stories from the Bible, but from the laughter and the costumes she guessed they had improvised in their mys-tery plays some more modern themes to entertain her people.

She thought, "*My* people. How are they mine? I feel the blood with my kin, but I am spiritual. I feel as though I have lost my bodily form."

Yet for all her spiritual yearnings, Christine relished the laughter and general merriment. Towards the end of the day, she could hear the men arguing about how big their teams of kick-ers should be. After all had drunk too much of brewstress

Denton's barley ale, they would kick a big solid leather ball, with as many as thirty or forty in each team. The men were supposed to compete at archery, as the by-laws for festive days and fairs dictated, but, if a lord or bishop did not attend, other sports that went better with wagers and ale were indulged in.

As the sun set, young William and Margaret went to pray with their sister at her grille and, despite her rules, Christine spoke of homely matters with her brother. She learned who had excelled at every sport and how a goose, unplucked and undrawn, was rolled in special clay and then put into the embers of a fire.

"Cooked it was in the fire, Chrissie," he enthused. "And when they split it open with a gentle blow of an axe it was so easy to thrust off all the feathers! It was ripe then for the feast!"

"The menfolk did drink the ale to quell the quacking of the goose," interrupted Margaret.

"Aye, almost a battle there was—over the goose," said young William.

"No manners there, even for the men in holy orders. So many there were. You know what is said: 'a fly or a friar in every dish,'" Margaret said with infectious laughter in her voice. "Do you know what they said about Ranulf the Miller?" she asked mischievously.

"No, I do not know," said Christine, suppressing a smile, "but you will surely tell me."

"What is the boldest thing in this world of ours?" declaimed Margaret solemnly. She paused for effect. "A miller's shirt, for daily it clasps a thief by the throat," she finished triumphantly. Christine smiled and young William yawned.

When their brother went home tired to Ashe Cottage, Christine spoke privately to Margaret for the first time since she had heard of her wish to work in the manor house. She could not tell her sister of the crime against herself, and so chose her words carefully: "I do not think it wise to enter into Sir Richard's service, but if you must, never be alone with him. He is evil and dangerous; he is a wolf. I counsel you from my heart. Do not think they are our betters. In soul, he is below the meanest pauper of this parish. I tell you true."

Margaret knew she was more familiar with the ways of the world than her sister. "Christine. I thank you," she said patiently, "but you are enclosed. You know little of the world outside your walls. I love you, for you are pure, but I do not have a call from God. I will see a little of the world, and where else can I go but Sir Richard's abode? To go out of this demesne is the same for me as a pilgrimage to Rome or Jerusalem. I have no choice but to work, for myself and for our family. Long days for little monies will I work, but I shall come home eventide to our father's home. A pilgrimage is more a danger or, were I to go a mile or so away into the Hurtwood, brigands could my life or honour steal away. You have forsaken our worldly life; I must venture more to live a little as our betters do."

Christine realised that she could not prevail, and tried to accept God's will. "Do as you must, my sister. I will pray for you through this long night. I shall not sleep. Good night to you." She closed the grille, leaving Margaret to skip home, dreaming of the new world she would soon encounter.

Christine prayed fervently not for one night but for a year for the soul and body of her sister. Her fears for Margaret...her fears for Margaret...Margaret's fate gnawed at her being... gnawed???

◁≋∞≋▷

He trailed off into more question marks. Duval struggled with himself, praying for guidance, but there was no answer. In his heart he knew there was no other way. He left his desk to run a cold bath, the second of the day. Although sometimes he would reward himself with heated water, tonight he needed to be severe, to force himself to think how he would recreate in a contemporary woman the purity of vision so absent in the present, how to alchemise

70

the base metal of the 1960s into the gold of 1330. He had tried before and he had not succeeded, because they had been too weak. They had all failed him, although the very process had helped to redefine his purpose, a project charged with all the grandeur of Jehovah. This time it had to work. And he had a young woman in mind, the "chosen one."

IV

The Chosen One

Duval liked the smells of night, savouring the evening scent of summer rain after days of dry heat, when the soil gave up a fecund perfume, the sexual aroma of Mother Earth. The rains dampened sounds from far away, but intensified the night calls of nearby woods and gardens. At night in rain or mist he would stroll with his collie along the Lime Walk and through the fields and copses, or over the southern hills to the King William IV, summoned by the low wooden beams in the bar and the winter fire. Tonight, however, there was no fire in the large stone fireplace. It was late September, and the nights were drawing in, but one or two whole days of sunshine had induced the landlord to hope that an Indian summer would still announce itself next day. A log fire would have been too ready a concession to autumn's arrival.

Walking with a dog allowed special dispensations from the strict laws of English social conventions. True, in the countryside, locals said "good morning" and "good evening," even to a stranger, if they passed on quieter lanes or paths. But walking with a small child or friendly dog permitted actual conversations, brief at first, and still within very firm conventions.

Duval normally didn't encourage such flouting of the English code of silence and reserve, and he had a special distaste for the endless variations of comments on the weather. Foreigners often found the custom bizarre, although it was quite simple. The actual weather conditions did not matter at all: the comment and response were an elementary voice test, a means of gauging vocabulary, grammar and, above all, accent; the first barrier in the rigid class system. If this test was failed, then passing conversations, even over the course of decades, might not get beyond the weather. They might even regress to a plain "hello" or, in extreme cases of mangled elocution, to a mere nod. Because it was socially embarrassing to regress to silence, the well-defined steps up and down the conversational ladder were taken very cautiously: hence the English reserve. But dogs were filed under the "extenuating circumstances" section of the social code.

Marda Stewart had probably never thought about the code, which had for generations been bred into the genes of middle-class English women, especially in the south. She simply liked dogs. Bobby, Duval's dog, with his mournful eyes and wagging tail, sauntered up to her three or four times during that late summer on the secluded walk down Rectory Lane from the bus stop on Upper Street. Marda had been living in Shere for nearly two months and she often took the short cut across the ford and through the small wood to gain access to Lower Street, where she had a two-roomed flat in a cottage near the Old Prison. The Tillingbourne river ran opposite, alongside the well-tended allotments.

On their first encounter, near the ford, Duval exchanged a nod with the young woman. On the second occasion, a week later, Bobby ran up to Marda as she was walking down Rectory Lane and dropped at her feet the stick he was carrying while looking up expectantly. She smiled, picked it up and threw it down the lane.

That gesture was sufficient for Duval to say "hello."

"What a lovely dog. What's its name?" responded Marda.

"His name is Bobby. Are you a dog lover?"

"I used to have a dog, when I was a child…it broke my heart when he died." She patted the dog on the head, and they said their goodbyes.

On the third meeting, three days later, they talked for a minute or two about the weather, while Bobby happily let Marda scratch him behind his ears.

Duval made it his business to walk along the same route at the same time nearly every day, but two weeks passed before they encountered each other again. This time Marda mentioned that she worked for a wine importer and had just returned from a ten-day business trip to France. And, crucially for English social conventions, they exchanged first names. Marda was an outgoing, friendly young woman with the confidence of the naive and a belief in the natural goodness of rural life.

That was the sum of their initial connection, yet Duval was carefully analysing Marda's potential. He guessed, accurately, that she was in her early twenties. She had well-tended hair, cut to the shoulders in a bob, and was slim and very pretty, at least to Duval. She wore very little make-up, which to Duval was a positive sign. Her voice had a slightly nasal twang which grated on his ears, but she seemed educated and intelligent enough to learn from him. She had an open, fresh complexion and an easy smile. It was the kind of innocence that Duval appreciated.

In his "local," the White Horse, he had overheard the self-appointed village Lothario say to the landlord, "Dan, have you checked out that smart blond bird I seen walking down past the Old Prison once or twice? Dresses well. Does she come in here somewhen?"

The landlord screwed up his face in concentration. "I think I know who you mean, but she 'asn't bin in 'ere. Anyway, you're the expert on the tarts aroun' Shere."

His customer took this as due praise. "Mystery she is," he mused. "Nice bit of skirt, but nobody knows her. Per'aps an 'oliday let in one of the cottages?"

And then the conversation drifted on to football. Despite the distorted consonants and slipped aspirates, which Duval detested, he continued to eavesdrop with intent while feigning patrician indifference, but the conversation remained bogged in the clichéd crudities of sports debate. That snatched information confirmed that Marda was not a local—all Duval really needed to know. After a few calls, disguising his distinctive voice, he found out her surname, her address and the company for which she worked. The letting agent for her flat was in Guildford: she had been renting it for almost two months, but she appeared to know no one in the village—Duval presumed that her work overseas kept her from making friends in Shere. Training someone from his own village who roughly matched his medieval vision appealed to his sense of historical perspective, but caution worked against selecting a girl on his own doorstep. He had to be extra careful, although in this case it might be worth a small risk.

The young woman was definitely a suitable case for his special treatment: the right age, probably sufficiently intelligent, fit enough to survive the rigours of confinement, certainly single, and—if he were lucky—even a virgin. Except for her dangerous but convenient proximity, she could well become an apprentice anchoress, real flesh to wrap around the metaphysical skeleton of Duval's beloved Christine.

Marda Stewart, of course, could not know that she was a potential candidate for a grotesque rapid-immersion course in religion. She regarded herself as not conventionally religious, but she believed in God, maybe a god or even gods. Despite her mother's former adherence to Rome, Marda had been christened an Anglican, but she had rarely been to a church after leaving school, although she did read a little about Eastern religions. She had always yearned to see faraway places, and her new job as personal assistant to the managing director of Phillips' Wine Company, despite all the hard work, was very satisfying. Her career had not looked so promising when she left her private girls' school at the age of eighteen. After a year working as a secretary in Weybridge, she had applied, unsuccessfully, for a job with British European Airways. So she found employment as a nanny in Lyon, where she spent a year improving her French and then moved to Paris. Surviving a variety of odd jobs, she developed a particular interest in food and wine, and finally secured her current job with an English wine importer with headquarters in Guildford. She enjoyed shuttling to and fro between England and France because it made her feel cosmopolitan.

As she was usually at home for less than two weeks in any one month, Marda had lived with her parents in Woking for a while, but at the age of twenty-three she decided it was time to have her own flat. Guildford was the obvious place, but she had fallen in love with Shere's sleepy, traditional atmosphere during her weekend hikes. The buses were reasonably frequent, and a friend from Guildford, Jenny, sometimes gave her a lift home in her Mini-Cooper, dropping her off at the top of Rectory Lane. It was quicker to walk down the hill rather than go through the centre of the village. And that was how she had bumped into the man with the wonderful voice and friendly dog.

Duval did not know the full biography of Marda Stewart yet; with a grim smile he decided to make it his business to rectify this deficiency.

It would all need planning and precision.

He found it difficult to concentrate in the White Horse, right in the centre of the village, where he felt people were watching him. He sometimes tried the second Shere pub, the Prince of Wales, but the landlady talked incessantly in a loud voice. Up the hill, tucked away in the woods, the King William IV allowed him to relax. Marda's potential had distracted him—as had a letter from an irritating American, some jumped-up professor who claimed to be an expert on anchoresses. The American had rather impertinently suggested that he should meet Duval during a forthcoming visit to England. The priest disliked uninvited visitors almost as much as he detested Americans and academics.

Duval felt he needed a little pick-me-up. In the dark Hogarthian bar of the William IV, nobody would stare if he pulled out a little jar of honey and added a few drops to his beer. It sweetened it and made it more like the mead of medieval England. Duval relished the taste of his customised drink. He liked to experiment with the flavours, the herbs and the potions of the Middle Ages. At home he could be far more adventurous, adding wormwood, sweet-gale, yarrow, meadow-sweet, cowslip, juniper berries and tree barks to his beer, or sometimes his tea. Despite the dangers, he had tried various permutations of henbane, the weed of witches. But his favourite additive was fly agaric, the red-capped mushroom that grew in abundance around Shere (its white cousin, the "death-cap," is never tasted twice). The Vikings were said to have spiced their ale with fly agaric before their raids, to put themselves in the right frame of mindlessness, and Duval restricted his usage of the mushroom to the occasions when he needed to be suitably aggressive. Tonight, in the William IV, a little honey in his beer was just fine. Before sipping it, he silently toasted Christine and the imminent arrival of a new companion for her.

Duval started to plan the transformation of Marda's life. The initial capture was always the trickiest bit, requiring the most specific planning. He thought hard for the best part of an hour; then, having made his decision, he purposefully swallowed the dregs of his customary one pint of beer and walked the twenty minutes from the William IV to his home in a state of controlled excitement. Even Bobby wagged his tail and seemed happy. Duval would be able to write well that evening. Marda Stewart would suffer great emotional pain, but finally she would transcend it, just as Christine had done.

1331

The second winter of Christine's entombment in the wall was not as hard as the first. Slowly, she had grown accustomed to a cell which was not much larger than a cupboard, and no more did she have to suppress the desire to run, for just one brief minute, in the fields, to let the wind race about her body, or to feel the freedom of rain on her face. She stored these sweet memories and embroidered them into her prayers and savoured them in her contemplation of God's gift of Nature. There was no doubt that she had diligently applied herself to her devotions: her reading had improved, and she could understand most of the Latin in her single book, while the Church Latin of the services was almost perfectly comprehensible. Father Peter continued with whatever extra education he could master himself before passing on his new learning to his dutiful pupil.

Even in her confessions, the subject of Sir Richard was never broached, not with Father Peter, her regular confessor, nor with the bishop, nor the visiting archdeacon who occasionally counselled her, received her confession or conducted Mass. Yet through her long isolation and his guilty kindness, Father Peter had become a confidant, no longer the accomplice to a crime, and he was the only person Christine could turn to on the matter of her sister:

"Father," she said one day, as he knelt in front of the quatrefoil, "year-long I have prayed hard for my sister. For six months now she has laboured in the manor for Sir Richard. Days she works at table and in the scullery, nights she returns to our cottage. My father tells me all is well, but I fear for her soul, and for her life. I know that I should be torn apart by the hounds of Hell were I to let her fall to Sir Richard's lust. He might treat her e'en worse than me. I spake to my father to guard her well, but naught can he do, 'ceptin' sendin' her away. Besides, she is now contracted to the lord, and he might rebuke my father were she to leave his demesne."

The priest understood her fears and tried to calm her. "Have you warned her of your own fate at Sir Richard's hands?" he asked plainly.

"I have told her to be beware, but I did not, I cannot, speak of my defilement," said Christine, shuddering.

Father Peter moved closer to the opening in the wall. "I will inform you very privately that Sir Richard has been over-ambitious. I hear tell his politicking within the court sits badly with the king. His manner with his bonded men, or his applying, here in England and to you, the *droit du seigneur*, matters not a fig to the royal court, but his taking of disputed land in other demesnes has made many enemies, not least the Dean of Guldenford, who claims Sir Richard has taken properties which the Church has been bestowed in legal writs. To have king and Church agin you is not fitting for a lord."

Christine was not reassured: "But Sir Richard is cunnin' like the fox. I do not portend his fall so quick, Father. And I worry still that Margaret be ill-used. She has not paid visit to me for two months or more, and my father shows hurt in his face when I ask of her, though he hides that hurt, or so he does attempt."

"There is naught you can do but pray," said Father Peter lamely.

"Father, women may only pray, but men may do bold acts. I am a weaker vessel which I shall pray God fills with purpose, hope and grace."

The next morning, after Matins, William visited his daughter to speak to her of Margaret, prompted, thought Christine, by her priest. She saw the lines of worry and fatigue etched in his face and knew in her heart that the news was bad. William hesitated, and when he spoke there was a catch in his voice.

"You have often spoken of your sister these weeks, and now I must tell you fairly. She has taken herself to Peaslake to be with our cousins there."

"Has she been by force compelled to leave the manor? By Sir Richard?" asked Christine.

William sighed. "Aye, that she has."

Relief coursed through her. "Then that is for her good to be away from his evil hand..." She saw her father's face. "Unless there be some crime or wrong done by her? Or, God forbid, to her?" The pain in her father's face seared Christine's heart.

"She is with child, Christine." He could not look at his daughter. "She says she was taken and forced by Sir Richard from near the start of her time at the manor. She was too fearful to speak to me."

William put his shaking hands to his face and tried to continue: "On the night of St. Reuben's feast day, she stumbled home all cuts and welts. She fell at my knees and told me all. That she were with child by Sir Richard and had just told him so. Thereupon he beat her, and took again of her, and his son Edward has taken of her too, when she lay terrified and barely knowing what day or month or year it be. She told me all in tears when she came home that night— those weeks ago—all bruised, and cut, and sore..."

William started to cry. Christine pulled aside the edge of her curtain and wiped the tears from his cheeks. She leaned through the outer grille and touched the tip of her head against his as their tears joined in shared pain.

Christine wanted to shout at her father, and demand to know why her family had kept the dreadful secret to themselves, but the agony on his face made her control her anger.

"Father, why did you not tell me of this before?" she asked gently.

"I wanted to, my child, but I have worried so much about your health; I dared not add to your privations here in this cold cell. I had delayed telling you, from fear...from love... searching to find good words for such terrible deeds. I ordered your mother to keep silent. When Father Peter told me of your constant prayers for Margaret, I was driven here by guilt. I am sorry to tell you all this now..."

"I forgive you, Father, but tell me, please, what has become of Margaret? How does she fare now? What did you do when she came home so defiled by those monsters?"

William could not answer; his shoulders shook uncontrollably as he tried to fight his anguish. Eventually he composed himself enough to speak: "I asked the reeve to arrange for me to see the lord. He made me wait eighteen days, saying he was conducting duties in London. Finally, in the great hall, Sir Richard spake to me with witnesses all around; before I could speak, he shouted that my daughter had shamed his house. That she was with child and so must depart. That there would be no bastardy in his household. He told me to send her away to furthest kin and let the child be raised in more Godly ways than I had raised thy sister.

"I was so angry I could not stop myself. 'Sire,' says me. 'I must speak out now, without your leave. My daughter tells me she was taken by main force, and by members of your household. This is not justice...'

"'Hold your insolence in my house,' Sir Richard did roar at me, his face all aflame. 'I have conducted enquiries full into your daughter's fall and ascertained that it were a village lad not connected with this house. Were you now to gainsay my word, here in front of witnesses, I will summon her to court ecclesiastic for the sin of childwrite. And if you persist in this calumny she will by Church courts be judged for fornication and bastardy. If one word more you utter against me in my house, you will also be sent from my sight and land. Leave me now whilst I have the patience not to draw my sword against your insults to me and to mine. Be gone, man, and avoid my face in case I lose my mercy. Next time I see your snivelling features, I will hang you in a cage as we do to Scottish rebels.' Then he started to scream: 'Out with you, you lying cur! Out, I say!'"

William shivered as he recalled the awful scene. "His armed men forced me from the house and I have sat with rage at home. With all my righteous hurt what can I do agin so strong a lord? I tell you true, but there is naught you can do except to pray His justice be done on earth." William pointed up to heaven.

Father and daughter sat silently. Then William stood suddenly, unable to endure his humiliation. "I must take my leave straightway," he said, not able to look into Christine's eyes. "Your mother needs more comfort than I."

"Comfort her well and tell her I do love her," said Christine through her tears. "And send word of my love to Margaret, too," she called out as the sound of her father's footsteps diminished.

Christine sat on the cold stone bench, then fell to her knees. She would intensify her rigorous devotions and pray for a sign to come at last.

She prayed all night, asking for God to guide her in how to avenge her family's wrongs. She knelt for hours, and stared and stared intently at the altar, willing some holy tears of blood to fall from the crucifix, but her Christ did not answer her. Drained and frustrated, she fought off sleep.

The long night became a day of prayer and fasting, but still Christ did not respond. Throughout the second day and night of prayer, she took no food nor water, and her thin frame shook uncontrollably. The lice and fleas roamed her body and she was too distracted to scratch or search them out.

Usually she needed to pray in seclusion, but she was interrupted that morning by a visit from Anna de Kempis. For once, she was welcome. "Perhaps you are the sign of God, Mistress de Kempis. I have prayed for guidance to leave my cell for urgent business to save the life if not the soul of my sister. Let us pray together and, then, please help me by unlatching the bolts of my door so that I can leave my cell."

Anna de Kempis's eyes widened in horror. "Oh, I cannot, holy anchoress, you are tempting me and God is tempting you. Were I to sin thus, I would be excommunicated, and tortured on the rack. I know God will strengthen you, just as when He gave fortitude to His Son on the Holy Cross. I know the pain, the terrible pain…"

She threw herself on the ground and started to kick her legs in the air and wave her arms and scream, and sob, and whimper, and then scream again. Christine had seen her share the agony of Christ on previous occasions and waited for her passion to pass, but Mistress de Kempis wailed for longer than before, and louder. Father Peter heard her cries and came to the north wall. He kneeled to comfort her and she threw her arms around him, sobbing more piteously.

The priest rocked her gently. "Ah, the Holy Spirit is leaving you for a while, Mistress de Kempis. Peace be with you now. Hush. Go and pray in the church, and I will speak to you after the Mass."

The wailing woman staggered off, and Father Peter spoke to Christine: "God works in strange ways with strange people."

"Father," moaned Christine, "God is ignoring my earnest supplications. He has not answered my prayers. Please undo the bolts. I must leave to help my sister."

The priest looked at her in amazement. "After all our devotions together, I cannot throw you to the Devil! What can you do that your father here in Shere and our Father in Heaven cannot? This is worse than foolishness, it is vanity. This is Satan's temptation—you must know that. You do know that, don't you?"

Not a little anger suffused his face. "I must be off to Mass, before Mistress de Kempis causes mayhem in my congregation," he said with unaccustomed terseness. "I shall pray for you. But I shall return soon to confirm that your resolve... and the bolts...are firm."

An hour later she heard her priest rattle the bolts, but he did not speak to her. Self-loathing, fear and doubt engulfed her, and she cried in long choking sobs until night fell upon the church.

At the end of the second day, a fever crept upon her, but she did not feel the touch of death. On the third night of her intense devotions, she felt the flood of warmth embracing her whole body. Through the mist over her eyes she peered at the crucifix. Did it move? Were there holy tears of blood? The mist cleared and there was nothing. The crucifix stared back, immobile, untouched, unresponsive.

She hid from the gaze of her mother when she brought her food, and the priest spoke only in communion prayers.

In her solitude, in darkness except for a little light which framed the edges of her curtain, she dreamed that her long nails were broken. Blood flowed from her fingertips, blood seeped from the iron nail that had been plunged over and over again into the frame of the trapdoor. She dreamed that she was tearing with bare hands against the crumbling mortar around the wooden frame.

She raised her bloodied hands in despair and, in the slim shaft of light, noticed two tiny holes appearing on the palms of her hand. She watched them grow, indefinably at first, then over the hours she could not be mistaken.

On the fourth day blood began to seep through, although there were no wounds in the palms. Then it stopped. On the fifth day the blood appeared to flow copiously for a few seconds when the Mass began. On the sixth day, it happened again.

She felt the gashes on her forehead, and imagined them as wounds from the crown of thorns. Her shoulders ached, perhaps from the weight of the Cross, she thought, and she babbled in tongues.

This she saw and heard and felt in her fever.

In truth, her hands were a mass of gore, her fingers were ten stumps tearing at the door frame, fumbling for the rusted bolts.

God, she believed, had answered her with the blessing of the stigmata.

⟨⟩∞⟨⟩

And God had answered Duval.

"Don't S-H-I-T on your own doorstep," the priest had said to himself and to Bobby more than once, when the dog made a fuss of local women. When occasionally he swore he would spell it out under his breath, as he didn't like to profane openly. He knew that Christians in medieval times believed that Christ's body was continually wounded by those who blasphemed in the course of their work.

Duval was cautious, meticulous in his planning, and usually his *modus operandi* demanded a geographical distance from his chosen ones. But, in this very special case, Marda had obviously been *presented* to him.

Reassured, he returned to his typewriter. For two nights ideas swept across his mind in invading hordes. The words raced onto the page. On the third day the words stopped, the ideas transformed into a vortex of contradictions. Perhaps he was being weak? Should he persist, retreat, wrestle with his muse, not advance into the world of flesh and those pale young girls, frightening in their innocence…? And yet, and yet their fear was so intoxicating. He adored that unique smell of terror which oozed from the flesh of young women, as pungent as the reek of cordite and rotting

86

cadavers on the battlefield, an abiding memory of his brief few months as a military chaplain in the Korean war. The aftermath of battle had appalled and terrified him, and he had been recalled in some disgrace, but now this aroma was sweet to him because it flowed from the women's demonic desire to live, and it came from every pore of their skin, especially from beneath their pinioned arms. Fear was the precondition for their new life, fear of one man helped them to fear and, ultimately, love the one true God.

Duval had finally decided. He knew that action would have to replace words and ideas, that the frisson of planning must succumb to the surge of adrenaline which always accompanied the capture. It was surely time.

V

The Capture

It was around seven on that chill early October evening when the bus dropped Marda Stewart at the top of Upper Street, and as she walked down Rectory Lane it was almost dark. Gathering the top of her anorak around her neck to ward off the cold, she felt pleased with herself: she had visited a number of car showrooms in Guildford, having saved enough money to buy a new Mini, but a basic Mini rather than the flash Cooper which her friend Jenny's father could easily afford to buy for his spoiled daughter. Marda had decided on a bright red one, although she hadn't signed the papers yet. She would take Jenny with her in a few days just to confirm that she had made the right choice. Marda had no mechanical bent at all; she had simply fallen in love with the sparkling little machine. She surprised herself by starting to hum "Yellow Submarine." Why not? Life was good…except for her brother. The new car had temporarily displaced bitter thoughts of Mark, while the pleasant memories of her former lover in France had almost totally slipped from her conscious mind.

Near the ford at the bottom of the lane she encountered Bobby, who bounced up to her in friendly recognition. She patted his head and carried on down the lane with the collie skipping around her feet.

On the other side of the small ford, by the faint light of a cottage window, she could see a green Morris estate with the back doors open. She could just make out a person whom she assumed was the dog's owner leaning over into the back of the car. It was difficult to be sure because the stream was surrounded by large trees and bushes, and the footbridge was indistinct in the darkness.

"Hello. Is that you…Michael? I found your dog at the top of the lane."

From the interior of the car came Duval's muffled voice: "Can you hold him a minute? I'm looking for his lead. He disappeared on our walk a while ago. Chasing rabbits…I have been out in the car looking for him…Where *is* that lead?"

Marda was now standing behind the Morris bending over to hold Bobby's collar, while the dog busied himself with licking her hand. She did not see Duval check all around to ensure that nobody else was in the secluded area. He would take her. He had the chloroform ready.

"What are you doing in there, Michael?" Her voice was so kind, so friendly, so trusting…

The first thing she would recognise was the force used to clamp the cloth around her mouth and an awful sickly chemical smell. For two or three seconds she would be too shocked to do anything except try to scream, but she would not be able to. Then she would try to break free, but he would hold her firmly around her waist. Nothingness would envelop her.

He put the bottle back in the cardboard box.

"I can't find the lead," he said, rummaging around in the back of car, and trying to appear slightly helpless.

"No need," said Marda smiling, "Bobby seems quite happy to stay with me."

Duval swivelled around and smiled in turn at his prey.

They talked about Bobby for a few minutes and Marda mentioned a forthcoming trip to France, to which she was looking forward. She then risked a personal question.

"May I ask what you do? I thought that perhaps you worked professionally with animals," she said tentatively.

"I am a priest," Duval replied. He thought she seemed a little surprised. "I don't often wear my dog collar when I am off duty."

"Where's your church?" asked Marda, trying to recover.

"In Guildford, quite close to St. Mary's, the old Saxon church near the castle."

"I like churches," said Marda. "In fact, occasionally I pop into St. Mary's. I love the ancient smell, the feeling of so much history."

"You are very welcome to visit mine, although it's not nearly as old. I'll jot down the address," he said, rifling around in his jacket for a pen and paper. "I have what I call 'surgery hours,' when my parishioners call in for tea and sympathy. I usually try to offer them some cake as well as the opportunity for confession." A small, slightly dry chuckle accompanied this remark.

Marda laughed ruefully. "I could certainly do with a sympathetic ear from someone. I've had a terrible row with my brother. I rarely see him, but when I do we always manage to argue... Anyway, I am sure you hear enough of family troubles. You don't need to hear mine. Sorry I mentioned it. I feel rather embarrassed, imposing on someone I hardly know. Terribly sorry," she said, obviously flustered.

Duval put on his best priestly manner.

"That's my job: to listen and to help. To all, whether they are Catholic or not."

"I'm not a Catholic, although my mother is—*was*—but it's nice to talk to you. You seem friendlier than most priests, although I don't suppose I know that many." She laughed a little too self-consciously, and Duval liked the girlishness of this grown woman.

"My surgery hours are usually between five and seven."

"I may take you up on that."

"Don't come if you don't want to. It must be your choice… We all have freedom of choice," he added gently.

"Well, I'd better get on," said Marda. "Thanks. I may call in to see you sometime. Bye." She patted Bobby on the head and walked the short distance to her flat.

Duval was pleased with himself, glad that he had not taken her. It would have been too risky, too impulsive, here on his home ground. He had selected her, and he felt that she had chosen him. He was sure she would come eventually to him. A few days later they chatted briefly near the ford, and he repeated his invitation to visit the church. She said she would call in when she returned from France, which would not be for a few weeks.

The next evening a demurely dressed young woman, looking very unsure of herself, walked into Duval's church. She gazed up at an elaborate chandelier and then at the high wooden supports of the ceiling; as her eyes became accustomed to the gloom, she caught a glimpse of a black surplice bustling from a passage near the side of the altar. It was Duval and he greeted her warmly.

"You look so different dressed as a priest," Marda said shyly. "It makes it so formal, rather than chatting to an old…well, a new friend."

Duval considered whether he should shake her hand, but decided against it. "Welcome, Marda," he said, showing surprise but also genuine pleasure at her arrival. "I'm on duty now. So please come into the vestry and have a cup of tea. And there is some coconut cake as well." He led her to a small office, full of old books. "Bit small and scruffy, I'm afraid, but most people find it cosy enough for a chat. I thought you were going to France."

"I am, but I had a stinking letter from Mark, you know, the brother I mentioned to you, and, well, I wanted to clear my head before I went away."

"Sugar?" said Duval.

"No thanks."

"Please sit down. That chair is more comfortable. Now tell me about your brother…"

"Well, I feel awkward talking about it."

When she started to pull out a blue packet of Gitanes cigarettes from her handbag, Duval noticed her long painted nails.

"Oh, I'm sorry. You don't smoke in church," Marda said, looking flustered again. "I'm just rather nervous."

"I don't smoke in the actual church, but I sometimes smoke my pipe here in my office. Smoke if you want. *Really.* Use my ashtray."

Duval disliked women smoking, but it was not the time to say that. Marda lit up the Gitane, sank back into her chair and sipped her tea.

"This tea tastes unusual… It's interesting, though. What is it?"

"I have an interest in herbs," said Duval, not looking at her. "It's my own mix. Some conventional Assam with a few of my own little additions… You were talking about your brother."

Marda put on a very diffident smile, with her chin down and her eyes up, as though she was a doe startled by a strange sound in the forest.

Duval waited for her to speak. When she did, the words tumbled out. "We're not really a close family and I don't feel I can talk about it with them. In fact, although my mother is a lapsed Catholic, my father is a staunch Anglican. He would have a blue fit if he knew I was here talking to a Catholic priest. I haven't told a soul I'm here, not even Jenny—she's my best friend in Guildford. Maybe it's crazy, but I wanted to talk to someone professionally, if you like. It's not religious, at all, so perhaps I shouldn't really be here."

"I'm glad you are," said Duval. "Very glad."

For ten or fifteen minutes the priest was told a tale of recent sibling rivalry, of two over-achievers close in age, with loving but distant parents. Duval listened carefully enough to offer the occasionally anodyne commiseration, but he was more intent on examining Marda's potential for the tasks he would set her. It was enough to sit and let her pour her heart out.

Suddenly Marda dried up. "I feel such a fool, telling you all my problems; I'm sure you have lots to do..." And she stood up to leave.

Duval stood with her. "It's good to talk. Confessions—or even informal chats like this—are often the first steps to resolving personal problems. Please call in again. If it helps, I am always ready to listen and provide whatever advice I can."

He offered his hand, and she shook it warmly. The priest escorted her to the side entrance of the church, passing two old women bent under the weight of their years, praying in a small side chapel, too engrossed in worship to notice the striking young woman. It was dark when she left the church.

If she comes again, thought Duval, she has chosen. She has exercised her own free will. It is her choice.

Duval did not have to wait long. The next evening, after work, Marda rushed in from the rain to apologise for unburdening herself. This time the church was empty.

The priest led her into his room, and offered her tea again. She was very reluctant to stop, but he insisted. He calmed her by asking, "Did it help, opening yourself up a little? That's all that matters; and, remember, it is my role in life to listen to people's problems. Priests can *sometimes* be useful, you know."

She drank her tea rapidly, trying to avoid any impression of imposing on this man whom she had so recently met.

"Michael...or should I call you 'Father' in church...?"

"Please call me 'Michael,' I insist."

"Well, *Michael*, I do appreciate your listening and your advice, but I must be truthful, I'm not into formal religion at all...no offence meant, of course." She laughed at her own clumsiness.

Michael laughed too. "None taken, I can assure you."

Marda wanted to put her cup down, to indicate politely that she was about to leave. She tried to get up from her seat, but slumped back down. She spoke, but she found it hard to enunciate correctly. The priest stood and watched as Marda's voice started to wind down to a quiet, slurring monotone. As her head slumped on to her chest and her empty cup and saucer fell to the floor and broke into pieces, Duval locked the door to his office.

⋖⋗⋗⋙⋘⋖

When she awoke from her drugged sleep Marda was lying in complete darkness on what felt like a wooden bench.

Too groggy to explore her mind, let alone her new environment, she just turned to her side and was copiously sick. She lay back prone on the bench and opened and closed her eyes. It didn't make any difference because it was completely black. She pinched herself to see if she was dreaming. For a moment she thought she was dead, until she heard herself croak: "Where the hell am I?"

Somehow that fragment of self-assertion made her feel a little better, although she had a pulsating headache. Her lips and mouth were bitter from a chemical taste and sour from the vomit. She desperately wanted to drink something. Anything. A part of her felt like falling asleep again, but her panic forced her to explore.

She stretched out her left hand to touch a cold stone wall to her side. Then she raised her right hand to just above her head and felt the same cold stone. She began to feel cold herself. What is this place? her mind screamed, terror welling up inside her. Some sort of burial vault in the church?

Her jacket had gone, so had her shoes. She tried to sit up, but the pain rushed to her head again and she lay back down. Slowly she felt her body with her hands, and realised that she was wearing just her bra and pants. For a second, indignation displaced some of the dread.

"The bastard," she said aloud. "The bastard. He's drugged me, locked me up somewhere in some cold dungeon or something...and he's taken my clothes." The thought suddenly took hold of her terrified mind that he could have raped her as well, and she began to sob uncontrollably. Then her common sense reasserted itself, and she realised that there was no bruising or pain between her legs. She would know if she had been violated.

"No. Not that. Thank God," she mumbled.

She forced herself to sit up again, despite the pounding in her head, and then swung her legs off the bench. Remembering the vomit she put first one foot then another on to the floor, very gingerly, away from where she had been sick, but when she tried to stand she fell back on the bench.

For two or three minutes Marda breathed hard in and out. Then she tried again, supporting herself by holding on to the bench, which was about two-and-a-half feet from the stone floor. At the foot of the bench she touched a hard, flat wooden surface which she tapped and realised was some kind of door. In complete darkness she traced both hands across the door, finding a square metal lock with no handle. At the far end of the door, about two feet away, was the facing wall; she felt along it very carefully, afraid that it might hold something jagged, cutting, cruel. For roughly the same length as the bench she touched the wall with her fingertips. It was cold stone. Dry in most places, with a little damp here and there. No moss, no slime. Reaching the far end of the facing wall, she touched the corner and felt her way along the wall opposite the door. This time she stepped in her own vomit and, in disgust, she sat back on the bench.

The self-disgust began to invade her whole being. Then anger seemed to ride the helter-skelter of a mind in turmoil. Cold, numbing fear was the next passenger. Fear kept coming back, accompanied by terror and panic. Despair sometimes joined the black company: Marda even thought of killing herself before her kidnapper could violate and murder her.

She was slipping into hysteria. She had to talk to someone, even herself. "So a little bloody square cell," she said aloud. It wasn't exactly square, but the sound of her own swearing made her more confident. "I don't care what they say about going nuts. I *am* going to talk to myself," she said, although her confidence did not sound very real.

Her introspection was disrupted by a scratching noise. It sounded far off, then she thought it was quite near. She wondered whether it was somebody, or something.

She shouted, "Who's that?" but then thought that she should remain quiet. She was panting with panic. Each breath, however, sounded to Marda like the chug of a steam train. Soon the scratching noise stopped. After a few minutes, with trembling hands, she wiped the cold sweat from her brow.

It was darker than all the darknesses she had ever experienced before. It was suffocating her. The darkness seemed so heavy that it was like a huge creature pressing down on her chest. Feeling herself drowning in the enveloping miasma, Marda wanted to strike out at her oppressor.

She began to mumble to herself. In the space of minutes— or was it hours?—she was catapulted through highs and lows. First, depression at the hopelessness of her situation.

Then euphoria in the certainty that it would last but a short time. For a few seconds she could pretend that it was all a nightmare, but then came the crashing reality. She roller-coasted from terror to resignation, to rebellion, a sense of abandonment, fear, hope, despair, anger…the will to live, to fight. She found herself screaming and then forced herself to think.

She wondered what the time was. Without a watch she felt herself to be lost on a sea of time, completely out of sight of any land. There was no time, only eternity; and that eternity was standing still. How long had it been since she had been attacked by "Michael"?

"I bet that's not his real name," she said quite loudly. Maybe the cell was bugged. "I don't care if you *can* hear me. You're a bastard! Let me *out* of here," she shouted.

Utterly desperate, she stood up and groped her way to the door and banged it with both her fists until they hurt. "Is there anybody out there?" she yelled hysterically. "Where am I? What do you want with me?" The clawing pains of extreme panic rippled through her stomach; she cried like a little girl for several minutes, then made a concerted effort to pull herself together.

She couldn't be sure, but Marda estimated that it had been a few hours or so since she was taken. So, she realised, it was a kidnap. But the wrong girl, she thought. Maybe they—Marda assumed a gang—were after Jenny, her friend with the rich father. But that was unlikely because she had spoken with this Michael on a number of occasions. And she had visited him in a church. Was he a bogus priest? It couldn't be mistaken identity. He had seemed so kind, so cultured. If he's so cultured what's he doing putting me in here? A pervert? A psychopath? "Oh, God. Maybe he wants me for that. Then he'll kill me." She started to cry again, but stopped herself. "Whimpering and wailing are not going to do you any good, my girl." The harsh-kind words said aloud reminded her of the times she had said them to comfort homesick younger girls in her boarding-school dormitory.

He seems a reasonable man and he's obviously educated, she thought. Maybe there's some mistake. I can talk to him. Explain. He'll apologise and let me go home. Home? Nobody's in my flat, she thought sourly. Nobody knows where I am. I'm not supposed to meet my boss in Bordeaux for a few days yet. I could be dead and buried by then.

She felt terrified and sick, and suddenly yearned for a cigarette, but he had taken all her belongings away. She could not believe what had happened to her, so she tried to organise her questions to make some sense of her living nightmare. In the confined space, she realised that she could smell her own fear, and this fear, she knew, was undermining her judgement. What judgement—how could she have trusted this priest? Who knows I'm here? No one except him. So who is he? Where is he now? What does he want? Where am I? Why, oh, why did he do this? What comes next? What if nothing is next…and I'm just left here to rot?

A talon of dread tore at her very being, and she shivered from terror as much as from the cold. Her breathing became laboured as she worked herself once again into a state of hysteria.

"Calm down, Marda," she said aloud to herself. "We can sort this bastard out."

Suddenly the "we" made her feel desperately alone, and she felt her whole life rushing before her. She so wanted to live. Once she had doubted the very existence of God, but now she wanted to be wrong about that. If there were a God, surely He could not be so cruel as to end her life here in this horrible dark place.

All her personal ambitions, plans for a career and tender unspoken hopes of love flashed through her mind in seconds. Now they were all gone. Now all she had was fear and darkness. She was entombed.

VI

T𝒽e Tomb

Duval was feeling good. This capture had been easier than the others, and it pleased him that he was becoming more efficient and ruthless. Somebody might have seen him put Marda into his car, but how? It was so secluded and dark behind the church. If someone had seen him, surely they would have shouted? No, he was safe. Guildford was not so far, and she had not stirred. That hurtbane potion had worked; an old trick, dating back to the Norman Conquest, which could topple a man for an hour or so if applied correctly.

It was dark driving through the almost unlit village of Shere, and even if someone had seen him in his car with his dog up front, nobody would think twice about it. His driveway at the top of a dead-end lane was completely obscured by trees and bushes. He had been taking a chance, but he had done it. No one would ever know.

He lit the big wood-burning stove in the kitchen, and relaxed in his wooden rocker. In front of him he contemplated the pile of Marda's belongings. First, he checked through her handbag and removed her address book, purse and keys, then, once the heat in the stove was intense, gradually fed its remaining contents into the fire. Her shoes, tights, skirt, blouse and jacket followed methodically. Duval hid the chloroform bottle in his attic, just in case he might need it for another chosen one. Marda's purse, address book, keys and watch he put in a secret drawer, to be examined later before their disposal.

After making a cup of tea, Duval treated himself to a hot bath and sat down at his study desk, giving his crucifix a lop-sided grin which any fly-on-the-wall onlooker might have interpreted as a wink. An aura of contentment settled upon him, and he recalled part of a medieval parody of a monk's prayer:

> *Meum pectus sauciat*
> *puellarum decor,*
> *et quas tactu nequeo,*
> *Sa item corde mechor.*

He loved the sound of Latin vowels, and the vigour of his own translation pleased him even more:

> Wounded to the quick am I
> By a young girl's beauty.
> She's beyond my touching?
> Well, can't the mind do duty?

"I shall write tonight. I can feel my words flowing," he confided to the crucifix.

July 1331

Christine knelt and thanked God for His mercy and His sign of the stigmata. She knew He would understand her leaving and He would condone the breaking of her vows by granting her a holy indulgence. Her bleeding hands were the perfect symbol of the Christian passion, absolute proof; no writhing and howling like Mistress de Kempis.

In her frenzy, Christine had managed to remove two of the stones that stood aligned with the bolts. Parts of her fingers had been worn almost to the bone, and deep gouges despoiled her arms.

To Christine, her own endeavours were God's miracles; her head was spinning, her senses dulled and vision blurred by pain. On the sixth day after she believed God had granted her the visible signs, she managed to make enough room for her thin wrist to move the bolts.

She kicked the trapdoor open with almost the last of her strength, climbed through it, and stepped blinking into direct light for the first time in two years. The breeze embraced her cheeks as she staggered through the churchyard on legs that had not taken more than one or two paces at a time in almost two years.

Christine recalled and felt overwhelmed by the story of Christ walking on the water, when His lightness of being had overcome gravity. She was following His holy steps, although she did not glide across the ground. In a misty twilight, she limped slowly and painfully to her father's house, where William opened the door to her weak knock. He could not speak, but Christine smiled on her father; he had visibly aged even more in these past weeks.

"Father. Look on these hands—God has blessed me with the stigmata. These holes are my Heavenly permission. He has told me I can leave the wall. I must be free to do His will outside this cell. His will shall be done."

William stared in stupefaction at his daughter's hands, seeing wounds from clawing at stone but no stigmata. He tenderly gave his arm to Christine to help her balance as he sat her down on a bench.

Helene ran to the girl, and grasped her tightly. "God be thanked, you needed to be free from that wall or you would have died."

They fed her, and bandaged her hands. Neither Helene nor William could tell their beloved first-born that torn hands did not a miracle make, that proof of the stigmata required more than bloodshed and fever.

❧∞❧

Duval fingered the knob on the end of the typewriter carriage, and rubbed the stump of his severed digit with his thumb while scrutinising his notes for a few minutes. He was drying up. Taking out a small riding crop from his desk drawer, he struck the top of his thigh as hard as he could. He punished himself thus five more times before returning to his work.

❧∞❧

Little is known about the period that Christine spent away from her cell...

❧∞❧

He stopped typing, angry with himself.

"Of course little is known. Most of this is the revelation I embrace when Christine speaks to me." He almost spat the words at his crucifix.

"Christine," he said aloud, "where are you? I have harvested another woman for you."

He could not feel the presence of the anchoress. "You are not in my head," he moaned. "Do you want me to visit you now?"

Duval left his study and checked in the kitchen to ensure that the trapdoor leading down into the cellar was bolted. Putting on his raincoat, he grabbed the lead and whistled for Bobby.

It was a short trudge in the rain down to St. James's. He instinctively did not want to be inside a church at that moment, so he walked around to the northern section and, leaning against the outside wall of the cell, he waited. After ten minutes he seemed to feel a force emanate from the cold, wet wall. Now he understood what Christine had endured, and what he had to write.

Within fifteen minutes, Bobby was curled up in front of the stove and Duval's fingers were dancing on the typewriter.

In the initial tumult of her reunion with her family, little was said about the alleged stigmata. The next day, at dawn, Christine set out for the journey to Peaslake, accompanied by her father. She asked her mother to tell Father Peter that she would seek out the bishop and explain her flight from the cell. If she could, she would renew her vows. But she had to see her sister, even if the price was excommunication.

Although exhausted emotionally by her recent trials, Christine—hooded to avoid any neighbours' stares—walked at first with relative ease. Every part of creation seemed to be bursting with life: she heard every bird-call, saw every leaf, and every tree proclaimed a miracle. The whole world was welcoming her and for a while the seriousness of her mission was transcended by God's bounteous earth. The sweet, rich smell of cow dung teased like jasmine, every sense was exaggerated beyond measure. But soon she grew tired, not of the green wetness, but because her body was not accustomed to walking, so her father made her stop every half-mile to rest.

William said very little, his thoughts consumed by his many burdens. During the third rest, sitting on a fallen oak tree, he finally asked, "Will the bishop allow your penance and return—even if that be your desire? Besides," he went on, "our family is in lowly esteem with Sir Richard. It may be that we all shall be banished by lord and bishop. Perhaps your mother and your brother should have journeyed with us, and then all flee together from Peaslake? While there, we are within the grasp of bishop and lord."

Christine felt none of his uncertainty. "Father, we must render unto Caesar what is Caesar's and to God what is God's. I will seek out the dean and bishop, as is my promise, and throw myself upon their wisdom and their mercy. The dean will advise about the injustice done by Sir Richard. Our lord bishop is no friend of Vachery Manor, either. This is known."

"I doubt not your piety, my daughter, but a village girl, two long years enclosed, may not judge too well the politicking of Church and nobility." He touched her cheek, drawn and pale with fasting. "But we must be on. 'Tis many a long stride to Peaslake, especially with your weak limbs. Or I may have to carry thee like a new-born lamb."

At the end of a bitter-sweet day of fatigue and yet rein-vigorated senses, Christine and her father arrived in the hamlet of Peaslake, where William's cousin lived in a row of three wooden houses rather grandly misnamed Queen's Cottages. One end of the cottages was adorned with a massive dung heap, and the other with a haystack. A pig rushed from the middle house, where Margaret was staying.

Adam, William's first cousin, greeted them at the door, hospitable despite his surprise.

"Welcome to my home, cousin," he said. "Good it is to see you. What be it? A year or more? And who be with you in the hood?" Adam started. "Heavens above, it be your Christine. Special leave from bishop then to see your Margaret?"

Christine just nodded as she stooped to enter the dank main room.

Adam's wife bustled with formalities and offered mead while the children and chickens were shooed out of the room, which was illuminated by a solitary rush light. On a rough straw palliasse Margaret lay sick, but she managed a smile for her closest kin.

Christine hugged her sister as silent tears merged into tiny rivulets chasing down their cheeks. Christine, reluctant to move from the embrace, eventually kneeled beside her sister and, making the sign of the Cross, said a prayer for the sick. The whole room fell quiet as the anchoress prayed.

Finally, Margaret broke the silence: "I be sick in my body, Chrissie, but you need not forsake your holy vows to visit me. Were I well, I would have come to your cell. Has a privilege been granted by the bishop?"

Christine shook her head. "Of bishops and lords will we parley anon, but first tell me what ails thee. Father said your confinement was not a goodly one."

"Two months or so I think will be my term," she said grimacing, "but the pains are on me now. The village midwife says it may be nigh, albeit before it be full-grow'd inside."

She winced as she said this and put both her hands on her extended belly.

Christine put her bony, wounded hands on her sister's firm ones. "I will tend you till your time. I will not leave my sister. If our father will speak with our kin here, I am sure that I can stay alongside you, to offer help and prayer as much I can."

William left the next day while Christine stayed in Peaslake, even though she was summoned by the bishop's man to hasten to Guldenford. Of the threats of ecclesiastic court she did not speak to Margaret.

Left much alone, the two sisters talked of childhood games. On the second night Christine, despite her wounded hands, spent an hour delousing her sister, as she used to do when they were at home together in Ashe Cottage. It was during this sisterly ritual that Margaret confided her story. No tears came now; the pain she had endured was beyond such manifestations. After the story was told, Margaret said, "May I bathe your hands and apply the potions, before new bandages?"

Christine nodded gratefully. Alone, the sisters were reunited in their torment. In turn, Christine finally shared her experience of Sir Richard to help ease her sister's pain and guilt. Both had suffered too much at their lord's unholy hand.

"I vow upon the Cross that I will take vengeance for you," said Christine. "I care not now for the hurts I endured, but will seek our rights by court, if justice there be in our troubled land. To the dean will I speak."

"I thank you," said Margaret, "but we are the poorest in this land. And e'en you have left your saintly course, so will the dean or bishop attend your words?"

"It will be well." Christine spoke with confidence. "God has answered my prayers, I promise. Now let us talk of your unborn son—for a boy-child I think it be."

Two weeks passed and Christine was joyous in the family atmosphere. Despite the tragic happenings she was rarely discomfited by the throng of bodies in the small, smoke-filled cottage, and she said her prayers either to herself or quietly in the vegetable garden at the rear, not wanting to stray too far from her sister.

There was no doctor in the hamlet, a deficiency which did not trouble the locals because the last one had leeched to death at least two of his patients. His occasional forays into surgery had resulted in even higher mortality, and he had moved to Guldenford to return to his real vocation as barber and pedlar of magic potions. In contrast, Matilda, the midwife, was much respected. William had left some groats to pay for her attentions to Margaret; he had been warned that the labour would be long and difficult.

It was made more difficult by threats from Sir Richard's armed men when they eventually visited Peaslake, so Adam arranged for Margaret to be carried in an ox-cart to a wood-man's hut deep in the forest. Christine did her best to make it more homely, but the move was dangerous.

Despite the best ministrations by the midwife and Christine, Margaret began to bleed copiously after a healthy son was pulled out feet first, after much struggling. The loss of blood was too much for the sixteen-year-old girl. They tried to staunch the flow with all the herbal remedies known, but to no avail.

Ghostly white, Margaret found the strength to cradle her son for a few minutes, and even managed these words: "Shall we name him William Adam...after my father, and the kindness of cousin Adam?"

"Hush, now. Sleep. Restore your strength," said the mid-wife with kind authority in her voice.

And sleep she did, for eternity.

William and Helene had been summoned; they arrived too late, just as a friar was conducting the final rites. After a few attempts at comforting words of Christian resurrection, the friar departed, his tonsured head showing sunburn as he ambled nonchalantly into the woods. What mattered a hasty funeral compared with his reward of a good meal?

After her own simple words of farewell, Helene cut her daughter's nails and put the parings, along with a lock of her hair, in a small cloth bag. This she would keep with other relics from her parents and her grandparents, unconsciously honour-ing a pagan order from long before the message of Christ found its way to these islands. William busied himself with con-structing a suitable wooden cross for the grave.

Christine prayed unceasingly for her sister's soul, but also planned her words for the bishop's court. She remained for another two days, hidden in the deepest wood, insisting that she would see her sister buried in Peaslake even though she had been warned that armed men awaited her. At the church, four soldiers stood guard, but they were Christian men, and allowed the funeral to be completed. Thereafter, without chains, she was taken to Guldenford.

❦

Duval looked at his watch. It was five o'clock in the morning, and his mind wandered back to other times. His earlier selections had been made away from Shere, one removed from Weybridge, two from the Dorking area, and one from Reigate. The first one had been selected in London, but that had been a mistake. Too rushed. Duval now knew he needed time to gauge their suitability, yet he also needed his anonymity in Shere. It was much easier to lose people in bigger towns, but Shere was small, perhaps too small. Marda, though, had been easy prey.

He usually liked to leave his guests in the cellar for a day or so on their own; they were much quieter, easier to manipulate, after the initial panic had subsided, but this time his curiosity was getting the better of him. Marda was going to be different, interesting and compliant, he felt sure. Duval bathed, scrubbing himself extra clean, then brewed some camomile tea and poured two cups.

Despite the thickness of the door to her cell, Marda could hear a muffled sound of another door opening somewhere outside. She sat up, tense and alert.

It must be him. Her mind was racing. Has he come to release me? To explain some terrible mistake? She dared not think of the alternatives.

She could make out footsteps on a stone floor outside. Something metallic slid across the outside of the door, and a shaft of light entered her tomb. She had not noticed the fifteen-inch-square indentation in the door, shielded by a solid metal grille on the outside.

Instinctively she edged towards the back of her cell and huddled in the far corner of her wooden bench. The presence of light seemed both magnificent and ominous as it jabbed at her eyes. Her dark world had been transformed only for seconds, but her fear made them seem acute, long minutes.

Duval's strong face peered in, transfixing Marda like a rabbit bewitched by a headlight. Not able to speak, she just trembled.

Duval spoke matter-of-factly: "I have brought you some herbal tea. You've had a difficult night. I am sure you need something."

He handed her a cup through the grille. Desperate for something to drink to take away the acrid taste in her mouth, she stood up to receive it as Duval passed it through the hatch, but she could only stare at him.

"Drink it," the priest said kindly, as though making small talk with a parishioner in his study. "It's camomile tea; I have just brewed it. Milk spoils it, but I put sugar in for you. I don't know if you take one or two spoonfuls, so I compromised by putting in one and a half. Sugar is good for shock."

Duval saw her hesitate as she drew the cup to her lips. She was like a deer in the Hurtwood, thirsty, quivering at the edge of a stream, sniffing a breeze tainted by the scent of man.

He smiled at her overwhelming vulnerability. "See," he said, "I am drinking mine. Take this one. It has just one sugar in it. There's nothing wrong with it."

He handed her his cup, half empty.

"You will need something. When your stomach has settled, I shall bring you some cornbread, if you like."

Marda stared at him as she carefully sipped the aromatic tea. A part of her felt like throwing it in his face, but her throat and mouth were screaming for some liquid, anything to drown the sour taste.

After the first sip, she gulped the remainder. It made her feel warm, and she found her voice. "Please, Michael," she said, breathing rapidly, "let me out of here. I don't know why I'm here. I'm sure there's been some terrible mistake. Just let me out with an apology, even without an apology, let me go home, and we can forget all about it."

The words cascaded, but Duval said nothing. He merely looked at her and smiled. In another context it could have been interpreted as gentle charm.

"There's no need for the police," Marda continued, her voice catching. "You can apologise. Explain if you can and let me go. Please. It's terrible in here, and it's very cold. Please let me have my clothes back and let me out."

Duval casually took a sip of his tea.

She watched him through the square in the door, bathed in the light from the corridor. It was almost as if she were looking at her own black-and-white television screen,

except that she could see the deep penetrating blue emptiness of his eyes. Cold blue counterpointed against the dark
metal frame of the grille, and then the yellow of the light,
enhancing the brown of his jacket, and the colours of his
checked shirt...She felt faint again, but willed herself to
challenge him.

"Speak to me," Marda pleaded. "Tell me why I'm here,
and when you'll let me out. Have I done something to
you? What? *Tell me*. What? Have you confused me with
somebody else? I've never done you any harm, so why did
you kidnap me? Why? *Please* tell me." She was crying now.
"My family has very little money. But if you want some,
I'm sure my father will give you what you ask. Please tell
me you'll let me go."

Finally Duval spoke. "There is no mistake, Marda. You
are the one I need, as I think you need me. You are assuredly
not a kidnap victim. You have been brought here for your
own good. Indeed, I could argue that you brought yourself
here...You have manifested your destiny, and I am a mere
catalyst. Trust me. You will even thank me...in time."

"What are you?" Marda shrieked. "A Russian spy or
something? I've got nothing to do with politics or anything.
I simply work for a wine company. I've never been to any
communist countries. You can check up on me. You'll know
I'm telling you the truth."

"I *have* checked on you," Duval said patiently. "I have
chosen you *because* of your truth. Now, if you are cold, I
will look for something to dress you in. In a few hours I
will bring you some refreshment. It isn't very nice in this
place so, with your co-operation, we can perhaps...later...look
for ways to make it more comfortable..."

Marda stared at him in rage now. "I don't *want* to be
comfortable here," she shouted. "I just want to get out.
Please. Where am I? Is this some sort of prison? Am I in
London? Who do you work for?"

"I work for no one but God."

Duval's words chilled Marda; not just the content, but the coldness of his tone, the deadly humourless conviction which so belied the smile. Duval seemed an embodiment of the belief that Christ never laughed. He spoke to her like a well-educated but bored post-office official helping a particularly stupid customer fill in a very simple form.

As he slid the grille across, the beam of light was removed; darkness reconquered the room and her soul.

She rushed to the grille to see if she could open it, but it was impossible from the inside. Putting her ear to the grille, she tried to catch some sound from the outside, and heard Duval say, "Hello, Julie. Hello, Denise. And you, Mary. Justine, you have company. And Dorothy, you used to be so lonely. You have a friend now." As he said each name, Marda could hear a tap as if on separate doors.

So I am in some kind of prison with other women, she thought. Somehow that made her feel better. She was still terrified, but she was less alone.

VII

The Bonds

Duval returned to his desk. He wanted to write while his universe was in perfect equilibrium.

August 1331

Christine, on her knees, kissed the bishop's ring, which was as opulent as his private chambers. The episcopal parlour was adorned with brightly coloured tapestries from Arras. Opus anglicanum embroidery, the handiwork of doting nuns, was displayed on a heavy carved oak table. This was some of the finest embroidery in Christendom, with workmanship so delicate and designs so very fine, threads of gold, yellow shading to green, and white to blue.

Christine had spent three days in the Dominican convent in Guldenford, where she had been starved of food and sleep and then forced to repeat a series of detailed confessions. In each the main theme had been that the step between ecstatic vision and sinful frenzy was very small, and she had willingly taken that fateful step to excommunication by abandoning her vows in order to follow the Great Tempter. Made public, against normal protocol, these confessions had been recorded on vellum and a summary presented to the dean, who had then summoned the bishop. It was his job to supervise petitions for Christine's excommunication as punishment for the abnegation of her vows. Thereafter, she could be handed over to secular authorities for trial and possible execution.

The bishop, however, had more worldly fish to fry on this Friday. Alone except for a scribe, he addressed Christine with due solemnity: "My child, I have read the summation of your confessions and I have..." He stopped, seeing her strained face. "Please, look up from the floor and at me. You seem pale. Scribe, place that stool for our errant sister...Sit, Christine."

Christine had been struggling, through her fear, hunger and exhaustion, to hold herself upright. "Thank you, my lord," she said gratefully.

"By all the rights," continued the bishop, "you should be before a court ecclesiastic. This may come, but I wanted to speak to you privily. To help. To counsel. To keep a sister in the faith. With due penance, perchance you can be absolved of your sins and avoid excommunication. But should you persuade the court to shrive you, then to be re-enclosed in St. James's church will require the special permit of our Holy Father the Pope. Do you understand?"

"I understand, my lord," Christine said meekly.

"Let me speak to you of God, and also of worldly things," intoned the bishop as he stroked his heavily embroidered rochet. "Firstly, your miracles. Your claimed miracles. I pray that God has visited you, my child. Let me see your palms."

Christine showed her open palms. He reached forward from his gilded chair and examined them carefully. "I see no stigmata, my child," he said kindly. "Were it now to happen before my eyes, and extra witnesses I could summon, this proof might be hailed as saintly. But one claim, with none as witness, will not persuade this bishopric—let alone the Pope—to grant your pardon."

Christine was silent. He pulled out a brocaded cloth of sarsenet and blew his nose into it, then he tried again to explain: "Saintliness, the desire for this lofty gift, may be the ultimate temptation. And your fasting to extremes...to die for our religion is much easier than to live absolutely for Christ. As you know now, solitude is a palace for the Beast."

The bishop saw a tiny tear in Christine's eyes, although she, who had suffered so much, now found it hard to cry. He wanted to take her mauled hands to comfort her, but knew he could not. "I believe in the truth of your vision which led you to enclosure in St. James's church," he said softly. "I sense your spiritual strength, my child, but let us leave the claim of miracles apart.

"I have read your extra deposition. You have accused Sir Richard of carnal violation of your virtue and that of your deceased sister, Margaret—God rest her soul. If true, this is devilish work. But your sister has gone to another place, and it rests upon your truth against your honoured master, Sir Richard. True, your calling to the anchorhold would give you extra worth, but you are a fugitive now from your cell."

The bishop's brow furrowed. "Fornication—especially by main force—is against God's law, and the Church condemns accordingly, but our custom is that bonded and free men of the demesnes have few redress in matters carnal against their lord, especially when he has a strong sword-arm and the knights to follow him.

"But I myself have remonstrations with Sir Richard." His voice dropped. "I will aid you to avenge your family's wrongs, but you must return my favour. Later I will explain all to you. Meanwhile, I swear you to absolute silence. Rest quiet in the convent, where I have forespoken to the Abbess Euphemia and instructed her to treat you well."

⋖⋗⋖⋗

Duval was happy and the writing flowed, yet even though his story was materialising, he felt his thoughts were being seduced back into the twentieth century. The Middle Ages shimmered around him, but they did not envelop him with images. His imagination was not seized with irresistible force by thoughts of the 1320s. Previously, his female trophies had allowed him, on occasion, an almost perfect escape into the fourteenth century, but now he found that Marda's face was assuming the likeness he had long ago invented for Christine. The more he tried to focus on the medieval Christine, the more he wanted to start his work on the living flesh and blood of Marda. This had not happened to him before and he found it unsettling, yet he could appreciate the delicious metamorphosis.

A few feet below the thick stone floor on which Duval's writing desk stood, Marda was desperately banging on the door again. Why hadn't the women Duval had spoken to said a word? Maybe their cells were too well sound-proofed. But surely they could hear her banging? Perhaps they were locked in another part of the prison? For several hours she had been consumed by an almost mindless rage, but some small part of her knew that others were suffering as she was, and she needed to speak to them.

She shouted a few of the names she had heard: "Denise! Dorothy!"

Maybe they were gagged or drugged? Not all of them, surely? How many people were in this hell-hole? Was her gaoler working alone or was he part of some bizarre and insidious organisation? There had to be other people involved, captors and captives.

She wanted her fellow-prisoners to help her, at least to tell her what was happening: knowing would make it easier. She could then survive whatever she had to go through to be released, or to answer whatever questions were needed to pass the test that would enable her to leave.

She tried banging on her door again, to no avail. She tried to estimate how long she had been in the dungeon. Fifteen hours? Sixteen?

Although she was only a light, social smoker, she suddenly felt the craving for a cigarette. A few puffs might relieve the tension cramps in her stomach, but she would not beg him for nicotine. Food and water were more important.

The heaviness of time became increasingly unendurable. In the darkness she was lost. Only the light—and his face on the black-and-white TV screen of the grille—would help her to gauge the passage of time. She felt as if she were being swilled around like a goldfish in a tiny polythene bag on the back of the rickety horse and cart of the rag-and-bone man. Tom—that was his name. He would shout "Rag-Bonnnn-er. Scrap metaaaal." He used to give her balloons when she was a little girl, but she had wanted a goldfish. She had felt sorry for the trapped fish, so she asked her father whether they ever suffered from seasickness. Were goldfish aware of water? She was beginning to feel the same about the concept of time. The hours, she suspected, would become meaningless; she could only measure time by her feelings. And all she felt now was fear.

Marda heard again the muffled opening of a second door and then a lower tone of the thudding closure of a door and a metallic click. She presumed he was locking the door into the corridor outside her—their—cells. Perhaps it wasn't "Michael." Perhaps it was a female warder or kidnapper. But by now she had begun to discount the kidnapping theory. That didn't make sense if five or six girls were all locked up together. For a fleeting moment she thought that it was all some elaborate practical joke. But that would be crazy, she realised, especially as she could have choked to death on whatever it was "they" had used to knock her out. Maybe it was illegal, criminal…or political. No, he was mad—as simple and as horrifying as that. If only she could make contact with the other women, she could find out what on earth was going on.

Unexpectedly, the grille slid open and the light flooded in. She heard his deep, cultured voice say with mock subservience, "Toast with marmalade, *mademoiselle*, and some more herbal tea. Please tell me if you would prefer coffee next time."

She had dreaded his coming, but, oh, the light. And food. And some kind of company. Even his. And that voice. It was almost comforting despite its terrifying chill.

Duval passed her a small plate with two pieces of toast and a mug. As he went to close the grille, Marda begged, "Please, leave it open a little, just so I can see what I'm doing." There was no response. "And please may I have my clothes?" she pleaded. Still he said nothing, but before he walked back up the corridor he left the grille open a few inches.

She crunched her way through the toast and gulped down the scented tea, desperate for nourishment. Only when she finished did she look to see if there was anything she could spot in the cell. The single feature she had missed was a small air vent which fed from the corridor into the inner wall of the cell.

Drinking the tea made Marda realise how much she needed to urinate. She wondered why she hadn't felt this need before. Was it shock, or perhaps she had been in the cell for less time than she thought? However long it was, she knew she had to respond to the call of nature immediately. Was Duval still there? She had not heard the outer door.

"Michael, are you there?" she called. She thought how best to placate him. "Thank you for the tea and toast," she said, trying to sound sincere. "But please can you let me go to the lavatory? I haven't been since before you...you...*brought* me here. Please." The panic in her voice was rising. "There is already a mess in here with my being sick. Please let me go to a bathroom, and then may I put some clothes on before I die of pneumonia?"

She heard him open the outside door. She couldn't see much out of the grille even when she stood on the wooden bench, and her attempts to push the grille open wider were futile. She could just make out what looked like another cell door opposite, and a stone and timber ceiling with an unusual light fitting.

"Hey! Hey!" she half-shouted, half-whispered. "Hey, is there anyone there? Can you hear me?" Her voice echoed a little in the corridor.

"*I* can hear you," Duval suddenly said, though she couldn't see him. "I will introduce you to the rest of your companions later. For the moment, you can use this." He appeared carrying a small porcelain chamber-pot, and proffered it through the grille.

"I can't use *that* thing," Marda snorted in disgust. "Please let me out to use a proper toilet."

Duval let the chamber-pot crash to the ground. The impact made Marda jump, then instinctively cower into a ball as she tried to avoid the flying shards and the noise so monstrously amplified in the confined space.

"You should do what I suggest," said Duval quietly, as the echoes died away. "Now you must wait."

"I can't wait," sobbed Marda. "And, oh God, please don't shut the light out." But there was total darkness, and then the noise of the closing of the outer door. And all Marda could think of was which corner of her cell she would use to relieve herself.

She squatted in the corner and felt her muscles relax, even as tears stung her eyes. There was nothing with which to dry herself. Later, sitting on her wooden bench, she felt her bowels churn. How could she live alongside her own faeces? She felt as though she had reverted to childhood. Faced with soiling herself, she would have to use the floor. He would control even her toilet habits.

Marda was cold, frightened and sickened by the stale smell of urine and vomit. For a fleeting second she thought of death: I would prefer suicide to suffering in this hell on earth. Then she became angry at such a thought. Damn you, whatever you are, I *will* survive, I will sort this out and get myself out of here. If I think like a victim, she told herself, I will become a victim. Her defiance, too, was only a passing impulse. She felt so weak, so vulnerable. She wanted to stay alive, and to stay sane.

Part of keeping sane was keeping time. It seemed that she'd been his captive for many hours, but she wasn't sure how many. If only he hadn't taken her watch. She also wondered where she was. How can it happen, she asked herself, that you have no idea which part of the country you are in?

Then, suddenly, the noise of the outer door. The footsteps. The sliding of the grille, the light. That face, the power in it. The voice, its innate sense of command.

"I hope you will do what I suggest this time," he said sternly. Clearly pleased with himself, he stood back and held up a large round canister for Marda to see. "I have brought you a portable lavatory. It's what they use in caravans, I believe. I have also brought you some cleaning materials and a rubbish bag so that you can tidy your...your room. To give you the toilet, I need to unlock your door. If we are to avoid unpleasantness, you will have to do as I ask. I am going to pass you through a pair of handcuffs. Please attach one manacle to your left wrist and the other to the small metal loop at the end of your bench. I am not going to harm you. I had a very alarming experience with one of the other ladies here who caught me off guard. This will not happen again."

More degradation, thought Marda. "Please don't expect me to handcuff myself," she beseeched him. "Can't you see I'm cold and sick and frightened. How could I attack you? You're twice my size."

"Here are the handcuffs," he said, undeterred. "Please do what I say."

Marda knew she could not stand the indignity of defecating on the tiny bit of floor space. Reluctantly, she took the cuffs, found the small loop on the bench and clamped one manacle to it, then encircled her left wrist with the cold metal of the other. Once Duval was sure she was secured, he unlocked the door and stepped in. The metal toilet was dumped on the floor, without ceremony. Marda, shivering in her bra and pants, handcuffed to a bench, could not have presented a more pitiful tableau.

Pity did not seem to be part of Duval's psychological make-up, however. He merely wrinkled his noise in distaste and said, "You'd better clean this room up. It doesn't smell very healthy in here. I'll return in fifteen minutes or so. If it's clean, I shall provide you with some clothing. I do appreciate that you may be cold."

He left the cell, locking the door behind him, then through the grille he offered her the key to the handcuffs. She could only just reach with her right hand. After she had undone the cuffs, he asked her to return them, with the key, through the opening. "This procedure we will observe carefully—until I can trust you. As I said, I shall be back in fifteen minutes. It would be to your advantage to make good use of this time by cleaning up."

He sounded like a headmaster, thought Marda.

Duval soon returned. The handcuff procedure was repeated and he removed the broom and cleaning bucket. Then he produced a shapeless black garment which he laid on the bench a few inches from Marda's bare thighs, goosepimpled with fear and cold. He did not touch her and he avoided her eyes. Quickly, he locked the door and handed her the key again through the grille. After undoing the manacles, she dutifully placed them in his cupped hand protruding through the grille.

"That is something for you to wear," he said pointing. "Please, it's warm, put it on."

Marda examined the coarse black wool.

"What's this?" she said, trying her best to humour him. "It looks like something someone graduated in."

"You have not graduated yet, Marda," said Duval, no amusement in his voice. "This is a garment that novice nuns must wear in the order of Saint Benedict."

"Am I in the cellar of a convent?" Marda asked quickly, thinking he had given her a clue.

"No," said Duval coldly. "Any more questions?"

"Have you got something that I can wear underneath this?" She fingered the heavy cloth. "It will be very rough and itchy next to my bare skin."

"It is usually worn by nuns without an undergown, so that is how you will wear it. It is not worn for pleasure. You have a choice. Wear it or not. It depends on how cold you get."

Marda's eyes narrowed and she gritted her teeth, but she did not say anything. And she was very cold, embarrassed at being in just her underclothes and still in shock; so she pulled the heavy black garment over her head and shuddered with the roughness. She stood stiffly, to try to keep the coarse gown away from her skin.

She still would not give in. "If you won't give me back my own shoes, may I ask whether there are witches' shoes to match this outfit?" she enquired sarcastically.

"Normally stout black boots, with extended laces, are worn with dark leggings," answered Duval with pedantic dignity. "I am sure something similar can be provided. What size shoe do you take?"

"Size…five," Marda replied guardedly.

Duval thought a moment. "I think one of the other girls has shoes that size. I will check."

Marda seized on this. "May I meet the 'other girls,' Michael?"

He smiled coldly and said, "Why not? As I told you, until I trust you, you will have to use these handcuffs." He handed them through the grille. "This time you will cuff both your hands together."

Reluctantly, and with difficulty, Marda did so. Duval opened the cell door and led her blinking into the light of the corridor. Her heart leapt and she even attempted to laugh: "This is not a good way to meet people. A barefoot nun in handcuffs."

Duval did not smile.

Once her eyes had accustomed themselves to the direct light, Marda saw that she was in the middle of a long hallway. Three doors—all with the same grilles—stood on either side. A total of six cells. In front of her was a short wooden staircase leading to a trapdoor. At the other end of the passage stood a large, well-lit crucifix attached to the stone wall.

"Is this a church?" she asked when she noticed the crucifix.

"In a way, yes," said Duval uncomfortably. Marda's eyes swept her newly enlarged world.

"Are you really a priest?" she dared to ask.

Duval looked at her sharply, then tried to dismiss her with a feeble laugh. "So many questions, young lady. You said you wanted to meet the other girls. Are you sure?"

Marda was suddenly uneasy at his tone. "Well," she said carefully, "I heard you speaking to other people. You spoke to Denise, and Dorothy, and some others. So I wondered about them. One gets a little short of company down here." She tried to shrug her shoulders, one of her mannerisms, but realised that the loose black shroud she was wearing tended to drown out such subtle gestures.

"All right, Marda." Duval's shrug was more obvious. He banged on the nearest door with the side of his fist. "This is Denise's room. I met her—let me think—about five years ago."

Marda's face froze: "She has been in there for *five years*?"

Duval met her stricken eyes, five inches below his. "Yes."

"Why are you doing this to her? Please let me see her…" Marda stopped herself. "Why isn't anyone answering? Have you gagged them? Or are they all well trained?" Marda tried to suppress her panic with a touch of mock sarcasm.

Duval knocked again on the door. "Denise, may we come in to see you?" He called out: "Speak up, my dear, I can't hear you. Ah, she has always been difficult," he said almost fondly. "Here, Marda, let me presume to open the door without her permission. Then I shall introduce you." Duval pulled out a ring of keys from his trousers and fiddled with the lock.

Marda wondered what Denise would look like after four years in his care, and tried to steel herself to stay calm, whatever she found. As Duval opened the door, an unpleasant smell burst upon her nostrils and she could not prevent herself from stepping back.

"Denise," said Duval, amused. "Never good at house-keeping, I'm afraid. Rather spoiled young lady." He opened the door wide and stepped into the cell.

"Denise," he said expansively, "say hello to Marda. Marda, this is Denise."

Duval gestured to Marda to follow him.

Marda did so, screamed and collapsed to the floor.

When she regained consciousness in the dark of her cell, Marda thought for a joyous second that she was in her bedroom in Woking. She remembered her big brown teddy with the torn ear. That memory could not keep the horror at bay, and the most awful image she had seen in her short life came back. She saw again the light flooding into the cell. A quick movement in the corner: a rat had been sitting on the bench, and had scampered into some dark hole when the door opened. Then the light had fallen on Denise. Her ankles had been tied to the base of the bench. She had no clothes. Her hair had grown so long it fell over her face and down towards her waist. She was gripping a wooden crucifix with both skeletal hands. Hands that had been frozen in death for over four years.

VIII

The Trial

Marda, after what she thought must be three days, begged God to free her from her tomb, or end her life mercifully soon. Traumatised, almost unable to speak, she was barely able to consume the dry toast and tepid drinks that Duval brought every day. But, after eating the food, she became immensely hungry. He hardly bothered to speak to her, let alone, in his perverse way, try to console her.

Most of the time she shook uncontrollably. For hours she would curl herself into a ball, rocking back and forth on her haunches, muttering to herself. Random flashes of memory coursed through her brain, and songs came into her tormented mind, snatches of old nursery rhymes, modern pop, Gilbert and Sullivan. Scraps of force-fed school poetry jumped from hidden corners of her brain. Sometimes she thought obsessively of food and devised ever more complex recipes for dinner parties she would hold when she was free. She could not sleep, could not take refuge in dreams or nightmares. She imagined herself stranded in a huge circular tank, the sides of which were impossibly high, and where there were no handholds, just a smooth, shiny metal surface. Water kept flooding into the tank, and she could survive only as long as her strength held out to keep swimming, knowing all the time that she wasn't going to escape and that eventually she would drown. After an interminable time, her panic became a rage, first against him and then turned against herself. What had she done to deserve such treatment? She felt like an animal. Waves of nausea swept over her, then feelings of abasement, of self-loathing, as she smelt her unwashed body, the reek intensified by the pungent aroma of abject fear.

Marda thought that he was probably mad, and now she knew without doubt that he was also a killer. The image of Denise's skeleton constantly marched through her mind.

After the initial shock subsided, she found that she was detaching herself from her body, becoming two people, the one frightened, childlike and compliant, the other a mature adult observing the deteriorating habits of this help-less woman-child. She clung to a certainty that she would be released soon, but should her inevitable freedom be delayed, she knew—without understanding why—that her best chance of psychological survival would be to hang on with all her reason to her own personality and not be bro-ken by captivity. Let the woman-child disintegrate; the real Marda would become stronger. Let him see the weaker woman, the one he wanted to control. She would play-act for him, but her inner core had to be safeguarded. When she was free, she would still be Marda Stewart. No one and nothing else. Until she was free again she must separate these two parts of her, these two personalities. She had to separate her reason from her fear. It was the only way to keep alive, to stay sane…yet she threatened her own sanity by continuously asking herself whether Duval's other vic-tims had attempted the same strategy—and failed.

September 1331

Christine left the audience with the bishop with fear in her heart, and yet hope that justice would be done. She feared excommunication and an eternity in Hell, but the fires of vengeance burned almost as fiercely. Christine was made to wait in the convent for two weeks.

She was anxious about being summoned to the court which the bishop had explained would take place in the Sheriff's Court in Guldenford castle. The petty court met every three weeks, she was told, but the Assizes were a very special event, where the King's travelling judges heard serious cases of crime. She dreaded, but steeled herself for, the confrontation with Sir Richard. The bishop's advocates visited her three times in the convent to rehearse her words. "What can I speak but the truth?" she kept saying, but she decided that lawyers did not understand truth.

They explained that her testimony about her lord's lewd behaviour was only a small part of the bishop's indictment, which was principally concerned with Sir Richard's theft of properties to which the Church lay claim. Despite the turmoil of the civil war, the rule still stood: no alienation of Church land without royal licence. True, the tyrant Edward II had, with his allies, despoiled much of the land of his opponents, including the fiefs of the clerics who had supported the insurrectionary barons, but the new king needed to restore his alliance with the Pope. The young king's position after his father's forced abdication and mysterious death was still tenuous. In sum, Edward III, the new king, needed the Church if he was to keep his throne.

In this case, the simplest solution for monarch and clergy was the death of one man by an arraignment for treason.

Sir Richard, although he had sympathised with the rebels, had carefully managed to avoid the fate of many knights and nobles who had fought the old king. He had not been exiled, nor had he forfeited lands, but the bishop was determined to regain for the Church the lands that Sir Richard had disseised and taken for himself. The knight would suffer, the bishop would prosper with the new archbishop's backing, and Christine was a mere pawn. She knew this, but she would play her part.

Nothing was said by Christine's guardian, the abbess, about excommunication. Instead, she decked out the anchoress in a new habit so that she would represent the Church in best holy orders—to impress the judges.

When the day came, the abbess accompanied her in a small open wagon drawn by two bay mares and driven by a male servant of the abbey. This was the first time Christine had travelled in such style, and it only added to her nervousness.

The dining hall of the castle had been transformed into a court room. On the high table sat three judges, with an elaborate canopy erected above their heads to emphasise their rank. Two had travelled from Canterbury and one from Winchester, carrying the writs with the king's great seal. Beside the judges sat the Bishop of Hereford, to advise on the laws of the Church. On benches along the side of the hall, local noblemen were arrayed; commoners, of course, were not allowed to sit in judgement on a knight.

This was English justice witnessed by Sir Richard's peers, but his fate was to be decided by high politics, not by law or natural justice, although justice it would be to Sir Richard's too numerous enemies. His attempts to play both sides in the civil war had succeeded for a while. Wisely, he had been in France during the climactic battle of Boroughbridge when the king's opponents had been defeated. He did not suffer in the first wave of massive recriminations, but he had not tempered his land hunger sufficiently. The bishop had bided his time, and now the last of Sir Richard's allies at the royal court had been removed.

The judges sat for three days while Sir Richard's alleged crimes were carefully recited. The lawyers debated the significance of the deeds of the lands claimed by the Bishop of

Winchester, while the last day was reserved for the destruction of the knight's position as dutiful custodian of the laws of the realm.

Sir Richard's tenants were paraded, and they confirmed that his enforcement of forest law was unduly harsh. The Charter of the Forest had been binding on countrymen for a century, but Sir Richard had claimed to be acting for the king, they said. Two men had been unjustly hanged for killing a deer; another man—Wat Smith—had suffered the loss of both his hands for carrying a longbow near a roe deer; a villager had been blinded, said the witnesses, for merely disturbing a royal deer. The prosecution then built up its case on cows and sheep and stolen acres. Commoners could not sit in judgement, but witnesses they could be: dyers, weavers and fullers chastised the crusader with pretty lies and practised truths. In short, Sir Richard had undeniably breached local custom and law.

The hall resounded to the phrase "*Quasi veteri more Anglicano,*" according to the old English custom. Two best beasts, not the traditional one, had been taken by the lord for heriot, death duty. Sir Richard had denied access to common land. Armed men had been levied for more than sixty days for the Scottish wars. And so it went on: Sir Richard's aggrieved bonded men came from the Welsh Marches, from his lands in Surrey and Kent. Occasionally men spoke well of their lord, especially those who had fought by his side, but complimentary words were silenced by the bishop's lawyers. Sir Richard's own learned advocates, sniffing the changes in the political climate, fell silent too.

Two hundred men, knights and nobles, filled the smoky hall; no woman spoke to the court until Christine was led in. The prosecution thundered that the lord's right of *prima nocte* was not acceptable in the settled lands of England, although it was admitted that it was not uncommon in the conquered parts of the Celtic territories.

Christine was asked to stand before the high table, with the bishop's chief lawyer by her side. He read out a brief description of who she was and whence she came.

The judge in the centre of the high table spoke first, although Christine could not understand his curious Latinised French. In English she said, "My lord, I do not comprehend your words for I am unlearned in such affairs."

The bishop's man translated into English, "Summarise your indictment against Sir Richard."

Christine had been told to be as brief as possible, and not to speak further unless the judges asked her to say more, which was not likely, they said.

So far Christine had not looked at Sir Richard, whom she had always remembered in his fine linen and purple tunic. Above all she recalled his jewelled dagger. This day he was dressed in a simple black robe, with no adornments. His feet were chained together, his face was dirty, and his beard bedraggled. He had aged ten years in the two since last she saw him. Although her enclosure had honed her hatred, the period of intense devotions permitted some pity to enter her soul.

She recited the lines the bishop had instructed. "I swear to God and King that I verily speak unto ye this day." She spoke quietly and nervously. "I am Christine of Shere, the daughter of William, also of Shere. I confirm the times the deposition states regarding Sir Richard's offences against my person and against my sister Margaret, now deceased. I confirm that Sir Richard..." She stopped staring at the floor and looked into her tormentor's face. The words died in her mouth.

The bishop's lawyer poked her with his finger. "Proceed," he said.

Christine continued: "He did...he did violate my chastity, by cruel force, and with no volition on my part. I had been betrothed to Simon, a tailor of Shere. In shame thereafter I did confess and was sworn by holy vows as an anchoress of St. James's church. There was I bound by my vows for life until—I beg the holy Mother Church for forgiveness—I did break these vows. I did this to aid my sister who had been made victim of Sir Richard's cruel lust for the months she had worked as scullery maid in Vachery Manor, the seat of Sir Richard. She was chaste until she was by Sir Richard employed. He and his son did by brute force violate my sister, and then she was with child—from their seed. She died in childbirth, and is now buried these three weeks past in Peaslake."

She stopped and coughed a little as the bishop's lawyer glared at her. "My father, William of Shere, did protest to Sir Richard," she went on, hesitantly, "but was dismissed from his presence with threats. My father has no debts to his lord, and has honoured all the tallages and obligations. Sir Richard has brought shame on our house, humble though it be. He has scorned our local customs as well as laws of king and Mother Church."

She spoke quietly and nervously, but she had delivered all that she had rehearsed. Nor had she lied, although she accepted that the bishop's lawyers could tutor her in words more befitting the court.

The judge did not question her, but spoke in French to the bishop's lawyer, saying, "You will translate this statement, taken in Latin, by our scribe, and this Christine of Shere will sign that it is a true account of her words sworn in this Court of Pleas."

The bishop's lawyer caught the sleeve of Christine's robe to indicate that she must leave. As she turned, she looked back at Sir Richard. She expected to see the fire of anger in his eyes, but instead they were dull; like his face, they showed no emotion. She wondered whether torture had broken his spirit.

The abbess took her back to the convent in her carriage. She did not at first converse with Christine, who knew not to speak unless addressed by her superior. Christine felt a cold emptiness in her heart. There was no joy, but she had had her moment of justice.

Eventually the Abbess Euphemia spoke, and with tenderness: "Christine, you acted bravely and well. The bishop has granted you to stay with us until the trial is complete. You may be taken before a bishop's court to be examined, to restore your vows if you are shriven well and are truly penitent. The bishop, I trust, will look with kindness on you. The King's Assizes, I know, will restore the lands belonging to the Church. And you have acted to the bishop's will."

Christine stayed five more days in the convent, until the King's Bench found Sir Richard guilty of all the charges. Although the king had not returned to the despotic ways of his father, the issue of Church land was dear to his benefactor, the Pope. It had been seven years since a knight had been thus dispossessed, for the king had need of noble support, not least for the wars in France and Scotland. For reasons of state, however, Sir Richard was stripped of all his chivalric rights. Knights were executed by beheading, but he was to be treated as a commoner.

On the appointed day, Christine was allowed to leave the abbey to join the common throng. The abbess insisted that Christine attend his hanging in the square, and she did not argue against the order.

As the abbess led Christine the short distance to the centre of the town, the townspeople respectfully stood back to let them pass. In the square, the crowd carried an effigy of Sir Richard on a pole, then burned it, and danced and sang round the flames.

After an hour or so of peasant revelries, Christine saw Sir Richard's broken body dragged by four horses through the cobbled streets of Guldenford. Battered and bloodied, he was hauled, scarcely conscious, to the steps of the single gallows, ten feet high. The people hissed and booed at him, while the mob nearest him spat. Gobbets of spittle streaked his face and robe, decorated with his coat of arms, but reversed so that they would never again be worn by any courtly family. Upon his head they placed a crown of nettles.

Two hooded men dragged Sir Richard up the wooden steps and thrust his head roughly into the dangling noose. The once proud lord showed no emotion; he seemed beyond caring or, perhaps, beyond any further earthly pain.

The sheriff, after reading out a short proclamation in Latin and English, concluded: "Such be the fate of all who dare rebel against the king."

The crowd roared back, "The king. The king. Death to all rebels against the king."

Sir Richard, looking up at the grey, overcast skies, tried to speak. Although the crowd ceased their tumult all that Christine heard was, "I deny all these unjust accusations and I curse ye all..."

He was silenced by the shouts of the crowd, and stones were pelted at his broken body. Soldiers tried to push the mob back as the sheriff gave the order to hoist him up.

Christine saw his bowed body straighten and jerk up into the air until, in the utter silence of the throng, she heard a sharp choking sound at which the crowd broke into loud laughter. His body dangled and twitched for many minutes before it grew still and they let him drop.

To all this Christine forced herself to bear personal witness, but she closed her eyes as the sheriff himself lowered Sir Richard from the gallows; deliberately allowing a tiny ember of life to remain within his body. The two hooded men threw the blue-faced victim on to a small bench and tied him down. After his robe was cut off with a large meat cleaver, the sheriff took the cleaver and slashed downwards through the dying man's stomach. He drew out the intestines and threw them on to a brazier. Still alive, Sir Richard, hearing and smelling the sizzling of his own innards, let out a groan like a dying ox.

The crowd did not shout for mercy, but the sheriff ordered one of the hooded men to wield the axe. After two strokes, Sir Richard's head tumbled on to the platform. As the blood spouted from the neck, the crowd raised their voices. A peasant cried out, "Justice! Justice!"

The hooded men took turns to quarter the body with the axe as the crowd cheered at every cut. The four quarters of his body were swarmed over by the crowd. With knives they scratched on his skin, and chanted verses from the Holy Scriptures denouncing arrogance and evil. Some of the more drunken members of the mob, particularly the women, started to sing and dance again. At this the abbess led her charge away.

In her convent cell, Christine was too overcome to offer more than perfunctory prayers, but she did finally manage to sleep. She dreamed of floating down a river of blood until her little boat reached an island. The boat steered itself to the shore, where she was greeted by her sister, dressed all in the finest white linen. She stretched out both arms to embrace the dead girl...

That was all she could remember the next morning, yet she felt that Margaret was thanking her for defending her memory and their family's honour.

After Matins, the abbess instructed Christine to return to her father's house. She thanked the abbess and took leave of the convent, but asked to be allowed to depart from the garden door via Castle Arch and through the "gates" or passageways of the town. She did not want to pass again through the square, explaining that she had witnessed too much suffering and pain, even if it was to an evildoer.

Yet as she walked alone through the great east gate of the town, she saw Sir Richard's head impaled on a pike above the wooden arch. Shuddering at the sight of his bloated face, she hurried past, knowing that his disembodied features would haunt her nightmares.

She had endured enough of man's inhumanity to man, and relished the tranquillity of the countryside after the foetid smells of the town, but at a crossroads a mile or so along the road, near the leper hospital, she beheld another cruel sight: a naked man buried head first, up to his waist. With caution she moved towards the strange apparition and touched his ankle, still warm. Transfixed by further horror, she did not notice an old leper woman watching her.

The woman, swathed in filthy rags, hailed Christine.

"What be this, mistress? Why bury a man like this?" Christine asked.

The woman, cackling, replied, "The judges made this so. The villeins were dealt with first before the king's men smote down Sir Richard."

Christine said gently, "Sir Richard's crimes are known to me, but what of this malfeasant here, naked in the sight of God and man?"

"I be sorry to offend a lady in holy orders," said the old woman, "but he be killed for his sodomy. Sometimes they hang 'em, sometimes they bury 'em so, to fit their crime. Have you no eyes afore today? 'Tis not uncommon in this town."

"I live a long way from here, in Shere."

The old woman looked confused. "Don't know all 'em villages roundabouts. But upon the holy tears of Christ, you be crying too. Did you know this man, assumin'—beggin' your forgiveness—that you can recognise his lower parts?"

Christine looked shocked. "No, I know him not. I cry for all the hurt and pain in this land. So many die by the hands of men, when there be pestilence enough from nature. I pray for His coming to cleanse this land."

"Amen," said the old woman, as she shuffled off with the help of her stick.

The long walk home did not daunt Christine, now strong with exercise, food and sated vengeance—but a vengeance that seemed empty with her Margaret lost from this world.

⋞⋙∞⋘⋟

Duval spent three long evenings editing the section describing Christine's months of freedom. His time was not entirely his own: he had to spend two days in Guildford on church duties, which included another fractious interview with the bishop, still fervent about new American methods

139

of modernising the two thousand years of tradition which graced the Church of Rome. Between the distractions in Guildford and his writing, Duval was not finding the time he wanted to spend with Marda.

He imagined her huddled in her cell. Of course he wanted her to feel comfortable, but it would only work if she did things his way. The other girls had been stubborn. They would not listen.

Especially Denise. Duval had not opened Denise's door for over four years, his mark of respect for the dead.

He remembered a buxom, strong girl, all kicking and screaming; lots of temper tantrums, including one that had caused him an injury. In the end he had left her to her own devices for a few days, but then, somehow, he hadn't felt like confronting her red face, bulging eyes, the endless shrieking. A few days had become a few weeks, and finally his conscience and curiosity impelled him into one brief visit to her cell. Thereafter, he had cut Denise out of his mind. Such a difficult girl.

He had left her to God. He did not kill her; she had simply died.

In his more contemplative moments, he sometimes likened his actions to the glorious Inquisition. It had never killed; the priests handed over their victims to the secular arm of the state, and it was *they* who burned heretics at the stake. When the sinners were handed over to secular authorities, the Church issued a prayer which, while asking that there be no shedding of blood, also had the effect of signifying by what manner of death the wrongdoer should glorify God. The Church thus absolved itself from all responsibility.

Nevertheless, seeing Denise's skeleton had shocked him. Afterwards, he had scrubbed his whole body for over an hour. A scintilla of remorse entered his heart.

If Duval had been a psychiatrist, and sane enough to analyse himself, he might have admitted that his own obsessive cleanliness was part of the denial of his actions, a way of relegating misdeeds to the lower levels of his subconscious; that even he, a murderer, disliked seeing corpses was perhaps also a subliminal defensive reaction to his own innate destructiveness.

Duval, in his conscious persona as a priest, could certainly understand why Marda was upset by the sight of Denise, but if the shock led her into the path of obedience it would have been worth it. It would save her life, maybe her soul, and make God and His servant happy.

No, he had done it for Marda's own good. He didn't want to mollycoddle the girl. He would keep his distance to give her time to settle down and, anyway, he was quite busy with his other work in Guildford.

But he always returned to the primary impulse of his life, the recreation of a spiritually successful anchoress in the modern world. To the outside secular world, Duval might seem a failure, a mere second-rate priest, an Oxbridge scholar who had wasted his potential. But his hidden devotional work, his search for the divine channel to the ultimate energy that suffused the planet, would be worth—if such baubles mattered—a thousand Nobel laureates.

Psychologically, this was a holy transformation of impotence into the experience of omnipotence. Through his work, Duval strove to become the master of his spiritual life, and hence the highest quality of spiritual life had to be nurtured in his chosen ones. He wanted to control, not destroy, and while that meant the issuing of punishments and threats of punishment, he was demanding *spiritual* surrender, not bodily annihilation. He craved power over his novices' inner lives.

He occasionally admitted to himself that he was stimulated by their helplessness, but the guests who failed him had been weak in mind and body—they had given up and chosen death. So he would try to distance himself, a little, from the cellar for a while, but he didn't want to become too forgetful. He would feed Marda, and when she was ready he could start his work on her.

On the fifth day after Marda's arrival, Duval decided to begin her induction course. He walked down the corridor, opened the grille, and through it spoke to her quietly, trying his best to be comforting. After all, he had some experience: he was a Catholic priest.

"Marda, how are you?" he said, his voice full of concern.

Marda cringed in the corner; she now equated the light with her tormentor.

"Are you cowering from me, or from the light? Is it too bright for you? I thought that perhaps you would have had enough of the darkness down here. Who is more foolish, I wonder, the child afraid of the dark, or the man afraid of the light? Ah, but I came to comfort you, not to philosophise…Really, how are you? I do care, you know."

Marda said nothing. Duval simply stared at his captive. After a minute or so, he tried again: "I *am* sorry that opening up Denise's room upset you." Duval continued ruefully, "It upset me, too. I hadn't opened it for a very long time."

Nausea rose in Marda's throat. "Did you leave her there to die?" she said, her voice breaking. "How long was she here for?"

"She was my guest for some six months," Duval explained calmly. "A very difficult guest from whom I removed food privileges because she wouldn't do as she was told. It was exasperating."

Marda stared at him in horror. "You mean you starved her to death?"

Duval shook his head. "That's not what I said. I think she chose death and starved herself, in effect. Just before her spirit left her I cleaned her body and performed the last rites. That was the least I could do."

Her mind raced with the implications of his words. "You mean...you really are a priest?"

"Yes." He smiled, and the play of light on the contours of his face made him seem even more disturbed.

"But how can a priest do this to young girls?"

"Do what?" Duval looked genuinely bewildered.

Marda was learning to be cautious. She searched for the right words. "Well, accommodate young...guests...in a cellar."

"I have a mission," he replied proudly. "Both in my church and in this sacred cellar."

Again Marda chose her words carefully. "May I ask how many girls have been your...your guests?"

"You are my sixth guest."

"Are all the others still here?"

"Yes."

"And they are all...dead?" Marda held her breath.

"Yes," said Duval regretfully. "They all failed me. Failed themselves really."

Again Duval smiled with his whole face but emanated no warmth. "But you, Marda, you will live because you will not fail me. I *know* you won't fail me. Let us forget about death and think about life. What can we do to make your life more comfortable?" he asked conversationally.

Marda thought carefully before replying. "Couldn't I live in a room upstairs?"

Duval furrowed his brow in thought. "That would be quite impossible now for a novice. Perhaps later, when I can trust you, yes."

"Trust me *how*?"

"Trust that you will learn what I shall try to teach you. That you will not try to run away before we have finished."

"Finished *what*?" Marda had no idea what he was talking about.

"I am required to teach you about God," said the priest earnestly. "I am obliged to teach you about the life of an anchoress. An anchoress is a woman devoted entirely to God. Later I shall tell you of Christine, about whom I have been writing, and how a woman can achieve everything through a contemplative life. I believe the modern approximation is…" he paused, searching for words to which she might relate, "to teach you to tune in, turn on and drop out. Dr. Timothy Leary, I believe. Have you heard of him?"

Marda shook her head, completely confused. Her intuition told her that she would survive only by pretending to be much less intelligent than she really was, and then making Duval feel superior by appearing to learn quickly what he wished her to. She had indeed read about Leary and had discussed his ideas with friends, but she knew that "no" would be the correct answer to the question. Somehow she sensed that he wanted, as did all men, or certainly all men with diminished egos, to explain things to her. Let him go ahead, then.

"Dr. Timothy Leary experimented with drugs in America," lectured Duval. "LSD—'acid,' it's called—can make a person explore their inner mind, he claims. Silly, really. The religious mystics had better, safer and more sustained visions without this 'acid.' Religion, approached properly, can give you a real 'trip'"—Duval waggled two fingers on each hand to provide the quotation marks—"if you want it enough."

"And when I have learned your religious course properly, I can go?" asked Marda hopefully.

"If you reach the level of attainment of which I think you may be capable, you will not only learn a new philosophy of life, but you will also be free to decide whether to stay or go." The lie came easily.

Marda forced a lopsided grin for Duval, then looked thoughtful. "How long will I take to pass your…exam, your examination?" she asked seriously.

"Historically speaking, a few—very few—people have reached the mystical stage in weeks. Others take a lot longer."

"What about those who fail?"

"As long as you are sincere and you try"—Duval's eyes glanced heavenwards—"God helps you to try and try again."

Marda's knees felt weak, but she struggled to stay engaged in this sinister tutorial. "But some fail, perhaps like the girls in the other cells?" She was not sure if she wanted him to answer this.

Through the grille, Duval looked at her kindly. "I don't want to hurt you. I want to look after you. Ensure you eat properly. Make sure you are warm. In return I merely expect you to listen to me and to answer me openly and honestly. We will start with a little Sunday school—Bible classes, if you like—and then as we progress and study and gain spiritual depth, I will try to explain why I have chosen you."

By now Marda was convinced she was dealing not only with a homicidal religious maniac but also a patronising bastard. The only course was to placate him and wait for an advantageous occasion to escape. Meanwhile, appeasing him meant food. Obviously the first lesson.

She took a deep breath. "The sooner we start, then, the better," she said brightly. "Is that OK with you, Michael?"

Duval looked at her with a slightly quizzical expression. "Indeed," he said thoughtfully.

Shifting his standing position, he composed himself to begin the lesson. "Let us talk about faith," he began. "My first definition of faith was provided by my old theology tutor. He told me that a philosopher is a blind man in a dark room looking for a black cat that isn't there, and a theologian is the man who finds it. I thought it was amusing the first time I heard it, but I soon realised that faith depends upon doubt. Believing in God unquestioningly sometimes, yes, but at other times doubting him. Doubt isn't the opposite of faith, it's a crucial element. Religion may be morally useful without necessarily being intellectually sustainable. So you could say that a believer is happier than a non-believer. Perhaps that's as valid as saying that a drunken man is happier than a sober one."

Marda wondered yet again whether he was merely trying to impress her or whether he wanted genuinely to engage her in conversation. Intuitively, she grasped that he wanted questions from an eager pupil.

"What is God like?" was Marda's first question, as she assumed an attentive posture on her bench.

"So you believe in God?" replied Duval, peering through the grille.

"Yes," she said. But what she really wanted to shout was, I cannot believe in God because long ago he would have destroyed evil men like you. How could God allow such an unspeakable evil? In other circumstances she might have wanted to discuss the holocaust, but for now she was keeping it simple.

"I can tell you that God is alive, Marda, because I spoke to Him this morning," said Duval smugly. "Perhaps you are surprised by such direct communication. You mentioned, I recall, that you are not a Catholic."

"No, I'm not," she replied defensively, "but that doesn't mean I'm hostile."

She started to cough suddenly, as the nauseating taste of bile rose in her mouth. She was shivering from the horror and unreality of her interrogation, but she knew she had to try to disguise her disgust. She patted her chest and coughed again. "Please excuse me; the cold is getting to me."

Duval waited for her to continue. The coughing fit gave Marda time to select her words. "I'm interested in religion but not really inspired by it. I told you, I think, that I was christened in the Church of England and then didn't really bother. I went through a period of doubting God's existence. You know how it is. Well, maybe you don't. That was a stupid remark," she said, feeling awkward.

But Duval answered her seriously. "I hope I am not an unthinking Catholic. My early conversion changed me. You don't know how much less tolerant I would be if I hadn't become a Catholic…" He paused, waiting for a response. Marda did not move a single muscle on her face, and there was silence for a few seconds. Then he continued, as though he was discussing the weather: "But I have my healthy scepticism. In some ways I tread my own path. I have my doubts about big organisations such as the Church. They grow bureaucratic, the arteries become sclerotic. They insist on absolutes. You know, the Curia in the Vatican is a bit like the Politburo in Moscow. Both Catholics and communists are alike in assuming that an opponent cannot be honest *and* intelligent. But I digress…"

He stopped, peered through the grille, and turned his gaze directly to Marda, "All right, let's start at the beginning. Who made you?"

"Well, God, I suppose." Marda was somewhat taken aback by the question.

"You are not sure."

"No," Marda paused, "but maybe there are various gods."

"No." Duval started to recite: "There is the one God, who is three—with His Son, Jesus Christ, and the Holy Ghost, the Holy Spirit if you like. Again, who made you?"

"God." Marda felt like a chastened schoolgirl.

"And why is there a God, do you think?"

"To guide us?" she hazarded.

He prompted her: "To provide moral limits, moral goalposts perhaps?"

"Yes," she said quickly, "that's a good way of putting it." Marda gathered her thoughts. "Um, I don't believe in organisations, either. Yes, I suppose I should know my Bible better, but I try to act according to my own conscience. I try to develop my talents—if I have any—to the best of my own ability, without hurting anybody else."

She paused to wipe her runny nose with the edge of her finger.

"I don't need an organisation to tell me what to do," she continued, "but I suppose that God's word has been interpreted over the centuries—by the Catholic Church and others—and that provides me with the essence of what I believe, as an individual. So, I suppose, God has provided us with morality."

Duval waited for her to finish, then said "I don't know if you understand the philosophical implications of what you have just said, but you are developing the theory of moral relativity."

"I don't have a theory; I just try to do what is right."

"Perhaps," replied Duval, shifting from one foot to the other, "but if we become too relative, too individualistic, then we might as well decide whether the earth is God's plaything, His golf ball if you like, or rather—to turn the argument on its head—maybe our role is not to worship God but to create him…that black cat which isn't there in the pitch-black room. But we do need God, whether we feel Him intellectually or emotionally. And so we are back to faith again."

He changed tack. "Let me play devil's advocate: if God cannot make us become better, then perhaps it's time to get rid of Him. No God, no faith, no nothing…God, however, is necessary for the human condition."

He sighed, enjoying flexing his intellectual muscles, but felt that at this stage it was probably rather in vain. *"Why* did God make *you,* Marda?"

Not to listen to you, you monster, Marda thought, keeping her face neutral.

"Take your time, Marda. I like a considered reply. Not just something flippant, off the top of your head, just to please me. I want the truth at all times. God will know if you lie, and we can hide nothing from Him. So let us try that again: why did God make you?"

"We both make the assumption that there is a God. Then His purpose would be for us to live on earth and be good Christians…or Muslims…or Buddhists, if that's what you believe. That's my first thought. But I know that some people want to live in heaven. I've never fancied the idea of harps and clouds and all that. I might when I'm sick and old, but not now. As for good Christians, what is 'good'? Presumably priests are supposed to be good." She bit her lip slightly, but Duval ignored her ironic parry.

"I am not good," he said, trying to sound humble, "but in my own small way I try to bring people to God."

Yes, thought Marda, you put the fear of God in people, but she continued to play along. "And, Michael," she asked, "are people who are not Christians not good? Can a Buddhist be a good person? Or a Jew? At least by our"—she emphasised the "our"—"definition, as Christians, I mean."

"Excellent, Marda," smiled Duval, "you are *thinking* about God. I suppose you have thought more about Him in the last few days than in all your life."

Marda's big eyes flickered nervously, but Duval carried on excitedly. "Let's try to learn the basic rules and then we can move on to debate. We can discuss good and evil later. I do believe there is evil, I must say. It is tempting to deny the existence of Satan since it removes the need to fight Him. It is so easy to slip back into moral relativism. You might know the saying: kill one person and you are a murderer, kill millions and you are a conqueror. But if you kill everyone, you are God."

Marda nodded politely, completely appalled.

"I enjoy talking to you, Marda," said Duval expansively. "I feel very confident about you, but we are running before we walk. Let us get back to God's purpose."

Duval stopped and stared at her for a moment, then continued, "Of course there is the classic dilemma. If God is perfectly loving, He must by definition wish to avoid evil, and if He is all-powerful He is able, also by definition, to abolish evil. But evil exists—I suppose you think me evil, Marda?—and therefore, God cannot be both omnipotent and perfectly loving. Do you see?

"Or take our situation here. Even if you think me evil, and let us agree that in some circumstances I may be evil—no one is perfect of course—then let me suggest that even here good can come from evil, that new life can come from old. Christ's crucifixion was an utterly despicable historical act, but from this sacrifice emerged the New Testament, Christianity and the possibility of redemption on a world scale. So what *seems* a bad action may actually be good. Do you understand?"

Marda frowned, and deliberately did not answer.

"I shall give you a Catechism to read and learn," Duval continued, not really having expected an answer. "Initially I shall allow you to have one hour's light a day to read the Catechism and a Bible which I shall also give you. If you use this period fruitfully, I shall extend the reading time. Later, if your studies go well, I shall give you some paper so you can make your own notes.

"When I go I want you to think about your soul."

Marda thought he was about to leave, but Duval rambled on about the soul and its immortality. She came to realise that often he wanted to indulge himself in long monologues. Despite his excellent memory, he would sometimes repeat himself.

When he touched on faith again, he suddenly asked Marda, "Where is God?"

Her mind had been wandering and she was not prepared for the question. "I'm sorry, I don't know," she stuttered.

"*Ubique*. The answer in the Catechism is 'God is everywhere,'" he said confidently.

"Well, He's not bloody well here, is He?" she blurted out, unable to hold back the tears any longer.

Duval stood back, disappointed. "Ah, Marda, you were doing so well until now. I don't like this kind of facetiousness—which, by the way, is also blasphemous. Since this is just the start, and you have had a difficult few days, I shall be lenient on this occasion. For two days you will have no light, and you will have only plain bread and water. Now I know you do need more nourishment, and I was about to add, for example, some cardamom to your coffee and put some fenugreek seeds in the bread; that is so good for your digestion. But if you insist on being a poor and recalcitrant pupil, you have only yourself to blame."

Marda was beyond caring what Duval thought of her. She grabbed the frame of the grille and brought her face close to the priest's. "Maybe my stomach can survive on bread and water," she shouted at him, "but my bare feet won't last much longer. Will you, please, give me the shoes and stockings you mentioned? The ones that are appropriate for this nun's habit."

The afterthought, more calmly expressed, was well targeted, but Duval ignored her, closed the grille and walked away.

Marda sat in the absolute silence, the absolute darkness, feeling proud of herself. A short time before she had been a quivering mass of abject terror. Now she had somehow managed to engage a maniac in a sustained philosophical discussion. She could pretend to play according to his rules. He wanted to control her mind and body, but he could control only her body. Her mind was hers, and she would beat him at his own game. Let him think he had the power;

she would somehow discover how to use it against him. Meanwhile, she would survive. She resolved not to allow herself to be foolishly flippant again, no matter what she felt like saying. In the lonely blackness she would train her body and her mind. No matter how her stomach was knotted in agonising fear, she would not show it. She would not be humiliated. That was how she would win.

And yet doubt and despair sapped her bouts of confidence. She wondered whether she could continue to subdue her intelligence, to get the balance right between her assumed mantle of dedicated student and docile victim. Her life teetered along a razor's edge every time he asked a question, so she would have to think hard and plan her words more carefully. She had plenty of time to think. She would use this time to her advantage, no matter how cold and desperate she was.

An hour later, Duval opened the grille without a word and threw in a brown paper bag. The grille was slammed shut and she heard his footsteps echo angrily down the corridor.

Marda tore open the bag and found clean woollen stockings, and shoes. They were a little large, but it made no difference to her feet, aching with cold.

Two days passed, and Duval opened the grille twice without speaking. Each time he handed in a clay jug of water and half a loaf of dark bread. Marda started to beg for some light on the first occasion, but the grille crashed shut before she could get the words out.

When it opened the second time, Marda said in rush, "Please give me a Bible so that I can read."

Duval still said nothing, leaving her standing in the darkness.

On the third day, he silently brought a wooden tray with strange, rather gritty coffee, a fruit she did not recognise and cold venison, heavily larded with horseradish. As soon as he passed the narrow tray through the grille, Marda seized it and began to devour the food.

The priest watched her gorge, then said in a clipped voice, "I have brought you a Bible. I will permit you light for one hour."

He flicked on a switch in the corridor.

"You can also have this tallow candle so that you can study as they did in olden times." She heard the now familiar sound of his heavy tread disappearing down the hall.

Spiritual and physical food, thought Marda. She scanned the cell, her first chance to see it in proper light. As she chewed greedily, she flicked open the first pages of the Bible: the Catholic Douay version. It was unfamiliar. She would have preferred the King James Bible, the one she had used at school, but realised it was ridiculous to worry about that.

Wiping her hands on her habit, she began to read the first line of the first book: "And in the beginning God created the Heavens and the Earth…"

"What am I beginning?" she asked herself. "And can I prolong the beginning to avoid the end?"

IX

The Inquisition

November 1332

For over a year Christine waited at her home. The bishop's court did not summon her, but Father Peter informed her that the bishop, true to his word, had petitioned the Pope for her re-enclosure. These months she spent in caring for her nephew, the child she had helped bring into the world. She watched tenderly as the wet nurse suckled him. It was, she knew, the last intimacy she would share.

Although the rhythms of the village embraced his household, William was subdued, despite the fact that the justification of his word and the restoration of his self-respect had been important to him. His wife Helene was sad, but pleased to have her family around her. Christine's brother was a support, too. But, above all, Christine loved the baby, and William hoped deep in his heart that she would stay. He did not want further change in his life. True, the new lord displayed due respect by ordering furniture to be made for a bedchamber at Vachery Manor, but the outside world had intervened too much in his once well-ordered life.

It was raining hard when Father Peter came to the door. The priest seemed to be full of his own self-importance because he was bearing a very important letter, although the essence of its content had been unofficially sent from Guldenford a few days before.

William welcomed him warmly. "Come in, Father Peter, and dry yourself by our hearth."

"Thank 'ee, Will," said the priest, letting his sodden hood fall on to his shoulders. Sitting on a stool by the open fire, despite his excited state he could not resist casting a covetous eye over the pork roasting on the spit.

William did not ignore the silent request. "Will you honour this home and join us in our meal?"

"I will most gladly, but pray let me read to you all this letter."

The whole family assembled within the minute to hear the first letter William had ever seen.

The priest looked with concern and affection at Christine, while playing to the gallery in his hour of triumph. "Aye, Christine. Good it be to see you in a womanly robe, but I can tell you that your habit should be readied."

The family members all stood while the priest raised the document in the air.

"I have here a copy of the response to the bishop's petition on your behalf. It is in best Church Latin."

"Tell us in our speech," said William impatiently.

The priest assumed a self-important stance, holding the letter with both hands, his arms fully extended. Allowing a few seconds for a dramatic pause, he said, "It begins thus: 'John, by divine permission Bishop of Winchester, to the Dean of Guldenford; we greet ye with grace and blessing.'"

He explained in detail rather than translated the inter-cession of the Bishop of Winchester with the Pope.

"This part of the letter speaks of our Christine. This is from our Holy Father. Heavens be praised, a letter from the Lord Pope about a humble villager here in Shere."

The priest was clearly relishing his role as papal emissary.

"Read it, Father," said Helene, almost unable to contain herself.

The priest nodded with exaggerated dignity. "'Our sister Christine, an anchoress of Shere, in your diocese, has by humble confession shown us that whereas at one time, as is known to ye, choosing enclosure in the life of an anchoress, she made a solemn vow of continence, promising to remain in that place. Now forswearing'—that is 'leaving,' William," he said with a gentle smile as he looked up at the frown on the carpenter's face—"'forswearing this life and conduct that she assumed, she has left her cell inconstantly and returned to the world. Now, with God's help, she has humbly petitioned us that she may be treated mercifully by the Apostolic See.'"

The overawed family looked at each other and, in turn, Father Peter glanced individually at each person in the room before continuing. "Her transgressions have been forgiven, William. Aye, Christine, the Pope himself has given you abso-lution."

Helene started to cry, while young William clapped his hands.

"Now, let me try again—by your leave, Christine," said the priest, a little less portentously, "but this is learned Latin. I have laboured in the church an hour or more to comprehend the words before I came to this house.

"'Therefore, we who strive for the salvation of the souls of her and all mankind with fervent longing, wishing to take care of her soul send ye, according to the rules of the Church, absolution for her, by authority of the Lord Pope, from the excommunication usually promul...promul...'" Father Peter coughed nervously and tried again: "'Promulgated against such persons. In the name of the Lord Jesus Christ, in the manner of a good father of a family rejoicing in the finding of a lost sheep, the said anchoress shall come humbly to ye within the space of four months from this our order that she shall re-enclose herself in the same place, lest by wandering any longer about the world she be exposed to the hunger of the rapacious wolf and, which Heaven forbid, her blood be required at your hands.'"

Christine sat down, and covered her face with her hands. The priest cast a quick glance at her before returning to the complexities of the document: "'After she has been re-enclosed there and has for some time conducted herself in worthy manner, and after she has made salutary penance in proportion to her sin, she will be accepted wholly into the Church. If these requirements be not met then she will lapse into the sentence of excommunication, and this present dispensation shall be absolutely of no moment.

"'Given at Avignon, the sixth day of the Kalends of August, in the sixteenth year of the Pontificate of the Lord Pope.'"

The priest's chest swelled with pride: "This is the Lord Pope speaking to us. Well, speaking to us through the Bishop of Winchester and then the Dean of Guldenford, but it is about our Christine—our sister again in the Church."

Father Peter then translated the attached letter by the Bishop of Winchester, enjoining the Dean of Guldenford to guard against Christine being torn apart again by the attacks of the Tempter.

"This was given at Farnham, the tenth day of the Kalends of November in the year of Our Lord 1332."

The family and the priest sat in silence for a full minute.

William was the first to speak: "We all thank our bishops for their pleas to the Lord Pope. I thank 'ee Father Peter. We will talk of this during perhaps one of our last family meals together with Christine. Father, will you take food with us now? Will you sit with us for our humble meal? And will you say a prayer?"

"Aye, with pleasure, but I will ask Christine to say a prayer over the bread. The Lord Pope has honoured her, not me."

Christine looked at the priest in horror. "It is not right, Father," she said. "I cannot lead a prayer in front of a priest, and fully ordained at that."

"Do what the Father says, Christine. He is honouring our house. I have lost one daughter, but I have regained another."

The priest laid both his hands on William's shoulders, and said solemnly: "No, Will, the Church has regained your daughter. She will return to her cell, and, with the Pope's blessing, for her natural life. Thanks be to God. Amen."

Christine now felt elated, justified and proud, but also a tinge of fear crept into her heart. The Pope himself had granted her absolution, but Hell's torments would be doubled were she to leave her cell again. For his part, William thought of the coldness of her stone cell, not the fires of damnation.

❦

John, Bishop of Winchester, was reluctant to officiate at the re-enclosure. Only three or so years earlier he had conducted the first such ceremony in the whole of the Suthrige, the district later known as Surrey. These were strange times indeed, he thought, as he made the arduous journey to Shere. Winchester ruled the richest diocese in all England, and he was a busy man, with much to do in his own palace. He did not like to travel far at his age, and, with only four armed escorts, he fretted about the wild robbers who roamed in the woods. The Pope, however, had sanctioned the re-enclosure, and so it had to be done.

Father Peter had readied St. James's church and himself for the visit of the sternest of bishops. In deference to the superior status of Winchester, the senior clerics of Guldenford had been invited to witness the re-enclosure, but not all were expected to attend, although Abbess Euphemia had declared her intention to see the re-sealing of the godly woman.

Christine's family and all of the village were preparing, too, for an act ordained by the Holy Father himself. Simon could not attend; he would break out in tears, just like Mistress Anna, he told William, and the carpenter understood well the lover's pain.

The night before the ceremony, Father Peter organised a small feast to honour the bishop's visit. John of Winchester was a guest of Vachery Manor, as the new lord had been eager to sanction Christine's respectability; William and Father Peter had sought and gained his permission for the ceremony. One feast was held for gentlefolk at the manor, and another for the villagers near the church.

Scot-ales were plentiful, although not so abundant as to induce drunkenness, but Noah Flood, whom everyone called Ark, became intoxicated on two ales and mocked the riches of the Church by dressing up as the village "pope," pretending to grant special indulgences to the revellers. A visiting par-doner rebuked him, and swore that no holy favours or relics would be sold in Shere for a year, whereupon the villagers threw the pardoner into the Tillingbourne. The wet and angry par-doner threatened to complain to the bishop, but Father Peter interceded, soothed the man, and prevented any disruption of the episcopal ceremonies.

Meanwhile, Christine had been summoned to the manor to speak to the bishop. It was troubling for her to retrace her steps along the Stations of the Cross she had endured those years before. Wearing her new habit, the gift of the Abbess Euphemia, she was led by the chamberlain to the bishop's rooms.

The Bishop of Winchester, tired after his long journey, made it plain that his spiritual counsel would be brief. Previously his patience and kindness towards Christine had been stimulated by her usefulness in the bitter legal conflict with FitzGeoffrey. Nevertheless, he had honoured his prom-ise to assist with a papal indulgence, no small matter when letters to Avignon could take many months, if the messengers survived the journey.

Bishop John told Christine to kneel at his feet.

"My child, the Holy Father has been bounteous in his mercy," he said with due reverence to Avignon, but also a marked irritation because he had a cold and, ever concerned for his health, had been forced to leave his apothecary behind in Winchester.

He sneezed loudly before continuing, "You must know that this indulgence is rare. If you repeat your crime against God, excommunication is inevitable. A second transgression of this kind will make you a heretic. It will affront God and the Papacy, as well as make a mockery of my two visitations here. You can seek out God, or you can face the stake and flames. It is a simple choice which should cleanse your mind of worldly thoughts, of family, of village. Your duty is to God, not man. Compare your eternal life with a score of years wallowing in the mud and dirt of the hovels of your kin. Have you compre/ hended this, with no doubt?"

Christine, kneeling, spoke humbly: "I have, my lord bishop. I cast aside all, except the Holy Mother Church. My life is devoted to the final mortal ecstasy of finding oneness with God, if it be granted me by faithful prayer and constant devotions."

The bishop made the sign of the cross: "Then so be it. You will spend the night alone in prayer at the altar of St. James's. In the morrow I will find you on your knees and lead you to your cell, with all the rites. May God be with you." He dismissed her in haste, and went to join his host for a supper of roast swan and heron.

Christine returned to Ashe Cottage for a final simple meal with her family. All were quiet over the bowls of soup and bread, followed by salted mackerel. All too soon for Helene, her daughter stood to embrace her. Then Christine enfolded herself in the arms of her brother and father. Her nephew,

Margaret's child, was asleep in a rough wooden cot. She would not wake him, but she bent over to kiss his little hand as Helene held back her tears. William escorted his daughter to the church as a full moon bathed the stone in celestial light. They held each other, but did not speak.

William, seemingly frozen in the moonlight, watched through the church door as Christine walked to the altar and prayed before it on her knees. He gazed on his first-born for long minutes, as the wind fluted through the willows that formed an ostentatious honour-guard for the stream's passage through the church grounds. A movement in the graveyard suddenly caught his eye: a roe deer had wandered from the Hurtwood. It stood motionless, staring at the carpenter. The deer remained stock-still for a few seconds, then bounded away.

William looked back through the church door at Christine's devotions, and waited until he could bear no more. If only my daughter had the freedom of that deer, he thought.

Christine prayed throughout the vigils of the night. She asked God to grant her the courage to overcome her fears and doubts. She had been tempted once into breaking her vows, and she could not immediately ignore the maternal urges that her baby nephew had aroused, but this craving would pass from a worldly body cast off when the secular life was renounced for the glories of the Holy Ghost. She prayed for forgiveness for leaving her cell, and for all those who had sought the help of bishops and Pope on her humble behalf.

Because she had been again in the tangible world, among the trees and wind and sun and, above all, people, Christine had lost the sense of being surrounded by the unseen; her material senses had been overwhelmed. In her cell, her previous isolation had refined not only her imagination but also her hearing, which had become very acute. In midsummer she had listened to the song of the grasshopper, at first soft, then gradually louder, stopping quite suddenly before the creature restarted its cycle. In the long evenings in her cell she had paused in her prayers to heed all God's creatures, especially the nightjars. She had often eavesdropped on the "co-ic" call of the male to its mate; afterwards she would wait for the churring sound of the unpaired males. Then, in the first week of September, the nightjars would fly southwards to unknown parts of the earth, and she would cherish those sounds deep within herself until the birds resumed their courtship in the spring.

In her renewed confinement she would hone her senses once more, and learn again how to transform the mystical nuances of enclosed life into the blessed touch of the hand of God, though she knew that it might be many years before she could personalise the external rhythms of nature into an immanent relationship with Him.

❦

Duval stopped typing and went to the bathroom situated next to his ground-floor study. He felt a little weak. When he denied Marda food, he usually fasted himself, and when he punished her, he had to punish himself. There was no need for a cold bath, he told himself. His third bath of the day would be a hot one; he could think and plan in the luxury of hot soapy water.

He needed to prepare his mind because he had an unwelcome appointment and he did not like meeting strangers. Above all, he did not like Americans, particularly ones who kept pestering him with letters, and he wondered whether he was doing the right thing in agreeing to meet this one.

In fact, Professor Irvine M. Gould had written only three letters; formally couched by the standards of Harvard, but irritatingly intimate according to the conservative norms of English address. The third letter had arrived that morning, and it had begun "Dear Michael." Duval was appalled at the man's presumption.

Gould was a medievalist who had initiated a somewhat one-sided correspondence with the priest on the subject of fourteenth-century mysticism. Duval had persuaded himself to answer the second letter, tolerating the foreigner's interest because it was a mutual one: Christine the anchoress. The professor's letters had been opaque, but had sufficiently piqued Duval's interest for him to agree—provisionally—to meet this interloper; "if you come to England," the priest had blithely written. And now the damned man had actually pitched up in Surrey.

Distrustful of such types, Duval needed time to work out what he would say to the pushy American who had somehow bamboozled him into conceding a meeting. He had two hours before the appointment, which was to take place in the Angel Hotel in Guildford.

Despite his agitated state, Duval was hungry and looked forward to eating that night. Strangely, he thought of meat, even though he had been a vegetarian for many years. He had always regarded his aversion to meat as a symbol of his inability to kill. He reproached himself for this regression, as well as his own nervousness, as he paced up and down his study in a bath towel. Surely he, Michael Duval, was a world authority on anchoresses, and certainly the unchallenged expert on Christine. Nevertheless, the tension forced him to set out early.

Duval parked near the recently completed Yvonne Arnaud Theatre, but did not get out of his car immediately; he sat there thinking, waiting to make a precise entry into the hotel. His Morris shone under the lights of the car park as though it were new, but it was a neon illusion: the car had not been properly cleaned for months. Once he had been fastidious in caring for his possessions, not least his body, but his clothing was beginning to look worn. Members of his congregation had commented to each other that their priest was looking a little seedy, certainly pale and thinner, and perhaps even somewhat scruffy. One had observed a certain wildness in those cold, blue, mesmerising eyes. Duval, however, had not noticed any change in himself.

Punctual to the minute when he walked into the hotel foyer, he asked the receptionist for Professor Gould, then spoke to the man himself, using the phone on the cramped reception desk. The American visitor said he would join him in the small lounge, "the one decorated with reproduction hunting prints." Duval sat alone in the lounge for a few minutes before a gangly, bespectacled figure with a full beard marched down the stairs, strode up to his table and asked, in an unexpected southern drawl, whether this was indeed Father Michael Duval that he was finally meeting.

Shaking hands, the two men sized each other up. The American's round spectacles and beard gave the impression of an identikit inhabitant of the ivory tower, while the tweedy jacket with leather elbow patches hinted at what later became apparent: the American was a passionate anglophile. For his part, Gould noticed that the priest was ill at ease, so he determined to be as friendly as possible, despite what he sensed as intellectual suspicion or even rivalry. That, at any rate, was the impression he had garnered from their brief correspondence, but maybe Duval would be more relaxed face to face.

The professor suggested dinner in the hotel. As they sat down in the empty restaurant, Gould explained that he was spending most of a sabbatical leave from Georgetown University in his beloved England. He had already visited the country home of Lewis Carroll, who, as the Reverend Charles Dodgson, had preached at the Saxon church in Guildford. The two enthusiasts of church history soon jettisoned all pretence of small talk: within five minutes they were becoming animated by the concepts of the new Guildford cathedral. Gould admired the original designs by

Edward Maufe while Duval did not, although their disagreements were politely academic.

Eventually, the priest asked Gould about his current research.

"Well, I've spent a lot of time in France in recent years, pursuing my work on the Inquisition..."

Duval cut in: "You speak French?"

"Not too well, but I've worked damned hard on being able to read medieval French and Latin. They look after their archives over there almost as well as you folks do here in Guildford."

"But what has the Inquisition got to do with English mystics?" Duval asked, a little cautiously. "Surely the Inquisition was a continental affair which hardly ever risked a trip across the water to England?"

The American nodded. "True, of course, but a large number of English people and Frenchmen living under English rule in France were taken by the Inquisition."

Duval side-tracked the professor into a discussion of the Inquisition's methods, a diversion eagerly followed until Duval commented: "Innocent IV's Bull *Ad Extirpanda* approved of the use of bodily torture only in Italy, professor."

"Yes, that's true, Father..."

"Please call me Michael," the priest said, a little too self-consciously.

"Oh, I'm 'Irv' to everyone back in Georgetown. Yeah, that's true, *Michael*, but by the end of the thirteenth century some form of physical torture was employed by the Inquisition throughout Europe."

Duval did not like to be contradicted, but he struggled to keep up the façade of professional charm and let the American develop his point.

"Initially, of course, inquisitors were not allowed to torture, but you'll remember that in 1256 Pope Alexander IV gave them the right to absolve one another mutually and grant special dispensations to their colleagues, so it was all hunky-dory. One inquisitor could torture and then his companion could absolve him. No guilt." The professor's eyes twinkled over the top of his spectacle frames.

"But torture was not as widespread as anti-Catholic propaganda would have us believe," insisted the cleric. "The records of torture are very limited. Libraries are stuffed full of records of patient attempts by the clergy to persuade people to recant, and there is little evidence to support your assertion."

The professor was too decent to suspect Duval's hypocrisy. He could not know that the priest's intellectual sophistry was in utter contrast to the primordial drives of Duval's debased secret life in the cellar; nor how easy it was for the very intelligent to lie, to separate the soul from the body, the mind from the heart, that very denial which was at the centre of Duval's existence.

So the well-meaning academic took his collocutor at face value, continuing the debate in all sincerity. "Ah, Michael, you can't argue *a posteriori* that the absence of such documents from the late thirteenth and early fourteenth centuries means that the inquisitors were more lenient. The verbal ingenuity displayed in the records to gloss over repeated torture suggests that it must have been common practice..."

"No, I don't agree, *Irv*." Duval's use of the Christian name was obviously strained. "Usually the mere sight of the instruments of torture was enough to extract confessions of heresy."

The professor would have been interested in debating the quality of the records, but Duval chased off after the instruments of the Inquisition: "I am sure you know that there were six main methods."

Gould knew the methods, and felt no need to discuss them. He thought he showed this in his face.

Duval, ignoring the hint, began to pontificate: "The ordeal by water entailed a prisoner being forced to swallow a quantity of water, either by means of a funnel or by soaking a piece of silk or linen jammed down the throat. When the prisoner's nose was blocked, and water was dripped continuously into his mouth, it could result in blood vessels bursting. Lenient treatment involved about two and half pints, and severe about five pints. Not very pleasant, I should imagine."

Gould fingered the menu, another cue which the priest either missed or deliberately ignored. Duval pressed on: "The ordeal by fire demanded that a prisoner was tied so that he could not move, and his feet were placed before a roaring fire. Fat was applied to his soles and they would be fried until a confession was obtained.

"The *strappado* was very common, of course. Prisoners, regardless of gender, were stripped to their undergarments and then had their ankles shackled and their hands secured firmly behind their back. The wrists were tied to a second rope that ran over a pulley in the ceiling. The poor heretic was hoisted about six feet above the floor, sometimes with iron weights attached to the feet, and left hanging there from wrists tied behind the back. And this was the *gentle* version of the *strappado*. The rack and the wheel were also popular. The *stivaletto*, or brodequins, were often used in Italy. Nasty way of crushing the bones, sort of an early type of vice."

The priest's delivery was rapid, almost staccato. He was obviously excited by the topic, thought the professor, who tried to look interested.

"The point I am making," Duval continued relentlessly, "is that I have researched the details in some considerable depth. Yes, there was torture, but not as much as the critics make out, and then only after non-violent investigations and trials which sometimes went on for years."

Gould was becoming increasingly bored by the rehearsal of information he knew in detail and cared little to talk about, but he understood fellow medievalists: too enthusiastic for their own good. Since Duval insisted on projecting his skewed history of the Inquisition, Gould tried to manoeuvre him into more contemporary interpretations.

"I still maintain," the professor said confidently, and a little provocatively, "that the six-hundred-year Catholic onslaught on supposed heretics killed between eight and ten million people. The last victim, you know, was hanged in Valencia in 1826—the Spaniards were always the most bloody-minded about what we might today term genocide. They targeted forcibly converted Jews and Muslims throughout Spain. And in Italy, remember, the Vatican turned a blind eye to the Nazi holocaust. But what I find curious is today's lesser-known inquisition, the *current* persecution of dissident Catholics, even in the USA…"

Duval interrupted him: "You are indulging in poetic licence. I thought America was the home of the free."

Gould smiled. "I'd like to think that, but the fact is the Vatican has simply renamed the Inquisition the 'Congregation for the Doctrine of the Faith.' They don't burn heretics any more, but they use anonymous reports—you would call them 'delations'—to silence anyone, especially theologians, who advocates or even discusses anything contentious, such as artificial birth control, for example."

Duval became slightly prickly. "I am not a theologian, but a simple priest with an interest in Church history; I am not privy to the intrigues of the modern Vatican."

Gould smiled tactfully: "Nor am I."

The professor was keen to move on to Duval's knowledge of the self-mortification techniques of English mystics. He did not know very much about herbal purgatives, and in the priest's single letter, as well as in one or two of his published articles, Gould had been impressed by the evidence of Duval's apparently encyclopaedic knowledge of the properties of medieval herbal cures.

Gould's mention of herbs prompted a long monologue, until finally he interrupted Duval's flow: "Michael, I don't believe that mystics used leeches for other than medical reasons. It couldn't be seen as any form of self-mortification. But there were one or two recorded examples of self-branding with a crucifix mark on the cheek."

Duval's face lit up. "Self-branding! Very interesting, Irv. I have never heard of that."

Gould asked the priest to cite evidence for his assertion that some anchorites habitually drank their own urine. He argued that there were only a few indirect non-clerical references to such practices. "Seems to be going a bit far, old boy," Gould said in deliberately mock-English fashion.

"Not at all, *Irv*. Even Gandhi, a regular imbiber of his own urine, quoted the example of the English mystics."

The hotel dining room was now almost empty, a condition perhaps not unrelated to the *outré* dinner conversation of the two enthusiasts, whose historical passion had increased the volume of their debate. Their conversation eclipsed their own meal, which was not discussed except for a few words about Duval's vegetarianism.

The evening drew to a close with a port. The priest decided that the occasion had turned out better than he had expected. Gould's private opinion was that the priest was a harmless and eccentric, if overenthusiastic, medievalist, although he could readily understand another scholar's passion for the period. Finally, they discussed Duval's research on the Anchoress of Shere, but Gould sensed that the priest was being deliberately cagey. After all, the kind of interpretative history in which Duval was engaged was not recognised by academia.

Gould explained that he was busy writing a paper on English anchoresses of the period, and hinted that he had discovered some new information about Christine Carpenter. Duval, although intrigued, was too proud to admit that the American might know more than he did on his specialist subject, but it was enough for both men to agree to meet again.

Shaking hands to say goodbye, the professor asked whether Duval would look at the almost-completed draft of his paper on Christine.

"I'll look forward to that," said the priest. Duval, however, was not looking forward at all to anyone contradicting his personal vision of Christine. He very much doubted whether the American would be able to add anything new to his long obsession, and he could not have tolerated any changes to his vision of the anchoress.

On the drive home, Duval thought of Marda. *She* would not change his vision of Christine. She would be made to fit what he already knew…over the following weeks and months and perhaps years.

⟨⟩⟨⟩

The American medievalist took up lodgings in the White Horse, close to St. James's church. Gould mentioned these arrangements to Duval, who immediately confined his pub visits to the William IV, up in the woods, away from prying foreigners.

In the evenings, amid the relaxed atmosphere of the White Horse bar, the American got to know a number of villagers by name as well as one or two commercial travellers who sometimes stayed in a nearby guesthouse. It was in the bar that the professor bumped into an earnest, strong-looking man in his mid-twenties. The earnest young man and the American soon realised that they were both making it their business to get to know the area; in their own way both men were searchers. After three or four evenings the two outsiders became drinking companions.

The well-built young man with the slightly affected upper-class accent had only recently become a "regular." In the last few weeks he had visited the bar nearly every night for supper, because it was a convenient watering-hole around the corner from his flat—although it wasn't really his. He dressed in regulation mufti for an army officer: cavalry twill trousers, check shirt and a sports jacket.

Captain Mark Stewart had taken special leave from his regiment in Germany. His commanding officer had been very understanding: "Do what you have to do," the "old man" had told him. And he would, since Mark Stewart was not the sort of person to give up. He had insisted, for example, that he and his father should keep up the rent on Marda's flat. He would use it as a base to find out where she was because he would never accept that Marda was dead...not until he found her body.

There were less than two years between the siblings, but he regretted that they had not been closer. He had gone off to Sandhurst when he was eighteen, and had spent most of the last five years away from Britain in Cyprus, Hong Kong and Belize, the ragged bits of empire that clung to a country which seemed to be shrinking as fast as that infamous pound in Harold Wilson's pocket.

In Shere, the army officer had gone out of his way to court the locals. His charm helped, especially with the younger women. The Guildford police, however, had been politely non-committal. "We have missing persons all over the place, sir. They often pop up in the most unexpected places. We're doing our best," the sergeant at the police headquarters had told him. Annoying variations on the same theme he had heard about a dozen times.

The officers in the tiny Shere police station were more sympathetic, however. Constable Ben McGregor was a fifty-eight-year-old Scot who looked older. He was popular in the village for his friendliness, but his distracted manner prompted some to suggest that his retirement would be a minor blessing. Still, there was little crime in Shere, and McGregor's friends put that down to a shrewd nosiness that was disguised by his vagueness. McGregor promised the army officer that he would "look into it." He did, and while his seniors in Guildford brushed the case aside, the constable not only sniffed around the Tillingbourne valley, but also in his own—slow—time started to check on the records of women who had gone missing in Surrey. McGregor found his task almost impossible, however: the records were in a hopeless mess. Nonetheless, he would keep at it, but time was short and his intuition and long experience might be more effective, he decided. He was an honest plodder in the best traditions of the Surrey police.

Marda's parents had started to badger the police three days after they last heard from her. She had always rung them just before and after her trips to France, and they were expecting her to arrive at their house with the new car she was so excited about. When they heard nothing, her parents contacted Jenny, her friend in Guildford, and then her employers. Finally, they rang the police in Shere. A week after Marda's disappearance a detective came to their Woking home, asked questions and took away two recent photographs. Marda's friends were questioned, but nobody had any information. It was two weeks before the Stewarts phoned West Berlin, where their son was on temporary attachment as liaison officer with the Americans. Captain Stewart immediately sought special compassionate leave.

He had now spent over a month searching in Shere and Guildford. He had used up most of his savings in expenses and to pay for printing leaflets displaying Marda's photograph. His father had contributed a reward of £5,000 for any information leading to her discovery. At first Mark Stewart called at the police stations in Shere or Guildford almost every day, but it was down to every few days now. The police were becoming mildly irritated with his amateur sleuthing, although they didn't display much emotion beyond, at times, polite exasperation.

Mark Stewart did not swallow the police theory that Marda had unexpectedy gone to France and disappeared there. He'd spent a week in Bordeaux and talked to Marda's former boyfriend, as well as her colleagues in the wine trade, but had found nothing. He knew Marda better: she would have phoned home before going abroad. He was convinced she was in England, probably in Surrey.

The only lead anyone had found was the possible identification by a bus driver, who remembered her pretty face from various trips but couldn't pinpoint when he had last seen her. Marda's Guildford friend, Jenny, had provided very little information except to list their haunts in the town. Mark had spent about half his time in Guildford, but he had a gut feeling, born of the cavalryman's overweening self-confidence, that Shere itself was a better target for his search. He had called at nearly every house in the village and at the surrounding farms, but nobody had any idea of Marda's whereabouts. A few, especially in the shops, recognised her photograph. And one or two loyal customers in the White Horse also remembered the attractive young woman. Since the pub was also the centre of village gossip, Stewart reconciled himself to spending most evenings there.

The officer had little in common with the locals, so he was pleased to bump into the companionable, if slightly offbeat, American.

❧∞❧

Deep in the cellar, Marda applied herself to her studies. Intellectual pursuits meant light, food and something to occupy her mind; anything was better than the hunger, the cold and the empty darkness. Even talking to *him* was better than nothingness; even *his* conversation was better than

174

being alone, thinking of the ghosts of those who had been tormented in the other cells.

Marda retreated more and more into herself. Often she thought she was becoming insane, laughing loudly, then immediately crying with rage and fear. After a bout of utter misery, Marda was sometimes surprised by the strength of her own inner resources. She wondered whether resourcefulness was like exercising a muscle: would it grow and develop? Was it something she could use again, more easily, when she was free? Or was it a finite quality: would the strength that she had acquired be subtracted from resources that she could no longer draw on in the future?

The cinema of her mind played back old films, and she tried to remember lines from her favourite films and television dramas. She could sometimes conjure up the face of her grandmother, who had died when Marda was ten; she longed for that sense of warmth and security generated when the old woman had read her stories about Winnie the Pooh or tales from Beatrix Potter. In the dankness, she struggled to remember smells and tastes from her youth: marzipan on cakes, the hint of sherry in trifles, bacon sizzling in the mornings. She rehearsed all the little chores she would do in her flat, the exciting projects she could undertake at work. Then the fear and hurt would overcome her imagination and memory; at other times boredom blanked out everything. The boredom was occasionally relieved by random flashes of memory, but they could degenerate into waking nightmares of the dead girl in the next cell. Gradually, she learned how to control the nightmares and to use them, to turn them into plays and stories of her own construction.

Perhaps Duval sensed her new strength and his diminishing control, or perhaps he feared that madness might overcome her because—for whatever reason—he relaxed the harshness of her regime. Her cell was often lit for five

175

or six hours a day. She was granted a small table and chair—the table could accommodate her books—and a small washing bowl when she wasn't studying. Every lesson, if it went well, would result in some favour: a coverlet, a pillow, and, most important, heat. It was probably early November; she had been imprisoned for a month by her reckoning. He would never tell her what day it was, and laughed at her requests for a newspaper.

"Read God's word, not the manifestos of Satan," he said. He also called newspapers "the Devil's dung," and she wondered whether he had ever been the target of a press investigation.

Initially he left her grille open and passed through an electric extension cable for a one-bar electric heater. Five or six hours' warmth helped. In the long hours of darkness, however, the cold stone soon stole away the heat. When the electric heater was removed, sometimes abruptly because of some theological mistake she had apparently made, she shivered beneath her blanket. She would construct a little tent and hide inside, helplessly smelling her body odour and her unwashed clothes.

She tried harder in her studies, and was allowed a change of clothes: fresh underwear and a clean habit. She wondered if the dead girls had worn them. Probably, but she had no choice if she wanted to live. Without them she would die of cold. After what she estimated to be five weeks, Duval gave her a small paraffin heater. It made the cell smell like a garage, but it gave her warmth.

Sometimes she received two full meals a day. The meals were eccentric mixtures, often heavily spiced and containing tastes and foods she could not identify, but generally the end result was palatable. Occasionally she would get only bread and water, as punishment for offences she could not fathom. Duval sometimes explained her alleged transgressions; at other times he would simply tell her to pray for understanding.

Yes, she prayed. Duval explained how to use a rosary, and she prayed to God with a will, fingering the beads he gave her. Some of her newfound faith was a disguise donned for Duval; part of it was to relieve the boredom. A little of it, she half-understood, was real. To avoid growing to hate herself, to hate the animal locked in a dark cage, she decided to search for God, or at least to try to comprehend what God's love might mean. She suspected that religious mania could result from long solitary confinement, but she reasoned that a measure of real faith would help her. Total immersion in religion was madness, his madness.

She began to realise that he was also a prisoner—of his own perniciously distorted vision—but in the darkness something had to fill the vacuum. After prayer, God seemed in fleeting moments to be a presence, not just a set of ancient beliefs. She understood the hypocrisy impelling her search for religion, but time hung around her neck like an albatross, and the possibility of God, the possibility of His intervention, might help to lighten her burden. She remembered her brother saying: "There weren't many atheists in fox-holes in the Great War." Now she, too, was at war—with the evil that lived upstairs.

When things went well, Duval would empty her portable toilet every day, but sometimes he would refuse for a few days. Occasionally her requests for food or an extra blanket were met with polite agreement; at other times they seemed to anger her captor. She could never work out whether it was simply the moods of a deranged man or some genuine "fault" on her part. She did realise that she was being manipulated into his version of submission, so she would simulate her version of meekness.

She tried to adjust to his Jekyll and Hyde personality. At times he was polite, almost shy, and very controlled, but he was also subject to fits of intense anger. She wondered if Duval contrived the fits to frighten her into submission.

Was there a conscious split between a volcanic core and the role-playing of the outwardly charming persona? At times he seemed possessed with almost medieval religious passions, and then in a second or so he would assume the mantle of a harmless country cleric.

She tried to appease his various moods, and to keep her requests to the minimum necessary for survival. Sometimes he offered her something she had not asked for. An exercise book was her first such gift. She started to keep a diary, secreting a few pages at a time in the small air vent above her bench. The diary was her only psychological contact with the outside world. Sometimes she wrote brief notes to her friend Jenny, sometimes to her mother, and occasionally to Mark. She had not corresponded regularly with him before, and she regretted that bitterly.

She pleaded with Duval, on one of the few occasions she had really begged, to phone her parents to say she was alive. But he ignored her request.

Later she asked whether she could write a note to them. She explained that he could post it anywhere in Britain, just a note saying, "I am alive. Please remember I'll always love you." She knew that her parents would be enduring mental agony, not knowing whether she was alive or dead. When she tried to insist, he kept the light off for two days.

She half-consoled herself by thinking that he could have agreed and simply burnt the letter.

She tried to find some meaning in her imprisonment: "At least I am learning something new—I didn't know my Bible at all before," she kept repeating to herself. Now she had read almost half of it. She tried to maintain some dignity, some independence, even though her whole world was controlled by that "pious, hypocritical maniac," as she dubbed him in her first diary entry.

She tried to understand him, but he was so reserved, so secretive. On matters religious or historical he would hold forth, but he wouldn't say anything about himself, and was even evasive if she enquired about his dog. She asked whether the dog could come down to spend a few hours with her in the cellar, and also mentioned that she could baby-sit Bobby if he went away. She genuinely wanted the dog's company, but also wanted to guarantee that Duval would return to her cell. She had panic attacks when she thought that he would just leave her, forget her, punish her, as he had Denise. She reckoned that he would not starve the dog as well as her. She tried not to think of the fate of her predecessors, forced to fast to death.

Whatever happened she would live. She would make herself interesting to him: a good pupil, lively and, given the circumstances, fun. He would be interested in keeping her alive. But the trouble was her sense of fun did not match his. He had a twisted sense of humour. He liked intellectual jokes, but sometimes her half-intellectual ones backfired. She was always dancing on theological eggshells.

She tried to engage him by preparing a written question: "If Christ did die for our sins, dare we make His martyrdom meaningless by not committing those sins ourselves?" It was half a question and half an attempt at a witticism, but it angered him.

He ignored the requests regarding the dog, but once or twice, when Marda had really worked at her lessons, Duval brought Bobby down to the cellar for a while. The sheer touch of another creature brought her unimaginable joy. And Bobby made such a fuss of her; he seemed to empathise with her plight. Dogs knew about these things, she told herself.

She couldn't understand why Duval never touched her. She didn't want him to, dreading it as loathsome, but the fact that he seemed to go out of his way to avoid any physical contact made her wonder whether he was sexually repressed. She laughed when she first thought of this. "Of course he's repressed—he's a Catholic priest," she said to herself in a loud whisper.

He needed order, and seemed strict and harsh about minor things. He was offended by the smell in the cell, and she wanted more than anything to have a bath, but this he would not allow, even though he himself seemed obsessed with bathing. She could hear the water running from his bath sometimes five or six times a day, because the waste and overflow pipes from the bathroom ran somewhere along the cellar corridor. So he was pernickety, to put it mildly. And although Marda did not have the intellectual background to apply Freudian insights or terminology, her shrewd instinct told her that, besides order and cleanliness, he demanded control. His fear of touch implied fear of love. Perhaps he could love only when he had total control and power over the object of his love. No, she decided, he cannot love; he can only control.

She tried to understand his mentality, because this knowledge might keep her alive that little bit longer. Celibacy could never be easy, but perhaps it had been easier when sex in public was taboo; now it was everywhere. Sex seemed to have been discovered in the 1960s, so maybe now it was that much harder for him. Perhaps he was a homosexual who, unlike some of his fellow priests, intended to remain chaste.

"Keeping women in bondage must be his kick" were the blunt words she entrusted to her diary. Duval's earnestness in his religious instruction seemed either to contradict or to confirm that; she wasn't sure which. On some days he spent three or four hours talking, teaching, instructing her in theology, and she had learned a great deal. Her rationale was straightforward: the more she learned, the more Duval would be losing if he let her die. Religion was her investment in her own future.

Perhaps she was going insane, but she also took some pleasure in acquiring new knowledge about a world she had never thought about before. She was an eager student because she had no distractions, except constant fear, and cold and hunger on occasion. The utter and comprehensive boredom of total darkness was a powerful incentive.

When she had started working in France, she had wondered what it would have been like to go to university. She often thought about it. And Duval may have been a killer, but as a teacher he was good. She started talking aloud to herself: "Good? A good teacher? Am I going mad? I'm captive to a monster. I'm not a student. I'm studying to fill my time. To keep my sanity."

Yet, despite herself, she started to enjoy learning. It was her only contact with the outside world. The Holy Land was a lot more rewarding than the dank nothingness of her cell. Her studies allowed her to escape from her fears for a while. And Christ's thoughts were usually healthier than her own morbid ones.

For the first lessons he spoke through the grille. Not only did this feel awkward, but the lessons were short. The longer the lesson, the more warmth, food and light. He seemed to want to be invited in. Marda sensed that she was not facing an immediate physical threat from him, not unless she really upset him by trying to escape, perhaps. She also wanted him to appreciate the discomfort of her cell, if he could be moved by such things.

She said, "Michael, why don't you come in and we can speak face to face? I would prefer to sit upstairs, but until you trust me can't we at least try to be civilised down here?"

She was trying to exercise some control over him. He understood that, but he accepted her co-operation. "All right, Marda," Duval said gently, "but we will go through the handcuff procedure, at least for a while."

Reluctantly, Marda agreed. She sat on the bench with her left hand cuffed, while he sat on the single chair that he had placed as far away from her as possible.

"Mmm. It is chilly in here," he said, as if he was reading an actor's line. "Do you mind if I turn up the heater a little?" He seemed shy, almost nervous. "I shall get you some more paraffin tonight...You have no objections to my smoking a pipe?"

"No."

"I do not approve of women smoking cigarettes. You smoke those French cigarettes, if I remember correctly."

Her eyes twinkled. "I do like to smoke Gitanes. My brother used to tease me, and said I was going all Brigitte Bardot on him. Is there...is there any chance of a pack or two? It might help to relieve my...my tension. And help me concentrate on my studies, of course," she said almost coquettishly.

"I will consider it," he said, lighting his pipe. The aromatic Dutch tobacco filled the room, and she noticed that he had a habit of breaking his matches in two and then putting the pieces back in the matchbox.

"I like that tobacco, Michael, and not just because it smothers some of the paraffin smell."

He ignored her small talk. "All right, Marda, let's discuss your knowledge of the Catechism again. I have mentioned that once you know enough, we could start the process of your confirmation. We'll have to adapt a bit because I cannot really ask the bishop to come here."

Marda almost said, "Can I go to the bishop, then?" But she knew well enough by now that he didn't like what she would call "smart-aleck" comments. She sometimes overreached herself in her attempts to spar with Duval, to keep lively a conversation with someone she knew to be far better educated than herself. It was very hard.

"Let us run through some of the basics," he said slightly impatiently. "What is faith?"

She replied eagerly: "Faith is a supernatural gift of God, which enables us to believe without doubting whatever God has revealed."

"Good. That is word perfect. How are you to know what God has revealed?"

"I am to know…to know…what God has revealed by the testimony, er, teaching, and authority of the Catholic Church." Marda looked a little embarrassed by her hesitation.

"There is no problem with a stumble. It is knowing and understanding. That is what counts. This is not an elocution lesson."

"Michael, may I interrupt? You have a wonderful voice. Did you learn to speak that way or was it something God-given?" Marda would never have used that adjective before. She did it unconsciously. With a start, she realised her vocabulary was altering.

"I was born with it."

"Where?"

He seemed reluctant to concede further information, then suddenly blurted out, "Not far from here…" And then again, he said, "Not far from here. Not far from here…"

A curtain descended and blanked out his motor functions and his speech; his eyes were glazed. Marda remained absolutely still, while Duval, triggered by some past trauma, explored his inner being.

Although he tended to live in the past, both professionally and personally, Duval did not talk about his own history. To anyone. He didn't even like thinking about his upbringing. At first he had tried to forget the whole business, then he attempted to change reality: Duval rejected, then falsified, most of the emotional experiences of his childhood. And he had eventually come to believe these lies as fact.

Especially, Duval tried not to think about his father, who was cold and authoritarian towards him when he was young. He had been attached to his mother, and had some fond memories of his childhood before the tragedy of his sister's mental illness and eventual suicide. After that he grew away from his mother. His conversion to Catholicism caused the final break in an already emotionally estranged family. The Church became his mother, yet although he loved Catholicism, he also hated parts of it.

Duval recovered almost immediately from his brief reverie, but even if it had lasted for eternity, he would never have fully recognised the element of destructiveness in his complex Oedipal relationship with his Church, which to him was both a protective and persecuting goddess.

Duval seemed not to notice that both he and Marda had been silent for over a minute. She had learned to remain very still and quiet when occasionally he slipped into these almost catatonic states.

"But enough of me. Let us get on," he said in a normal voice, as though he were in the middle of an Oxbridge tutorial.

Silence again ensued as he fiddled with his pipe for a few seconds.

"I will ask *you* a personal question before we carry on. You have an unusual name. What does it mean?"

"Oh, Michael, you don't want to know…"

"Yes, I do. Please tell me."

"Well, it's the name of a mountain pass in Somalia. My father served there during the war and he just liked the sound of it."

"How very noble of him." Duval smiled. "Yes, it's a pretty name, and it sounds like 'martyr.' That's what I thought when I first heard it…'And the desert shall rejoice, and blossom as the rose.' Isaiah, chapter thirty-five, verse one."

He stopped himself and his voice became a fraction sterner: "Now the Apostles' creed. How does mortal sin kill the soul?"

Marda was disconcerted by his gloss on her name, but she could not allow herself to be side-tracked; she had to be ready: "Mortal sin kills the soul by depriving it of sanctifying grace, which is the supernatural life of the soul."

Marda did not want to ponder on mortal sins like murder and possibly get lost in a blind alley where she would have to confront him. "And of course a venial sin is an offence," she said, "which does not kill the soul, yet displeases God and often leads to mortal sin…"

She looked up at him. "You have told me a lot about the soul, Michael."

She tried to use his name often; it bred a familiarity, a touch of friendship. You don't kill your friends, Marda thought. Did the others try to be friends, too? Or were they all too "difficult," as he put it? Was she less brave than the rest or simply wiser? Or nicer? She kept wondering.

"If the soul's immortal, Michael, how can sin kill it?"

He answered the question, not very satisfactorily thought Marda, but she wouldn't dare say so. He also tried to explain that the invisible part of the human being, the soul, was not restrained by Einstein's laws of space and time. But he did respond eagerly and in depth, so Marda assumed that it was a good question. The longer the answer, the better the question was her rule of thumb. She had learned that without going to university.

He asked her to define "hope"; then she was asked to explain "prayer."

Marda replied quickly. "Prayer is the raising up of the mind and heart to God…is that right?"

Duval sucked on his pipe and nodded.

Marda was sincere in wanting to learn all about prayer. There was no dissimulation here. Duval seemed to know most of the time if she was acting, so she was always trying to play double bluff, and therefore sometimes not even admitting things to herself in his presence.

"Good, good. Now the Ten Commandments."

Marda rattled them off. She slowed on "Honour thy father and thy mother" but only slightly, and then only marginally speeded up on "Thou shalt not kill." She was learning as much about diplomacy as theology.

"Are you saying grace before your food?"

"Oh, yes," she said. She risked direct lies occasionally.

"Another aspect of the Christian's daily exercise, then. How should you begin your day?"

She scratched her ribs and wondered if she had lice, but no emotion showed in her reply: "I should begin the day by making the sign of the Cross as I wake up in the morning and by saying some kind of short prayer, for example, 'O my God, I offer my heart and soul to You.'"

Duval seemed pleased. "You are learning quickly. In a few weeks we can get you to confirmation stage, and then on to taking part in Holy Communion. I will also explain penance and absolution."

"Michael, speaking as someone who knew so little about religion, I am grateful for"—she was going to say "your time," but she stopped herself—"for your patience, but may I ask what level I am supposed to reach?" She wanted to say something about the fact that, to her knowledge, there had never been a female Pope, but that would certainly have come into his definition of facetiousness.

"I will explain more later. Perhaps first I will show you some of the history I am writing. Not quite yet. It needs some editing, but it is the story of a woman's purification, and I hope it will make things clearer."

Marda didn't push him.

In these "seminars," as he called them, he soon dispensed with the handcuffs. Initially he locked the door behind him and watched her carefully, but as the weeks passed, and she made no attempt to escape, he grew more relaxed. There had been no "removal of privileges" for at least ten days. He seems to like me, she thought.

Marda's cell was tolerably warm. She had light for up to twelve hours a day, and an extra towel. Her little library had extended beyond the Bible and *Lives of the Saints*—she had enjoyed particularly a history of the Crusades and a book of religious poetry. In the dismal dark world she inhabited, Hopkins's "Glory be to God for dappled things" took on a very special meaning, of hope for light, literally, in the future. She desperately wanted to get out, of course, and above all to reassure her family, but somehow she didn't think Duval intended to kill her. She tried to find out what he really wanted from her. Was he simply trying to convert her? Secure one good Catholic conversion before he died or...What if something did happen to him? If he were knocked over by the proverbial bus or had a heart attack? No one would find her. She would starve.

She started trying to keep a little store of food at the end of the bench, but one night she awoke to find a scratching sound next to her ear. Instinctively covering her face with her hand, she felt the brush of damp fur across her arm as something scuttled off her bed.

Marda screamed. She hated rats.

She wondered whether someone, in years to come, would find her, dead, with a rat sitting on her skeleton.

Marda tried to brush aside such terrifyingly negative thoughts; she would think constructively. Yes, she would find its hole, and block it when she had some light, but she would keep her little food store. She would make a small bag and hang it from one of the grilles of the air vent when it was dark, then hide it each morning. She didn't want him to have the slightest suspicion of her plan.

Plan? I should be thinking of a plan to get out, she said to herself.

She estimated that in a few days—maybe, maybe, please—he would allow her to go upstairs, but first she would ask if she could walk in the corridor. Meanwhile, she did some press-ups on the bench during the long dark hours, to tire herself because she was sleeping so badly. She fretted about her physical deterioration.

She had asked Duval for a mirror to see what she looked like, to see how pale she was.

"Such vanity is entirely unnecessary," he had said dismissively.

"Will you tell me then how I look, after so long down here?"

He had said she looked just fine. But what else could he say?

X

The Good Book

Duval cut out a small section of a newspaper and stared at it for five minutes. Before carefully folding it and putting it in the drawer of his desk, he wrote on the clipping:

"*Surrey Advertiser,* 19th November 1967, page 7."

FRENCH POLICE DRAW BLANK

French police in Bordeaux have discounted the reports of a recent sighting of Miss Marda Stewart, 23, the missing Guildford employee of Phillips' Wine Company. Miss Stewart was last seen in Guildford on 7 October 1967. She is believed to have travelled to France the following day. Two recent reports of her in the Bordeaux region have been checked by police and discounted.

A spokesman for the Surrey police, Superintendent Terence Dawkins, said, "We are maintaining our search for Miss Stewart, but we believe she is more likely to be found in France. Hence our close co-operation with the French authorities, who are continuing to follow up leads on the Continent."

Marda had also been busy writing, trying hard to connect with the world outside her cell:

Dearest Jenny,

This is my third letter to you. Still imprisoned here. I shall try to escape by talking about our everyday life. Such thoughts keep me sane.

I don't know what the people at work must think. I suppose that Michelle—who always wanted to go on the French trips—has replaced me. I suppose the police have been on to you. What did you say I wonder? Did they take you to my flat in Shere?

What has happened to my flat? Has Dad kept up the rent for me? And all my records? Do you have them, especially the Kinks LP, the one we always used to play. I wish I could hear it now. I told you all about Him in my previous letters, so I'd better bring you up to date on Events.

I'm not so cold any more. He lets me have a heater and usually gives me enough paraffin—Parrafin (spelling?)—OK heating oil—to keep it going. And although I've lost a lot of weight I'm not hungry *all* the time. I told you about the rat. He's come back once or twice, but he seems as afraid of me as I am of him. But I still have my little store of food, perhaps it can keep me going for a few days if something happens to him—Him, not the rat. I can tell the difference! What if the police find him and he doesn't talk? What if they lock him up?

I hate him. He is so frightening. Michael, I told you his name, his surname is Duval. He is Father Michael but I call him Michael. I am trying really hard to be his friend so he doesn't kill me, like he did the others. Oh, Jenny, I so want to live—there's so much I want to do. Just one hour—even half an hour—to be with you, going shopping or to the theatre in Guildford. Just one drink in the King's Head.

Sometimes I don't hate him as much. I have learned a lot. Mainly about religion. In some ways I hate God for letting me be here, being imprisoned by one of His priests. Perhaps he is not a real priest, after all, but he certainly knows a lot about religion. And I have learned about history. Every now and then I think I am in a crazy university, but I could walk out of a university and just go back to work and enjoy my life with you, and my other friends. And my family. I wish you could tell them that I love them so much. I could even hug my brother and tell him I love him too. I have never told him that.

Have you seen Jim at all? I promised to ring him back. Of course I couldn't. If only I could tell him that I wasn't ignoring him.

Oh! My poor parents. If only they could know that I'm not dead. Not yet. Not by a long way. I try to keep fit by press-ups and running on the spot. I suppose I must look awful but I don't know because I haven't looked in a mirror. I have had to give up smoking, which is one "plus," I suppose. I've asked him for some ciggies, especially my own brand. I'd love a puff before going to bed. I never go to sleep straightaway. I'm either too cold or hungry or sometimes just too frightened. I have dreams—bad dreams— about seeing Denise's body. Well, skeleton. It's in the next cell to mine. There are five skeletons, I think, all within a few feet of me. It's creepy. More than creepy, as you can imagine. Could you really imagine my situation? I am afraid to write how I really feel, to give in to total despair.

I am trying to be brave. I remember some of the mountaineering things we tried and how I failed some of the courses. I think I could do all that now. Sometimes I think I can be brave but then I get floods, yes floods, of fear. I cry until my body aches. I have even thought of trying to kill myself, but I don't know how. Then I say NO! I will come through this! Talking to you helps, you know.

At other times I feel OK. Like he needs me. If he needs me, he won't kill me. Am I right? Even when I am so scared I try to look happy, just so that he likes talking to me. I have to act, but he seems to know when I'm acting. He is clever; perhaps cunning is a better word.

There are times when he is almost nice. I almost feel sorry for him. Like if I was free I would help him. I couldn't really, of course, because he has killed all those girls.

I wish I knew what to do. I have thought of trying to hit him hard and make a run for the door, but he is a big man. Looks athletic, although I would think he is about 45. He's got strong hands. I don't think I could get the better of him.

I felt better starting this letter. Now I feel it's pretty useless. But thanks anyway. I look forward to seeing you soon.

Always your very, very best friend,

All my love,
Marda

PS. I still would like to go to Portugal with you for Christmas. I hope you haven't given away my ticket!

PPS. Reading this letter for the twentieth time makes life sound so superficial. I want to do the ordinary things, but most of all I want to see the sun, feel rain on my face, hold someone's hand, run for just a few yards, to live for a few minutes without fear, to tell my Mum how I adore her, to put my arms around my brother, to hear my father's voice. It is these little things that really really count. Please remember that.

Marda wiped her tears on one of the two towels that Duval had given her. She carefully folded the letter as small as it would go, then standing on the bench, she pushed it into the air vent.

"Useless mail box," she said aloud. She suddenly remembered a joke from her childhood: "What's the difference between a post box and an elephant's bum?"

"I don't know," she said in a silly Mickey Mouse voice. "What *is* the difference?"

"You don't know? Well, I wouldn't send *you* to post a letter!"

She laughed hysterically, and then burst into tears again. Shaking, she pretended to light a cigarette, and thought that in the films tough guys smoked and didn't cry. She felt that her life now was just like some terrible B-movie, except she couldn't walk out in the middle of it. She coughed from the imagined smoke and that stopped the tears, but not the pain in her head. She'd had a bad cold for about a week; although he had brought her some aspirins, they didn't help. She did not beg to be taken upstairs. That wouldn't have worked, but she told him that nearly two months of no fresh air was driving her mad. "If only I could see the sky!" she said.

She worried about her health, as she had not menstruated since her incarceration. Perhaps my body is going haywire, she told herself.

Then she began irrationally to fear that somehow he had made her pregnant; that maybe she had been drugged again. She developed a brooding fear that she had been impregnated by the Devil, that some dark beast lurked in her womb, even though her weight loss told her that this was impossible. She hadn't even thought about sex since her capture, so perhaps part of her was closing down for the duration. She wondered whether it would be temporary; she prayed that her ability to bear children was not being taken away by the monster upstairs.

The next morning he knocked on her door before unlocking it.

"How are we this morning?" he asked cheerfully.

"I feel awful, Michael. My headache's getting worse," she said, her voice racked with self-pity. "Can I please just walk around in fresher air outside in the corridor? And I don't want to see any more rooms, I promise. I won't try to escape. You can see I'm too weak." She was sitting limply on her bench.

He came in and helped her up, the first time he had touched her since he had captured her. She looked at him in surprise, and he drew back his hand, as if he had suffered an electric shock.

"No, Michael. Don't be afraid of touching me," she said reassuringly. "I appreciate your trying to help me up. May I walk a little outside the room?"

He gestured towards the open door. "The cellar door is locked, but I will permit you to walk up and down to give your legs a bit of exercise, and the air is a little fresher out there because the main door has been open for a while."

She hesitantly stepped through the door into the corridor, and walked gently up and down with childlike pleasure, despite her cold. She didn't speak for a few minutes, then she said abruptly, "What is the weather like outside? Raining I expect."

"No, it's dry, but very windy."

"Has there been snow at all? Are we into November yet?"

"It's actually the fifth of December."

She stopped walking, and her pale face seemed to sag into total lifelessness. "I've been here since the seventh of October," she said in disbelief. "That's nearly two months. I had no idea it was that long...I must have lost track completely. I should have kept a calendar from the start, but I was sort of lost for those first few weeks, wasn't I?"

He gave her a look bordering on kindness: "You were a bit."

"But I am better now?" She spoke as though she were a little child.

"Yes, and we get on better," he said in an avuncular fashion.

"You're not, not going to kill me?"

"No, I never had any intention of doing you any harm, as I told you. You are my pupil."

Marda thought she would quit while she was still ahead. She changed the subject: "What's that big crucifix for?"

"That came from my first church in East Anglia. They were renovating the place, and I was the only one who wanted it. I've had it for twenty-odd years. Sentimental foolishness, really."

That was one of the first signs of sentiment he had confessed to, she realised.

"But why put it in the cellar?"

"No room upstairs, and I had intended this to be a holy place. But it hasn't...worked out. It's become like a graveyard. Well, until you came. So, let's make sure you get well and we can proceed with your seminars, so you can come upstairs out of this draughty place, at least for our teaching sessions. I must admit I get a bit uncomfortable down here, too." He seemed to be assessing how much he could show of himself.

He assumed again the role of kind uncle. "But all in good time. All right, you get back to bed—I know it's still early—but if you feel weak, may I suggest a drop of corn spirit with a little milk, honey and lemon? A good old remedy for a cold."

She nodded. "Thank you, that would be nice. Even nicer—although not conventional medicine—would be some Gitanes. Just one?" she said with an exaggerated wheedling tone.

Duval said nothing as he led her back to her cell, closing the door without locking it.

Marda sat on the bed and pulled the blankets over her clothing. She became more alert. He's left the door unlocked and the light on, she thought. For the first time. And he touched me. He's either going soft or he's fattening me up...for something awful. She heard him unlock the main door to the cellar and come down the stairs.

After knocking on the door, he came in with a steaming glass of medicine.

"Here, sip this. I'll turn up your heater. I've also brought you something different to read. My opus. It's called *Anchoress of Shere*. I call it an 'interpretative history.' I've researched the basic facts extensively, although some of the documentary evidence is scanty. This is real history, founded on real truth. I think I have taught you enough for you be able to appreciate what I've been trying to do."

He paused; then, with a gloss of modesty in his tone, he said, "Great literature, they say, is the clever orchestration of platitudes. I hope I've avoided some of the platitudes even if I've been playing on a one-string fiddle. So few good books are written nowadays, because those who can write rarely know anything. I don't really know how to write, but I do know the most important thing is man's, or in this case woman's, relationship with God."

Duval appeared embarrassed by his explanation. His arms seemed disinclined to obey his own words, as though giving her his book was impossible. Reluctantly he offered her the text, and she politely received it with both hands. Duval would not let go of the manuscript until he had finished speaking. Later, in the utter darkness, when Marda was reflecting on this contrary behaviour, she thought it was like Dracula being forced to open up his coffin in daylight. Duval and the book were almost one.

A few minutes later, he returned to the cell.

"To me, writing has perhaps been a lonely substitute for conversation," he said confessionally. "Talking to you means a lot to me, so I would like you to read my work and say what you think about it. I won't be too hurt if you say you don't like it. It's not finished yet. I have to add the conclusion, and even the rest needs a lot of editing. The typing isn't perfect, either… I'm being too defensive, I know, but you are the first person I've shown it to. I hope you are well enough to read it… Take your time."

He looked at her face. He rarely looked straight into her eyes, but this time he did.

She smiled to give him more confidence. "I'll make time, Michael."

"Yes, I suppose you have lots of time. I'm sorry to have to detain you."

She saw this as a psychological breakthrough, even though he locked the door on the way out.

It was ten o'clock in the morning when she started to read. She had seen his watch; normally it was covered by his shirt or jacket. Perhaps that, too, was a concession.

◈◈◈

He was obviously pleased with her progress when he came back at two o'clock—he announced the time—carrying a tray with a large cooked meal in a scrubbed wooden bowl. He also gave her a pack of Gitanes, for which she thanked him profusely. Duval made some small talk, but avoided asking her opinion before he left. She ate her meal, smoked two cigarettes and continued with her reading.

Later, he brought her coffee, and this time he couldn't contain his curiosity: "How far have you got with it? You don't have to read it in one go, but I'm pleased that it's held your interest for so long. Well, my child?"

Marda had been planning her response. She had been terrified by the story. Despite her rapid religious training she had not understood all its meaning, but it told her much about his state of mind and revealed even more about his plans for her. Although she was heartened by Christine's escape, Duval's ideal of spiritual fulfilment through life incarceration within a wall chilled her already cold and pained body.

She had practised over and over what she would say. A bad response could be dangerous, she knew. She realised what his writing meant to him. It was more than an obsession: he was acting out a deadly fantasy.

She did her very best to smile, a simulation of deep contentment. "It's fascinating, Michael. Truly." She realised that the "truly" was too quick, too desperate, too gushing. "No, I have to be a little careful because I haven't finished it yet. I am up to the bit where Christine meets the bishop in Guildford...I didn't know that it used to be called Guldenford...Please let me finish the book. I will have some questions because I don't understand everything, and I *do* want to understand it all."

She tried to be convincing. Marda had a naturally kind disposition, but it was extremely hard for her to applaud a prospectus for her own premature burial in stone.

Duval's face beamed with pleasure. "No, don't rush it. I value your opinion. There is no one else I would show it to."

Marda was cautious now: "Did you show this to your other…guests?"

"Good Lord, no. I told you, you are special. And to be honest I have rewritten a lot since you've been here. Since I met you the first time in Shere, I've done a great deal of work on it. If it's ever published…of course I don't know if it's good enough. Sometimes I think it's too personal to publish. Too important. I don't know much about publishers, agents…all that London business…but, yes, *if* it is ever published, I would like to dedicate it to you. With your blessing."

Marda often found it hard to follow her captor's logic, but she recovered quickly from this surprise. "Michael, no one has ever asked whether they could dedicate a book to me before. I don't know what to say."

Now Duval had become the child of their relationship. "Well, I'm jumping the gun a bit. You'll have to finish reading the draft there. I mean you don't *have* to, but if you would, then I have to polish up the whole thing. You know, then get it looked over by a proper editor, *et cetera, et cetera*."

Marda sensed the power reversal again. He seemed like a schoolboy, her captive for the moment, but she had learned how volatile he could be. She was afraid of uttering a fatally incorrect phrase. "Michael, please let me finish your"—she almost said "masterpiece" but wisely refrained—"book. I want to see what happens next."

That was the correct reply.

"I'll leave the main door open and your grille a little way open, if it's not too cold, then you can shout if you want some coffee or something. How is your cold?"

She couldn't resist a cliché: "A day in bed with a good book is what I needed." She attempted a wan smile.

He was not generally susceptible to flattery, except about his book. He was well on his way to believing himself to be an author.

"Thank you for your support. I'll leave you to it, then," he said enthusiastically.

Marda returned to the hardships of the Middle Ages; they helped her forget a little of her own suffering.

February 1333

Simon was not quite as tall as the woman he had loved all his young life. Broad-shouldered and very strong, he worked hard in the fields as well as long hours on his delicate task of making clothes. Christine had shunned him, told him to forget, but he could not. His father had warned him: "Ne'er go within three arrow-shots of the carpenter's home," but Simon could not help his feelings. He called upon William the Carpenter from time to time.

William was fashioning two benches for Simon's cottage in exchange for some woven fustian.

"'Tis good to labour in oak; they be the monarchs of the forest," said William.

Simon did not reply, but then said, "Is she in goodly health, Master William?"

William sighed heavily. "Aye, the many months in the world, despite the trial, have granted some rosiness to her cheeks, just as when she was a girl in the fields. Done her well, indeed. I doubt that she would have lived, being alone in the wall, if the death of her sister were brought to her there."

"I am well pleased at those tidings, sir, but I wish her rude health would allow her to speak with me."

"So still she denies you, Simon?"

"Aye. She will not speak to me; she just prayed aloud over my pleas. Then she began to act like a mummer, as if I were not there—that be some weeks ago." Simon spoke with infinite sadness.

William put his hand on Simon's shoulder. "You know she cannot speak of earthly matters with you. Her rule is strict: she can speak to her family, but briefly, about her daily needs—all else is to be spiritual. She means not to hurt you. I know she does it to make you forget. It is some years since we did make preparations for the nuptials, so 'tis time you married another, though I would gladly have taken thee as my son."

Simon walked towards the open fire and stared into the flames. He was lost in thoughts which William did not interrupt. When finally he spoke again Simon's voice was tinged with a slight tremor: "I did tell my heart that once my Christine had left the cell, she would not go back. Her leaving gave me hope again, the hope that I had buried for two years."

"Simon, I have told you this oftentimes: you must not tarry. You are a handsome lad, the wish of many a maiden in this parish. Go: take another. With my blessing."

"Sir, I cannot. While Christine lives, I cannot." Simon's face was full of emotion.

"This is foolishness," said William. "Life is short and hard; you need sons and daughters to care for you when strength departs from your limbs. And if you do not heed me, then for your own sake take yourself away: you are a craftsman, and strong to labour. Escape this demesne or seek permission of our new lord, if you must."

"My father who did not become my father, you have seen into my thoughts. I shall take my love away. Perhaps in foreign lands, I can forget your daughter, sir."

XI

The Testament

Duval was pleased with both his writing and his guest. As he had always hoped, his interests were coalescing because they were mutually inspiring. His relationship with the Bishop of Guildford, however, was deteriorating, if it were possible for it to become any worse. It reached a nadir during lunch the next day: the bishop, surprisingly, had invited Duval to a meal in the Napier Hotel, an ornate red-brick Edwardian edifice near the River Wey. Duval was a little taken aback by the written invitation, but it was the kind of gesture the Americanised cleric might make. "A good public relations move, as they would say in the US of A," Duval said aloud in an exaggerated southern drawl. The invitation worried him—he realised that it would be more than a friendly chat over good wine.

Bishop Templeton was already sitting at a reserved table when Duval arrived promptly at one. Duval's superior indulged himself, while sipping sherry, in a zestful diatribe about cricket for twenty minutes before moving on to Church matters.

Templeton launched immediately into his views on the liberal trends in the American Church, complaining that the papacy was using its strength to downgrade the role of theologians and fill vacant bishoprics with yes-men. "Rome," he said, in his nasal version of received pronunciation, "is trying to reverse all the progressive developments we have made on the Pill, on marriage annulments and upon attitudes towards sex, including homosexuality."

Duval's energetic views on the principle of individual relationships with God made him a natural opponent of the over-centralised, over-dogmatic Church, but like all zealous converts he was at heart a traditionalist. Besides, he felt he had to engage the bishop in Church matters beyond Guildford, if only to distract him.

"Surely, Your Grace, the papacy is by definition authoritarian." Duval's voice was not as confident as his words. "There is a very long history supporting the papal right to appoint bishops. Christ did not form a subcommittee of apostles, did He? He did not take a vote on the subject of His own crucifixion."

Bishop Templeton raised his eyebrows slightly, and recommenced his tirade: "Maybe not, but recently cardinals have been treated like altar boys. There is a culture of fear, a culture of passivity... Rome is out of touch, especially with the Church in the Third World. Take the 'liberation' theology in Latin America. We can't stand against it because if we do so we'll lose the people. We have to understand the constant conflicts between authority and conscience. And we must be on the side of conscience."

"But where do you stop?" Duval asked with some passion. "The history of the Catholic Church has depended on its unity, its uniformity. It has survived all other empires in history because of its centralising strength. If you start saying that Latin America can do this, Africa can do that, there will be another schism. You have to hold the line..."

"Against the tide of moral relativism?" The bishop bestowed upon his words a smug smile.

"Yes. Absolutely," Duval said indignantly.

"And so Rome becomes as rigid as Moscow?" countered the bishop. "QED, I'd say."

Duval had recently said as much to Marda. He was losing the argument, so he switched to another tack: "Perhaps, your Grace, it's not a question of papal dogma. I accept the Pope's infallibility on matters spiritual. I think some of the errors made, and there have been many, relate more to personal factors—old age, tiredness and stress. Clearly the cardinals and bishops should support the pontiff more whole-heartedly, not add further problems."

"What further problems?" Templeton tilted his head quizzically, and looked directly at the priest.

"Well, I mean specifically abandoning the old rites and rituals," Duval said. "The liberal position often regards these shibboleths as meaningless gibberish. They say they have to 'dump' Latin services for the sake of the worldwide flock. I know that few could understand the liturgy, but it is not mumbo jumbo. In word and form Church Latin is beautiful, the crystallisation of fifteen hundred years of intellect, of a love of God and a healthy terror of His divine anger."

Duval was into his stride now: "Trendy guerrilla priests in South America or folksy fathers in New York strumming guitars will not create a populist, or popular, Church, but will destroy the authority built up over centuries."

Duval examined the bishop's expression to see whether he should continue. He did not see a stop sign. "I do not deny the need for Rome to be flexible, but this... this... socio-logical Church will no longer stand as a beacon against evil. Soon anything will go. The brightest and most sincere priests will leave and soon there will be few male priests, celibate or not. You will have to ordain women, God forbid!

Why not make the Pope a woman? That's the logical conclusion to liberalism."

The bishop smiled; he thought they were both now debating for the sake of it, not from principle. None of these things was likely to happen. He couldn't quite accept that Duval was in deadly earnest.

Over dessert, Templeton came to the point of the lunch: "Michael, I know we've had our difficulties in the past, and I've always tried to, er, smooth them over and find a way forward. But it would seem that, in spite of not inconsiderable effort on my part, some of the problems are coming to a head."

Duval looked only slightly pained: "You are referring," he said, "to complaints from my congregation, I presume."

"Yes and other little sundries that keep occurring. I don't need to rehearse them again. The Lord knows, I've tried to help you: you've been given reduced responsibilities for some three years now. You are almost *sine cura*, although admittedly partly at your own request so you can complete your, er, book. How's it coming along, by the way? Have you found a publisher yet?"

"It is almost completed." Duval was guarded.

"When may I see something of it?" asked the bishop politely. "You have always been so reluctant to let anyone see it."

Duval shifted in his seat. "Well, Bishop, it is rather unorthodox. It is, as I explained in the synopsis, a modern interpretation of the role of contemplation in the fourteenth century. It is not a scholarly work as such, but rather an attempt to interest modern, by which I mean popular, readers in this neglected area of Church practice. That's my concession to populism, if you like, and it is mainly aimed at women readers. I think sometimes we tend to neglect the largest group within the Catholic community, don't you?"

The bishop ignored the diversionary cue: "It's a pity, then, that it's women who've complained about you, but I shan't dwell on the details because we have discussed this already. However, I do look forward to seeing your book. And I would expect you to show it to your superiors before it's published, especially if, despite your conservatism, it's perhaps a mite unorthodox—but don't let me put you off. You know that I'm trying to move the Church forward as fast as I can, without undermining her sacred tenets, of course."

The bishop patted the small golden cross that hung from his neck. "What I really wanted to talk to you about was a change of direction for *you*. In the light of the flurry of criticisms, I don't want you to suffer any possible scandal..."

"But..."

"Hear me out, Michael. I want to do what's best for you, and this is what I've decided. I think a period of missionary work in South America might suit you."

"Bishop, I must object..."

"You can see some of this newfangled liberation theology at first hand. With your intellectual gifts I'm sure you will begin to understand the new theories and you will certainly master Spanish quickly. In fact, I've arranged a language course for you for three months in a seminary near La Paz."

"Bolivia?" asked Duval, unable to conceal his astonishment.

"Indeed," continued Templeton firmly. "After that there are two missionary stations in rather more remote parts of the country which would benefit from your talents. Once you're there you can decide which one is suitable. After all, you have shown a great interest in anchorites, so you can hardly object to being cut off from the busy world for a while, can you? Consider it not as the back of beyond, but as God's front-line. It would provide precisely the right sort of spiritual refreshment."

Duval's face clouded, while Templeton fiddled with the stem of his wineglass before continuing. "Some of the women in your congregation find your behaviour decidedly odd. I have already cautioned you informally and in writing. Sometimes you seem to be behaving as if the outside world does not exist. I have to pull you out before anything untoward happens. I will simply *not* tolerate a scandal in my diocese. Need to nip things in the bud and all that. Frankly, Michael, Guildford needs a change from you, and you need a change as well. A fresh challenge."

Duval was fuming, but there was little he would be permitted to say, especially after his little disquisition on the need for authority in the Church. Intellectually, he had boxed himself in, and both he and the bishop knew it.

"When do you plan to send me?"

The bishop inhaled deeply. "I shall give you time—say, four to six months—to wind up your affairs. I shall release you, with immediate effect, from all your remaining duties to allow you the chance to prepare, perhaps start on some Spanish, and to sort out your house. Yours by inheritance, is it not?"

"Yes, yes," Duval said distractedly. "I don't want to sell it. I had always wanted to retire here. Rather sentimental, really. Belonged to an aunt. It's a sort of family association."

"Quite, quite. I understand."

"And my dog?"

"Ah, these encumbrances you have on your ministry, Michael. I'm sure someone can be found to care for the poor creature while you're away."

Templeton has never owned a dog, thought Michael.

The bishop coughed politely as he cleared his throat for the disagreeable details. "I don't want to *order* you to go to South America, Michael. The Church doesn't do that any more. *I* don't want to do that, but I fervently believe that it's right for everyone, for you, for the Church."

Michael wanted to say, "And for you, you patronising old soak."

"Just think about it for a while. My assistant will provide you with all the details. Think about it very seriously, Michael."

By this time Bishop Templeton was enjoying his third glass of wine, and was more inclined to return to the state of English cricket. Duval had no interest in the subject, but was obliged to nod and smile in the right places until lunch had finished, promptly at 2:15 p.m., and the bishop elegantly dismissed him.

⋘∞⋙

Duval drove his old Morris at full speed on his return to Shere, realising his life had just been altered forever. He considered his alternatives: theoretically he could leave the Church, but it was his whole life. All that he owned was his house, although Duval had never thought of himself as materialistic. The house meant nothing to him in terms of pounds, shillings and pence, but his work in Shere, his writing, and now Marda—these were not *things*, they were tools of his spiritual work, not material goods. They were his vocation, they were not shameful worldliness.

And Marda was at home waiting for him. He was finally achieving what he had worked on for years, and now it was all threatened by a sanctimonious sports obsessive who believed he was a trendsetter. Duval wanted to get drunk and then resign from the Church, but he could do little except curse the bishop.

Unconsciously, his vanity had propelled him into believing that the Church needed him as much as he needed it. He was altering reality to preserve his sanity. He was afraid of being alone, not least alone and without the Church; regardless of how much he railed against it, he would be lost without her mantle of protection.

He hated Templeton and all his kind, but just as he wanted to control, so, too, he understood that, in the final analysis, he had to be subservient to the authority of Rome and its episcopal appointees, even if they were bibulous oafs such as Templeton. But Duval would not give in, even though the Church had failed him yet again. *He* had not failed; the *Church* had failed to understand his mission. The more the success of that mission seemed to fade, as near-victory slipped into defeat, the more destructive his soul became.

In his subconscious, probably, and certainly in the rambling confessions in his diary, Duval the erstwhile spiritual champion was becoming more and more Duval the destroyer. Perhaps something deep inside his psyche, well hidden, told him that he could never succeed in his mission, that he never really wanted to. His psychotic streak was enhanced by his paranoia. He was a gambler who was satisfying what he truly wanted, to appease his hatred and his lust for destruction without compassion.

He still had some compassion for "her," and, for that matter, his dog. But everything else was like background music on the radio, the real world had become barely observed wallpaper in a room full of frenzied lunatics. He was only interested in *his* thoughts, desires, wishes and plans; other people mattered only in that they could be used for his own ends.

Duval was not completely psychotic, however. The sadist in him demanded his victims' surrender, but not necessarily their annihilation. He could still control himself, despite the traumatic news from Templeton. He could still maintain his denial of the contradictions which permeated his existence: a vegetarian who killed people; a priest who imprisoned innocents; a theologian who could not love yet who preached Christ's message of charity and hope; a man obsessed by compulsive cleanliness who forced his would-be disciples to live in their own squalor. He was stimulated only by the helpless, not by the strong. On the surface he showed courtesy and correctness, but these social graces were a superficial veneer over his demonic inner drive. Perhaps only a priest could juggle for so long with so many masks.

For Duval there was still the ideal of the anchoress. He had once loved his mother, but she had failed him, and he had come to love the Church instead. He had been passed over for promotion. As a keen Latin scholar he had wanted to work in the Vatican, but had been turned down, then he had failed as a military chaplain, and had finally ended up in a dead-end post in Guildford. The Church had rejected him even though he was convinced of the power of his spiritual views. In the end only God could know, and so Duval would submit only to Him. He liked to quote from St. Paul: "If you are led by the spirit, no law can touch you"; no law of Church or Caesar really mattered when it came to the search for absolute truth, so he would explore the only route to God available to mortals—holy, absolutely solitary contemplation. Duval had attempted to follow this path on numerous retreats in the most austere of monasteries, but he understood in the end that it was not his vocation. Nevertheless, the path was righteous, and this had led to his study of the extreme mystics of the Middle Ages.

After his sister's death, he had cut himself off from his mother and grown to hate all women. The Virgin Mary was a respite, the temporary but vital exception to a total misogyny that would have toppled him into insanity. Then he reached out to one mystic, one holy anchoress, whom he had pursued for years in thought and writing, but for all his love for the historical Christine, she needed a physical embodiment. He sought living flesh to clothe the skeleton of Christine, which haunted his mind, but that flesh had rotted in his cellar. Only Marda now stood between him and total madness, only she could save him and his vision. She had become both Marda and Christine.

When he reached his house the thought of Marda calmed him. She was his now, but he could possess her only for six more months, at the very most. He would have to accelerate his special ministry for her. Yes, if she became totally acquiescent to his plans, he would leave the Church and maintain his life with her. He could just afford to retire, keep her and share their spiritual union, together until death. But what if she refused to understand that this would be a perfect future for her? He might be forced to let her starve herself to death. Duval dreaded the thought of losing her. He would, for her own good, *make* her believe. She would live then, with him, forever. Marda would be his lasting spiritual project, but he couldn't contemplate another failure. No, he would make her believe, and he would complete his book. He gave himself three months.

The first thing he did was to make a pot of coffee and take it down to Marda's cell. He desperately needed to be with her, the one living person who brought some meaning to his life.

Marda, who had learned that it was wise to be supportive, noticed at once that he was troubled. "What is it, Michael?" she asked solicitously. "Has someone died? Or has someone stolen your book—you told me you had only one copy?"

"No, Marda"—sometimes when he was angry he refused to address her directly; she felt good to be a person with a name rather than an animal in a living tomb—"I still have the manuscript. I haven't finished it yet. There is much more we have to do until it is complete. No, it's my bishop again."

Marda had not heard him mention the bishop in such terms. That there was a chain of command, that there was somebody in charge of him, sent a fresh surge of hope rushing around her brain.

"What has he done, Michael?"

"He wants to send me away from here. From my work, from you."

Marda realised that a sign of relief could be fatal. She listened intently as Duval explained the bishop's plans for him.

"Do you have to go?" she said cautiously.

"No, I could resign and stay here with you. It depends on you."

"How?"

"Well, your studies have gone well. You are a willing and able student. I like teaching you."

"But what is all this learning for? Do you want me to become a nun in a convent?"

"No, I don't want you ever to leave me." He said this with an utter conviction that horrified Marda.

"Then what? Surely you don't want to keep me locked up here for ever."

"No, of course not."

They were both standing in the cell, a few feet apart, their eyes locked on one another.

"Then I don't understand. May I ask: do you intend to leave the Church in order to get married? To *me*?"

Duval appeared shocked, but he managed a hollow laugh. "Good Lord, no. It's quite simple what I want. I want to share my life with you, but on a spiritual level. I want you to become"—he had never really defined it so succinctly to himself, let alone to any of his guests—"to become, as it were, a modern anchoress...I will always teach you and spiritually support your seclusion. I intend to renovate a room upstairs that will be more comfortable. You would be secluded from the world, but it would have a small window, in the shape of a quatrefoil, looking on to the rear garden. You need some light, not this dungeon."

He hesitated, uneasy at how this young girl could make him seem foolish. "But a period of penance," he said with forced authority in his voice, "is good for the contemplative life. I want above all for you to desire this yourself. In the end I cannot force this vocation upon you."

"So if I said no, you would let me go?" She knew she was risking all with this question.

Duval hesitated for a second. "No, I cannot let you leave me."

"Even if I swear on all the religious meaning you have given me that I won't tell anyone, the police, my family…"

"It's not that I don't trust you, although it would be hard to hide so many months' absence."

He looked uncomfortable as he tried to do something with his hands. He searched around in his jacket pocket for his pipe and started to fill it with tobacco. Marda sat on her bench, deflated.

"I cannot bear you to live without me," he confessed. "Perhaps I should say I cannot bear to live without you."

Marda wanted to contrast his comments about her spiritual renunciation and the hypocrisy of his wanting to possess people, but she said, "If you go to South America, can't you free me then? You will be so far away and I'll be grateful for all you have taught me. I've been cold and hungry and I did hate you at first, but I've learned so much. I've come to understand a great deal about life and intellectual ideas. If you go, will you let *me* go?"

Then a final stab at persuasion: "Perhaps *I* could come to South America?"

Duval looked at her, incredulous but half-pleased. "I don't think the bishop has a female companion in mind. I haven't decided anything yet. Perhaps you are right: if I do go to South America I can let you go then. Unless you decide you *want* to stay with me…I need to think, Marda. And so do you. I shall give you a small fustian kerchief to embroider. It will aid your reflections."

He walked out and carefully locked the cell door.

⪻⊱∞⪼⪼

Duval, sitting bolt upright in his cold bath, beat himself with a walking stick. His self-mortification was brief, but some of his anger and frustration were lifted. Deliberately not shaving after his bath, he threw on some old clothes and slouched on the wooden seat by his desk. He glared at his typewriter for a while before rolling in the first white page.

⪻⊱∞⪼⪼

July 1333

Christine, crouching on her bench, stared at the pattern on the embroidery she was doing as part of her penance. It felt strange being enclosed again after the months of sunshine, greenery and people, but the smells and sounds of Guldenford, the bustle of a visit to the town, even the domestic clamour in Ashe Cottage, had been overwhelming.

She summoned her senses to commune again with nature, to commune again with her God by worshipping the sounds of His Creation. Before dawn she listened intently to the churring of a nightjar; the song thrush then began its beguilingly repetitive chorus. She anticipated eagerly the two entirely different songs of the wood warbler, and, although she could not see them, she knew that the wood pigeons and stock doves would squabble with the jackdaws. Her hearing was beginning to reach the intense levels of her previous enclosure, and she could almost sense the beating of tiny wings as butterflies perched on the ledge of her external grille. That summer the large tortoiseshell butterfly, with its tiger-like markings, and the peacock butterfly, with two blue-black eyes on its wings, would affirm the glory of the Creation and her place within it. As the light faded, the woodcocks' duck-like call announced Vespers, and, at Compline, the tawny owls promised food to their hungry youngsters. When a moth fluttered on to her ledge, she knew that the long-eared brown bats, one of the most delicate of God's creatures, would emerge from their roost in the church's eaves to feed. To complete the cycle, the nightjar sang once more to announce that it would share its nocturnal nesting duties with its mate. All awaiting the miracle of another sunrise.

Nature would aid her contemplation, her insight into God; perhaps soon the *calor*, the heat of divine approval, would descend on her, and finally she would reach the *canor*, the ability to hear the sound of heaven, the *musica spiritualis*.

That was the future. As she listened to the Mass in the church of St. James, she took stock of her past life: the events that had led to her calling as an anchoress and the two years enclosed in the cell; the horrific news that her sister had been grossly abused at the hands of the same tormentor, her search for guidance and what she believed was the blessed sign from God; her escape in time to comfort poor Margaret and the birth of her nephew; her sister's death; the harrowing trial and Sir Richard's punishment; the blessed personal interces-sion of the Pope himself and, finally, her re-enclosure. Her short life had been very full, and now it was time for reflec-tion, peace...

"Christine, are you ready for communion?"

The familiar voice startled her, but she responded quickly. "Aye, Father Peter," she said resolutely. "I shall commune here forever. Enough venturin' have I done for life. By the grace of God, I shall die within these sacred walls."

⟨⟩∞⟨⟩

Duval stopped writing and rubbed both his hands over the stubble of his beard. Although Christine had inhabited his inner life for years, he could no longer see the face he had long imagined. Now he saw only Marda. Before, he had hoped to instruct Marda by example—Christine's example—and by slow, methodical preparation. But Templeton, the

Church, were stealing his time away, risking the corruption of his vision. He needed to write more directly for Marda, because his inspiration was not diminishing, it was changing.

The keys of his typewriter waited sullenly, mocking his determination to define his mission. A sudden rush of energy surged through him, and he started to jab at the keys.

⋘⋙

Yet there was a paradox: only by participating in the divine do we become human. Christine—Marda—could not know it, but there was a God-shaped hole in her consciousness. All cultures in all time have created an archetype, an image of God, a model of how hapless humans should behave. All the philosophers in all of time have groped to shape the symbols, the replicas of the divine world. They searched for unity of purpose, whereas in the modern world we tend to see autonomy and independence as supreme values.

Man is teleological by nature: he must search for God to prove himself human, or more than human, with that greater sense of self. After an intense emotion of tragedy or pleasure, it is a common experience to feel that we have missed something greater that remains just beyond our grasp.

Those who think they have grasped it simply make their own God. They assume that He loves what we love and detests what we detest, but this endorses our prejudices instead of forcing us to transcend them. Personalising God can produce a fatalism, a facile belief that any and all disasters are the will of God. "It is the will of Allah," say Muslims. We accept things that are normally unacceptable.

There is a mighty difference in making God like ourselves and then blaming Him for everything, and each one of us having the right to seek for ourselves the Godhead. For so long, the Catholic Church has discouraged the individual route to God because it threatened the very basis of its authority. Mysticism was rife in the immediate aftermath of Jesus, but

217

then Christianity became fossilised. For a brief period in the Middle Ages, the Church allowed mysticism—what it called the individual path—to flourish. Some of the mystics, the solitary seekers after truth, were canonised; some were burnt as heretics. Soon the Church in Europe crushed all individualism with the power of the Holy Office of the Inquisition. Yet in England, where the inquisitors of the Holy Office rarely ventured, mysticism was entrenched in the soul of the Mother Church. Only a few records survive of these enlightened ones: the unknown author of *The Cloud of Unknowing*, together with Richard Rolle, Walter Hinton and the saintly Julian of Norwich. The greatest of these visionaries discovered the insights to which the mystics of Islam and Judaism also alluded.

Although each great religion has produced magnificent visions which are culturally conditioned, each shares a similar concept of the true searcher being able to ascend to a vision of God; something that human adventurers who have honed their spiritual talent have always wanted to do. The mystical experience of God has characteristics that are common to all faiths in all times. These spiritual voyagers have sought a journey through the imagination, not through a process of scientific or logical reasoning.

Yet all established religions have feared these individual journeys, and so most mystics became outcasts...

❦

Duval felt the silence of his study, the contrast with the frenzy inside his head. He thought of his pupil entombed below, the vessel of all his hopes. He believed in Marda, but could she really understand his mission? For her sake he hoped fervently that she could, because it would save her life. He had done his work, at a more rapid pace it was true, but in the end it was her role, her destiny, to understand. Yes, she *could* understand. He was simplifying two thousand years of the search for God into just a few pages...

Mysticism is still unpopular in Christianity; today the word is allied with charlatans, gurus and hippies. These self-indulgent cranks seek three things on their selfish path: to feel in control; to feel good about themselves; and to feel that there is a future. But for these misguided people, individualism comes first and last. They have abandoned searching—the ego is enough for them. And their chemical drugs.

Yet the themes of inner contemplation seen in yoga or Buddhism and the fashion for psychoanalysis all display a form of mysticism. It is no accident that both Freud and Jung turned instinctively to myths to explain and explore the inner world of the psyche. So today there is a need for an alternative to a purely scientific explanation of our existence. It may be the only way of preventing the destruction of this world—unless we hold fast to the notion that God will not allow His Creation to become a nuclear wasteland. Perhaps God Himself will bring His Armageddon in the last decades of this second millennium, as a prelude to His Second Coming. Time is short, Marda. I feel events pressing on us. These must be the End Times. I can almost smell the destruction of the world.

Yet the discipline of solitary contemplation can help the skilled and sensitive soul to return to the One, the primordial beginning of mankind, and the ability to create a constant state of God's presence by tapping into the energy field which surrounds this Earth, God's energy for God's Earth. But such a journey to the centre of light and energy, and to the centre of the mind, can entail great personal risks because one soul may not be able to endure what it finds there. Madness is always nudging at our elbow.

I, myself, fight off madness every day, and I walk in the world. A world I often hate, despite God's creatures, perhaps because of God's creatures...

So defeat, despair and loneliness affect us all, but especially the solitary seekers. The mystical journey can be undertaken only with the guiding hand of a tutor, a sympathetic and patient expert, who can monitor the experience and guide the apprentice past and beyond the terrors, to give him or her strength when it is needed. Marda, let me be your true guide. But there are also false guides. Pseudo-science says the patient in psychoanalysis needs the guidance of a therapist, except that this is a selfish search for the ego inside, not God outside.

The joy and peace of enlightenment through solitary contemplation can only be attained for a few minutes at a time, and after a titanic struggle between the spirit and the world, God and the Devil as it were. Then, finally, the overflowing taste of God's sweetness comes as the reward. The soul has to battle its way out of the darkness that is its natural habitat.

There are many ways, all arduous, of achieving this glimpse of spiritual Nirvana, Valhalla, Paradise, Heaven...call it what you will. One example I have tried is a form of Christian yoga, where breathing exercises systematically help to wean the mind away from the passions of pride, fear, greed, lust and anger which tie it to the ego. The self has to be forgotten in the search for the light. Charismatic sects claim literally to see this light which transforms, but the instant "cure" of the evangelicals is no substitute for the long, sure process of learning the love of God.

God is not necessarily an external objective fact, but an essentially subjective and personal enlightenment. The path to God is not, therefore, necessarily taken via a building, an organisation or even reason, but through the creative God-given imagination. The Catholic Church cannot admit that God, in some profound sense, may be a product of the imagination, but it is self-evident that imagination must be the basis of faith. I can see that you have real imagination, Marda.

Imagination is the motor behind all major advances—in science and art as well as religion. The imaginative idea of God, the absent reality, has inspired men and women since the Creation, because it transcends all sectarian divides. The only way we can conceive of a God who remains imperceptible to the senses and impervious to logical proof is by means of symbols and visions, which it is the duty of the imagination to interpret.

That symbol, Marda, is often a woman...

❧∞❧

Duval realised he was writing his testament exclusively for Marda. His long-suppressed subconscious motivations were being explained by him, to him. He was being as explicit as he could in order to direct her soul and save her life. The priest wondered whether he should end his own life if Marda could not, or would not, understand his desperate attempts to help her. It would be easy: fly agaric and hemlock in a vial.

A movement in the darkened study distracted the writer: Bobby rubbed against his legs and looked with devoted eyes at his master. Duval, feeling ashamed of himself, instantly dismissed thoughts of suicide; for the moment he was needed. He would not cave in to the pressures of spiritual minnows such as Templeton. Patting Bobby affectionately, he returned to his manifesto for his modern anchoress.

❧∞❧

The youthful mystical poet Dante Alighieri was inspired when he saw Beatrice Portinari in Florence. His love for Beatrice became the symbol of spiritual love in *The Divine Comedy*, where he constructs an imaginary journey through hell, purgatory and heaven to reach a vision of God.

Since each man or woman can have a unique experience of God, it follows that no one religion can express the whole of the supernatural mystery. Any moral chauvinism about one's own faith at the expense of other people's is therefore unacceptable, since no single faith can contain the whole truth about God. To a hidebound Catholic this would be heresy. But a true man or woman of God should be equally at home in a temple, chapel, synagogue or mosque, since all provide a valid meaning of God. The pure vision of God is not imagined by conflicting faiths but by a coalition of them.

God is alive, not dead, as is suggested by some current thinkers. Auschwitz killed our God, say some Jews. The socialist utopia has replaced Him; besides, He never existed, say the Marxists. Since we are on the point of creating our own Armageddon with nuclear weapons, man, not God, will destroy the world, say the liberals. Even if God exists, then it is necessary to reject Him since the idea of God negates our freedom, or so the existentialists argue. And some say that religion is an immaturity which science will overcome.

But can we feel positive about a godless humanism so soon after the Holocaust, or confident of scientific rationalism in the shadow of Hiroshima? Frankly, I could never trust man's rationality after the Americans dropped their damnable atomic bombs. So the search for God is a necessity for all mankind; a deep-rooted anxiety is part and parcel of the human condition. This anxiety is not neurotic; it is ineradicable and no therapy can dispel it. We constantly fear the terror of extinction, both individually and collectively, as we watch our bodies slowly but surely decay. As long as there is death, there must be God.

The whole idea of human life has been directed towards the future. We experience our lives as incomplete or unfinished. We always want more: to find that "something" out there that is beyond us. If Marxism dies, as it must, God as utopia will return to more than just the few pilgrim souls. Marxism is merely a temporary secular religion. As for science, in its core is God. Even Einstein appreciated mystical religion. Science may one day find the Great Mechanic of the universe, but the scientific method is not required. Subjective experience, fired by our imaginations, is the true way. This requires long periods of training and considerable time, helped by an expert. We can create God within ourselves. God cannot come ready-made and pre-packaged. He cannot be conjured up by the instant ecstasy of the revivalist preacher.

Human beings cannot endure the emptiness and desolation of no God. The truth is...

⋙⋯⋘

The phone rang. It was the American professor wanting to meet for a chat over a beer. Duval put him off with a curtness bordering on rudeness.

The priest looked back over his hours of writing. He knew he was losing his way with Christine's story. He wanted so desperately to work on the final chapters of the successful search for ecstatic visions, but he had drifted off into a prospectus for Marda. Re-reading it, he knew he was rambling. He wasn't sure what he wanted to say: to describe the purpose of an anchoress in straightforward language was almost impossible. He would work on the draft again in the hope that Marda would understand it and act on it.

Beneath him Marda was also trying to distil her hopes for the future.

Dear Jenny,

Middle of December (I think) 1967

Michael has told me he might have to go to South America. That means that I can leave my cell. Or I can stay with him forever, he says. Not in here, though. That is the most important thing, getting out of this coal-hole. I cannot survive much longer in this tomb. He says he doesn't want to marry me, which I thought at first might be his ambition. Which is to the good because he is far too old for me, but in different circumstances I might even have been a little flattered. It would be really odd for a Catholic priest to ask me to marry him, I know.

He has been much kinder to me and we get on very well—under the circumstances. I can exercise in the corridor and he has promised me a room upstairs. I still won't be able to go out but at least I shall be in a proper room. Perhaps I can even go into the kitchen, or—who knows—watch a little TV, if I can persuade him to hire one. I miss *Coronation Street* and the *Forsyte Saga*. If you are allowed to visit me—I may be allowed some visitors—you will have to bring me up to date.

I am quite happy to learn more about religion because I do feel closer to God, both emotionally and intellectually. I know I never was an intellectual or anything before, especially as I wasn't that brilliant at school. But I am learning, growing inside my head.

Sometimes I think my head will expand to bursting point with the new ideas. I had never thought of becoming a nun but I am sure there are some good aspects to it. I suppose you could say I have already converted to Roman Catholicism. It's good to have a religious belief in life. Something to explain death.

If Michael leaves—I don't know if he will—then I shall have to change my life anyway. If we both leave this house then he will go to South America, but I intend—at the very least—to become a regular churchgoer. I know that I have sinned many times in my life.

And I would like to go to university. I know that I am a bit too old, but some colleges take mature students, I think.

I feel much more positive about life and religion. I know that Michael doesn't mean to hurt me. He has been so kind after the first difficult period when I had to learn to settle in. He gives me cigarettes and recently even newspapers.

But I do miss you and my family so much. I miss someone to hold. I miss the sun so much. I have forgotten what the colour green is. I want to see fields, and trees, even a blade of grass. I miss my freedom, even if only to choose what I do with my life. Michael says that Jesus Christ is the key which unlocks the doors of the prison cell of our own making. Perhaps that is right. I do know that enslavement against your will is the worst condition of life. I want to choose freedom, if only for the chance to be a better person. There is so much I want to do.

As always, your best, best friend.

Love
Marda

PS. Have a lovely Christmas. Please remember that we will be celebrating the birthday of Christ. Perhaps you will go to church and say a prayer for me. I certainly shall be praying for you.

Dear Christine,

I suppose this is a little crazy, but I feel I need to talk to you, somehow, despite the gap of over 600 years. I have been reading your story, and trying so hard to understand you. Michael has explained the spiritual aspects of your search, but I want to know how you feel...about being cut off from your family above all. I suppose they can...

Marda crossed out the present tense, and shifted to the past tense.

...could at least talk to you, but didn't you feel like hugging them, especially your little brother or nephew? I would give anything to hug mine. Or talk to my parents at least. God must give strength...to us both, but does that mean that He gives more strength the more we are cut off from those we love? How did you cut off your feelings for Simon? It must have been such a difficult thing to give up all hope of having children, but life must have been very different in your time. I have been reading about the Middle Ages. Sometimes, I wish I could hold your hand and lead you through today's Guildford—the place you called Guldenford. There are cars, trains, jet planes, TV. I wonder whether all these modern inventions would have affected your faith, your desire to be secluded? Was it easier then than now? God doesn't change, but we do. How do we adapt?

I haven't finished your story yet, but I hope—no, I pray—that you found what you were searching for. I will write to you again when I know more about you.

With affection,
Marda

<figure>❧∞☙</figure>

Marda wrote a series of letters throughout the rest of the afternoon, using pages from her supply of exercise books. When she had finished, she climbed on to her bench and managed to winkle out the tiny folded squares that constituted her previous archive in the air vent. She destroyed the old ones by soaking them in the well of the paraffin heater and letting them burn bit by bit. Clearing away the ashes, she put them in her waste bin. Satisfied with her rewriting of history, she put the new letters in the vent.

Duval brought down some coffee and slices of chocolate cake around 5:30. That's what his watch said, but she didn't know whether it was morning or afternoon; the nature of the food indicated it was probably the latter.

He seemed much more relaxed, so she asked about his book: "I've read up to her returning to St. James's church. I know there's an Amen at the end, but you said you were still working on a conclusion. If you've finished it, can I see it? I know so much about Christine up to the age of twenty-two—is that right?—but what about her later years as an anchoress? Did she stay there, or did she leave again?"

Michael smiled at her transparency. "I haven't finished the conclusion, but I will show you soon."

He talked for a while on what he had read about Bolivia. At the end of his long monologue, Marda said simply, "Seems all jungles and revolutions."

As she finished her last piece of cake, she said, in a patently wheedling tone, "Michael, I have a favour to ask. I don't like to think about…the other rooms. But from what I have learned—from what you have taught me—I would like your other guests to have a proper burial." She paused, trying to read his facial expression, but she could not discern the impact of her question.

Marda continued, "I suppose it would be too…difficult…to arrange a church burial, but couldn't you do something in the garden? You said it's quite secluded. And then you could say a blessing, even though it's not holy ground. Excuse my presuming to tell you about Christian rites, but it would seem proper. Or have I spoken out of turn?"

"No, I had considered the same thing myself," said Duval in a very conciliatory fashion. "They were suicides, they starved themselves, so I felt I could not take them to consecrated ground. But they should be treated with some dignity. It would be wrong to leave them where they are, especially if I do go to Bolivia. *If.*

"I should have done it before. I do apologise to you for not giving them a Christian burial. I will do it in the next few days, but I will tell you beforehand. I shall close your door and close the grille—I don't want you to get upset again."

Smiling, he added, "Is that to your satisfaction?" He enquired as though he were promising to take a favourite young niece to the funfair.

Marda heard the faint chime of a doorbell for the first time. She realised that he must have left the main cellar door open for the sound to carry this far.

He pretended to look unconcerned. "Ah, I was not expecting a visitor. Too late for the post. Perhaps somebody to do with the local elections, or a Jehovah's Witness."

The bell rang again. He quickly excused himself and, without shutting the cell door, hurried up the stairs.

Marda waited for a few seconds, and then put her head around the door. She ran along the corridor and up the short wooden stairs to the main cellar trapdoor, begging God that it would be unlocked. She tried the handle gently at first, then more and more frantically while trying to avoid being too noisy. It was locked. She thought of trying to shout through it. To scream. To bang.

She didn't.

Marda returned to her cell, her eyes brimming with tears, the first for more than a month. She sat picking up bits of cake crumbs with her fingers and waited.

He returned within ten minutes, seriously agitated.

"Who was it?" Marda tried to ask as casually as she could.

"Bishop Templeton. Insufferable intrusion. Some excuse to drop off information about Bolivia. Said that he had to visit a friend in Shere anyway. He just wanted to snoop around my house. Blast him!"

Marda didn't know what to say; she let him rant. Eventually she said, "The bishop doesn't understand what you're trying to do. You always get men higher up in a bureaucracy who are afraid of new ideas."

Duval turned on her. "Don't give me this Job's false comforter routine. If I hadn't locked the door, you would have been out screaming for the bishop to lock *me* up, I know. Don't *lie* to me."

Marda looked at his blazing eyes and felt utterly forlorn. She didn't think he could have heard her fiddling with the lock.

"No, no, Michael. I was sitting here waiting for you. I was just trying to be kind because you seemed so upset. I want to help you."

"You're a liar. Just like the rest of them." As he stormed out of the cell, he spluttered, "Yes, I'll bury them, and you...if I can't trust you."

He locked the cell door, switched the light off and closed the grille.

Marda felt the fear again, that same cold fear of her early incarceration. She prayed that it was not entirely her fault, just a tantrum because of the bishop's unexpected visit. He had been severely rattled. She would not cry, she swore to herself, but she needed to do something, not just endure as a passive victim of his moods.

She sank on to her bench and lit up a cigarette. For a change, it was quite warm in the cell; she pulled up her robe and rubbed her legs a little, feeling the hairs she had not shaved for months. As she puffed a smoke ring in the dim light of the paraffin heater, she moved her hand up her legs to remind herself of human touch. Utter desolation closed in on her soul, as she longed to touch someone who loved her. And to be held. She was held now by the dark, cold walls of a tomb.

She pulled her bare legs to her chest and curled into a foetal position. Through the black despair she thought of her mother's comforting arms around her when she'd suffered nightmares as a child. She was not a promiscuous person, but she had always enjoyed physical contact. Marda remembered the warmth and kindness of her first real lover, Gerard. Where is he now? she wondered. Hours of gentle passion on balmy evenings in Bordeaux seemed to belong to the memory of another person, another life, another planet; that kind of intimacy was almost impossible to imagine, then, now or ever again. She worried that her sexuality had drained away for all time.

She recalled how intense and sensual Gerard had been, the immaculate manners over dinner and in bed, so strong and yet so tender. He loved to undress her slowly, delicately, patiently; "Rushing love-making is as ungraceful as galloping through a fine meal," he had told her in his lilting French, grinning boyishly, with his charm an essential ingredient of his being—rather than the often superficial tactic of the English. Effortlessly but with utter concentration, he would ensure her orgasm before he penetrated her—she remembered how she would involuntarily arch her back and raise herself into the air, and he would laugh, and kiss her, and continue to satisfy her, not ending until her series of orgasms, and her moans and shouting, had excited him sufficiently to reach his own climax. And then he would hold her closely in his arms, and say that he loved her, and she believed him then—and she believed him now, and would tell him so over and over again, in the most romantic language on earth, if only he were here...

She stroked her arms and then her legs, trying to stimulate her dying senses. Tentatively, she massaged her inner thigh. She had not touched herself like this since she was a teenager, and it felt good. All sexual thoughts had evaporated the moment she had been captured. Occasionally, and very weakly, they drifted back, but she tried to suppress them, for her only connection with humanity was her gaoler. She knew precious little about sadomasochism, yet she feared that new sexual stirrings might somehow be connected with him. She shuddered at such a depraved idea.

She willed the priest from her thoughts, and forced herself to concentrate on Gerard: his jet-black hair, his tanned limbs, the smile which reminded her of a schoolboy pirate, the little notes he sent her, the occasional bouquet of flowers, and always his sense of mischief and irreverence. And she spoke to the darkness: "Why did I stop seeing you? We never quarrelled, and there has never been anyone else, at least for me...if only I could reach out and phone you, to say I'm sorry I've been out of touch, and that I love you." She had never been able to say it to Gerard's face, but she could now.

Her struggle for sheer survival had dominated nearly all her thoughts, but her longing for human touch, physical contact, sexual passion, all overwhelmed her. Suddenly, and just for a moment, she needed sexual release more than anything in the world, and just as suddenly she decided on what she must do with her tormentor.

XII

The Last Supper

The opportunity arrived sooner than she had intended. It seemed like the middle of the night when Duval stormed in without knocking. The light blinded her for a few seconds and, as usual, she had no idea of night and day unless he told her. It was disorienting, as was being woken up so abruptly.

"Get out," he ordered. "Get out, now."

"I can go? Leave?" she asked groggily.

"You can leave your room and go to the corridor. The cellar door is double locked, so there's no point in trying to get out again. Stay out there while I search your room."

He seemed to go berserk as he threw her blankets on the floor and searched through her books. He removed her notebooks, then looked in every little cranny of the heater and wash-basin, and under her portable toilet.

Now fully awake and thoroughly alarmed, she asked, "What's wrong, Michael? What are you looking for? I haven't done anything. I haven't got anything."

His unshaven face was flushed with anger. "Shut up. Shut up! Don't make me any angrier than I am."

Petrified, she kept quiet, and retreated shivering to the end of the corridor near the large crucifix.

"Aha! Your little pigeonhole," he said with an exaggerated note of triumph. Taking out a penknife, he edged the letters out of the air vent. With the notebook in his hand and her letters in his pocket, he walked out into the corridor.

"Get back in there," he barked. "I suspected you were keeping a diary."

He locked the door and turned off the light. It remained dark for an hour, then twelve hours and then, so she guessed, for twenty-four hours. She had a water bottle and the scraps of food she had stored, so she did not feel hungry for the first day.

He's taking a long time reading my few notes and letters, she thought. Has he gone away?

Then, after what she estimated were two days, she wondered whether he had deserted her as he had deserted Denise—just leaving her to rot. It couldn't be, not after all her stratagems of appeasement.

The heater had run out of paraffin, and the room temperature moved slowly towards zero. Putting on the cardigan he had allowed her, she wrapped the blankets tightly around herself.

She tried to think, despite the cold. "Thank God, I destroyed my original letters," she told herself. "Those new ones should satisfy him."

She wondered whether she had been plausible, because lying didn't come naturally to her. She was pleased that she had taken precautions, but would he believe them? She had to be extra attentive to each nuance of his every mood in future.

She forced herself to relive good memories from the past: she was surprised how often Mrs. Violet Jenkins, from Wales but an inspiring teacher of English, surfaced in her catalogue of heroes. Schooldays hadn't seemed so good at the time, but in retrospect Mrs. Jenkins had been very kind, very encouraging. She would be surprised to learn that her star pupil was reading the English mystics, and occasionally Gerard Manley Hopkins for light relief. *The Cloud of Unknowing* would certainly impress her, if only she could be told about it. If only. Marda's thoughts involuntarily turned to school meals. They didn't seem worth eating then, but her hunger pangs transformed them into bacchanalian feasts.

She began to pray, and surprised herself by quoting word perfectly from some of the prayers she had been taught by the monster upstairs. She questioned her sanity for the umpteenth time that day, or was it night? The black hole of timelessness was sucking her into madness. Finally, she drifted off into a nightmare in which she was transformed into a slave in some far-off time. She was chained in a medieval kitchen, forced to scrub and clean pots in a dungeon. She was beaten, but at least she encountered different tormentors; one or two even exchanged kind words and gave her scraps of food…

A sound came as if from a long, long tunnel, and she jumped when she realised it was a knock. On her door. *A knock.* That was a good sign.

The light went on and she managed to say, "Come in."

He came in, trying, she thought, not to look in the slightest bit sheepish.

"Excuse my intrusion," he said politely. "I don't like reading other people's private things, but I had to know. Were you telling the truth in your letters?"

"Yes."

"Why did you write them?"

"I had to keep some—even imaginary—contact with the outside world."

He snorted slightly.

"Are you hungry?" He said this almost tenderly.

"Yes, I'm starving. And it's really cold in here."

He turned his back to walk out and then spun around on his heels. He looked at her without speaking for a few seconds, seeming to take in the whole room, her whole subterranean existence. Finally, he said, "It's Christmas Eve, so I wondered whether you would like a special meal. I have cooked a turkey. I don't eat meat, but it seems right to offer you some on this eve of the feast."

Marda thought: that's as close as he is going to get to offering me an apology. "Oh, thank you," she said appreciatively. "I'd like to help you. I'm not a bad cook, you know. I could help with the trimmings."

Smiling, he said, "I can prepare it all myself, but thank you. I will lay out the table...upstairs...in the warm. I don't expect to have any callers this late. I rarely have callers at all, especially on Christmas Eve. I will ask you to put on your handcuffs again, just as a precaution."

Marda was ecstatic at the thought of leaving the cellar, even for a short time. "If you would like to get yourself ready, I will come back for you in about an hour...with some heating oil."

Her excitement was genuine. She beamed when she said, "I don't really have much to change into. And is there any chance of having my—first—bath?"

"Your habit will do fine...and I will think about the bath," he added grudgingly. He locked the door and left the light on.

When he came back she had combed her hair and washed as best she could. She looked at her bitten nails, but there was nothing she could do about them. She had never bitten them before. He had refused to give her make-up, but the soap was fragrant. Duval himself seemed to be a bit more spruce than normal, she thought.

Duval was making an effort, especially since he had noticed that he was starting to let himself go a bit—not shaving regularly, wearing the same stained shirt for two days.

After leading her along the corridor with both her hands cuffed together, he helped her up the stairs and through the thick wooden door of the cellar. The flat trapdoor was heavy, so he climbed first and held it open.

The kitchen exploded into her consciousness. Everyday objects such as a bottle of milk, a loaf of Hovis and pots and pans were miracles, wonderful reminders of real life, heaven after the gloom. She marvelled at the tiles, the big enamel teapot and the red-checked cloth covering a tray. This was life, life, life. Light, colour, good smells, comforts, food, but—above all—light. She wanted to cry, laugh, sing, dance, shout, all at the same time, but controlling herself, aware he was watching her every movement, she merely indulged in the unbridled pleasure of staring at all the amazing artefacts of a living kitchen.

She noticed that he had carefully laid out two places on a large pine kitchen table. The bottle of dry French wine made her almost scream with joy.

To add to her pleasure, Duval let Bobby in from an inside door. The dog leapt up at Marda and she patted him furiously.

The priest seemed pleased with himself, but still very cautious. He said, "I hope you will excuse our eating in the kitchen. It is the most secure room on the ground floor. And, if you don't mind, I will have to handcuff one of your hands to the table."

She didn't know whether she should push her luck. "Michael, it's Christmas Eve and I take it the other doors are locked. Please let me enjoy just one meal and let me eat properly. Please let's have a civilised meal together."

He smiled with a slight frown as if to say I half-believe you.

"One move that I don't like and I will return you to the cellar. If you even *think* of trying to escape…"

"Michael, I *want* to have a meal with you. It's Christmas."

"If what your letters say is true, then I might believe you. What if you are trying to bluff me? And why did you write to Christine?"

She started fiddling with the end of the tablecloth, but she knew she had to maintain eye contact: "Michael, those letters were like my diary, my lifeline to the outside world. I needed to talk to my friends—including Christine. She has become like a friend. They were just meant for me, though. Would I lie to myself?"

After he had undone her handcuffs, he smiled again, in his lopsided way, and said, "Let's not argue tonight. Please sit down, Marda. May I pour you some wine?"

Except for the corn spirit, she had not tasted alcohol for nearly three months. "You bet," she said eagerly.

He pulled out for her a real chair and she actually sat at a proper table; and, in warmth and light, this was paradise for Marda. She watched him pour the wine into a crystal glass and place it in front of her. She stopped herself for all of a minute, and then drank the whole glass in one gulp.

"'Scuse my manners, but I needed that." The unaccustomed taste made her hiccup slightly.

Sitting down opposite her, he poured himself a glass which he sipped deliberately. Savouring his wine, with no mock pretension he said, "This is from Bordeaux; it's a good year."

"It's lovely, Michael, thank you. I've spent some time there, as you know, working with wines, so I appreciate your thoughtfulness in getting a Bordeaux. Thank you so much."

"Since you are so appreciative, I have decided to allow you a bath, a quick one. I don't want to spend hours on guard outside the door. I shall give you ten minutes. Do you agree?"

A look of unadulterated delight transfixed Marda's face. "Oh, yes. Oh, yes!" she said delightedly. "Now?"

"Yes. The window is firmly shuttered from the outside so there is no point in trying to get out. The water is hot, and there is a spare towel on the chair."

He unlocked the kitchen door and, holding her firmly by the arm, led her along a gloomy passageway next to the kitchen. He pushed her gently ahead into a darkened room, switching on the light before she could become anxious.

"Help yourself," he said expansively. "Remember, though, I will be outside the door, in case you try any funny business. There's no lock inside, but I promise I shall not disturb you, so long as you are not more than ten minutes. Fair enough?"

She nodded, her eyes wide with anticipation.

Duval closed the door, leaving her alone in the most spartan bathroom she had ever seen. A forty-watt bulb illuminated the white enamel sink, bath and toilet, all scrupulously clean. Alongside the bath stood a simple wooden chair, painted brown. An old heavy-duty wooden towel rail had been treated to white paint, but long ago. There was nothing else, except a threadbare towel, soap and toilet paper. She had hoped there would be a mirror.

The next ten minutes passed in a blur of ecstasy: the luxury of a real toilet, while she ran the bath, then the bliss of deep, hot water enveloping her body, the glide of the soap caressing her limbs, the chance to end the itching in her scalp, her body tingling, revived by heat and cleanliness and the smell of Lux soap, this was almost the world she came from...

"You have one more minute, Marda." His voice ruptured her reverie, and hate suffused her being; her first luxury in months, and again he was rationing her.

"Right, Michael, coming out in a moment." She jumped on to the cold white-tiled floor, wiping herself furiously. Only half-dry, she threw on her habit in fear that he would enter the bathroom while she was naked. She wanted to be ready before he came in to enforce his time limit. And she needed to make some effort to clean the bath: she used the towel to wipe off the tidemark from water dirtied by her first proper wash in months.

He gave her two minutes, and knocked; she opened the door, her hair still dripping.

"Happy, now?" he enquired.

"Yes, ready to eat," she said, as he loomed behind her, gesturing the way back to the kitchen.

They sat at the table, both nervous of initiating conversation, until Duval said, "Were you really so afraid of me in the beginning? I know that the herbal drug must have been very unpleasant, but I did my best to keep you happy. Am I such an ogre?"

She held out her glass and he refilled it.

"How can I answer that, Michael? As you said, let's not argue. Let's just enjoy the meal. I can't wait." Again, she patted the dog which was now asleep under the table.

Duval had heated some canned tomato soup, for which he apologised. To Marda it tasted superb.

As he prepared the food, he was careful not to turn his back on her. Whether he was being ultra-cautious or just nervous in her presence, she wasn't sure.

When he served up the main course Marda tried hard not to gobble it down. He ate only the vegetables, while she revelled in the turkey.

"This is excellent, Michael," she said with her mouth full and not caring. "I didn't know you were such a good cook."

"So that's what you think of my cuisine over the last three months?"

They both laughed. He relaxed and, after the second glass of wine, so did Marda—a little.

"Hmm," she said, after beginning the third glass. She never was much of a drinker, but this wine tasted so delicious. "Hmmm, lovely wine. So I have been here nearly three months; that's a very long holiday from work."

"Yes. And I hope you will stay a little longer, Christine."

Marda went utterly cold and numbness overtook her brain.

"*Marda*, sorry. I suppose I have been working too hard on my book." He did not appear in the least embarrassed by the confusion.

Marda managed to recover and changed tack by asking about the Christmas decorations in Guildford, and whether it was snowing. Did he know what films were showing locally? The day before she was taken by Duval she had read a review of *Bonnie and Clyde*. When asked whether he had seen the film, he told her that he never went to the cinema. Who was in the pantomime in the theatre? And she asked him to summarise what had happened internationally. He mentioned some political event in Africa, and she joked that it was perhaps warmer there than in Bolivia. Marda sucked in the fresh information as though it were the very tangible essence of freedom, vicarious freedom.

He had bought a small fruit trifle, a dessert she had always enjoyed. Over the cheese and biscuits she asked him about the football league, but he knew nothing. So she asked him what Harold Wilson had been up to. That was a little easier for him.

"I'm a bit of a newspaper fan, like to keep up with the news, sort of a family tradition," she explained.

"Since you have constantly asked me for newspapers, as a special concession, I have been ordering various periodicals for you, but I have been examining them to see if they are a suitable complement to your instruction," he said. "*The Times* may have some merit, but the music papers you mentioned are soaked in sin."

"OK, I won't ask about music, but would you tell me what's been happening the world?"

Duval told her that Clement Attlee had died, and so had Che Guevara. He tried to respond to the concerns of a different generation when he realised that she was interested in the death of the charismatic guerrilla leader whose picture was pinned on the wall of nearly every college student's room. Joan Baez, he told her, had been arrested during an anti-Vietnam war protest, and Charles de Gaulle had vetoed British entry into the Common Market. He seemed so knowledgeable that Marda quizzed him on his views on the new Europe.

Eventually she asked, "If you don't normally read the newspapers and don't own a TV, where do you get your information?"

"Mainly from the radio. The BBC keeps me in touch with the world."

"Would you put the radio on?" she pleaded.

"Which station?" he replied without any demur, taking the dust cover off an old Dansette transistor radio.

"Can you find the new Radio 1? You know, the pop music station." He didn't, but he played with the dial.

"Oh, oh, it's the Bee Gees. *Please* leave that station on. I love them." The haunting strains of "Massachusetts" filled the kitchen.

The priest could not disguise a slight grimace. "Do you mind if I lower it?"

"No, but please leave it on."

He lowered the volume slightly, then rummaged around in a kitchen cabinet. "Would you like some port?"

Marda was a bit giggly now.

"Yes, pleeeease."

She swigged down the port. Her body, partly anaesthetised after so much pain and fear, craved more alcohol. "Excuse me being a little pig, but can I have some more please?" She held out the empty glass.

Marda was not emulating his archetype of the austere Christine, he thought, but his guest had endured a long preliminary penance. There had to be occasional rewards, even of meat and wine, before she could make her own decision to renounce such indulgences. And, after all, it was Christmas, a traditional time for feasting.

So Duval, with no apparent reluctance, poured her a second glass of port. He had not touched his first.

"Have you got me a Christmas present then?" she said jokingly.

He looked at her with raised eyebrows. "As a matter of fact I have," he said, barely concealing the sense of his own largesse.

She was about to say, "I hope it's not a bleeding Bible," but she wasn't that drunk.

"I have bought you a dress. I hope it's the right size."

Marda pretended to look cross. "You're not supposed to tell me because it spoils the surprise. Please let me see it."

As he pulled a gift-wrapped package out of a drawer in the pine kitchen dresser, she practically seized it from his hands and ripped it open. At any other time she would have opened it very carefully to save the paper to use again.

"Oh Michael, it's lovely," she cooed. "Blue is my favourite colour. But I thought you wanted me to wear a religious habit."

"I want you to have a choice. That's my point. I don't often wear my clerical garb here in the house. Tonight is an occasion where you could wear a dress so you can go downstairs and try it on if you like."

"May I use your bathroom to change? I don't want to spoil the lovely meal by going down…down there…not just yet."

"If you want to, but I shall wait by the door, if you don't mind," he said a little warily.

Under escort, she went to the bathroom to change, emerging with her new dress on and the habit over her arm.

Once back in the kitchen, she deposited the stale clothing on a chair. Marda turned to him and asked expectantly, "How do you like it?"

His face indicated obvious pleasure.

Encouraged, she gave a modest impression of a model's twirl, then stood next to him.

He reached out with his hand to brush her cheek, ever so gently and momentarily, and then turned red with embarrassment.

"Oh, you've gone all shy, Michael. I just wanted to show how pleased I am with your present. Come on, do you like it?"

He looked lost for words, but managed to say quietly, "You look ethereal."

"That's the first time you've paid me that kind of compliment. Why, thank you, kind sir." Disbelievingly, Marda heard her own words echoing in the room; suddenly a flash from *Gone With The Wind* intruded upon her mind: she was imitating Scarlett, and Rhett had not been fooled, had he? She knew she was no actress, but she was warm, clean, well-fed and rather tipsy. There might not be a better time. She understood that she was about to take the biggest risk of her short life. He was an apparently celibate priest who was also a deranged killer. Not an ideal choice. She would pretend, she would try to be the world's greatest actress, to find a chance to escape, or to immobilise him, perhaps even to kill him. She was utterly desperate to seize what might be her only opportunity.

She sat on his lap.

He froze.

"Don't, Michael," she said almost crossly. "I won't hurt you. Don't be silly."

Taking hold of his hands, she put them around her waist. Hesitantly he conceded, although he held her limply.

Marda heard herself say, "I know I don't look very sexy in these boots and socks, but it's a nice dress and—hey—it makes me feel like a woman again. And I don't have any make-up on. Treat me like a woman, Michael, not a student. Don't freeze me out."

She pecked him lightly on the cheek, almost recoiling as the stubble rippled along her lips, but he did relax a little. She willed herself to recall her lover in France, trying to picture every fine feature of his face, then, as she squirmed a little on Duval's lap, her dress rode up along her thighs.

"Don't you find me attractive?" she asked provocatively. "You always avoid touching me."

He closed his eyes.

"I know I've got a bit skinny and pale, but has being locked up made me so ugly? I haven't looked in a mirror since I came here. Look at me, don't you find me attractive?"

"Of course I do," he said, almost stuttering.

"Please open your eyes. Am I so frightening?"

The traditional wood stove in the kitchen was pumping out heat. Marda, returning to her own seat, took off her shoes and socks, then skipped around on the bare linoleum, humming to herself. The drink had fortified her, while he seemed relaxed, trusting almost, she thought, and this might be her last chance. She swallowed hard and, as she twirled around, she pulled off her dress while grabbing a tea towel to cover her breasts.

"Look at me. Don't you want me? Isn't this what you really wanted me to be?"

She flicked the towel into the air, leaving herself naked except for her pants.

"Do you want to see me naked? Is that what you want? Then I'll do it for you. Here."

She tugged off her pants, covering herself with her hands as she walked towards him.

Panic swept his face, he stood up and retreated until his back was pressed against the main kitchen door.

She followed him, standing on tiptoes to put her arms around his neck, and whispered, "You can hold me if you like. Do what you like with me…as long as you don't hurt me. Take me to your bedroom now if you want to. Anywhere, but not down there in the coal-hole."

As she pressed her naked body against him, he uttered a half-suppressed croak.

"Go on, kiss me if you want," she said aggressively.

Reluctantly, almost like an automaton, he leaned forward to kiss her on the lips lightly as she squeezed against him.

Out of the corner of her eye she could see the large knife he had used to carve the turkey, and she desperately tried to estimate whether she could reach it. Marda pressed hard against him to move him towards the sideboard where the knife lay, tantalisingly close. She edged him towards it, keeping his back to the knife. Pressed against him, she felt the surprising roughness of his tweed jacket against her naked breasts.

She was sure he was not aware of the knife. Marda steeled herself to kill, but her most pressing fear was whether she could be quick enough to reach the knife before he reacted. She prayed that he would keep his eyes shut.

"Stop. Stop. Don't kiss me any more, Christine," he barked in a pained, almost strangled voice. He seized her hand and, with surprising strength, dragged her towards the trapdoor. "You're the Whore of Babylon. The scarlet-coloured beast. Go to the pit where you belong."

"No, please, please don't put me back. Please," she begged. "I'll put my clothes on. No!" she shouted at the top of her voice. "Michael. Don't."

The last thing she heard on the radio as the trapdoor closed was the current hit song by the Spencer Davis Trio: "Somebody help me, yeah. Won't somebody tell me what I've done wrong?"

XIII

The Officer

That night Mark Stewart was waiting for Irvine Gould in the White Horse bar, and he was one or two drinks ahead of the amiable professor.

"Hi, Mark, sorry I'm late," the gangly American said in his watered-down southern drawl.

Mark gave him a half-hearted salute. "I take it that you'll have your customary pint of best English ale. Can't take the stuff any more myself after German lagers. Too flat, too warm…" He ordered a pint at the bar. "But if you're determined on researching the habits of the locals, then you might as well understand the reason for their flatulence."

Professor Gould realised that Mark was masking his fear for his sister with an external bluffness that was typical of the British officer class.

"Any news today about Marda?"

Mark shook his head slowly. "Bugger all, professor. I've spent a week ingratiating myself with a bunch of gypsies who've been camped near the common for about six months. The police suggested I try them out. Some of the locals have visited their Madame Rosa. I had my fortune told, but nobody had seen Marda. Anyway, I don't think she'd get involved with them."

"What did the crystal ball say? A tall dark stranger would change your life?"

"No, it's a lot of balls, but I thought I needed to jolly them along. I didn't find out anything. The police aren't too helpful, except for that old so-and-so in Shere, Constable Ben McGregor. He keeps sniffing around, hasn't come up with much, but at least he's trying. As for the rest...I don't know. Anyway, how's *your* research? I still don't understand you colonials being so keen on tracing family trees."

The professor gulped down his pint. He had noticed how the locals tended to do just that. When in Rome..."As I think I told you," he said, belching into his hand, "my interest in genealogy is only a sideline. Medieval church history is my bag, as the saying goes." The professor sometimes liked to think he was "cool"; he believed he could "relate" to the flower-power movement, for example. "My bag, man," he said self-mockingly, "my area of specialisation. They've got great church records in this area, especially in Guildford."

The captain, joining in the self-parody, felt it was his duty to play up to the professor's stereotypical image of the English gentleman. "Sounds a bit dull to me, old boy."

"Not at all. Fourteenth-century England was as bloody and as lively as Vietnam. Your guys were fighting all over France, pacifying the Welsh and kicking the crap out of the Scots, although the Scots gave as good as they got. And the English were fighting each other. It's no wonder that so many hooked up with the Church."

Gould had already explained his interest in St. James's church and its unique architectural heritage. "I've been working my butt off to finish a paper on the church and its anchoress."

"Bit far from the sea for mermaids, aren't we?"

248

"Everyone around here knows about the anchoress. You mean to say you don't?"

"Only joking. English sense of humour."

The academic ignored the jibe. "I can see your glass is empty. Let me get you another."

Over the next round of drinks, Gould explained his work on female hermits, and Christine Carpenter in particular; as well as the possibility of an interesting French connection to Christine. The professor meant to keep his description short and sharp, but he was an academic, and his learning and enthusiasm resulted in a long monologue.

"Sorry, Mark, I must be boring you."

"No, not at all, but I can't understand why an eighteen-year-old bird would want to lock herself away in a bloody wall. Sounds a bit insane, not to mention insanitary, to me."

"No, it's a fascinating case, and I have some really interesting new material that I unearthed in Bordeaux. So few English—or American—scholars work on French medieval records. They were so bureaucratic then…"

"They still are, Irvine. They still are. I'm glad the Frogs are out of NATO, I can tell you…"

"Yep, can't stand us Yanks running the show. The trouble with us is that we're fixers, not preventers. We could have soothed de Gaulle's feelings and prevented this cock-up. Same back home. I despair when a failed movie actor becomes governor of California. I know they're weird out there but *Reagan*. How could they?"

Mark Stewart enjoyed teasing the professor, despite the fact that Gould's lazy drawl made him suspect the man was falling asleep in mid-sentence.

"Politics and films are the same in the USA. Washington is one big B-movie, always looking for the happy ending." Mark was trying to coax the anglophile into xenophobia.

"No, I guess you're right. We could learn a lot from you Europeans, except how to stand up to the Russians. You guys are so weak the Russians could march to the Channel tomorrow."

Mark let it go because he had learned from their earlier conversations that Gould was a passionate advocate of nuclear disarmament, who wanted to ditch the bomb and force the West Europeans to build up bigger conventional armies...until the Russians were ready to talk peace.

The professor continued, "But culture, that's different. I wince when I see American tourists over here. Why do they all look fat and stupid? It's better over there, honestly, but we still spend more on chewing gum than books. We can't spell any more. All those fast-food signs, the letter 'U' for 'you,' and all that. America is becoming a monument to bad grammar and trivia. We measure our art in dollars, love in the number of orgasms, and churches have become supermarkets, or the other way around."

Gould took another big swig of his beer.

"And the South! Heck, I regard myself as a loyal southerner, but it's like Palestine before Christ; there are more prophets than rocks, and each one of them wants his own church. I just wish more architects would find God. If they do find a good design, in typical American fashion—if you've got a good thing, overdo it. I don't know, Mark, all these prophets, all these lousy churches and yet God, the great architect, has died. God has expired and fifty thousand do-gooding social workers have sprung up in His place."

"Don't be so hard on yourself, buddy," Mark said in an atrocious imitation of Gould. "Your films are great. That's what'll change the world. I think that the future will have a slight American accent, lots of Coca-Cola and bugger-all communists."

The professor laughed. "I hate the Coca-Colaisation of the world. That's where the Gaullists are right. We need individuality. That's why Sergeant Pepper is British. That's why I love you Brits, you have so many eccentrics. Here eccentricity is tolerated, even encouraged. Back home, so much of being an American is not to let your individuality become a social embarrassment, a nuisance in the commercially conformist drive for happy consumers."

"You're not a Marxist, are you, Irv?"

The professor ignored the dig. Despite his attempts to ape the current flamboyant vocabulary, he was a scholar and too deeply immersed in his period to pass convincingly for a member of the beat generation. He was not a political activist, despite his hostility to American involvement in Vietnam and his pro-disarmament views. His real world was the Middle Ages, and he could not help but return to it. "I've found some incredible material on the Anchoress of Shere—Christine Carpenter—in an abbey near Bordeaux. I should get a few more articles and a conference paper out of it at least."

The army officer did not understand the world of academic papers and conferences, which seemed a waste of time to him. But he appreciated the professor's passionate energy, so he put on his best intently listening face.

"The trouble is, the local historian—amateur historian— a Catholic priest who's written one or two minor things about Christine and the traditions of anchorites—male anchoresses, that is—is rather elusive. I wrote to him from the States, and we've met once. He lives just outside Shere. Now he's surely an English eccentric, a bit of a recluse, I guess. Harmless nut, but he knows his stuff. Bit cocky about his knowledge of the Shere anchoress; might be able to make him eat his words, though. I called him to say that I've almost finished my paper and he gave me the brush-off. Weird. You'd think a priest would be vaguely polite, especially if he's an historian who's in my field. I'll try again before I leave. Maybe I caught him on a bad day."

The Englishman looked pensive. "I don't remember meeting a priest when I went round with the reward leaflets," Mark said. "What's his name?"

"Duval. Father Duval. He lives at Hillside, an old rectory about a mile or so from here. Kind of difficult to find. Have you come across it in your wanderings?"

"No. I've checked out nearly every house or farm around Shere, using the electoral roll. But perhaps a priest might not be on it. I could have missed a few people. I'll find the house on the OS map I'm using," said Mark, with a renewed interest in the conversation.

"Well, I hope he's more polite to you than he was to me."

"Anyway, have you eaten, Irv? No? OK, let's see what grub is on offer."

❧⚜❧

The next day Mark went to Guildford to see Jenny. He enjoyed her company, and not just because she was such a good friend of his sister and somebody who could guide him around the town. Under different circumstances, she could have been special to him. Jenny was obviously extremely distressed by the mystery of her friend's disappearance, and she recognised Mark's angst hidden beneath the officer's bluster. Intuitively, they leaned on each other for mutual comfort. Mark opened up about his feelings in a way that he had never done before, and he learned much about himself and about his sister. He wanted so much to share his feelings with Marda, and was tempted to sublimate his emotional frustrations in a more practical way with Jenny.

One evening as he left her flat she held him, chastely, in an almost sisterly fashion, and said, "If you love Marda enough, and I think you do, and if you are determined enough, and I am sure you are, you will find her. I believe that with my whole heart."

Mark thanked her and kissed her gently on the cheek. Jenny's support meant a lot.

His search, however, was more important than his habitual philandering. Mark felt good about that—not much had come between him and his sex drive before. But his loneliness and fear about his sister were forgotten one evening when a quiet meal with Jenny was transformed into hours of gentle but intense sex. He had never needed to lose himself like this before. Previously, he had treated women in the same way he planned his military exercises: tactics, surprise, mobility, feints, and even aggression if necessary; women were prizes to be seized. Being with Jenny was so different that he almost cried after they made love. The loss of Marda, and Jenny's empathy, accelerated his maturity: he understood consciously for the first time that tenderness had nothing to do with any kind of victory. Jenny's comforting embrace and Professor Gould's company in the pub were the few bright spots on a black landscape for Mark Stewart.

Two days after the chat with Gould, Mark decided to visit Hillside. There was a small cottage a quarter of a mile away which had been empty when he had last called. He went back there, and then walked over to the priest's home.

Mark opened the rusty gate and climbed up the stone steps to the front door. The house had a run-down feel, weeds were running riot in the garden. It looked rather uninhabited, except there were curtains, which were drawn. The professor had told him someone lived there, however, so Mark knocked on the door; then he noticed a bell and tried that. He rang again and waited.

He could hear a shuffle inside. Sounds like an old man, he thought. Eventually, after hearing two locks click, the door opened a foot. A much younger, bigger man than the army officer had expected peered out of the gap.

"What do you want?" the man asked brusquely.

"Er, I'm sorry to disturb you. Are you Father Duval?"

"Yes, what do you want?"

"My name is Captain Mark Stewart. I am looking for a missing woman…"

Even before Mark produced a leaflet, he thought he noticed an odd shift in the priest's eyes. The officer had been involved in a number of interrogation courses in Berlin, and, despite his bluff cavalryman's manner, he didn't miss much. He recorded it all mentally.

"Have you ever seen this woman, please? She lived in Shere."

Duval's manner changed a little. He opened the door a few inches wider, and he was a touch more polite. Mark noted the nuances.

After Duval had looked at the leaflet for a few seconds, he said, "No, I'm sorry. I've not seen her."

"Thank you for your time. May I leave a leaflet with you? If you do hear or see anything, please contact any of the numbers listed…There is a reward."

Mark had said the same phrases a thousand times. Too late, he realised it was inappropriate to say this to a Catholic priest, so he covered his awkwardness by adding: "Not that you would be motivated by money, sir, but perhaps you would mention it to your parishioners."

"Yes, of course." Duval was a little taken aback; not many people knew of his religious vocation in Shere, but the priest managed a smile. "And Merry Christmas to you," he added. Mark thanked him and took his leave. The door closed quickly behind him.

As he walked slowly down the steps Mark decided that he would visit Duval again. He stopped by the gate, spending deliberately long seconds lighting a cigarette in hands cupped against the wind, his eyes taking in every detail of the house. As he walked back to the village he wondered whether his desperation was making him look for villains in the wrong places, seeing even priestly academics as suspects. But he had to act on any lead, any clue, anything at all. He thought Duval was lying. It was in his eyes. But a Catholic priest? Mark started to worry about his own mental state. Maybe he was going over the top because he had given himself just one more week in Shere. He had to return to his regiment soon: he couldn't test his commanding officer's patience too much.

⋘∗⋙

That night in the White Horse, after he had recounted the day's events, Mark asked the professor to tell him more about the reclusive priest. The officer realised that, in intelligence terms, he was breaking cover, but he had always relied upon his instincts, not manuals of fieldcraft. Gould was a good man, he knew. Mark had always liked the openness of Americans, at least those he had met in professional life. And he needed a mate to talk to—he was surprised how much he missed the camaraderie of the officers' mess.

"Tell me about this priest of yours," Mark said bluntly.

"Can't say much more than what I've already told you. He's had one or two undistinguished articles in the *Bulletin of the Institute of Historical Research,* and there's a small book published by the loopy medievalists in Exeter; he had an essay in there on Julian of Norwich. This stuff is really only for the specialists."

"But why do you think he's so unfriendly towards you? If there are so few specialists why isn't he interested in another one?"

"Could be rivalry. Local historians get very protective about their patches. And academic historians specialise in back-stabbing and being bitchy. They argue about university politics like crazy because usually the stakes are so low. And we all get paid zilch so we're mostly bitter and twisted old so-and-sos. But he's also a priest. They can be crabby, especially having to do without women."

That last sentence tripped a switch in Mark's clouded, unhappy mind.

255

"A man without a woman, living in a secluded place. It's a recipe for mischief. Look at the navy…"

The American laughed. "Hell, don't jump to dopey conclusions, Mark. He may be an oddball, but why should you connect him with your sister? I did notice that he's a pipe-smoker who breaks his matches in two and puts them back in the box. Supposed to be a sign of suppressed aggression. But that's not a hanging offence, Mark. You can't run around accusing priests of…whatever."

The professor didn't want to say murder, although that's what he meant.

"I am convinced she's still alive, and I intend to find her. I may be clutching at straws, but if this mysterious Duval character has anything to hide, I'll find it."

Gould looked at him warily. "Forget it, Mark. I told you, I've met him, and he's an innocuous medieval buff. A priest, remember."

"Yes, you're right. I'm just frustrated about going back with bugger all. C'mon. It's Christmas. Let's have another drink."

Mark went off to buy a round. He didn't want to annoy his new friend by pressing him on the priest, but a seed had been planted and now it was germinating. Impulsively, he asked the barman if he knew Father Duval.

"Well, lots of people come in 'ere, not sure if I know him, but you could try in the Prince of Wales up the road."

Mark bought the man a drink and tried again. The drink obviously helped.

"I'm not sure of his name," said the barman, "but there is a fellow who comes in sometimes with his dog. It's said he's a Catholic priest, but he don't wear his religious gear in here. Sits by there," he said, pointing, "and has a quiet pint. Don't bother people. Bit of a loner. Lives up at the old rectory, I believe. Lives on his own, so they say. But you could ask Jim over at the shop. He knows who does what and where roundabout 'ere. But it won't have nuthin' to do with your sister, though, if he's a priest an' all that."

The next morning Mark discovered from the shopkeeper that a few months back Father Duval's food order had increased. "Said he had an aunt visiting when I mentioned it. I thought it was strange because he's been ordering the same thing for years," said the shopkeeper, in the slightly conspiratorial tone in which village gossips specialise. "And he started ordering cigarettes, even though he smokes a pipe. Nothing odd there, lots of people smoke both. But when I mentioned it, he stopped coming in here, except for the very occasional thing. Must have upset him. Don't like doing that to my customers."

Mark left after thanking him again for putting up a leaflet in his window.

Next he called into the newsagent and contrived to find out what Duval read, using his easy charm to persuade the young female assistant to check the order book. Mark discovered that the priest was a new customer for newspaper delivery: *The Times* daily and, recently, the *New Musical Express* weekly. The officer made a quip about the priest being an ageing beatnik. The young lady was thanked and invited "sometime" for a drink in the White Horse. It was a typical English invitation—sometime meant never. Mark was too busy trying to reconcile the strange combination of reading matter in which Duval indulged.

The captain resolved to go again to Duval's house to confront him, on the pretext of asking whether the priest would take some more leaflets and leave them in his church; upon reflection, he thought better of it, because it was too obvious. He needed time to think, but he wondered whether Marda had time. He had discounted the idea of her going off on walkabout. There was no way that she would have done that to their parents. Amnesia, despite the detective yarns, was extremely rare. And nobody had been found.

The only chance she was still alive was that she was somehow being kept against her will…somewhere. He knew he was chasing after phantoms of his own imagination, but he had to do *something*.

That night Gould tried to solve his problem. "I'm sure that Duval is not your man," said the professor. "Sure, he's weird, but he's an intellectual. We're all weird."

"If you think you're weird, you should meet some of the senior officers in my regiment."

"Seriously, Mark, maybe I can find a way of asking, obliquely, about him when I see the Bishop of Guildford later on this week—Friday in fact. Bishop Templeton should know something of the priest, it's his diocese. The bishop isn't a historian, but he's fairly switched on to church architecture in the area, so I wrote to him from the States to arrange a meeting."

Mark looked downcast. "I'm supposed to leave on Friday."

"Why don't you catch your flight and I can contact you if I find out anything? If I may be frank, Mark, I do think you're branding the wrong steer. Look, I know you're desperate to find out anything you can about your sister, but don't get fixated on a Catholic priest. They've got a reputation in Ireland for getting lonely parishioners knocked up, but I've never heard of them kidnapping or doing worse things to young women."

"I'm sure you're right, Irv, but he's not Irish. Why do we always associate priests with being Irish?"

"Because it's the jewel in the papal crown," the American said in his classroom style. "The Emerald Isle is the most Catholic place on earth, and the Pope wants to keep it that way. No rubbers. No abortions. No porno mags or skin-flicks. It's like feudalism, really; the state backs the Church in its primitive authoritarianism. The real Irish problem is that the brightest ones become priests and are generally celibate, whereas the Jewish problem is the cleverest ones become rabbis—and you know what large families they have. I can say that, by the way, because I'm a Catholic with Jewish relatives."

"I didn't know that professors could indulge in such racial stereotyping."

"Sure, we do it all the time. The stereotyping of ideas is politics. Refining stereotypes is philosophy."

"Sounds too philosophical for me, Irv. My view is that the clever Irish all emigrated to America; the thickos stayed behind to listen to the Pope and give us Brits a hard time over Northern Ireland."

"Yes, you're still in the army. You might be needed if things blow up in Ulster, unless we Americans can get you out of there first." The professor smiled mischievously. "But we still need you in Germany. So go back. I have another month left of my sabbatical. You can leave some leaflets with me, and I'll check with Constable McGregor at the Shere police station before I go. If I hear anything, I'll phone you, I promise. Don't wreck your military career on top of everything else."

"Yes, you're right. I'm making an ass of myself. We'll have a farewell drink on Thursday, then I'll bugger off to Woking before I get my flight from Heathrow. Thanks, Irv, I'm glad I got to know you. It's been a bloody tough few months."

XIV

The Fallen Woman

The previous months had been even tougher for Marda, but they had been a time of joy and peace compared with her suffering after Christmas Eve. She had ventured all when she had thrown herself at her captor; she had ended up degrading herself and risking her life. It was a conscious strategy, not a drunken whim, although the alcohol had made it a little easier. Realising that he was utterly repressed, she had hoped somehow to distract him, to find a way out, perhaps from the bathroom. She had prayed that someone might call. She knew more than enough about his character to realise that playing the sexual card to a psychotic misogynist was extremely dangerous, but she had wanted to create a smokescreen to confuse him while she sought a means of escape. She had not really planned to kill him; that had come to her *in extremis*, when her self-abasement into public nudity had forced her to accept the final option, to kill or be killed. Marda had fallen back on the last resort of a young female: sexual allure. And it had failed. He was more monster than man, she realised finally. She had gambled all and lost.

In one way she was relieved, because he hadn't raped her nor, almost as bad, made love to her with her apparent consent. She didn't know whether she could have gone through with it. If he was undressed and also off-guard, she had been fully prepared to bolt out of the house without any clothes on. That wouldn't have mattered as long as she was out of the prison. The windows would have been closed, perhaps secured, and the doors certainly locked; yet it was an opportunity for freedom which she had lost.

For the first few hours she sat in her cell trying to keep warm with her blankets bound tightly around her. Her new dress and habit had been left in the kitchen. Luckily he had left her with some heating oil, and she managed to fill up the paraffin stove in the dark. She was careful not to spill any of the precious fluid. She had some warmth, maybe enough for six to eight hours, depending on how low she kept the flame, and she had half a bottle of water. She was full from her meal, but she had no extra food, so she tried to stop herself vomiting up the meal after the trauma of the evening; she needed that food inside her. Marda retched, but did not vomit. She tried to control her breathing; she swallowed some water, which helped. She knew he would starve her again, although she tried not to think of what else he would do. The least was that he would probably sulk for a few days, but she would survive somehow. Eventually, she would find a way of escaping, even if it meant killing him.

Had he realised, somehow, somewhere in his subconscious, that she was edging him towards the knife? She was terrified of this because sometimes she thought he could read her mind.

For two days she sat in the dark. She rationed her cigarettes to one every four hours, or what she guessed was four hours. She did the same with her water and heat. The light was off so she lived inside her mind. What else could she do? Either submit totally to the life he wanted her to lead, some crazed notion of being a hermit, or defy him completely. She had endured so much, but she felt her mind was still robust, although she knew she was not strong enough to overcome him physically—even if she could catch him unawares. If she had reached the knife, could she have plunged it into his back? After two days in the cold and dark she knew the answer was "yes." She thought of the morality of being a murderer, too, but she would have killed in self-defence, under massive provocation. He did it to innocent people because he was deranged. She asked herself yet again if she was descending into the depths of insanity, and she wondered what had made him so crazy. Or was he always like that? Was he born mad, had he suffered some tragedy? Or had religion turned his brain?

She hummed the anthem of her times, "We shall overcome," to herself; "Yes, I will survive, at any cost," she kept saying to herself. She would keep up her mental and physical strength, and she would find a loophole in his defence. Then she would kill him if she had to. But what if he just left her to rot? No matter what, she would try once more to be friendly and interesting to him, but first he had to come down to the cellar.

She always knew when he was in the house because she would hear the bath water running every few hours.

On the third day, she was frantic with cold and hunger. She tried banging on the door, but she knew that the sound did not carry up through the stone floor, nor through the thick wooden cellar door. She would have to wait for him, or death.

On the fourth day, eventually, he came with bread and water. In a weak voice she managed some questions and apologies, but he said nothing. Four or five hours later he came back with coffee and oil for the heater, but he refused to respond to her at all. The coffee was grittier than usual, and the taste was a little more tart; she had learned that he was a creature of habit, so she wondered why he had changed his brand.

She was sleeping badly but she felt very tired, and thought that she might get a good night's—or was it day's—sleep. Just as she nodded off, there was a slight tap on the door. It woke her up, and she said, "Come in."

The tapping continued for a while, and she shouted more loudly for Duval to enter. The door opened slowly, and she saw a thin arm, carrying a candle, move timidly around the edge of the door.

A frail figure of a woman, dressed in a rough white woollen dress, entered the room very slowly, as though she were sleepwalking. Marda was too astounded to speak. The woman, or rather the girl, probably in her mid-twenties, once pretty but now haggard, with a face lined as if by years of pain, did not speak; she just stared at Marda.

Marda shifted along her bed and gestured to the girl to sit down, but the stranger just stood. Eventually, she knelt as if in prayer and finally broke the silence. Her voice was thin, distant, weak: "You are Marda of Shere."

Marda struggled to speak. "Yes…but who are you?"

"I am also from Shere, and my given name is Christine."

Marda tried to think quickly. Was this zombie a survivor from Duval's earlier guest list? Was she completely insane?

"Why are you here? How long have you been in this prison? Is there a way out? How have you survived, and where…?"

The visitor did not appear to grasp the urgency or intent of the flood of questions. "This has been my sole abode for many years, and I do not choose to leave. God has selected this place for me, and you are also a chosen one."

Marda wanted to tell her to get lost, but instead she heard unbidden words spring from her own mouth: "God may be consciously experienced, but He remains incomprehensible, and my path is to search for His light, even though I may not attain the divine ecstasy."

The visitor slowly rose from her kneeling position and leaned over as if to kiss Marda, but a few inches from her face the girl whispered in Marda's ear, "Beware the lion of pride and the bear of sloth."

Marda heard herself say in reply, "I have sinned with my pride and laziness in the search for the light, but I will repent."

"Remember, my sister in Christ," said the visitor, "you may suffer a state of utter dereliction by God, but you must understand that abandonment comes before attainment of that cloud of knowing." And she turned towards the open door.

A part of Marda wanted to say, "If you got in here, how the hell do you get out?" But her speech would not match her thoughts. Instead her mouth said, "Will I see you again soon?"

The figure did not answer, but walked soundlessly out of the cell. Marda's brain told her body to run through the open door, to follow her, to find a way out, to discover if there were some hidden exit, but her body refused to obey the commands of her brain, and the door slammed shut.

Despite the astounding experience, Marda inexplicably fell asleep; when she awoke in complete darkness, she did not know which dimension she was in, whether she was alive or dead, asleep or dreaming. She recalled the visit vividly. Had it been a more than usually realistic dream? Or had it actually happened? Was she now certifiably insane, or the victim of another of Duval's sinister chemistry experiments? She could hardly ask his advice on the matter.

A few hours later her tormentor arrived. Even if she had wanted to broach the sensitive question of the unscheduled visitor to her maximum-security establishment, it was clear that Duval was still refusing to speak. He did, however, leave more substantial food, and a big bottle of water. He also left the light on for a few hours. This carried on for days.

Finally he came with food and a voice. "I hope you have learned a good lesson," he said cruelly.

Marda was too afraid to risk saying the wrong thing, and it was not the time to raise questions about her perception of reality, so she waited. She was becoming an expert at waiting.

"You're not ugly, but you will not be able to use sexual blandishments on me."

"May I speak, Michael?" she asked meekly.

"Of course."

"I apologise if I upset you. It was the drink and the sense of freedom. Please forgive me. I had meant to please you, not upset you. Please can we continue the lessons?"

In a harsh voice he said, "I shall bring you food and heat and leave the light on. Use this opportunity to read your Bible and pray for forgiveness from our Lord."

"I will. I will. May I have my clothes back? At least my habit."

"It is ironic—is it not?—that you should ask for a habit, not a worldly dress. Perhaps it is more than just the cold. I hope so. I shall come back with some more heating oil. It is very cold in here, I must admit."

"Thank you," she said with real sincerity.

Ten minutes later he came back with two large containers of oil. "This should keep you warm for a week," he said in his best distant manner. "When the room is really warm, I'll come back with more food and new books."

"Thank you very much."

He also emptied her portable toilet.

About two hours later he returned. After days of darkness and loneliness she felt as though she were on a crowded aircraft. Her spirits lifted after he had brought in a tray of food, until she saw him produce the handcuffs from his pocket. She tried to sound sweet and lively, but not too pushy: "Are you taking me upstairs again? Please, I would love to get out of here for a while. And will you give me back something to wear, please?"

"Perhaps later. Please handcuff yourself to the end of your bench," he said with cold politeness.

"Why, Michael? I can't go anywhere."

She did not want to argue because she wanted the food. She took the cuffs and clicked the lever shut across the loop and the other metal circle around her left wrist, while trying to hold the blankets covering her naked body.

Duval leaned forward and pulled the blanket off her.

"Please *don't,* Michael," she said, trembling with fear.

He stared at her naked form. "You were throwing yourself at me last week," he spluttered with outrage. "Now you pretend to be modest."

She huddled into a ball, trying to cover her nakedness.

"So the coy young thing now."

"Please. I offered myself to you before. When I was... drunk. But I *offered,* please don't take me against my will."

"I promise I will not touch you, except to take hold of your leg here."

As he said this, he produced another set of cuffs from his jacket pocket.

"Please don't, Michael." Fear made her raise her voice, which she was trying to keep calm to avoid angering him further.

Chained as she was, she tried to pull her legs up, but he forced them down and cuffed her right ankle to the loop at the bottom of her bench. Now she was spread-eagled, facing outwards on her bench, with just her right hand to cover her naked body.

"What do you want to do?" she cried almost hysterically.

"Nothing. I want to look at you."

He stared at her for a few minutes while she tried to stop herself crying. She wanted to shout that he was a lunatic, a filthy, perverted bastard, but she was hardly in a position to risk anything that would trigger him into an uncontrollable frenzy.

"I have some information about a member of your family."

She was astounded. "Really? My family, but how? What?"

"I will tell you if you do something for me."

"Do what?" she said, unable to mask the suspicion in her voice.

"I have some holy water, mixed with body oil, which I want you to rub over yourself. And I want to watch you do it."

She looked hard into his eyes, to try to read him, but it was no good. He did not, however, try to escape her gaze as he usually did. Marda said, "I will put oil on myself, if you give me some news of my family. What could you know about them?"

"I have met someone who is apparently your brother."

Marda squealed in delight. "My brother?"

"Captain Stewart, I believe. Strong-looking chap, in his mid- to late twenties."

"Yes, yes. That's him!"

"He gave me this."

Her tormentor showed the leaflet to the frightened girl.

"Oh, Mark. Mark. What did he say to you? What did you say to him?"

"I will tell you if you'll oblige by letting me watch you rub this ointment on to yourself. It is harmless. It is based on the gimmicks they sell in Lourdes, more water than oil. I have added a few perfumed plants from the Hurtwood. Smell it."

Opening the bottle, he put it under her nose. He poured a little into his hand, and rubbed it vigorously over his face.

"Observe, it's not caustic soda. I am not a sadist. But I need to see you do this. I want to show you that I do not find you unattractive. And you are safer, let us say, restrained by steel rather than by my religious vows or your sexual guiles. Do this for me, and I will tell you as much as I can about your brother and his Sherlock Holmes play-acting."

Reluctantly Marda took the bottle, while Duval sat and watched her.

With her free hand, she poured a little on to her arms and legs, then rubbed the mixture into her skin, while he lit up his pipe, broke the dead match in two and put it back inside the matchbox.

Marda used his annoying habit as an excuse to stop. "Please don't stop," he insisted. "I want you to rub it all over yourself...to rub it into your breasts and thighs." He sounded like a doctor telling a patient how to take a prescription.

"Please don't make me do this," she said, as tears teased the corners of her eyes. "So far you have tried to teach me uplifting things, about the Bible, about life, civilisation, history. This is degrading, just not like you."

His anger had abated somewhat, and the schoolmaster voice began to take over: "I tried to instruct you in spiritual matters, but I see you are addicted to the ways of the flesh. So be it. I no longer respect you in the way I did before."

Marda wondered whether he was a repressed homosexual, or perhaps he was just massively repressed, full stop: what normal male would have reacted so aggressively to her naked form? Now he had revealed himself as a voyeur. Whatever was wrong with him, she was terrified of the repercussions of the traumatic dinner.

To Duval, Marda was now far less like Christine. He tended to be ultra-deferential with the few women he met whom he deemed his intellectual or social superiors. With women he regarded as inferiors, his sadism grew more pronounced. He had abandoned the almost masochistic worship of Marda as Christine; now he was beginning to despise his young prisoner as a fallen woman, not worthy of his religious dedication.

Marda pleaded, "Please don't hurt me or starve me like the others, please don't."

"I won't if you do precisely what I say," he said. "Please continue rubbing in the oil."

She did so for a few more minutes, embarrassed, and in silence; a silence interrupted only by the sound of Duval sucking on his pipe. Her goosepimples grew hard with cold and fear.

"That is enough," he ordered.

He gave her back the blankets.

"I have one more request," he said, as he pulled out a pair of scissors from his jacket pocket. Marda was now really frightened.

"Don't be afraid. I would like to cut a small lock from your hair."

Marda's memory raced back to the scene of Christine's mother cutting a lock from the hair of the dead Margaret.

"Please don't scalp me, just take a small piece if you really have to."

"Thank you." He leaned over, cut a small section of her hair and put it into his top pocket.

"Now let me unlock the cuffs."

Marda was suddenly reminded of her dentist. He is so clinical, she thought. He's like a medical specialist explaining his methods to a nervous patient.

He undid her right foot first. She thought of striking him with her right hand as he bent over her ankle, but she could do little while her left hand was cuffed. Having unlocked the other handcuff, he moved back quickly to face her.

"Please tell me more about my brother," she pleaded.

"He was staying in your flat, I understand. He has spent the last two months looking for you."

"Where am I?"

"You are not much more than a mile from your flat, just outside Shere."

A look of amazement came over her face.

"He came here to give me this leaflet and to ask if I had seen you. The leaflets are all over Shere. Of course, I had to lie...unfortunately. He left quite satisfied. I understand that after two months of fruitless search he has left the village. He has gone back to his regiment in Germany, or so I'm told."

"How do you know all this?"

"Village tittle-tattle, and I've seen one or two articles in the local rag. Constable McGregor, our local protector, sometimes chats to me when I am out walking Bobby. Quite a little chatterbox is our PC McGregor. And too nosy for his own good, I'm afraid. Rather irritating Scotsman, but he is a useful source of information. And, of course, my brief meeting with that fine young man, your brother, was also interesting. But everybody has given up. They will not find you, Marda, so if I were you I would try to behave myself. I have a short time to decide whether to leave this place and go to South America or stay here, but I cannot just let you go. That would be too dangerous."

Marda felt bile rise in her throat, but anger made her speak: "You have lied to me all along!"

"Be reasonable," he said smirking. "I know you must think me a little mad, but I am not mad enough to let you just walk out of here."

"But you promised you wouldn't hurt me, or leave me to die of hunger."

"I don't *want* to hurt you, but decisions must be made soon, and you can help me make them by doing exactly what I ask of you. Today is a good start. It is the fifth of January, the beginning of a new year. Let's both make some firm resolutions to improve our lives. You seem a little more comfortable down here now." There was no sarcasm in his voice. "I shall take my leave and, if I may, I shall keep what remains of the 'holy'"—he deployed his habit of physically apostrophising words with his fingers—"oil. I would like to see you use it again, perhaps a little more adventurously next time."

He locked the door and left the light on, while Marda read and re-read the leaflet he had left.

Duval bathed in cold water and scourged himself with a scrubbing brush as penance for his act of voyeurism. Cleansed, he returned to his writing. His new appreciation of Marda, or rather his depreciation, gave him some fresh ideas. Initially, he had been concerned with Christine's visions during her re-enclosure. This original text would form a major part of his conclusion, but perhaps Christine might have been more rigorous in her self-mortification, especially when she returned to her cell. He decided to rework some passages of his history.

To help his work, he mixed a potion of fly agaric. Although highly lethal in its natural state, if the mushroom is dried and ground, and carefully measured, it can be added to honey and water to form a mind-expanding drug. Duval was cautious with himself in these experiments, but he had laced the drinks of all his guests and was satisfied that the mushroom was safe, and indeed rather interesting, in small doses. He swallowed the potion and sat in front of his typewriter.

❦

The first thing the visitor saw was the wall painting. St. Christopher was always placed opposite the main door of a church, because it was believed that whosoever looked upon a figure of the saint would be free from sudden death that day, and this would allow time for the sinner to repent. The visitor marvelled at the varied blues of the sea, and the crimson sails of the ships that St. Christopher was towing in his mighty hands. Even the painted eyes of the saint appeared to take on

272

a kaleidoscope of colour and form, while the air around the painting curved and buckled under the weight of the visible atoms.

And the sounds were magnified: the visitor could hear insects hopping in the nave, and the birds sang so loudly outside the church that every syllable echoed in his brain. Every sound was comprehensible, too: the birds were arguing about food, the locations of their nests, and even warning of the stranger who had just walked into the church.

The visitor floated through a bewitching landscape of sound and colour, warmth and peace and light; the whole world was in harmony with his movements. The tall stranger moved towards the cell and passed through the stones and sat on the bench. The woman was not startled by his presence.

She spoke calmly: "Where are you from, dressed in that strange garb?"

"I am from a different place and time," he replied gently.

"From Heaven?" Christine asked.

"Neither Heaven nor Hell."

"From purgatory, then?" she asked sweetly.

"From six hundred years in the future, from the twentieth century, a place which might appear like Hell to you, sweet Christine."

She did not ask how he knew her name, but knelt and kissed Father Duval's hand.

⋘⋙

The priest stopped typing, and read the words on the white page. He smiled and thought, "My vision, my pure vision of Christine, but not for others to read. Sweet indulgence, but not my history."

He looked at his crucifix, and acknowledged the need for penance. The penance for pride: first to kneel and kiss the ground, then to stare at dead men's—or in this case, dead women's—bones to remind the sinner of the transience of mortal life. He made his way into the cellar to visit

273

Denise. Yes, she had been proud, and defiant, too. She had fought back, and rammed a full container of paraffin against his hand. He lost a part of his finger—caught in a car door, he had told the doctor in casualty. That was his penance then. But he had made her suffer for the injury to his hand, and for hiding notes, portions of a diary. Yes, he had thought Denise was coming to believe in him, but she had been lying all along. She had hated him, even boasted of injuring him, she had not wanted to learn, and his patience had reached its final limit. He looked upon her skeleton and wondered where her soul had gone.

He returned to his study, ready to continue with his project, to complete the life of Christine Carpenter. The effects of the potion had almost worn off and he could become a serious writer again.

March 1334

Despite Father Peter's protestations, Christine embarked upon a rigorous course of self-denial for the sin of abandoning her calling. Besides four extra hours of prayer on her knees every day, she requested herbs to purge her stomach, bloated after months of decadent living, although in truth she was still too thin. And she asked to be leeched—Father Peter prevented this. The anchoress took to scourging herself, and wearing the hair shirt which was reluctantly granted to her, while all the time she prayed for proof positive of a stigmata. When, after months of prayer and self-denial, it did not come, she begged to be branded on the cheek with a hot iron in the shape of the Cross. Father Peter grew angry, and worried, because he feared that her devotion was turning into mania.

William tried to dissuade her from extreme devotions: "The body cannot suffer the demands of thy spirit. Please eat and rest and do not scourge thyself."

She said, almost petulantly, "My punishments are naught compared with those inflicted on our Saviour."

"Aye, child, but you must not presume to be too much like Christ."

"No, father, I wish to be near Christ in every way."

William could not overcome his daughter's stubborn resolve, but to his great concern and anger there was one who could reach out to her: Mistress Anna de Kempis. Her fantastic passions were now welcomed by the anchoress of Shere. Anna secretly brought her purgatives and the hedgehog belt which Father Peter had refused.

❦

Writing this section excited Duval. Some of these ideas, he thought, could be adapted for Marda: perhaps, for example, some cuts on her palms, a stigmata as it were. The vision of her blood dripping slowly into his mouth made him shudder. Branding on the cheek, suggested by the garrulous American, was a new concept to Duval, but one worth considering. He would thank the professor next time he saw him. Yes, he was sorry that he had been so curt with the man the last time they had spoken.

❦

Eight miles away, Professor Irvine Gould was reading *The Times* while waiting outside Bishop Templeton's office. The bishop's assistant made him a cup of tea.

"So sorry to keep you waiting, professor," he said. "The bishop's meeting is running late. He'll be with you in a few minutes, I'm sure."

A few minutes later the bishop did arrive. "Terribly sorry, Professor." Gould still marvelled at how often the Brits said "sorry." "Held up in a meeting...Ah, good, you have some tea. Do bring it with you..."

The American was led into a sumptuous book-lined study with a large and expensive free-standing globe set in a mahogany frame. It was more like the study of the president of an Ivy League university, too spoiled by oil-rich alumni, a little too decadent for the workplace of a man of the cloth. Gould thought that it might have suited the Vatican, but in Guildford it looked out of place.

"Please sit down, Professor." The bishop talked with practised bonhomie. "I was *so* pleased to receive your letter. Glad to meet someone who is a fellow student of church architecture. I must apologise—I haven't read your paper in its entirety, the one you *very kindly* sent me—on late Gothic experiments in—what was it again?"

"Cathedrals in southern England, Bishop."

"Ah, yes, but I will read it as soon as I can. Now, what can I do for you?"

The professor explained that he wanted access to certain medieval church records that dealt with monastic orders in Guildford.

"Yes, yes, no problem there." The professor noticed the cleric's nasal delivery. "If we have what you want you can look through them. I'll get in touch with our archivist as soon as we finish our chat." A *short* chat was implied. "By the way, what do you think of Gibberd's design?"

The bishop was clearly in no mood for extended small talk, but the professor responded to his comments on the new Catholic cathedral recently consecrated in Liverpool: "If I may say so, Bishop, it looks like a UFO."

"Precisely my view. Although I think we should be a little adventurous from time to time, I'm afraid I do prefer classical form. Mind you, I hope I am progressive in matters of theology."

The American felt he could proceed: "I worry about new church architecture. Churches aren't looking like churches any more. Some resemble gyms; others are like spaceships or hangars or theatres in the round. I worry this might be a portent of a kind of cultural collapse. It's important to recognise that in matters of religion, especially Catholicism, based as they are on faith and obedience, form really is substance. Life will imitate art, if you like. What a thing appears to be, it is. It doesn't look like a church, therefore it isn't a church, therefore we don't go there to worship God."

"Are you suggesting, Professor, that there is a direct correlation between ecclesiastical modernism and religious dysfunction?"

"I sure am, Bishop. Apses and chancels and vestries, the norm for fifteen hundred years, are succumbing to bizarre notions of modernity and so-called relevance. Even existing churches are being deformed—when they're not turned into markets or theatres or bingo halls. Cathedrals are ransacked by modern-day architectural barbarians. Pulpits and altars are smashed. It's as though Cromwell's thugs are doing a grand tour of Britain, and America is worse."

The bishop had started to fidget, and Gould made a gesture to leave, wondering whether his brief burst of intellectual debate was considered "bad form." As he got up from his seat, however, the American remembered something else he wanted to ask about: "I don't know if you're acquainted with a priest I know, Father Michael Duval?"

"Indeed I am."

"I've met him once to talk about my research on anchorites, and I wanted him to see my draft on a local anchoress before I leave. I did phone and, er, he was a little bit off, actually…" He smiled as he said the last phrase because it sounded so English to him.

"Yes, Duval is one of my people. Difficult fellow at times, very bright of course; too bright for his parishioners sometimes, but he's going away to South America very soon. Probably preoccupied with moving. Sorry about that."

Gould ticked off another "sorry" on his mental list while they shook hands.

"If there's *anything* you need, just get in touch with my secretary," said the bishop without much conviction. "He will introduce you to the archivist. I'll give him a ring now to clear the way. Enjoy the rest of your stay."

The professor knew a bum's rush when he was given one. "Thank you, Bishop. Thank you very much." And he added a final anglicism—"Cheerio."

⋖⋗

The bishop was angry. Sitting back, he lit one of his favourite Cuban cigars and ruminated on the second piece of disquieting information he had received about Duval that day. One of his curates lived in Albury, a few miles from Shere, and Bishop Templeton had asked him to keep an eye on Duval. The curate reported that Duval was furiously busy building some kind of swimming pool in the garden or perhaps burying an elephant.

Anyway, that's what Constable McGregor had told the curate.

"Burying rubbish, I expect," the curate told the apparently uncurious policeman. "He's going to move to South America. Getting rid of old stuff probably. Or maybe doing up the garden to help sell the house."

The bishop instructed the curate to keep things quiet, as Duval was getting a bit odd, you know, tapping the side of his forehead as he said it. A couple of years out in the wilds of South America would probably do him a lot of good.

The bishop would make sure that Duval was out of his hair just as soon as possible. One day it might be *Cardinal* Templeton. No lunatic obsessed with mystics was going to sully his reputation.

⋖⋗

Captain Mark Stewart was certainly risking *his* reputation. He didn't catch the plane to West Germany; his final trip to the police station had confirmed his hunch about Duval.

278

During a long farewell chat, PC McGregor rambled on about all sorts of village trivia, mentioning *en passant* that it was an odd time of year to be digging a rockery at the old rectory. Mark appeared to let it pass. He logged this in his mind but would have not acted upon it if—crucially—he had not noticed French cigarettes on sale in the village shop where, just before leaving the village, he popped in to buy his own brand.

"Don't often see Gitanes," he had observed casually to the shopkeeper.

"No, Mr. Duval ordered some and I got a few spare. Must be fashionable or something. Smells like old rope to me. Nobody else bothers with them now that your sister's not here…oh, I'm sorry."

Mark felt like kicking himself for not asking about the cigarette brand the first time. "Not good form for an intelligence officer," he said to himself as he left the shop.

❖

My colonel will go ape, Mark thought. I'll ring him on Monday to explain. Explain what? That I'm sitting in some wood with my army poncho on, soaking wet, freezing my bollocks off, doing an "OP" on some vicar who's digging a duck pond in his back garden. My head's throbbing from a boozy farewell to Irv. I didn't get on that plane and I didn't tell Irv I wasn't going. Been too bloody long in Berlin—that's my problem.

He remembered his old intelligence instructor: "Need-to-know principle. Vital to security, *sah! Don't you ever forget, Captain Stewart, sah!*" He could hardly forget, could he? He'd been hanging upside down over a bucket of shit at the time in a mock interrogation which seemed real enough, even now.

Mark moved out of Marda's flat and booked into a guesthouse five miles away. After parking his car on the far

279

side of Hoe Lane woods, he walked across country to the rear of Duval's house, the former rectory. Fortunately, there was a small hillock, sprinkled with Scots pines, giving a reasonable view of the place. He put his thermals on, but even these and his hip flask did little to keep out the January cold. He had learned his field craft in the Brecon Beacons, although it was never as brass-monkeys as this.

Mark sat there through the whole day, but the only movement, apart from the dog running around the garden, was Duval digging for about twenty-five minutes at dawn. Funny time and season to dig. If he was the villain, this wasn't good, Mark reckoned. The officer needed all his training to control the fear that his sister was already dead. Fear paralysed action, he knew all too well. He had to block out emotions and concentrate on logic, a plan of action. If it was a grave Duval was preparing, Mark would have to move soon, but he couldn't just burst into the house. He would have to wait until the bastard went out. He reasoned that Duval might walk the dog or go to the shop or do some bloody thing.

The dog kept dashing into the garden and sniffing around the area where Duval had been digging. At midday the animal spent some time retrieving a large bone, which he carried into the house.

Nothing at all happened for the rest of the afternoon, nothing except endless rain and sleet. The colder he became, the more Mark began to wonder whether he was wasting his time.

Ten hours of sitting in the rain finally brought its reward. Despite the very poor light, shortly after four o'clock, using his army binoculars, Mark saw movement in the front garden. He heard the dog bark before he realised that Duval was following the animal through the front gate. He waited a few minutes, hoping that it wasn't just a chance for the dog to crap. No, the animal had a garden for that, so it must be a proper walk. Mark had a safety margin of, at most, perhaps ten minutes. He had to go for it.

Pulling his balaclava over his head, he stood up, aching all over, and realised how out of condition he was. Not risking a torch, he scrambled through the bushes, wet branches whipping at him. He scaled the six-foot wall and found himself next to a big ditch at the rear of the house. "Looks a bit big for a grave," he muttered. He was slightly consoled by that.

He dashed around to the front garden and peered through the hedge to see if anybody was coming up the lane. Not much traffic likely in a narrow lane with no exit. He held his breath and listened hard: nothing except the distant revving of a car engine. Mark ran around the rear and tried the back door. Locked, of course. All the windows were closed. He went carefully to the front door and tried that, just in case.

"OK, a bit of breaking and entering is called for here," he said to himself.

He found a large stone near the front path and then returned to the back.

This must be the kitchen. Why didn't the bugger leave me some lights on?

Averting his face, he whacked the window with the stone. The wind swallowed some of the sound. He cleared away the glass with hands protected by thick sheepskin gloves, and then fiddled with the handle; it was locked. Putting his torch in his mouth, he hacked away at the wood around the window lock with his commando knife until it gave way. He got the window open and pitched himself into the open space.

The torch showed him the way down, via a wide pine shelf, on to the lino floor. There was little point in stealth, as he was hardly a cat burglar. It was more like a Special Air

Service assault, and he had failed the SAS selection course, he reminded himself. So let's do better this time.

He hadn't expected the internal doors to be locked, but they were. What's the priest hiding in here?

He thought of shouting to see if Marda was there, but, no, he would "recce" the house just in case somebody was around. Duval was reputed to live alone, but he would check. They would have to be deaf or dead not to have heard the window breaking, but there was a strong wind...

Pulling a short crowbar out of his belt, he jemmied the kitchen door open— it gave way fairly easily. In the hall a grandfather clock chimed.

This is like something out of Hitchcock, Mark thought. Must remember to be careful if there's a shower.

After examining all the rooms on the lower floor, he carefully tiptoed up the stairs to explore the bedrooms, then the bathroom downstairs; Duval didn't have a shower.

Right, there's no bastard in. I'll check all the rooms downstairs again, then take a quick look around any out-houses and have a shufti at that big hole in the garden.

The captain snooped around the ground floor again, finding nothing unusual. Reluctantly, he made his way back to the kitchen to get out through the broken window. As he stepped across the floor his footsteps produced a slightly hollow sound near the stove.

A bloody cellar!

He whipped away a large mat to discover the inset handle of a trapdoor. There were two inlaid bolts; he shifted them open. He pulled the handle but the door wouldn't budge. There was a lock in the trapdoor with a keyhole. Using all his weight he jemmied the heavy door open, tugged it upright and flicked the torch around to find a light. Nobody would see the light from outside. He found the switch and the light revealed a cellar with a large crucifix at one end and six doors.

Mark's heartbeat raced even faster.

Fuck, this could be it.

"Marda! Marda! Marda!" he shouted.

Her grille was closed, but she could hear the shouts.

"Mark!" she screamed, banging on the door with all her strength. Her heart pounded with massive expectation.

Mark's brain almost leapt through his skull.

"Marda. Oh, God. I'll get you out." He ran to the door where the pounding was coming from and opened the grille from the outside. He shone the torch in to see the ghostly, tear-streaked face of his sister; a face suddenly transformed by excitement, relief, and the passionate joy of having survived. Now she would be safe.

"Mark. Thank God! Thank God! Get me out of here. Please get me out," she gasped in a frenzy of exhilaration.

"You'll be all right. You'll be all right," he kept repeating. "Are you OK?" It was a stupid question.

He thrust his arms through the grille opening and grasped Marda's hands. She leaned to kiss him on the cheek.

"Get me out of here, Mark. Now. Now. Please. I can't rot in here for another minute. Please... Where is that fucking maniac priest?" she screamed at him.

"Out walking his dog, but stop worrying about him. You're safe now." The captain tried to jemmy the door open, but the lock was too strong. The raised edge of the door-frame prevented effective leverage.

"Do you know where the keys are kept?" he said, trying to sound as if he was in total control while his heart was banging like a bass drum.

"I don't know. Hell, I don't know, but get me out of here. Please."

"I'll go back into the kitchen and see if I can find the keys, or something bigger to force this door open."

"Don't leave me, Mark."

"Back in a second, Modge." Marda hadn't heard her childhood nickname for years.

Mark raced back along the short corridor and clambered up the stairs. Just as his head came up through the trapdoor, instant and massive pain jettisoned him into oblivion.

Duval had swung a vicious blow with a large lead candleholder. It crashed into the captain's right temple and Mark flopped down the stairs and collapsed inert into a mangled heap.

XV

The Final Chapter

"A daring rescue attempt. Failed, I'm afraid, but our latter-day Sherlock Holmes might have his Dr. Watson."

Marda screamed with the full force of her lungs at the sound of Duval's cold and controlled voice echoing down the corridor.

"Quite a family reunion, Marda," he said, slightly out of breath. "I've never had two members of the same family as guests in my little establishment. In fact it's also the first time I've had a male guest. How interesting."

"You've killed him, you bloody maniac!" Marda heard herself shouting.

"Language. Language, young lady," said Duval with deadly calm. "There's no need to shout. It will be bread and water for you again. Christine will not like this. She hath taken unto…"

"What have you done to him? I heard you drag him into the next cell. Is Mark all right?" Marda lowered her voice a little.

"I think he will wake up with a nasty headache." Duval displayed the hint of a mad grin as he peered into her cell.

"How could you? He was just trying to help. He was being a good brother...a good Christian, caring for his sister. I don't think you know what a Christian is, let alone a good one."

"Of course I do," the priest intoned sanctimoniously. "It was a Christian act of charity to accommodate your brother next to you, and he has Denise of course for company. I have buried the rest of my guests, as you requested. If your brother hadn't so rudely interrupted us, I would have interred poor Denise as well. Now she will have to wait."

Duval, standing almost triumphantly in the corridor, clasped his hands together, then stretched them back, making his joints click. She had never seen him do that before.

"Marda, we're fast approaching decision time," he said portentously. "Some of the recent events indicate that I should be away for a while—let things settle down for a year or two. The bishop has urged me to get a move on, and, for once, I might agree with him. A nice long holiday in South America is becoming more and more attractive."

"Will you let us both out of this place?" Marda whispered.

"How can I? I might have trusted you, but your brother would never have understood my vocation. If only he hadn't been so nosy."

Marda tried to cover all the angles: "Couldn't you leave us some food, and then contact someone to let us out when you're safely in South America?"

He stroked the stubble on his chin, as if he were musing on a major philosophical issue. "Perhaps."

"Couldn't you put me in with my brother so that I can see if he's alive?"

"Ah, three in a cell would be a little uncomfortable, don't you think?"

"No, no, I don't mind. I would give anything just to hold him. Would you see if he needs anything? Please, for me?"

"He can stay where he is. I don't think he wants any help. I shall leave you two to your own devices for a while."

The grille clicked back into place, plunging Marda back into darkness and utter misery.

⊰⧓⊱

Professor Gould had spent the rest of Friday and part of Saturday in the municipal archives. He had unearthed some useful information, but he couldn't concentrate because he kept thinking of Mark Stewart, his new army friend. He would ring him in Germany on Monday because Mark had said he would be back at the base then. The captain would be interested to hear that Duval was going to South America. The professor also considered visiting the elusive priest again, as he had only a few more weeks left of his sabbatical. He was convinced that his friend Mark had been barking up the wrong tree. Actually he was barking mad, to use another one of his favourite Anglicisms, to think that Duval was some kind of kidnapper. He would tell his friend about South America, but he was also concerned with his own research interests.

The professor desperately wanted Duval to offer an opinion on his paper about Christine Carpenter's life in France. It was certain that she was the same anchoress, because there was a detailed cross-reference to the papal indulgence granted in Avignon in 1332. The indulgence had been granted, no doubt about that, but Christine had not been re-enclosed. Something had made her change her mind, presumably something very convincing. Perhaps a more earthly love.

The local Inquisition records clearly stated that Christine was interrogated on two occasions in the small French fortress of Saint Sardos, after she had taken refuge in the English territory of Agenais. The English wars over Gascony

287

meant that, in this period, parts of France were sometimes English and at other times controlled by the French king.

The record of Christine's interrogation detailed, in exquisite Latin, that she was thirty-eight and a widow who had borne two children. There was a reference to her former husband being a seaman from the Cinque ports. He was not named, but the document stated that he was also a former native of Shere. The French Catholic authorities seemed to have been more concerned with the possibility of her being an English spy rather than with her probable status as an ex-communicant. She had been briefly accused by her Inquisitors of being a renegade Cathar, but the heresy line had not been pursued. She had been held, possibly tortured—there was an obscure reference to "pressure"—and finally released after six months. That was it. Probably she had then returned to an English stronghold such as Bordeaux, where she may have rejoined her children.

It was amazing, Gould thought, how details of the fourteenth century could be updated in the twentieth; that was the magic of historical research. He saw himself as an academic detective: provided you had the patience and the languages, medieval records were a goldmine of clues. So many had survived for hundreds of years, but it was tragic that equally as many had been destroyed by the savagery of the Second World War. How could original manuscripts from the Dark Ages be destroyed by the new dark age of Nazism and now, worse, suffer possible total destruction by nuclear warfare?

Professor Gould shook himself out of his intellectual reverie and decided he needed a drink. He walked down from his bedroom to enjoy a real citadel of English culture: the bar of the White Horse.

⋐⋛∞⋚⋑

Marda kept shouting to her brother through the closed grille. She didn't know if he could hear her, or whether he was alive or dead, but she shouted till she was hoarse. She sat in the dark swathed in her blankets, wondering whether she was better off or not. Her brother had momentarily given her massive hope, but now perhaps he was dead. The madman was probably going to kill them both, but his fear of tactility suggested to her that he would not murder them physically with his own hands. He would wait and let them starve. That was his way of doing things. But it would take time, and he was running out of that. If Mark knew where she was, presumably so did others, and they would come soon. The lunatic would try to escape from Shere. There were so many questions, and only Mark could answer them.

After two or three hours she heard a muffled thump on a door. She rushed to her door and banged hard. Another thump came back. He was alive!

She tried to prise the grille open a little. She had tried before, but now she somehow summoned extra strength. She attempted to force it open using her pen. It moved just a little and she shouted, "Can you hear me, Mark?"

"Just about." The hoarse shout clearly emanated from a pain-racked body.

"Are you badly hurt?" Marda asked.

"A blinding headache and a bad gash on my head, but I'll live."

"I can't really hear you."

"I am shouting. I'm OK. I'm sorry I messed up, but I promise I'll get you out."

"Does anyone else know you are here?"

"Not exactly, but there's an American—an A-MER-I-CAN," he enunciated each syllable, "called Professor Gould. I've told him about my suspicions. He's staying at the White Horse."

In her agitated state, Marda threw all caution to the wind. Duval might have been eavesdropping, but she had to find out as much as possible from her brother. "Will the American do anything?"

"I doubt it. I told him I was going back to Germany, but he does know I suspect that maniac. How long have you been here? Since you went missing?"

Marda tried to tell him as much as possible in short shouted sentences. They talked—despite the difficulties—till both their throats were aching with pain. She told him what she knew about the other girls and about the bishop's pressures on Duval.

"What will we do if he comes back?" she asked.

"I'll throttle the evil bastard as soon as I get my hands on him," Mark said, expressing an aggression which belied his predicament.

"That's why he'll leave us to rot for a few days. He sulks. And he's probably afraid of you...like all bullies. I can only pray..."

"Did you say 'pray'?"

"Yes."

"Have you gone all religious down here?"

Marda hesitated, not because her tormentor might be listening, but because she was examining her soul. "Maybe... No, I hate religion now. I can only *hope* that the American tells the police." She thought of Duval. "Yes, I'm sure the police will be here soon."

From what he had heard through the open trap door, Duval very much doubted that.

❖

Professor Gould did not contact the police. He had no reason to do so, but he did call again at Duval's house on the Monday following his meeting with the bishop. There was no reply, but he left a note.

Dear Father Duval

I'm sorry I keep missing you. I am returning to the USA in the next week or so and need urgently to speak to you regarding your research on the Anchoress of Shere. I have new information on her life outside Shere. Believe she left her cell a second time or more likely was not re-enclosed, despite the papal indulgence. Died in France. Please contact me at the White Horse (room 3) where I am staying. Look forward to hearing from you soon.

Yours sincerely,

Irvine M. Gould

Duval heard Gould ring his doorbell, and observed him from behind the curtain in the main bedroom. When he had read the note, angrily he crumpled it up.

He had been prepared to talk to the professor if the note had been civil. But bloody Yanks, know-all bastards who know nothing, another invention to get a free conference trip or promotion. Just like the bishop, more interested in position than in truth. He refused absolutely to believe that Christine had not died in her cell. He was, however, severely discomfited by the note, especially after his recent dramas. His quiet life was becoming too disrupted by outsiders—he would have to get rid of them, clear up all the mess and get out for a while.

He rang the bishop, who was unavailable, and left a message with his secretary to explain that he would follow the bishop's "advice" as soon as possible. He was now eager to undertake the challenge of a new ministry in South America, he said.

He had to sell his car, perhaps arrange to rent out his house, perhaps not. He didn't need the money, and tenants might dig around in the garden. Yes, he must finish his bit of landscaping, and he didn't care that the garden centre thought it was a bad idea to create a rockery and pond in January. It would have to be landscaped before he left, and he would have to do it all himself, just in case. Then there was the dog. He didn't want to give Bobby away; maybe somebody would offer him a good home, but he would prefer to take the animal with him. He was mentally preparing for his departure; he must make a start on his Spanish. And he had had very little time to do the final edit on his book. On top of all that, Constable McGregor had become more inquisitive than was healthy. The usual innocuous chat, Duval thought, had turned into slightly pointed questions about his garden, and the policeman had asked whether a Captain Stewart had called on him. It was getting too hectic, and pressure made Duval more aggressive.

With all this rush he put his problems in the cellar at the back of his mind. After three days, however, he decided he had better attend to them. It was quiet when he climbed down the stairs with some food and water. He walked past the new inmate and knocked on Marda's door. He didn't hear anything as he put on her light and looked through the grille.

She was lying on the bed asleep or dazed. He was wary.

"Christine, wake up. I have some food for you. I'm sorry I haven't been down for a while, but I've been busy."

She stirred when the light went on.

"Are you sick?"

"Yes. Very. Thanks to you," she said in a croaking voice.

"Still a little fire left in the belly I see. I shall open the grille fully and pass through the food and water. That should make you feel better."

She was now more alert. "Thank you. I need food badly. And some heat."

"We shall see."

He started to walk away.

"What about my brother?"

"I am sure his fat can sustain him for a while," Duval said matter-of-factly.

"No, no, please don't go. He's suffering badly from concussion and he's lost quite a bit of blood. Please let him have some—all—of my food. But we both need some water, please."

Duval carried on walking away.

"No, no, you can't kill him, not after all he's gone through. I'll do anything. Please. I promise I'll come to South America. Anything, but please let my brother live. Let me join him."

The lights went off and the cellar door was shut.

Marda agonised over her brother's condition, but her mind swirled into other nightmares besides Mark's possible death. In a feverish state, she saw herself married to Duval in the Shere church. Lapsing back into reality, she was violently sick. The image of Denise and Mark lying on top of each other, clutching each other in death, kept impinging on her semi-consciousness. She tried to keep a grip on her sanity. She so wanted to see her brother, but irrationally she was afraid that he would be shocked by the psychological and physical changes in her. Mark had seen her face, but her body had withered. She felt sub-human, worse than an animal, after so many months in the black hole. When she hoped for freedom, when she dreamed that she and her brother could float out into the greenness outside, she shuddered with panic. She was shocked to find that she had developed a fear of leaving the womb, of entering the world outside, which she had almost forgotten. She prayed to God for His help to save Mark and grant them both the sweet mercy of freedom. She remembered that even St. Peter—or was it St. Paul?—had denied Christ three times. Perhaps her memory was fading, along with her strength, or perhaps her religious instruction had been too superficial. Later, in freedom, she might want to learn more. Perhaps.

Sometimes she could not separate dreams from reality. On occasion her nightmares seemed so real that she wondered whether Duval had drugged her again. She recalled the strange, acrid taste in her mouth. She half-remembered the smell of burning flesh, then the pain and the scar of the cross Duval branded on her cheek. Fever took hold, loosening her grip on reality.

At other times she felt entirely lucid. Food and water and heat helped. She was almost herself when Duval came back with a sheaf of papers that he handed through the grille.

"You said you would do anything," he said in a voice that had altered in some distinct but indefinable way. "I would like you to read the final chapter of my book. Your comments, even now, would be appreciated. The rest is finished, and all collated in a tidy pile on my desk. Your end and Christine's will run in tandem. As you must realise, it is fitting that thou and the anchoress will be sanctified together in the Holy Spirit. The bishop hath spoken unto me..."

Duval rambled on in a strange monotone, his cold eyes flashing, while Marda tried to understand his disjointed words as he lapsed into medieval English.

Finally, she could take no more: "Would you, please, give my brother something to eat and drink? I beg you."

"I will ponder upon that when thou hast read my final chapter."

"OK, I'll do it, but come back soon," she said urgently.

She read the final section but couldn't really take it in, no matter how much she concentrated. She was weak, ill, cold, frightened and desperately concerned about her brother: not the ideal circumstances for literary criticism. She must, however, make some sense of it because he was bound to quiz her.

She was dismayed by the passages on Christine's sudden switch to extreme self-mortification, which said much about Duval's increasingly volatile state of mind. The priest's personality was disintegrating, not Christine's; Marda had grown to like and empathise with the anchoress of Shere.

Duval's sick fascination with cuts, purges and whips boded ill for Marda unless she and Mark escaped soon. The rest of the writing seemed to be about Christine's ecstatic last years in her cell, the return of her visions and her final death, still in the wall, at the age of thirty-three, the same age as Christ when He was crucified. Then followed a few final gushing paragraphs about her possible canonisation. Same twisted sort of stuff as before, but she would steel herself to be complimentary. She was the tamest and lamest of critics.

For the next two days Duval brought food and water intermittently for Marda, and once some heating oil and a packet of cigarettes. He didn't ask about the final chapter, and refused to discuss it even when she raised the subject.

She tried a series of variations on "it's a masterpiece, but please feed my brother." Yet no matter what she said, he seemed like stone. Mark occasionally shouted incoherently, but for the most part he was silent.

After hours of stillness and darkness, she heard the adjacent cell door opening and a dragging sound.

"Please open the grille. Let me see my brother," she begged.

The priest said nothing. For half an hour she heard strange noises, and then screams. He was torturing Mark.

"Stop it, please, I'll do anything," she shouted for the hundredth time.

She continued to hear the low moaning which echoed in the corridor. Perhaps it was another victim. Maybe it was the American, Gould, who had also been grabbed by Duval. She shouted to her brother, but he did not—or could not—respond.

A sound of sawing filled the corridor. She tried to shout again, but she had no voice left.

It was one of Duval's final acts in the cellar. He knew he had but a short time left. No one had come looking for the army officer, so he must have been working alone, but it was time to get out. First, though, he wanted to see if his historical description of Sir Richard's demise was accurate. How long could a man survive the tearing out of his intestines? Yes, he wanted to know that. For a while a strong man could perhaps hold on, and he wondered how difficult it was to quarter a grown man. Soon he would know that, too. It would be unpleasant but necessary work.

Marda was reaching the outer limits of her endurance, yet she needed to know what dreadful thing was happening. Then, if the monster kept her much longer, she would try somehow to kill herself. She explored the possibilities quickly in her mind, but then dismissed them. "No, no, no, I have come this far, I won't give up," she said to herself in a whisper.

Duval suddenly slid open the grille and announced coldly, "I regret to inform you that your brother is about to die."

Marda launched herself at the door as her tormentor slammed shut the grille. She could not cry any more. She lay on her rough bench, lurching in and out of consciousness, her exhausted nervous system mercifully relieving her tortured mind, but only momentarily.

An hour or so after she had last seen Duval, she heard the cellar door again.

She knew it was her turn to die.

He unlocked her door without knocking.

Wide-eyed and unkempt, Duval said, "Marda, sometimes moving events can create the required state for visionary experiences. You have read all of my book so you should understand what Christine experienced. And how she became what she became."

The priest wiped his brow, dripping with sweat.

"Christine saw an evil man die, Sir Richard, yet she prayed to see the re-enactment of the death of the very best of men: our Lord Jesus Christ. You tell me Mark has been a good Christian brother. So be it. Mary witnessed the death of her son; you are privileged to see the death of thy goodly brother."

Marda, barely conscious, tried to concentrate on Duval's slurred speech.

"This may be your last chance to understand completely what, for so long, I have been attempting to create in this cellar. Please come with me. Let the Lord be praised."

Marda staggered off her bench, still cloaked in her blankets. She was very weak now, and suffering from hypothermia. Her legs could hardly carry her. Yet, even given her desperate state, he insisted on attaching one of her hands to a handcuff and locking her to a pipe running along the wall. A screen made of old sheets covered the end of the corridor.

"Be prepared," he warned.

She could never have prepared herself for what she was about to see.

XVI

The Flood

Duval tore down the screen to reveal the young man's arms tied to the spars of the great wooden crucifix, his legs supported by a short plank. The officer's anguished, tear-stained face was slumped on his chest, while the blood on the wounded forehead had congealed into an ugly brown lump. His chest displayed a series of small injuries as though bits of flesh had been scooped out with a razor-sharp spoon. Blood oozed from the wounds on to his shirt, which had been wrapped around his waist like a loin-cloth.

Marda did not faint. To the contrary, steel entered her soul. Adrenaline surged through her body and the exhaustion and pain vanished. She could see by the heaving of her brother's chest that he was still alive.

Marda screamed at Duval, "Let him down! Let him down, you fucking bastard."

"No, I cannot do that. You must see him die, Christine." In his frenzy Duval's voice had moved up an octave.

"First I must hammer in the nails, but it will be swift. Not like the crucifixion of our Lord. I shall break his legs and then it will be over quickly."

Marda, screaming at him to stop, tried to wrench herself out of her handcuffs. She had lost much weight, but she could not slide her wrist out of the restraints. Her eyes bulged as the priest produced a claw hammer and long nails from a Gladstone bag.

Her eyes fell upon a large white candle, one of the three arrayed like an altar decoration near the base of the cross. She could just reach the nearest one, while Duval was busying himself standing on a stool to reach up and force the nails into her brother's outstretched palms. Mark pulled up his head from his chest and stared in abject horror at Duval for a brief second before lapsing back into a stupor.

Marda had reached out to the candle with her free hand, and pulled it upright towards her. Without hesitation she poured the hot wax on to her manacled wrist. With massive control, she suppressed the scream of pain that rose within her. She tugged hard and the lubricated wrist slipped out of the metal restraint.

A primeval imperative took command of her as she leapt, like a crazed she-wolf, at the surprised priest, knocking him off the stool with the force of her attack. She tore at his eyes and his hair as he attempted to back off, utterly confused. Then she kneed him very forcefully in the groin, and he went down groaning. With her fists she lashed out again at the big man, and then, with her bare heel, gave him a stupendous kick in the crotch for good measure. She heard the wrenching of tissue.

The priest cried for her mercy, but she could not see anything but fire nor hear anything but a loud drumming. Again and again she pummelled him while he curled into a ball and cried in pain. She stepped over him, grabbed the hammer and rained his body with blows; from her unknown reserve of hate and anger, she found the strength to beat him almost senseless.

She turned quickly to her brother and, standing on the stool, used the V-shaped claw at the other end of the hammer head to lever the ropes off his wrists and over his hands. Taking his weight on herself, she half-fell and half-staggered to the floor. She hugged him for a few seconds before dragging him into her cell and manoeuvring his groaning body on to the bench. She poured water into his mouth, slowly at first, then more to help rehydrate him. That done, she rushed into the corridor to check on Duval.

He was gone. The cellar door, she knew, would be locked. Much stronger than she realised, he must have crawled up the stairs. Perhaps she should have ignored her instincts and gone for help, but she could not leave Mark hanging on the cross. She had no time now to consider her future; all that mattered was the immediate safety of her brother. After washing his wounds, she did her best to bandage them with strips of her bedding.

"Oh God, let him live," she shouted.

Duval had crawled into his bathroom and run a deep, steaming bath to help ease the pain in his limbs and the searing agony in his groin. Then he staggered into the kitchen and poured himself some brandy. Taking a generous slug, he limped slowly into the hall, where he noticed a large brown envelope protruding through the letterbox. He tugged it out and glanced at the cover. It said, "By hand from Irvine M. Gould." He moved painfully back to the bathroom to turn off the taps.

He eased his aching body into the bath and began to compose himself, to think himself out of his conundrum: I'll leave that pair down there for a while. Let them starve. He'll be dead soon and she'll be too shocked to resist. I'll have to kill her; she deserves it for betraying me. How could I have ever thought that she was sincere? The ungrateful bitch. How could she have turned on me, after all that I've done for her? I'll bury them both and get away from this place. Nobody knows they are here. Nobody's come looking for the brother.

The brandy and hot water relaxed him a little, and the pain began to subside. He was sore, especially around the groin; the bruising would be bad, but there were no broken bones. He was taken aback by her hidden strength; obviously he had fed her too well.

He soaked himself and pondered on his future away from Shere. Wallowing in the comfort of the bath for a long time, he felt the water grow cold and let some of it out, then re-ran water from the hot tap. As he waited for the half-empty bath to refill he leaned out to reach the envelope on the chair beside the bath.

Curious, he opened it. It contained about thirty sheets of paper. The first page was entitled "The French Adventures of the Anchoress of Shere: Research Findings of the Saint Sardos Archives by Professor Irvine M. Gould."

The water was getting a little too hot. Putting Gould's essay back on the chair, Duval bent forward and turned on the cold tap, balancing the force of the two jets to give himself a pleasant temperature.

With wet hands, he picked up the papers again. His first reaction was that the essay was typical American fantasy. "France?" he said venomously under his breath. "It's not possible."

He started to read very quickly, sickened and enthralled at the same time. After perusing a few more pages, his throat became constricted and dry. He grabbed a towel and stepped dripping out of the bath. Clutching the offending document, now damp in his hands, he closed the bathroom door and limped back to the kitchen. In his state of double shock, from the beating and Gould's literary stab in his back, he did not notice that he had left the taps running.

Naked, except for the towel, he slumped into the rocker near the wood-burning stove. Although he rarely drank spirits, he swallowed his second double brandy in one gulp and turned back to the beginning of Gould's version of the life of the Anchoress of Shere. He read it carefully through to the end while drinking another brandy. He read it again. Disbelief and scorn turned to enraged despair as Gould piled up the documentary evidence, the irrefutable records. The American's research had been rigorous, with little conjecture. Gould had apparently proven that the anchoress had not chosen to return to the enclosure. He even suggested, quite convincingly, that the entombment had been forced on her—Christine had witnessed a murder involving a cleric in Vachery Manor, and the Church had connived at her enclosure to shut her up. She was compelled to undertake a vow of silence and enclosure, or her father would be exiled. As an extra inducement, her family was bought off with money and a small parcel of land. Poor Christine was no more than a victim of a conspiracy. She was never a visionary. Such was Gould's interpretation from the evidence of the French archives. It made a mockery of Duval's life work, and vindicated Gould's remark that he would make the priest eat his words. Duval's whole world collapsed around him.

Bobby came up and licked his hand, but the priest pushed the animal away. He opened the door of the wood stove, ready to project the offending article into the fire, but at the last moment hesitated and instead forced himself to read it again, much more slowly this time, stopping only to throw on a few dirty clothes that were piled on a kitchen chair.

Then he started to read it yet again, as though utter concentration on the text could transform its content. This time, after he had finished the first page, he started to chew at the end of the A4 sheet and then to bite it. "This is C–R–A–P," he said bitterly, instinctively conforming to his habit of spelling out expletives. Then, with a manic laugh, he said, "And I'll make it into C–R–A–P, too."

Eventually, he masticated the whole page into a pulp that he swallowed. After another long swig of the brandy, from the bottle this time, he did the same with the second page. Then the third. On the fifth page, he started to choke. He tried to retch, but could not, because the sticky pulp had jammed in his windpipe. He coughed and retched, but it would not budge. He tried to reach into his throat with his fingers. Struggling for air, his eyes felt as if they would explode, but he could not scream. He retched again and then nearly collapsed, but he stretched out to the door, desperate for fresh air. He managed to stagger blindly into the garden. In his frenzy to breathe, and without any light, he fell headlong into the large hole he had dug; a grave not designed for its own creator. Duval's collie stood guard on the edge of the hole, whining to the moon.

⊰⊱∞⊰⊱

In the cellar Marda did everything she could to help her brother. She gave him water and tried to make him take some of the food she had held back from her own meagre supplies. He was unable to eat anything, but the water helped to ease the parched agony in his throat.

In a while his eyes opened and he moaned, and she tried to soothe him: "Help will come soon. Hold on, Mark."

His eyes closed again. She made sure that he was covered by her blankets before going into the corridor to check the cellar door. It was locked, but she had light and the freedom to roam in the corridor. Some freedom, she thought.

Then she noticed that water was running into the corridor from the vents near the staircase. Soon an inch or so covered the floor of the corridor. It seemed to be a natural reservoir for wherever the water was coming from, on the other side of the vent. She stood on the stool to try to block the vent with the curtain material which Duval had used to veil his diabolical attempt to crucify her brother, but the force of the water made all her attempts useless. Then it hit her: My God, he's going to drown us!

Time had become elastic for Marda. For a few seconds it seemed interminable, but then it became shockingly brief as she measured her lifespan in hours. The monster had taken Mark's watch: she estimated that probably twenty-four hours had passed since Duval's escape, but in her state of emotional distress she could have been wildly inaccurate. Her brother, though, was still alive; she cradled him in her arms to give him extra warmth, but the water was rising in her cell. It seemed to be rising more rapidly, as though, perhaps, the pressure of the escaping water had damaged other water pipes in the house. The water was cold. And it was now about eighteen inches deep. Soon it would flow over the bench, and she did not want her brother to suffer any more.

Eventually, with the very last reserves of strength, she dragged him to the stairs that led to the trapdoor. It was uncomfortable, but it was the highest point in the cellar. Somehow she managed to pull him to the top steps, where she held him, breathing erratically but swathed in blankets, like two marooned sailors together on a tiny raft.

Very soon, or so it seemed to Marda, the water was about four feet deep in a cellar transformed into a large underground cistern. Bizarrely, she recalled the poem that Churchill had quoted during the darkest days of the Second World War, the words her father had so loved to repeat.

> For while the tired waves, vainly breaking
> Seem here no painful inch to gain
> Far back through creeks and inlets making
> Comes silent, flooding in, the main.

It seemed a sick joke now.

Soon the water would reach the top of the stairs. She could not believe that after all they had gone through they would die by drowning, in the middle of winter in land-locked Shere; especially in a cellar where she had so often been short of water to drink. She tried with every ounce of her being to push up the trapdoor, but she knew it was double locked. She couldn't understand why Duval had decided to kill them by drowning. Marda wondered whether he had recovered from the extremes of his mania and so perhaps did not want to murder them with his own hands. But why damage one's own house? She could not see the logic, but logic was a stupid thing to expect from a homicidal madman.

Before the flood fused the cellar lights, she saw the pages of the final chapter of Duval's crazy book floating in the corridor. She tasted again the dread of his anger.

As they huddled in the cold darkness waiting for death, Marda kept telling her brother how much she loved him. Every now and then he groaned in response to words he could no longer hear properly.

She would not die alone, as she had feared for so long, but that would have been preferable to making her brother die with her. Mark would have been alive and well in Germany if he had not searched for her. It was her fault, she told herself. Why had they both been deserted by the world, she wondered? She thought of Christ's final words on the Cross. With all his faith, even He had felt forsaken.

⋘∞⋙

Three days before, Professor Gould had dutifully phoned Germany, but was told that Captain Stewart was still in England. Delayed flights or something, he said to himself. He phoned two days later and got the same answer.

Now worried, he left his lodgings and walked across the square, past the war memorial and through the lych-gate. As he traversed the graveyard, Gould marvelled again at the instant changeability of the British weather: within seconds an overcast sky was sundered by a desperate winter sun, and yet despite the brief sunshine a stiff breeze arose. At its crescendo the wind's piping in the trees prompted the erratic shadows to launch into a jig, focusing a rustic *son et lumière* on the western porch of the ancient building. This was almost a divine invitation into the sanctuary of St. James's church. For the umpteenth time the professor peered into what remained of Christine's cell. As he looked into the black hole that was the quatrefoil, he wondered if he had been rather slow, too lost in the Middle Ages to realise what was happening around him in the present day. He resolved immediately to visit the police station, where he was told that the car belonging to Mark Stewart had been found abandoned.

He said little to the police, but he did not return to the White Horse, despite a storm that chased away the interlude of sun. Clutching his umbrella against the wind and lashing rain, he walked to the old rectory. He had just a few days left in England, and he had his excuse to see Duval, to discover the priest's reactions to his "French" article, and ask whether Mark had visited again.

Finally and slowly, the professor realised that Duval, Marda and her brother were fusing into a related tragedy. His brilliant mind, like many of his kind, had missed the obvious, but he was still not sure. As he rang and rang the bell, the whining of the dog inside the house reinforced his concern. The clergyman's car was in the drive—if Duval had gone out on foot for an extended period, he would probably have taken the dog.

"Where the heck is Duval?" he said to himself.

Gould went around the back of the house and found the kitchen door very slightly ajar. He knocked, waited and knocked again.

"Father Duval...Michael...Are you there?"

No reply.

He waited for two minutes.

Minutes that meant life and death in the cellar below. By pressing her head against the inside of the trapdoor, Marda could keep her nose above water, but it was far more difficult to keep Mark's slumped head in the same position.

Professor Gould waited another thirty seconds.

Then he did a very un-English thing: he walked into the kitchen.

It was deserted except for the dog, who gave him a very cursory greeting then dashed outside. In the gloom of the late winter afternoon, Gould could see a strange mess of paper on the kitchen table. Pages from his article lay strewn on the floor.

He called out quietly, and then noticed that the floor of the kitchen was wet—a part of the floor in the corner was under an inch or so of water. The movement of the water had pushed a rug to one side. He saw a trapdoor and a sense of foreboding welled up inside him.

Obviously there had been some accident. He should go for the police, for Gould was the most law-abiding of men.

He shouted, "Father Duval!"

He heard a muffled response—somewhere. Then a banging from beneath the kitchen. He pulled the sodden rug aside from the trapdoor and strained at the bolts. Because of the suction of the water that had drained through, he had great difficulty in lifting it.

When he did, two startled eyes peered out of the gloom.

No sound came from the mouth below the eyes; eyes which showed the horror that silenced the tongue.

"Marda Stewart?"

A faint "yes" came from the lips.

"Give me your hand," he said gently.

"No, get my brother out of here first," she whispered, struggling to find the strength to speak. "He's still alive... just."

Gould carefully helped them both out of the tomb.

XVII

The Crucifixion

Marda did not remember much of the immediate frenzy that followed Gould's phone call to the police and ambulance service, when blue uniforms and white coats filled the kitchen. She did remember being carried into an ambulance, placed alongside her brother, and something being injected into her arm. She had been starved and tortured for months, she had been traumatised by Duval's attempted crucifixion of her brother, and she had just endured a lengthy immersion in icy water. No wonder, for the moment, Marda's physical reserves were utterly depleted. The ambulance was warm and safe; lulled by the unaccustomed comfort, she drifted into sleep.

An hour after her deliverance she was wheeled on a mobile stretcher into the casualty department of the Royal Surrey County Hospital, by which time she was feeling reasonably alert again. Marda had been too long a helpless victim. Duval had not only been the lord of her life and death, but also the lord of the manner of death. Despite the months of agonising pretence and her ploys to appease or manipulate him, there had been little ambiguity in the relationship, merely a crude juxtaposition of the powerful and the powerless. Her life had depended on him alone. She had had to be grateful to this single embodiment of her fate for everything that happened to her—food and water and light—and, more importantly, for the things that did not happen to her. And yet her spirit had not been broken. The hardest steel had reinforced her will when she had finally confronted Duval, physically and psychologically. No more would she be dictated to. She had been transformed by her terrible ordeal; from now on, no matter how unconventional she might appear, she would choose her own path. Her body, showing obvious signs of maltreatment, had temporarily been subdued, but her will, her mental stamina, was not only undiminished but eager to continue the battle against her tormentor. With an acute stab of fear in the depths of her stomach, she sensed that it was not all over yet.

As the nurses prepared to move her into the starched white sheets of a bed, she said, "Where's my brother? I need to see him now."

The staff were used to the truculent behaviour of patients suffering from shock. A nurse, younger than Marda, said gently, "He's in intensive care. Don't worry, we'll look after him. Please let me help you into bed; the doctors want to have a good look at you. We've heard what a horrible time you've had and…"

Marda very calmly interrupted her, "I would like to borrow some clothes, please. A dressing-gown or something. I absolutely insist on seeing my brother."

The young nurse recognised the patient's determination and went to fetch the ward sister, leaving Marda to sit on the bed, swaddled once again in a blanket. She was even more resolved to break the cycle of her victimisation.

Despite the sister's remonstrations and the duty doctor's best efforts, Marda absolutely refused to be admitted formally to the hospital, even though she submitted to a brief medical examination. Legally, she could not be kept against her will. And she did not have to be told that she was malnourished. She showered in the hospital, and was loaned some clothes and shoes by a concerned nurse. In the nurses' staff room, over a steaming cup of tea, she gave an initial briefing to a very considerate detective inspector.

The briefing was interrupted by a tumultuous welcome from her father and mother when they arrived; they embraced Marda in a tight scrum of intense relief and passionate endearments. Marda enfolded them both, not ever, ever wanting to let them go, while all three cried, talked and kissed at the same time. It was her parents who finally persuaded the doctors to let them see Mark.

They peered through an inspection window in the intensive care unit, and saw that Mark was fitted with a phalanx of tubes and suspended bottles.

A specialist spoke in a soft, assuring tone: "He's very weak at the moment, but he's a fit young man and I believe he will pull through. The best thing you can do is to let us get on with it. If you'd like to sit in the waiting room, I should be able to update you in an hour or so."

For an hour the Stewart family talked intensely about their experiences, although Marda felt she could not disclose the full extent of her horrific ordeal to her parents, anxious as they were about her and even more distracted by Mark's condition.

Finally, they were told by the specialist that Mark was expected, all things being equal, to make a full recovery.

The jubilation was disturbed by the detective inspector, who apologised for his intervention: "Miss Stewart, I really am sorry to press you at this sensitive time, but we are obviously very anxious to catch Duval. The doctors say I can talk to you, and, if you feel well enough, I would like a few words in private, if possible."

Marda drank more tea in a quiet corner of the staff room, where she was joined by Professor Gould, who had also been debriefed by the police; she showed obvious pleasure at the American's arrival.

Marda did not want to argue with her parents, who would surely try to insist that she stay in hospital. She asked the inspector, "Is it safe to return to my flat, if my parents are told to meet me there?"

The policeman tried briefly to persuade her to stay in hospital, but she was adamant. Eventually he said, "I will send one of my officers to your flat, and ask your parents to join you there. We have set up an operations room in Shere police station, so the village will be very safe."

Gould, who had said very little, spoke directly to the inspector: "If Marda is so insistent on checking herself out of this hospital, may I presume to escort her back to Shere?"

The inspector excused himself to speak to one of his uniformed subordinates.

He soon returned and said, slightly begrudgingly, "OK, Professor Gould, I'll get a key from Mr. Stewart, and arrange for the parents to go there later, when they are sure Captain Stewart's on the mend. But please go to Shere directly. We don't want to lose Marda again. Is that clear?"

"Of course, Inspector, and thank you," said Gould.

So Marda was released from hospital on the understanding that she would undergo further police interviews and medical examinations later, and she returned with Gould to Shere. For the moment she had done all she could for her brother, but now she wanted to know what had happened to Duval. And she wanted revenge.

⟨⟫⟨⟩⟫⟩

It was eight o'clock in the evening as Professor Irvine Gould drove Marda Stewart back to Shere from the hospital in Guildford.

312

"You really should have stayed in for twenty-four hours' observation, Marda," the American said with deep concern.

"Freedom is enough, Professor," she replied forcefully, as she savoured the lights, the people, the smell of newness in the hired car. "Freedom is enough for the moment."

"Are you sure you want to go back to your apartment? It'll be cold. And, even with a police guard there, Duval is still on the loose."

"No offence, Professor, I appreciate your concern, I really do," she said, touching his arm, "but I've had enough of being told what to do and when. I've been living like a robot for too long. I know where I have to go first...Take me back, please, to Duval's house."

"Where?" Gould was astonished. "Why there of all places?" He slowed the car instinctively. Like most men, he found it almost impossible to concentrate on two important matters at once.

"There are things I must collect before the police ransack the place."

"The police will be there now."

"Precisely," said Marda, with complete determination.

The professor, reluctantly, did what he was told. He wanted to appease her, to delay the breakdown he thought was inevitable. He had served in Korea, and had witnessed numerous breakdowns caused by stress and trauma.

He parked outside Hillside, next to a police car, and a large lorry from the Water Board which was pumping out the cellar. Gould helped Marda up the stairs; she was still weak, and wearing someone else's clothes.

PC McGregor and the sergeant on duty at the house were astounded to see her back. She explained that she had come to collect Bobby en route to joining the police at her flat.

"Aye, I was wondering what we were going to do with him," said the amiable constable. "Nice little beggar. I don't see why you shouldn't look after him. But you need to leave the crime scene immediately. I'm breaking all the rules because you've gone through hell. So be quick, and then, please, go straight home."

They let her into the house to collect the dog. Alone for a few seconds, she sneaked into the study and saw on the desk a file of papers, amongst them a typescript with a cover sheet saying "Anchoress of Shere by Michael Duval." Marda hid the papers in her bulky borrowed anorak: Christine Carpenter, too, must be freed from Duval's evil.

With a sense of utter relief she led the dog to Gould's car, and away from her prison. She thanked the two policemen, and then impulsively kissed Gould on the cheek.

"Thank you, Professor."

"For what? For being so dumb? For taking so long to put two and two together?"

"For saving me, Mark...and Bobby here," she added, hugging the dog.

The professor looked sheepish. "I wish I could have done a damn sight more and a damn sight sooner."

"I don't want to go to an empty, unguarded flat. Until the police get there, will you please take me somewhere warm and safe, where I can have a proper bath? I want to get rid of the smell of this place, of him, of that bastard Duval."

Saying his name seemed instantly to undermine the front she was putting on: she was nearly hysterical.

Gould tried to calm her: "All right, but once we've cleaned you up we must go back to the police at your apartment."

As they drove the half-mile to the White Horse, Marda's pulse was racing and her body surged once again with adrenaline. Despite her extended trauma, she wanted to get out and see the whole world as soon as possible. She could not believe how alive the outside was, how sweet the air smelt, how wonderful it was to be free. She could now truly relate to how Christine felt when she escaped from the wall. But she also wanted to touch things; she felt the smoothness of the anorak she had borrowed, the plastic of the car seat, and, to Gould's slight embarrassment, the roughness of the jacket he was wearing.

Gould became aware of her intense femininity, in spite of the pain etched on her face. Despite himself, he wondered whether she would automatically regard him as an old man, even though he was only ten or fifteen years her senior. Mark had talked a lot about his sister, and Gould liked what he had heard about her character. And he felt he wanted to make amends for taking so long to put the jigsaw together, a delay that could have killed both brother and sister. Why were academics so impractical? he asked himself.

Marda's emotions were too crowded to think beyond the moment. Gould was a friend of her brother's, and her saviour. And because of, or in spite of, her ordeal, she felt instinctively at ease with him, not least because he was, she sensed, the polar opposite of the loathsome Duval. That was enough, for the time being. Her nerves jangled with all the stimuli which even the dark, cold winter's night could not disguise: a car-horn beeping, the powerful colours of the traffic lights, the glowing shop windows…she could stop where she wanted, speak whenever she wanted to, cry, laugh, sing, run…Duval had missed out so many little elements of freedom in his book, she thought; he could never have understood how Christine had really felt, not just because Duval was a man, but because he was incapable of genuine empathy.

The car stopped abruptly outside the White Horse, a hundred yards from Marda's home. The village gossips had already been electrified by the rumours of Marda's discovery and the police manhunt, so the bar was fuller than usual. Gould's entry into the pub with a dishevelled and now famous ex-captive, in clothes far too big for her and leading a dog, inspired a swell of excitement not seen since VE Day. The trio ignored the stares and the few cheers, and swept up the stairs into the professor's room.

"I need a good soak," said Marda rather imperiously. Seeming to have regained some control, she did not ask his permission as she rushed into the en-suite bathroom.

"Please would you order me some tea and, yes, orange juice, and as many sandwiches as possible," she called back to him, a little more politely. "I'll have my bath first, but I just want to *see* some food."

"You go ahead and I'll go downstairs and fix that up."

She put her head around the bathroom door. "Please don't be long. I don't want to be alone, not for a very, very long time. May I use your phone," she said brightly, "to ring my friend Jenny?"

The professor carefully locked the door to the room and went downstairs. He ordered the refreshments, and spoke to the very attentive landlady: "May I borrow some women's clothes for Miss Stewart, and may I use your phone to make a quick call?"

"Anything you like, Professor, this is the busiest we've been in months. Like Piccadilly Circus." And then in a soft voice: "How is she?"

"As fine as can be expected. She's had a very rough ride."

The landlady led him to the phone in the room behind the bar, and promised to deliver the clothes within minutes. Gould then dutifully rang Shere police station to inform them where Marda was.

Politely refusing the numerous offers of congratulatory drinks from the over-curious crowd at the bar, he trotted up the stairs and unlocked his room. The bathroom door was half-open and the air was hot and steamy.

"Are you OK, Marda?"

There was no response.

He shouted this time, nearer the door: "Is everything OK?"

He heard the lavatory flush.

"Yes, I'm cleaner, but still starving and parched."

"Oh, good. I've scrounged some clothes for you. Much more your size. They're on their way. I've rung the police and told them where we are. I don't want them to think you've disappeared again. A respectable professor taking a beautiful young lady and a dog to his room is not something I could hide for long—if I read you English correctly... Especially when I asked the landlady for some women's clothes." He hoped a little levity would help the girl.

The professor knew that Marda should be in hospital, where she would have received expert attention, yet he also admired her pluck. He was trying to jolly the girl along, hoping he might help to stop her collapsing. He knew that such anguish could not be suppressed for long, especially at the moment of safety, when the body, so long enduring, often gives up in abject surrender. One remedy was to keep talking, because it helped to let it all out, bit by bit. His job was to calm her down until she could receive proper medical help.

She came out, wearing a towel wrapped turban-style around her head and another large one around her body.

"*Two big* towels; you are spoiled, professor. Mostly they have a single little one in English hotels."

She retreated into a small armchair. She had been obsessed by her starved frame when she was in her cell, but now the elation of freedom helped her transcend such concerns.

"I look like Twiggy, don't I? I'll have to eat six meals a day for a month," she said, a little self-consciously, and with a slight tinge of suppressed hysteria in her voice.

She was interrupted by a knock on the door. Marda jumped slightly.

"Don't worry. You're safe now," Gould said reassuringly. "Come in."

The landlady came in with the clothes that Gould had requested, and a large tray of sandwiches, tea and orange juice, which the ex-captive fell upon.

The landlady said, "Hope everything will be all right now that you're free. If there's anything you want—make-up or anything of that sort, just ask me, love." And, before leaving, she gave Marda a little hug. Marda wanted to say thank you but her mouth was too full of food, so she just nodded her appreciation.

After she had demolished five or six more sandwiches over the next twenty minutes, Marda began to ask a thousand questions. She begged for a cigarette, and Gould gave her one of his Marlboros. She was smoking, eating, drinking and talking in a frenzy.

"Take it easy, Marda, you'll be sick," Gould warned.

She tried on the borrowed clothes, gabbling all the time. "They fit reasonably well; they'll do until I get to my flat; presumably my clothes will still be there, don't you think, Professor? Might be a bit damp, though." Her words were barely comprehensible through the thick ham sandwich wedged in her mouth.

"Marda, seeing as we're sharing a bathroom, at least call me Irvine. My friends call me Irv."

"OK, *Irv*." She got up, and walked back into the bathroom to remove some food stuck in her teeth.

"Why did you call the police?" she asked distractedly through the open door.

"Well, for one thing, because the police need to know where you are right now, especially since Duval hasn't been caught. I wanted to check that there is a policeman in your flat. And they mentioned again your not staying in hospital."

"Professor, I couldn't stand to be locked in any more, even in a hospital."

She came out of the bathroom again and faced him squarely. "I will go to the hospital tomorrow, and every day, to see my brother. I'll have a check-up, but I can't be ordered to be in one place. I have to be physically free. Free. Free. At last." She hiccupped as a result of her hasty eating, put her hand to her mouth, swallowed, and added very plaintively, "Don't you understand?"

"Slow down, Marda. The police will have to ask you lots of questions."

She lit another cigarette, took a long drag, and coughed. "I have a question for you, Professor, I mean Irvine. *Irv*. Mark mentioned that you knew Duval. What exactly is your connection with him?"

"My research on Christine, the Anchoress of Shere."

It was the very last thing that she wanted to hear at that moment.

"You're not another maniac who's obsessed with locking people up, are you?" She said this without alarm in her voice, because her brother had spoken highly of the professor during their shouted exchanges in the cellar.

"No, no," replied Gould. "I've been working on an article on her life in France, but you don't want to hear any more about an obscure fourteenth-century *religieuse*, I'm sure. And, incidentally, I didn't know Duval at all really. Just read a few of his articles and met him briefly."

The slightly defensive tone in the professor's voice prompted Marda to indulge in a small smile for the first time since her release: "Actually, I'm a world authority on the subject of Christine Carpenter," she said. "That's what the pile of papers there is about. It's Duval's book. The only copy, I think. The one he forced me to read again and again while he kept me in his awful prison."

"To be honest, I can understand you returning for the dog, but going back into that prison just for a book...I don't get it."

Marda took another bite from a sandwich. "I can't really explain, but somehow I wanted her—Christine—to be free of him as well. We both had to get out of his clutches. In some way I identified with her. Who knows? You can take it to read. But look after it."

"I can see it's precious to you. I will read it, and presumably so will the police."

"No," said Marda emphatically. "The police would take it and keep it as evidence. It's private, and it's mine. Some of the stuff he wrote was absolutely mad, but she is—was—separate from him. I'm sure she was a good person. I think I deserve to keep the book after all I've gone through."

"All right, Marda, if it's that important to you. Technically, you have stolen police evidence, but let's not make a fuss about it now. I'll put it in the hotel strong-box later, if you like. I think it will be safe on the coffee table for the moment..."

There was another knock on the door and the sound of heavy boots shuffling outside.

"Sergeant Terence Davidson, Surrey police, sir."

Soon the room seemed to be full of doctors, uniformed policemen and plain-clothes detectives. Marda's friend Jenny was allowed in for ten minutes, and they hugged and kissed and promised to do a hundred things together once the policemen and doctors had finished their business.

Prompted by Gould, who was rapidly becoming her psychological mentor, his decency substituted for the evil of Duval, Marda briefed the police on her months in captivity; the professor insisted that she stay in the comfort of the hotel room rather than go to Shere police station. She would sign a full written statement the next day, once the doctors had given their agreement that she was fit enough. Meanwhile, the police needed some leads for their manhunt.

Marda tried to remain calm at the centre of this maelstrom. She did not cry, although she would, long and hard; but later, after it was all over, and with friends rather than strangers. After the initial police interview, everyone was asked to leave the room while a local doctor gave her a second, more detailed, check-up. Fifteen minutes later they all trooped back into the professor's room.

"Rather run down and undernourished, but I'm sure she will be fine in a few weeks." The doctor meant, but did not say, *physically* fine.

Marda smoked too many cigarettes and drank pints of orange juice, interspersed with cups of tea and visits to the bathroom every ten minutes.

The outpouring of her experiences was not only a necessary police procedure, but also a useful psychological catharsis. Gould was always at her side as a prompter or comforter, until Superintendent Woodward arrived and asked to speak to him.

Leaving a policewoman with Marda, they went downstairs to the emptying bar to talk. The landlord, thrilled that the White Horse had become the centre of a manhunt, offered them tea.

After brief preliminaries, the police officer said, "We've got a full alert out for Duval, and at first light we'll comb the woods for him. His car has been towed to the police station. He won't get far. We had a sighting of a second car in the vicinity of the old rectory and it was registered to the car pool at the cathedral in Guildford. He might have sought help there. If so, we'll get him straight away."

The superintendent realised he had said too much: the Church connection could become sensitive.

"You'd better catch him fast, Superintendent. He's killed five or six women, and almost finished off poor Mark. And Mark's a bloody good bloke." Gould threw in another of his favourite English expressions. "The hospital expects him to pull through, thank heavens, probably because he's in good shape thanks to his army training. You know that Duval tried to crucify him?"

"That is utterly bizarre, although I must say that I find Catholicism generally rather…er, medieval," said the policeman, scratching his head nervously.

"Well, it's hardly anything to do with modern Catholicism, of course. But, historically, it's not entirely bizarre."

The superintendent looked at the American as though he were an alien.

"It ties in with my own research. It *is* my field," the professor said defensively. "A few medieval mystics actually believed they could eat of the flesh and blood of a crucified man, albeit preferably a holy man or woman. To put it crudely, just an extreme and perverted form of holy communion. Some devil-worshippers, and indeed some Christians, attached significance to such acts. That *could* explain it." The professor noticed the disbelieving look on the policeman's face, and added a caveat: "*Perhaps*—it's only a theory."

"Sounds a very unsavoury practice to me, Professor. Not normally the sort of crime we're used to around here. You'll be talking about flying witches next." He took his leave, adding, "The sooner we get this unholy priest under lock and key the better. Goodnight."

⋘⋙

The unholy priest was hiding near the spot where his last victim had taken up his observation post a little more than a week before. The rest of the world would undoubtedly have defined Duval as mad, but insanity takes many forms and the deviant priest was still very capable of avoiding capture, not least because he possessed the extra cunning of the hunted.

The priest had to make his final arrangements before leaving the country. The traumatic recent events had shocked him into a semblance of rational introspection and an ability to question his own sanity. Standing in the darkness of the woods, a cold logic penetrated his brain. Regrets started to swamp him, not moral regrets, but frustration with his own behaviour. If only he hadn't drunk so much and then nearly choked in his kitchen. He cursed himself for falling into a hole he had dug himself.

"May all the demons in Hell be forever damned for leading me into such utter folly," he said aloud.

He unscrambled his brain for an answer: psychologically, he had taken too long to recover from his beating. That was it. How could he know that his own disciple would turn on him? Who could have anticipated such betrayal? Her strength had been amazing, and her anger. The ungrateful witch.

And Gould's deceitful article had shaken his whole being, undermining a lifetime of work. But it was foolish to succumb to Gould's lies. He would recover and prove the American to be a forger and a charlatan. Yes, God would give him a second chance to finish his work.

The Almighty was on Duval's side; he had proof of that. God had saved him: stopped him choking to death, and sent the bishop's curate to the house to discover him lying in the half-finished grave and pull him out. Yes, that was a resurrection.

The curate, concerned for Duval's mental and physical health, had driven him back to the episcopal palace in Guildford. But Templeton, incandescent with rage at the priest's filthy and drunken condition, had simply locked him in a bedroom to sober up. He had been left there for over a day, his only visitor the bishop's secretary bringing him tea and unbuttered toast.

"His Grace does not wish to see you today," the man said. "He feels that a period of contemplation would be beneficial to you"—further evidence, as if Duval needed it, that the bishop was not God's man and did not understand the priest's holy calling.

"His Grace is going on a retreat," the secretary continued. "He has left you these written instructions concerning the travel arrangements and other details regarding your posting in Bolivia." With that he left the room, locking the door carefully behind him.

Duval sat stunned for a while, chewing on the unappetising dry toast. Late that evening he finally gathered his wits together and clambered out through the window of the locked room. And the bishop would get the car back, and the transistor radio he borrowed. It wasn't theft.

Time had been lost, though. Duval estimated he had been away from his house for around forty-eight hours. Thanks to the bishop's desire to banish him to South America, he had his escape route organised, but first he needed to get back into his house. He heard the initial news reports of the police cordoning his home on the radio he had "borrowed" from the bishop. He knew the place would be swarming with police, poking around in the cellar, digging up the garden; at first light they would start sweeping the woods. But the last thing they would expect him to do would be to go back to his own house.

⊰⧓⊱

Bishop Templeton was a seriously troubled man, but he knew where he would find solace. It had worked before: a day or two of isolation in a small monastery on the edge of Dartmoor. The abbot was an old friend. The bishop could pray, walk, and think there. He told his secretary to cancel all appointments for the next forty-eight hours.

The bishop departed for Dartmoor just two hours before the police arrived at his palace. Templeton drove himself, because he wanted to think, not engage in polite small talk with his driver. He brooded on Duval. God, he had tried to help the man, but he had been kicked in the teeth. The bishop blamed himself. He had been too indulgent. Too kind. His own reputation would be called into question if Duval were involved in any further scandals. The image of the Catholic Church had to be preserved at all costs; two thousands years of history had to be cherished. Human imperfection, he knew, would always threaten Rome's ideals. But Duval would soon be in South America, and no longer his responsibility. The bishop smiled, and started to look foward to his retreat.

But when Templeton arrived at the monastery, a message from the Surrey police, relayed by the abbot, forced him to turn the car round and drive back to Guildford immediately. He had not been indulgent; he had inadvertently succoured a mass murderer. The bishop's life and career were in ruins.

⊰⊱⋈⊰⊱

Little did Duval know it, but the bishop's absence had bought him the extra time he needed.

From his vantange point overlooking the old rectory he watched as an ambulance took away Denise's remains; various senior officers came and went, and for a while the place was a brightly lit circus. By three o'clock in the morning, however, just one panda car remained outside his house. If he was lucky, it would be occupied by the senile PC McGregor, probably asleep.

Duval was right: it was McGregor in the car, but the deeply superstitious officer was too frightened to sleep. Having locked all his doors to keep the devil-priest away, he was sitting rigid, with the police radio on and a truncheon on his lap. A tartan-patterned thermos flask lay empty on the front passenger seat.

Duval knew he would have to take his chance. He had to get back into the house, and he had wasted too much time already.

Duval would have liked to have taken his dog; that was now impossible, but there was one thing without which he would not leave Britain: his only typescript of the "Anchoress of Shere." He had almost completed it, but not quite. Busybodies had interrupted him when he was on the eve of finalising this all-consuming life project. His experiments on twentieth century women had not worked out as he had hoped, but his spiritual insights, the comparative work which linked the fourteenth and twentieth centuries, had to be recorded for posterity. Yes, despite Gould's lies, there were hundreds of years of mystical insight encapsulated in his work as well as twenty years of his own humble endeavours to add to this long sweep of history. He must finish it, and he had to take it with him. He was incensed with himself for not arranging a copy earlier, but events had crowded in on him.

Duval once more dismissed Gould's work as fraud, sloppy research or crass ignorance. The shock of reading the American's work had been overwhelming, but now he'd had time to think it through. He would cross-check Gould's findings, reveal the professor to be a cheat. He was the better historian, and he would be proven right in the end.

Frenzied thoughts hammered away in Duval's brain as he cautiously penetrated the dank copse at the rear of his garden. He scaled the wall by the big laburnum tree and peered over the top. No one was there...except a roe buck grazing near the wall. The animal stared at him before bolting back into the Hurtwood. There were no lights on, and as he crept through the garden he almost fell again into his recent excavations.

A yellow notice had been pasted on the back door: "No Entry—Police Investigation." Duval looked at the repaired window and prided himself on his handiwork, necessitated by the failed rescuer's vandalism. Ah, that was when he'd had time, and peace, before *they* all disrupted his sacred mission.

He rummaged in the flowerpot near the window to find the hidden doorkey. Opening the door slowly, despite the gloom he realised that everything in his kitchen had been moved. He was very indignant at the intrusion into his home. And everything was so damp, as though the interfering morons had hosed down his kitchen.

Moving into the hall very carefully, he felt that the carpet underfoot was soggy, and a cold, wet, musty smell pervaded the house. Perplexed, he made his way into the study. All the curtains were closed, and no outside observer could see him. He could not put on the lights, so he felt his way to the desk.

The book was not where it should be. "They must have moved it," he said aloud. He fumbled through the drawers of his desk and around the rest of the room. "They can't have taken it, not yet! Why would those interfering bureaucratic clods be interested in my historical work? Perhaps it's somewhere else in the house?"

He went upstairs for his small case and some clothes, and rummaged some more in search of his precious typescript.

"Maybe they've taken my passport," he said to himself, "but they wouldn't have taken my book. It can't be possible!"

He went back to the kitchen and lifted up the trapdoor, then leaned down to turn on the light-switch. No one outside would notice the light in the cellar, but it wouldn't work. He got his torch from the kitchen, descended the stairs, and was shocked to find two feet of water in the corridor. He had no idea why it was flooded.

All the cell doors were open. He looked into the sodden mess of Marda's room, searching for his final chapter, even looking in the air vent. It was hopeless. He hardly gave a thought to his former charges, simply assuming the police had taken the brother and sister away, alive or dead. But Gould; perhaps he had the book? The American was jealous enough to steal it, or perhaps the police had asked his advice on the meaning of the text. "Find Gould, maybe find my book," he said aloud.

He stared up and down the cellar corridor and his eyes alighted on the large crucifix. And then he knew what had to be done.

He tore at the crucifix with furious strength, but it was fixed firmly on the wall. He went back up to the kitchen for tools, and returned to loosen the fixtures and drag it off the wall. The cross was heavy, but he could just about pull it, dripping, up to the steps. His manic strength enabled him to stagger up the stairs with his load. He stopped for a moment, to draw breath and to think.

Frantically assembling the things he would need, he put them in a small hold-all that he hoisted over one shoulder. Over the other he dragged the cross to the front door. It was too heavy to carry very far, and he saw that the police had removed his old Morris from the drive. His rage was mounting to fever pitch.

Constable McGregor, dozing in the front seat of his police car parked on the road outside, awoke to the sound of a hammer smashing through the driver's window. He did not have the time to raise his hands to protect his face as the hammer smashed twice into his skull. The third blow blinded him. He gurgled blood as his left hand reached out and fell lifeless on the tartan thermos flask. Duval wrenched the door open and, in frustrated rage, battered the policeman's head until it was a shapeless crimson pulp.

It was less than a mile to St. James's church from Hillside. Duval drove the police car with the rear doors open, the spar of the cross protruding. It was very dangerous. But Duval didn't really care any more about anything, except how to tease out a little more time. He needed just a short breathing space to complete what he had to do. The journey along the winding lane between the dark hedges took just over a minute.

One hundred yards in front of the church, the village square was silent and deserted; the rear of St. James's, shrouded in trees, was in total darkness. Shere was unusual in having no street lighting; the local council had decided that it would spoil the medieval ambience of the village.

Leaving the car and the crucifix in the lane behind the church, he crept through the shadows to the edge of the square.

The White Horse was in darkness, as was the lane beside it. No lights were on in the upper floor. Duval used the hammer to force the rear door of the pub open, and carefully ascended the stairs to the residents' floor. He knocked gently on the door to room number three, Gould's room. There was no answer. One heave of his shoulders broke the flimsy lock. Cautiously switching on the light, he entered the room; it was unoccupied. He could see a manuscript on the coffee table. It was his work, his life's work. He seized it with both hands, and left quietly and quickly.

Keeping to the shadows, he walked along the stream side of the square. He glanced over his shoulder and saw two police cars, a hundred and fifty yards away, parked between the stone bridge and Marda's flat. No one would expect him to be in the centre of Shere; that was the last place anyone would be looking, but he still had to move fast.

In the pitch darkness, he managed somehow to drag the heavy crucifix from the car to the side porch of the church. The door was never locked; even with the rise in crime, a village church was nearly always safe from vandals or thieves. Exhausted and soaked in sweat, he sat down on the pew nearest to the medieval site of Christine Carpenter's cell. He looked with sadness on the sacred quatrefoil and squint, the last time he would gaze upon these relics of her life. These relics of *his* life, too.

He lit a candle and placed it at the base of the quatrefoil on the floor of the church. Alongside he placed his typescript, his offering to the holy Christine. Perhaps now, in his infamy, people would recognise his book, his lengthy intellectual toil.

Christine had prayed so long, so hard, for Jesus Christ to answer her; to provide a sign, to make the crucifix weep those tears of absolution. Now tears would weep for her. The agony of crucifixion would be displayed before her eyes.

The crucifix lay flat, shadowed by the flickering candle. One arm of the crucifix still had a nail protruding from where it had been fixed in the cellar. He hammered six-inch nails into the other spar and into the small spar on the base. Duval had practised a crucifixion recently. He had failed then, but nobody would stop him now.

Once the nails were in place, he carried the cross to the edge of the chancel, a short distance from the place where Christine had sought absolution. He propped the cross at a forty-five-degree angle to the wall. Using the thick cross-spar at the base as a step, he stretched his arms along the span of the cross and gazed longingly at the two squints, the windows of Christine's cell, the lights of her tiny universe. His book stood reverentially at the base of her anchorhold, flickering in the candlelight of remembrance. Tears would fall from the crucifix before her very eyes.

Duval felt the salt taste on the edge of his mouth. Balanced precariously on the cross-spar at the base of the cross, he removed his jacket, shirt and trousers. He was too engrossed in his spiritual dedication to feel the cold, but it would take a supreme act of will to force his wrists and feet through the beckoning nails.

The powerful presence of the saintly anchoress would be appeased by the blood of crucifixion, the ultimate act of worship. But Duval asked himself whether he was strong enough, let alone holy enough, to imitate his Saviour.

⊰❊⊱

Despite the lateness of the hour, Marda's parents had made her flat warm and inviting. And, despite the presence of the police guard and the lanky American, Marda was smothered with family affection, and the dog was curled up in front of an electric heater. It was a time of joy and concern: a daughter returned, a son recovering in intensive care. Marda's father and the professor demolished most of a bottle of Scotch, while the two women and the police officer consumed endless cups of tea.

Marda tried to explain her feelings, the complete desperation she had felt while in her prison, her total anguish at the manner of her brother's treatment by Duval, the lengths to which Mark had gone to save her.

"But I also feel so strong," she said. "I survived the ordeal and I'm alive! Perhaps God, after all, answered my prayers…"

She stopped, surprised to realise how important these prayers had been to her sanity. She wondered, too, if she could continue to be strong, to survive the coming weeks, especially, God forbid, if Mark did not pull through.

Her mother seemed to read her thoughts. "It might be hard, coming to grips with life again. A new life, for it will never be the same," she said, putting both her arms around the emaciated girl. Her very last reserves of strength utterly depleted, Marda fell soundly asleep on her mother's shoulder.

⋘∘⋙

The knock on the flat door came at eight o'clock in the morning, when it was still almost dark outside. The policeman opened the door and was met by his breathless superintendent, who enhanced the drama of his message by trying to underplay it: "We've found him," he said, trying to control his excitement. "In the church. We've called off the alert."

"So you trapped him there?" Gould asked.

Superintendent Woodward led Gould outside to answer him, because he thought the details might upset the already distressed Stewart family. "No, he was already dead. Crucified, it appears."

Gould looked at the policeman in amazement.

"This is just preliminary, you understand. One of my men saw a police car at the rear of the church and went in. I've just taken the message on the car radio. One of my men is missing, too. I'm going straight to the church now, but I wanted to tell the Stewarts first."

"May I come with you, Superintendent?" asked the professor.

The policeman nodded, and the two men hastened to the nearby church.

Gould had seen thousands of depictions of crucifixions, but nothing could have prepared him for the reality: the head was slumped on the chest and dried, matted smudges of blood and strands of tissue disfigured the body, especially around the wrists and feet.

The three policemen and the academic just stared.

Gould was the first to ask: "Why is his face so smashed up?"

He waited a long moment before adding, "Are you sure it's Duval? You said one of your men was missing. It must be damned difficult to crucify yourself."

The policemen looked at him in horror. They did not want to believe it could be one of their own.

Shere's doctor had had a busy night. Arriving a few minutes after Gould, he cleaned up the face a little and suggested that it was the body of a man in his late fifties or early sixties. Too old, probably, for Duval, but even the sergeant at McGregor's own station was not sure.

"I'm sorry, Super," he said, his voice strained. "I've never seen old McGregor with no clothes on, and the face is unrecognisable. There are no rings an' all, but he's missing and it could be him."

The body was not positively identified until two hours later. The official alert was renewed, and the sweep of the woods was begun. It had given Duval, however, that extra margin of time. He had used it well: at that very moment, Father Duval was contentedly smoking his pipe on board a small fishing boat en route to Ireland.

The professor walked back to Marda's flat, alongside the Tillingbourne. The weeping willows, bent in anguish, matched his mood. He did not want to inflict more pain on the Stewarts, so he explained that the police would bring further news shortly.

When, a few minutes later, the superintendent told the assembled Stewart family that the dead man was a policeman who had been guarding Duval's house, Marda and the professor stared at each other. There was a profound intensity and understanding in that look.

"Why did he go back to the house?" Marda's father asked.

"It's amazing how many murderers are drawn back to the scene of their crimes, even when it's highly dangerous to return," the superintendent said confidently.

"No, Superintendent." Marda's voice sounded suddenly very tired. "He was looking for a book, one he has worked on for years."

Marda said no more. She knew intuitively that Duval had found his book. A glance at Gould told him not to say anything, not to alarm her parents any more than was necessary; the news that Duval was still loose on a murderous spree was more than enough. Marda wondered whether her long isolation had honed some sixth sense.

"Since I clearly know so little of the psychology of the man," said the superintendent, barely disguising his emotions, "may I ask why—*why*—he would have killed my officer in this horrific way, and in a church of all places?"

Gould felt Marda had answered enough police questions already. "He was obsessed by the Anchoress of Shere, Superintendent. It was his consuming passion. I suppose he will burn in hell."

"*After* we catch him, Professor. And we *will*. He's killed one of my men, and I won't stop looking for him." The policeman paused to manage his anger. "But it's odd that he remained such a cold and calculating criminal for so long, but now seems to have gone berserk."

"Maybe because Marda stood up to him," said Gould, tentatively. "Perhaps I played a part, a small one. I uncovered some new data on your Anchoress of Shere. Maybe it finally got to be too much for him. Perhaps the enormity of his crimes affected his conscience, if he had one. I suppose in all senses of the word the game was up."

"It's a strange game you historians play," the superintendent said brusquely.

The phone rang for the superintendent and the room started to buzz with police jargon.

Sensing Gould's hurt at the policeman's probably unintended slight, Marda walked over to him and sat on the arm of his chair. She touched his hand gently.

"I haven't thanked you properly for helping me…and my brother. *I* don't lump all you history nuts together, I promise."

"I should be comforting you, Marda," Gould said, looking up at her. "I would like to. When all the police stuff is sorted out, when you've spent some time with your folks, when your brother's out of hospital…when you've done some grieving for yourself, I guess…would you visit me in the States? I live in a lovely historical part of Georgetown."

"Yes, I'd like that. Later, I'll need to talk things through, to try to understand what's happened to me, and inside me. I know I can talk to you."

"And when you're all talked out, no more medieval history, OK?"

"No more history, Professor Irvine Gould. No more history. When I've recovered I'll look forward to the future."

She squeezed his hand. He responded with the sensitive strength of both his scholar's soft hands. Marda appreciated a gentle, tactile man. That touch was to prevent Marda hating men and God, and would be her resurrection. After so long in a tomb it was, for her, the most important gesture on earth.

XVIII

The Redemption

Sand lizards scurried from walkers who trespassed on their territory, while at night foxes scavenged among the litter discarded by careless picnickers. The Hurtwood, however, no longer beckoned to Marda, despite the enticingly warm summer of 1968. She had said farewell to Shere forever, but Christine's ghost remained with her. Perhaps one day, in the hereafter, the shades of both women would together heed the summons of St. James's church as the bells tolled the Grandsire carillon.

But for now bells meant death; Marda attended the funerals of all her five prison companions. She tried to console the families of the other women, but telling them the whole truth would hurt them, and her, too much. It was enough that the bodies had been recovered and identified, and that the families could begin to grieve, knowing that their loved ones had been properly laid to rest. That was far better than spending a whole life not knowing what had happened to a daughter or a sister. Marda also attended the memorial service for Constable McGregor, and silently thanked him for trying to help her.

After so much sadness, Marda needed time to become herself again. True, she had regained her former weight, and her high cheekbones had lost their gauntness. Her lips were plump once more, and the rosy colour had long since returned to her face. She needed more time, however, for healing the woman inside. Her employers granted her extended leave to recover at her family home, while her job was kept open. She restarted in September, almost a year after her ordeal had begun.

The regiment put on a good show for the returning hero. Captain Mark Stewart was unable to resume active duty for a year, but he could manage a desk job in the interim. Marda had helped him through his convalescence, and now they were as close as any brother and sister could be. Marda had indeed found a new strength in her imprisonment, not least the strength to love unreservedly, unselfishly. She dissuaded Mark from waging a one-man crusade to find Duval, but Superintendent Woodward was true to his word; he never gave up. Despite his efforts, though, an intensive international police search continued to draw a blank. Woodward also tried to trace Duval through his attachment to Catholicism, but the impenetrable labyrinth of the Church was too complex.

Marda spent a lot of time with Jenny, who persuaded her to contact Gerard. The Frenchman did visit the Stewart family home in Woking, but Marda and Gerard had become strangers. They promised to meet regularly for lunch in Bordeaux, but that promise fizzled out into occasional and desultory chats over coffee.

Every day during her recuperation she played in the garden with Bobby, her new and faithful friend; the dog followed her every step. He, too, seemed reluctant to be alone again.

Professor Gould rang her regularly and wrote long amusing letters. She grew to like him more and more.

When a package arrived with an American stamp in mid-June, she rushed to open it. It contained a book entitled "Christine Carpenter: The Anchoress of Shere."

Her blood turned to ice as she began to read the covering letter.

Dear Marda

In the final analysis, the core of the Christian message is forgiveness. You don't need a Church for this, because you of all people should know that you can speak to God directly. The springs of sanctity and sadism come from the same source, and I may have inadvertently erred towards the latter. So I have asked God and my confessor to forgive the hurt I have done you, and your brother, and my other guests, but still I hope you learned something from me. And from Christine.

Perhaps you should take your American to France. Get him to re-check those bogus documents on which he bases the false claims of Christine's alleged sojourn in San Sardos.

I retain little from my time in Shere except my unpublished book, a copy of which I enclose. I realise that it can never, should never, be published. It is perhaps too tragic, like the love story of Tristan and Isolde, but Christine and I are separated by over 600 years. It was impossible, but I did my best to recreate her and her vision. I chose you to do that. You failed me in this, but perhaps it was a noble failure.

I am fortunate in being a member of the universal Church. I did not take up my posting in Bolivia, and I will have left America before you receive this letter. There is much more to see of this world

before I go to the next, whether Heaven or Hell.
Who knows?

Christian love,

Michael Duval.

PS. Please look after Bobby. One day I may come
back for him.

Epilogue

I received that letter thirty years ago. Whether it was a hoax or genuine I cannot know for sure, although the police questioned its authenticity. In my opinion, it may well have been genuine because of its peculiar tone. That Duval should have information about my new life was unsettling, and I wondered to what sort of international network he had access. Nevertheless, I tried to put it all behind me, and I am very pleased to say that I never saw him again. Although Duval was never caught, like Lord Lucan he became a famous untried murderer. Lucan killed one person; Duval was infamous as a serial killer, although serial killing has become more commonplace today.

I did see Professor Gould frequently; we became firm friends, and for a while even more than that. Just before Irvine died, at the tragically young age of forty-seven, he let me have his personal diary of the Shere events and copies of his academic work relating to Christine Carpenter. He explained that he had kept the diary secret for so long because it confessed his love for me. I knew how much he loved me, and I responded as passionately as I was able. We did discuss marriage, but eventually I decided that this was not the right path for me.

Irvine's papers also gave me further insight into anchoresses in general, and of course Christine in particular. I have spent a lifetime wondering which biographical version was correct. Naturally, I trusted Irvine's scholarship and integrity, and it is much easier to believe that Christine married Simon and brought up a family in France. This Hollywood version is certainly more acceptable in our modern era. Duval was criminally insane, and his historical gifts were questionable, but the essence of his description of Christine's search for truth might, after all, be more in tune with the spirit of the medieval age. And the purer dimensions of that quest may also be of relevance today.

I tried to recreate the whole paradoxical story, years later it is true, from what I had read and what I remembered, assisted by Irvine's scholarship, because it is my story as well as Christine's. Perhaps I have allowed it to be told now for her sake as much as for my own.

After I wrote a very amateurish account of the Shere events, I locked the manuscript away for many years. Recently I was diagnosed as having a terminal illness; after much heart-searching, I thought again about my story. In 1968 I refused to be interviewed by the newspapers and, in those days, the media would respect such a request. No one, except the police, interviewed me.

Finally, I was persuaded by my cousin to talk to a writer whom she trusted. He has edited and fleshed out the story, partly from his own research and partly from extensive interviews with me, my family, ex-policemen and Church authorities.

It was agreed that, after my death, the book would be published in a popular form, provided I could disassociate myself from any parts that I thought were untrue. Although the core of the story is entirely accurate, I must insist that some of the passages relating to sexuality, as well as sections on the Catholic faith, do not reflect my views today.

Most importantly, I do not believe that the Roman Catholic Church protected Duval; the police made extensive enquiries and found no evidence of this. It was on this understanding that I undertook legally to transfer my copyright.

Besides this book, the most evident legacy I have of that period is the small cross Duval branded on my cheek in the last stage of my captivity. When I was younger I intended to have it disguised by cosmetic surgery, but somehow I always managed to put off seeing a surgeon. In my vanity I grew to accept it as my own stigmata.

Duval was a truly evil man, and should stand utterly condemned by Church and state. Someone, such as myself, who actually suffered at his hands could never justify his actions, but I did learn one vital truth from my incarceration: sometimes good can emerge from evil. At the secular level of existence, I am pleased, for example, that Mark and Jenny have given me such charming nephews and nieces. At the more important spiritual level, Christ's crucifixion was the most abominable event in history, but from it came the promised redemption of the whole world.

I close by giving my thanks to the sisters of the Convent of the Immaculate Conception, who have enabled me for over twenty-five years to devote my love to the glory of Our Lord. When this is published, I shall have died and God will be my judge.

Sister Agnes (Marda Stewart)
Convent of the Immaculate Conception
Ranmore, Sussex
November 1998

To receive a free catalog of other Poisoned Pen Press titles, please contact us in one of the following ways:

Phone: 1-800-421-3976
Facsimile: 1-480-949-1707
Email: info@poisonedpenpress.com
Website: www.poisonedpenpress.com

Poisoned Pen Press
6962 E. First Ave. Ste 103
Scottsdale, AZ 85251